Traitor
Born

Books by Amy A. Bartol

The Secondborn Series

Secondborn
Traitor Born
Rebel Born (forthcoming)

The Kricket Series

Under Different Stars
Sea of Stars
Darken the Stars

The Premonition Series

Inescapable
Intuition
Indebted
Incendiary
Iniquity

"The Divided" (short story)

Traitor Born

AMY A. BARTOL

47N⬡RTH

Text copyright © 2018 by Amy A. Bartol
All rights reserved.

Published by 47North, Seattle

www.apub.com

Amazon, the Amazon logo, and 47North are trademarks of Amazon.com, Inc., or its affiliates.

ISBN-13: 9781503936911
ISBN-10: 1503936910

Cover design by Shasti O'Leary Soudant

Printed in the United States of America

To Jason Kirk, for the eleventh hour

Nine Fates of the Republic

FATE OF VIRTUES

Symbol: Halo. Firstborn moniker: Gold. Secondborn moniker: Silver.

The Fate of Virtues is the most powerful caste, the center of the political structure and seat of governmental power in the Fates Republic. Its leader—Clarity Fabian Bowie—is called "The Virtue" and his wife, Adora Wenn-Bowie, is the "Fated Virtue."

The First Family of Virtues (line of succession)
　　Fabian Bowie (The Virtue)
　　Grisholm Wenn-Bowie (Firstborn Commander)
　　Balmora Virtue (Secondborn Commander)

The Second Family of Virtues
　　Firstborn Rasmussen Keating
　　Secondborn Orwell Virtue

FATE OF SWORDS

Symbol: Broadsword. Firstborn moniker: Gold. Secondborn moniker: Silver.

The Fate of Swords is the military caste. Its leader—Clarity Othala St. Sismode—is called "The Sword." Her husband, Kennet Abjorn, is the "Fated Sword," an honorary title, as he is not in line to succeed should Othala die. The heir apparent is their firstborn son. Roselle St. Sismode is known only as Roselle Sword after being Transitioned into the secondborn military.

The First Family of Swords (line of succession)
    Othala St. Sismode (The Sword)
    Gabriel St. Sismode (Firstborn Sword)
    Roselle Sword (Secondborn Sword)

The Second Family of Swords
    Firstborn Harkness Ambersol
    Secondborn Hamlet Sword

FATE OF STARS

Symbol: Shooting Star. Firstborn moniker: Gold. Secondborn moniker: Silver.

Highly skilled in technical engineering, the Fate of Stars is responsible for energy and mining, including metals and elements used in the production of energy. Its leader—Clarity Aksel Vuke—is called "The Star."

The Second Family of Stars
    Firstborn Daltrey Leon
    Secondborn Kendall Star (deceased)

FATE OF ATOMS

Symbol: Carbon Atom. Firstborn moniker: Gold. Secondborn moniker: Silver.

Specializing in science, engineering, medicine, and technology, the duties of the Fate of Atoms overlap, to some degree, with those of the Fate of Stars.

FATE OF SUNS

Symbol: Sun. Firstborn moniker: Gold. Secondborn moniker: Silver.

The Fate of Suns is responsible for agriculture and most food production.

FATE OF DIAMONDS

Symbol: Glimmering Diamond. Firstborn: White moniker. Secondborn: Blue moniker.

The Fate of Diamonds produces media, art, music, and other forms of entertainment and manages public relations, writers, and actors.

FATE OF MOONS

Symbol: Full Moon. Firstborn moniker: Gold. Secondborn moniker: Silver.

The Fate of Moons is responsible for social work and advocacy. Its leader—Clarity Toussaint Jowell—is called "The Moon."

FATE OF SEAS

Symbol: Cresting Wave. Firstborn moniker: Aqua Blue. Secondborn moniker: White.

The Fate of Seas is responsible for fishing and ship building.

FATE OF STONES

Symbol: Mountain Range. Firstborn moniker: Gold. Secondborn moniker: Brown.

The Fate of Stones is the servant caste and performs tasks ranging from janitorial services and sewage management to factory work and assorted nonmilitary functions.

CENSUS

Symbol: Peregrine.

Census is a governmental entity that operates outside the nine Fates of the Republic. It is composed of agents whose mission is to hunt down and kill unauthorized thirdborns and their abettors. The Census uniform is a white military dress shirt, black trousers, black boots, and a long tailored leather coat. Census bases are located underground, beneath the Sword military Trees like the Stone Forest Base and the Twilight Forest Base.

SWORD MILITARY RANKS

Firstborn

Exo—This rank is higher than all other ranks with the exception of Admiral and Clarity. Exos wear black uniforms. Clifton Salloway is an Exo.

Iono—Iono soldiers are tasked with protecting the heads of Fates, the Clarities, and their families. Ionos wear gray uniforms. Dune Kodaline was an Iono soldier when posted at the Sword Palace.

Secondborn

Thermo—the highest secondborn military rank. Thermos wear sky-blue uniforms.

Meso—the second secondborn military rank. Mesos wear royal-blue uniforms.

Strato—the third secondborn military rank. Stratos wear midnight-blue uniforms. This is Hawthorne Trugrave's rank when he meets Roselle.

Tropo—the lowest secondborn military rank. Tropos wear beige and brown uniforms. This is Roselle's rank on her Transition Day.

Prologue

I'm a Fate traitor. I've betrayed everything I once believed in.

The starry sky outside the window of our airship blurs with streaks of midnight. Maybe I'd be sorry for what I've done tonight if my brother hadn't tried to murder me. I don't know. My thoughts are chaotic. Savage fear constricts my throat and chokes my breath. I shouldn't blame Gabriel for wanting me dead. It's self-preservation. Plenty of powerful people are conspiring to slaughter him—replace the firstborn with his secondborn sister. They view me as the stronger St. Sismode. The one who will crush their enemies for them.

My family never expected me to live this long.

Mother has been trying to have me executed since I became a soldier in the secondborn military. She wants to protect her firstborn son from all threats to his ascension to the Sword. In Othala's mind, I must die to save Gabriel. Secondborns like me are nothing more than pawns. Chattel. To be bartered away or killed without thought.

I'm beginning to hate her for that.

I rest my forehead against the cool glass of the airship's window. My warm breath hides the night behind a small circle of white fog. I wouldn't be alive if not for Hawthorne.

He's been lying to me since the day we met.

Goose bumps rise on my arms. I try to rub them away. Hawthorne is firstborn now, but he still has the heart of a secondborn soldier. Saving me has become a thing for him—from Census and psychotic Agent Crow, from war and the horrific battlefield in the Fate of Stars . . . from loneliness.

But he lied to me. He's been my brother's spy. How can I ever trust him again?

A painful ache brutalizes my hollow chest. Hawthorne has risked everything to help me. He warned me about Gabriel's plan to assassinate me. Our escape through the Tyburn Fountain will be discovered. The bloodthirsty maginot that tried to eviscerate me will be exhumed. Even though we crushed the cyborg wolfhound in the belly of a rubbish collector, I fear the secrets it could reveal if it's recovered.

To be fair, I haven't told Hawthorne everything I've done either. He doesn't know about my pact with our enemies, the Gates of Dawn, or that I've stolen monikers and traded the identification processors for the lives of Edgerton and Hammon, our two best friends. I have no plans to tell him either.

Sitting up straight in my seat, I glance at The Virtue, Fabian Bowie. He paces in circles around the exquisite apartment of his luxurious Verringer aircraft. Strong and cunning, he emanates ruthless aggression. I've personally witnessed him order the assassination of some of his closest allies for little more than an affront to his considerable ego. What makes him most dangerous is his insatiable appetite for power.

And now he has taken a disturbing interest in me.

In the soft interior light of the airship, the golden rose-shaped pin on his uniform's lapel winks at me. Our ruler has joined the Rose Garden Society, the secret purpose of which is to see me one day take my mother's place as The Sword. I'm the "rose" they want in power. Fabian's wearing of the symbol seals Gabriel's death warrant. Even after my brother and mother's attempt to have me assassinated, I still don't want my brother to die. Gabriel's addiction to Rush, a powerful drug, doesn't allow him to think clearly. He doesn't know what he's doing.

He's scared—and he should be.

Chewing on my bottom lip, I pluck dirt and grass from the tattered sleeve of my gown. Clifton Salloway is responsible for Clarity Bowie's personal interference in my life. The firstborn arms dealer and owner of Salloway Munitions has left nothing to chance in his desire to place me in power. He has been my constant ally over the past year. Unlike Reykin and the Gates of Dawn, who want to use me to take down the Fates of the Republic, Clifton is very much interested in maintaining the status quo. The only thing he wants to change is my status, from secondborn to firstborn. Well, that, and he'd like to be more than just my commanding officer.

My hands wring. My knees tremble. By now, the malware that I uploaded into my favorite maginot should be infiltrating the industrial systems of the Fate of Swords. Unless someone detects the worm, Reykin and the Gates of Dawn will be able to access everything they need—from within the intelligence centers of the Fate of Swords—to operate their network of spies.

I should feel some shame or remorse, not only for forsaking my family but for committing treason. This isn't what I was raised to do.

But I don't feel guilty. What I feel is terror . . . and maybe . . . maybe somewhere beneath fear, a purpose.

Chapter 1
Pain

Pain. It's the one thing that reminds me I'm alive.

The unfortunate part about relying on pain is the disturbing lack of it in the Fate of Virtues. The firstborn residents of the Halo Palace pursue only pleasure and beauty and avoid any discomfort. With so little pain to go around, I no longer know if I'm real. Maybe everything is fantasy. Maybe only this shell of a world exists.

My opponent's eyes shine with burning shafts of golden light, reflecting my fusionblade. The lightweight silver hilt of my sword in my grip spits molten energy from its strike port. The man facing me wants to cut my heart out with his equally lethal sword. But I'm like a seek-and-destroy algorithm that he doesn't understand.

Firstborn Malcolm Burton's dark hair tangles in wet clumps on his brow. He raises the back of his left hand to his tense jaw. Golden light from Malcolm's sword-shaped moniker quivers over his flushed cheek. I bet Malcolm never saw this coming when he awoke this morning. He's been mentor to Grisholm Wenn-Bowie, the heir to the Fate of Virtues, for years, and as the firstborn son of Edmund Burton, my mother's military arms dealer, he has never had to fight for the position. The Burtons are part of the Sword aristocracy. It's beneath Malcolm's status to spar with me, a secondborn, but The Virtue insisted.

The tips of Malcolm's ears turn red, and he hisses when my weapon burns the flesh of his upper arm. Lucky for him I switched my fusionblade to training mode. He gets to keep his appendage, but the black fabric of his Exo uniform ignites where I struck him, curling at the edges with orange embers.

"It's time for me . . ." Malcolm says between panting breaths, "to stop . . . going . . . easy on you." His pride is shaken. His free hand pats out the small flame. Tendrils of smoke and the scent of singed skin assail me. I'm used to it. With my ex-mentor, Dune, it was usually my flesh that burned.

"By all means," I reply, "stop." I pause to allow Malcolm to recover and reset. Using my thumb, I dial the energy output of my fusionblade back up to the most lethal setting. Malcolm's sword never left kill mode. I should keep that in mind.

"I normally don't fight women," he growls, his dark eyebrows drawing together scornfully. "Or secondborns."

I show no emotion. "A fusionblade is a great equalizer. It doesn't care about gender, size, strength, or birth order." Dune used to say this to me whenever I complained about losing to him.

When Malcolm's ready, I half-heartedly block his lopsided strike with my own assault, beating him back several feet. A part of me longs to feel the scorching heat of his blade, any pain to replace the hollowness in my chest. My ego, however, won't allow it. Losing even an inch of ground to Malcolm is more than I can bear.

I'm isolated in the gilded cage of the Halo Palace—cut off. Everything could use a restart. Especially Grisholm. I glance at the twenty-two-year-old Firstborn Commander. He's above us on the observation balcony, overlooking our sparring circle. A shaft of sunlight kisses his skin. His elbow leans on the arm of a throne of gold, and he rests his chin on his fist, his halo-shaped moniker projecting a glow onto his sultry smile, as if to encircle and highlight it.

A steep flight of gleaming gold steps separates him from us. Golden Gothic pillars support the balcony, fanning out at the high ceiling like ribs. Near each pillar, a hovering stinger drone buzzes. The automated, black-armored assault guards resemble wasps that emit a hum as they ping the monikers in the room, ensuring that no unauthorized person gets too close to the heir to the Fates Republic.

Grisholm lifts his head from his hand and swipes the holographic screen of his moniker. The glass wall behind him opens, allowing a soft breeze from the roiling sea to tussle his hair. The long golden curtains decorating the royal sparring circle flap and billow in the wind. At Grisholm's back, over two thousand stone steps descend to the ocean. I run them a few times a day.

"Here's some sea air for you, Malcolm," Grisholm calls from above. "You're looking a little overheated."

"I'm just getting"—Malcolm pants—"warmed up." He tries to avoid my fusionblade, but he's too slow. I dial down the weapon so that I only burn him with the searing tip across his thigh. He winces and lurches away. I let him put some space between us while I glance up at Grisholm again.

Grisholm should be training, not lazing around watching us. He's weak with Malcolm as a mentor and military attaché. Privilege, not merit, must have played a part in the decision to employ Malcolm in that role. Or caution. Fear of Grisholm being hurt has risen to a level I haven't encountered before—not even my brother, Gabriel, has been this sheltered from pain.

At the other end of the gallery, Clarity Bowie observes the sparring match. He summoned me today to Grisholm's training facility, sending his personal valet with a handwritten note. In it, The Virtue hinted that I might be an improvement in the role of Grisholm's mentor. I peer up. The leader leans against the railing, his elbows resting on the marble. He's well built for a middle-aged man. The strength of his stare bores into us. I wonder if he knows I'm only playing with Firstborn

Malcolm—prolonging this battle—hoping his son's mentor will do something amazing so he can keep his job.

Beside Clarity Bowie, Dune watches me silently. My heartbeat drums harder. I haven't had a private moment with my former mentor since coming here. He greeted me when I arrived two nights ago, and we walked together from the airship across the butterfly sanctuary in the south lawn. We talked only of trivialities because The Virtue had been present. Dune's look, at the time, demanded discretion, but I already knew this lavish fortress would be infested with hidden-camera drones and listening devices, just like the Sword Palace. I'd hoped that we'd be able to meet alone at some point, but Dune's duties with the demanding ruler of Virtue are such that it hasn't been possible.

Malcolm trips when I sidestep his advance. He tries to right himself. I give him a shove in the back with my foot to send him farther from me. He huffs and puffs, winded by the exertion. I haven't broken a sweat.

Dune's appearance hasn't changed. Even standing a few steps behind his sovereign at the railing, he's the taller, more powerful-looking figure. His long dark hair is swept from his face in a knot at the back of his head. The length of his hair hangs to his shoulders, not a bit of gray in it or in his beard. The intensity of his sand-colored eyes weighs on me. He stares, unblinking.

Malcolm barrels at me with his sword aloft, exposing every inch of himself for me to carve up. I duck under his downward swing, raising my fusionblade and angling it just short of the firstborn's ear. Several locks of his stylish hair float to the floor. His cheeks burn with fury. Guffaws from Grisholm fill the air. The firstborn claps and shouts, "I was just saying how your hair needed a new style, ol' boy!" Grisholm's voice booms through the automated voice amplification in the room, making him sound like a god on high.

Malcolm says nothing. He grits his teeth and lowers his head, careening toward me again, overwrought-gorilla style. Wrapping the fabric of the banner hanging from the ceiling around my wrist, I clutch it in my fist and swing away. My feet touch down in the center of the sparring circle. I release the drape. It floats backward, covering Malcolm's face in a swath of gold. He snarls, snatching it away from his eyes.

"*Roselle!*" Dune barks. I flinch.

Immediately, I attack Malcolm, swinging my fusionblade with blurring speed. It whirls, making shadows bleed with golden light. Malcolm lurches back until he stumbles and falls at the edge of the circle. His sword tumbles out of reach. Chin pointing at the ceiling, he cowers at my feet. The deadly point of my sword singes the hairs on his throat. Sweat slides down his cheeks, and his Adam's apple bobs in silent agony.

We wait, neither of us moving. Cold fear whistles through me. Malcolm feels it, too, if his shudder is any indication. *Will The Virtue order Malcolm's death?* My stomach curls and knots, but my hands stay steady. Patience is power in its truest form.

If I must kill him, his pain ends. Mine lives on.

Malcolm's eyes stare up—the color of November moons.

"Roselle, you may"—The Virtue pauses; Malcolm holds his breath—"execute him."

Malcolm emits a strangled sob.

Grisholm jumps to his feet. "*Wait! Hold, Roselle! Father!*"

I remain still, awaiting confirmation of the kill order.

"He's Edmund Burton's firstborn!" Grisholm pleads. "Burton Weapons Manufacturing supplies all of the munitions to our military."

The Virtue glowers at his son from across the open air of the balcony level. "Not anymore. We have new contracts. Salloway Munitions will supply our weapons, as well as new armor for our Sword soldiers. Clifton has developed secret military vehicles—ones that won't drop out of the sky if fusion power is disrupted."

"Well, that's good news," Grisholm replies with a note of desperation, "but why kill Malcolm? He has nothing to do with the military contracts. He has been my loyal friend for years."

Gripping the marble railing, The Virtue's knuckles turn bloodless. "Edmund Burton is Othala's man."

Grisholm raises his shoulders in confusion. "So?"

"So, he'd be the one to supply The Sword with the kind of support she'd need for a military coup."

Grisholm chuckles in derision. "That's absurd. Othala St. Sismode can barely look you in the eyes, let alone overthrow you."

"You're blind," The Virtue snarls. "I've raised a fool!"

"Then enlighten me."

"Othala will do anything to protect her firstborn."

"Protect Gabriel from whom?"

"From us," Grisholm's father replies.

"Because of her!" Grisholm points to me. "Because you brought her here!"

"Roselle's a much better choice to stand by your side and defend you from our enemies than Gabriel. He's weak. Your enemies will destroy you with him running the Fate of Swords. Roselle will make them cower at your feet." The Virtue tips his head in my direction. Malcolm trembles in fear.

"Malcolm isn't my enemy!" Grisholm retorts.

"He has taught you nothing!" his father says scornfully. "You can barely hold a sword!"

"No one's allowed to hurt me!" Exasperation drips from Grisholm's tone.

"That changes today!" The Virtue replies.

"You cannot kill Malcolm for following the rules you yourself set forth!" A part of me feels a grudging respect for Grisholm as he points out his father's hypocrisy. He knows loyalty.

"I can do whatever I like. I'm The Virtue."

"She's not firstborn. This goes against everything we believe in!"

"Exceptions have to be made from time to time to maintain power," The Virtue replies.

"Malcolm is more valuable to you alive," Dune interjects, the low resonance of his voice bolstered by the amplifiers. "Burton won't help Othala if you hold his firstborn and secondborn sons. Keeping Malcolm close and detaining his secondborn brother, Kendrick, would serve to collar Edmund's ambitions, instead of giving him a reason to strike."

"You really expect a coup?" Grisholm asks. The Firstborn Commander's arrogant smirk is absent now.

"I expect nothing less." The Virtue's attention drifts to me. He waves two fingers in dismissal. "Malcolm lives . . . for now."

I withdraw my fusionblade from Malcolm's throat. With a flick of my wrist, the surging energy of my sword dies. The firstborn Exo slumps in a serpentine sprawl, panting on the floor, hissing curses under his breath.

I move to the center of the circle and face The Virtue. Malcolm stays where he is, staring at the mat. Our ruthless leader calls in Exo soldiers to take Malcolm away, and the thick, muscular men in the ebony uniforms and capes of the royal guard approach. Malcolm gets to his feet, and they drag him away by his arms. His black boots skate along the cold floor before disappearing behind golden doors.

"Well done, Dune." The Virtue beams. "She's everything I'd hoped for when I sent you to be her mentor." I suppress a gasp. I had no idea that Clarity Bowie had played a part in selecting my mentor.

Both The Virtue and Grisholm stare at me with such intensity that they miss the cold-blooded hatred in the shifting sand of Dune's gaze. They misread my mentor—I don't even think they can see the dark rage dawning behind the gates of his exquisite control.

I shiver.

"Roselle"—The Virtue gestures to his son—"you will immediately begin instructing Grisholm in the art of combat and strategy." I knew this was coming the moment they told me I had to fight Grisholm's mentor, but even so, an uneasiness creeps through me.

"Father, please!" Grisholm snarls. "She's *secondborn*."

"A secondborn with uncanny skill."

"She's a woman!"

"Then you should have no problem besting her," his father taunts.

"She's strange and unpredictable."

"Exactly what you need. Roselle, you have my permission to use your own discretion in training my son."

I nod, hiding my supreme irritation with this turn of events. The Virtue turns to leave. "My moniker's communications have been blocked," I call to him. "My access to messaging has been restricted."

The Virtue pauses, facing me once more. "I'm aware of that."

"I want full access restored."

"Why? Whom do you wish to contact?"

Hawthorne, I think, but his question feels dangerous. Instead, I reply, "Commander Salloway."

"Ah. Clifton." He smirks. "He's insisted upon seeing you, Roselle. He's adamant that we discuss your work schedule at Salloway Munitions."

"Grant me access to my moniker's communicator, and I'll arrange everything now."

"I'm sorry. That's just not possible."

"Why not?" I frown.

"It's for your own protection."

"I can protect myself."

His bottom lip pushes out in a dubious look. "I'm sure it's no secret to you that your mother and your brother want you dead. They have ways of getting to you."

"It's a family matter."

"Your welfare concerns me, Roselle. Your moniker could be tracked through those you contact. I've restricted access to your locator. You may thank me now for protecting you."

I want to argue with him, but the stern set of his jaw tells me that now is not the time. "Thank you," I mutter. The Virtue dismisses me, turns, and leaves. An almost-imperceptible lowering of Dune's chin is enough of an acknowledgment to say, "You did well." He follows The Virtue out.

Moving to the golden stairs, I slowly climb to where Grisholm stands with his hands on his hips, glaring at me. His nostrils flare in anger. I stop beside him. The view of the sea beyond the cliff at his back is breathtaking. The salty breeze stirs my brown hair, blowing unsecured wisps that have slipped from my ponytail to batter my cheeks.

Grisholm's hot breath assaults my earlobe. "Let me make something very clear, Roselle. You are nothing. The moment I'm The Virtue, you'll be dealt with." My eyes don't stray from the sea. It takes all my strength not to cut him down with my fusionblade. He leaves through the private doors to his personal wing of the Halo Palace, followed closely by a swarm of hovering stingers. I stand motionless, contemplating the precariousness of my new position as hated mentor to the future ruler of the world.

Chapter 2
Domestic Bliss

I return to my apartment inside the Halo Palace. My private quarters are on a corridor near Grisholm's sparring circle. The rooms are posh by the standards of my former capsule in the air-barracks, but they fall short of the elegance of my penthouse apartment at the top of Clifton's sword-shaped skyscraper in the Fate of Swords. What I love most about this apartment is that it overlooks a formal rose and topiary garden and the sea beneath the jagged cliff beyond it.

Blue lights flash over my silver sword-shaped moniker when I place it beneath the scanner on the panel next to the door. The golden door slides open, and the heavy clicking and shuffling of metal footsteps on marble floor greet me.

No one attends to me here. The secondborns who work in The Virtue's Halo Palace find it beneath their stations to assist a secondborn Sword. To compensate for this, a "mechadome," a domestic robot with artificial intelligence, was assigned to me. They're usually humanoid in appearance with sophisticated communication and domestic skills. Mine is not.

My newly commissioned mechadome waddles over from the drawing room.

My lips twitch into a smile. It's clear this domestic servant has been resurrected from a scrap pile. Its two round, lens-like eyes, located in the center of its nearly neckless head, glow red. It uses infrared to find me in the wide foyer. The dented iron veneer of the three-foot-tall, hydrogen-powered domestic assistant doesn't have a bit of shine to it. Lines of rusted round-headed fasteners run down either side of its plump torso.

Out of curiosity, I researched my new mechadome. In its former life, this little bot was a sewer worker with few artificial intelligence capabilities. It had no domestic skills whatsoever until it was assigned to me. Only the bare minimum of upgrades have been applied to its operating system, according to the rudimentary diagnostic I ran. The potbellied robot strikes me as someone's idea of a supremely funny prank meant to make me feel less than welcome here. I suspect Grisholm had something to do with it. The Firstborn Commander's joke couldn't have backfired worse, though, because I find this squat, burly brute endearing.

"How has your day been, Phoenix?" I ask.

The mechadome shifts its weight from wide metal foot to wide metal foot and back—*clang, clang, clang*—and its glowing red eyes stare up at me.

I unfasten the armor clasps of my heat resistant hauberk and pull it over my head. Holding out the metallic mesh garment, I let go. As it falls, Phoenix lifts its short, cannon-barrel-shaped arm. The hollow appendage whines, and a powerful vacuum sucks the armor to it, catching it before it hits the floor.

Straightening my black tank top back into place over my abdomen, I realize that this little unit probably used to suck up sewage—a thought I don't want to dwell on when it brings me my dinner later this evening.

Phoenix uses its other longer arm with the clawlike hand to secure the armor. The mechadome makes an awkward turn because its hover mode no longer works. With more clanging noises, it crosses the foyer at a toddling pace, depositing my hauberk into a transparent case. The thickset bot programs the storage unit to sanitize the armor. I pat its iron head on my way by to check the parcel chute.

The bin is empty—nothing from Hawthorne to let me know if he's alive.

I cross through the drawing room to the message console on the wall in the den and take out the hologram pad. Lifting the antiquated handheld device, normally used by the administrative arm of the Halo Palace, I switch on the pad. An automated virtual image of a Stone-Fated secondborn appears, in holographic form, with a message: "Your request for a manual and tools to repair a Class 5Z Mechanized Sanitation Unit has been denied. You do not hold the moniker classification for this task. Please requisition a Star-Fated or Atom-Fated representative for further assistance." The hologram winks out.

I growl in frustration. Using the handheld hologram pad, I record and send a request for a Star to visit my apartment. I shove the message pad aside. I'm irritated, for the millionth time since arriving here, about the restrictions on my moniker communications.

I squat down. "Don't worry, Phee. I'll get your hover mode fixed soon." Phoenix responds by shifting its feet—three quick *clangs*—reminding me of the maginots' tails wagging.

Straightening, I leave the den and walk to the winding stairs near the drawing room. As I climb them, I hear Phoenix behind me ramming repeatedly into the bottom step, trying to follow me. It turns on its powerful vacuum arm and angles it down. Reversing the flow of air, it blows a stream of wind, acting as a propulsion system. The squat little bot almost levitates to the first step. "Stay, Phoenix," I order. It stills. The air system powers down.

The expression on its little face is almost forlorn. Its eyes glow brighter red. Its portal mouth, which is where it attaches to a power source to recharge its hydrogen power cells, can curve up or down to show the bare minimum of humanlike expression. The oblong opening is in a definite frown. "I'll be right back." I feel a bit stupid for talking to it this way. I don't know the extent of its intelligence or whether it has genuine feelings, but still I'm acting as if it has both.

I jog up to my bedroom suite to take a quick shower. When I'm finished, I wrap a robe around myself and move to stand in front of the holographic mirror in the dressing closet adjacent to the bathroom. The mirror reflects my image with a holographic list of categories on its right side. I select "Casual Wear" by touching the air button. My image in the mirror becomes garbed in a champagne-colored silk blouse with off-white leather pants that taper at the leg. I swipe away the leather with a gesture of my hand. I want something that will suit my mood, which isn't bright. The leather pants are replaced by cherry-red cotton leggings. I wrinkle my nose and keep swiping.

I was advised by the Stone-Fated attendant who gave me the tour of the Halo Palace that I'm not to wear any symbols of the Sword second-born military while in residence here. Instead, I'm to dress like Sword aristocracy. The Palace agent fell short of telling me to comport myself as if I'm firstborn, but it was implied in his rhetoric. I have outfits for a myriad of occasions, from formal to beachwear, but everything in my clothing lists is stylish and feminine and fits the profile of a wealthy firstborn.

Tailored black high-waisted trousers finally catch my eye. Pausing on them, I swipe through a range of different tops to pair with them, settling on a clingy, long-sleeved black top with an asymmetrical neckline. All the appropriate undergarments that accessorize the outfit display as well. I order them. About seven minutes later, the outfit arrives through the air-driven clothing conveyor chute inside the dressing closet. The items are packaged in separate garment bags that store neatly in clothing cubbies until I send the garments back in them later.

The black heels I order have a wait time of thirty minutes. Barefoot but dressed, I go back to the bathroom. As I'm twisting my hair into a smooth knot at the base of my head, the door of my apartment bleeps in melodic tones.

"You have a visitor," a sultry male voice says from the apartment's speaker system. The heavy metallic ring of Phoenix's feet begins in earnest below—*clang, clang, clang, clang—*

"Who is it?" I ask, securing my hair with a few pins.

"Secondborn Kinjin Star," replies the simulated voice.

Clang, clang, clang, clang, clang—

Smoothing the last hairs into place, I leave the bathroom and descend the stairs. "Open the front door," I command, hurrying across the drawing room to the foyer. The apartment door opens, and the young woman outside gazes down at Phoenix at her feet. The mechadome shifts noisily from side to side.

The Star-Fated woman looks up at me as I approach. "I read the order, but I thought it was keyed in wrong. You have a Class 5Z Mechanized Sanitation Unit as a domestic assistant?" Her brown eyes sparkle with restrained mirth. She rests her hand on the knee of her lemon-colored uniform, bending toward Phoenix in fascination. The silver belt around her waist holds magnetized tools. In her hand is a silver case.

"They're the up-and-coming thing," I reply, my lip twisting with sarcasm. "Everyone will have to have one soon. Please come in." I move aside, allowing her in. "This one has seen better days, though. The hover module doesn't work on either of its feet." The door slides closed behind her.

"Is there a place I can work?" she asks, appearing as if she's making mental notes of all the tests she'd like to run on my little bot.

"This way." I sweep my arm toward the long table in the formal dining area. Phoenix toddles along behind me like a puppy. At Kinjin's urging, I help lift Phoenix off the floor and onto the marble tabletop.

"Thanks," she says. "These little units are heavy. Their outsides are iron, and their insides are lined with lead."

She wipes her forehead with the back of her hand and goes to work pulling rusted fasteners from Phoenix's abdomen. As she works, I watch, asking questions when she pulls out soldering tools and replacement wiring. She runs upgrades on the operating system. After minutes of poking around, Kinjin pulls out a blackened metal part.

"I don't have a replacement component for this," she explains with a sheepish expression. "The lead is fine, but the receptor nodes on either side of it have shorted, and its boards are shot." She sets pieces of lead on the marble table. "The hover mode won't work without them. I can requisition replacement parts, but it will take several weeks because it's not a high-priority item."

"Is there somewhere I could get them?"

Her eyes turn up toward the ceiling, and her cheeks puff out. "There's a small repair shop in the downtown city center of Purity. They might have them. I can give you coordinates, if you'd like." I nod. She closes and secures Phoenix's iron casing. As she repacks her tools in her silver case, she reaches for the damaged lead parts.

"Can I keep those? I can show them to the technician at the shop. It might be easier," I explain, palming the parts and shoving them in a nearby drawer before she can say no.

"Sure." Kinjin shrugs. Together, we lift Phoenix down from the table. The stout bot seems no less functional for the loss of the small lead bits. Kinjin packs up her tools while Phoenix waddles around sucking up dust from the floor with its vacuum arm. When she's finished, Kinjin says, "I'll contact you when I get the parts."

I nod. We walk together to the foyer. Once we're away from Phoenix and the noise of the vacuum, a thought occurs to me. "I wonder . . ." I want to be subtle about what I say next. It pertains to Firstborn Reykin Winterstrom, my contact in the Gates of Dawn resistance. He told me he's looking for his secondborn brother, Ransom. If I could somehow find this secondborn Star, I'd have something to barter with Reykin and the Gates of Dawn the next time they want something from me. "Kinjin, do you happen to know an engineer by the name of Ransom Star?"

A flicker of recognition crosses her face. "That's an unusual name," she replies.

"Yes," I agree, offering nothing further.

"It doesn't sound familiar." Her eyes shift away, as if she's afraid to look at me.

"Oh. Well, I'll notify you if by chance I can get those parts sooner than you can."

Kinjin nods without glancing my way. "You have a pleasant evening."

"And you, as well." The door closes behind the Star, leaving me to wonder why she lied.

Once Kinjin is gone, I panic. *That was a supremely stupid risk to have taken for a negotiating tool I'm not even sure would be useful. I just blurted out Ransom Winterstrom's name, as if a name like that couldn't get me killed! As if a connection to Reykin Winterstrom and the Gates of Dawn isn't the most dangerous aspect of my life. Everything is a mess.* My hands tremble. I close them into fists.

Suddenly, this apartment is too small. I need to escape it. Going to the bureau drawer where I stashed the lead pieces, I yank it open. I could leave. I could cloak my moniker with the lead parts and just run away, but where would I go? Not back to Swords—not without speaking to Gabriel first. The moment I cross back into my Fate, I'll be cut down—unless it's in secret, and for that I'd need a plan.

My forehead dampens with sweat—my breathing hitches erratically, my heart drumming out of control. Even though I don't want to admit to myself that I'm suffering from a severe form of panic, I know the symptoms, which are common among Swords before and during the trauma of combat—and even long after they're away from any fighting. I drop the lead back into the drawer and close it.

Moving to a holographic screen in the drawing room, I explain my symptoms in gasping breaths to the Atom-Fated physician on duty. As I wait for a chet to arrive, I pace between the large white-linen sofa and the glass doors that lead to the balcony. The view of the sea beneath the cliff in the distance is gorgeous, but it does nothing to calm my anxiety. Nor does the formal rose garden directly below my balcony.

The musical bleep from the front door sets me further on edge. The automated voice announces the medical drone's arrival. Phoenix trundles toward it, but I easily pass the mechadome and answer the door myself. A silver, bullet-shaped medical drone awaits me in the corridor. It scans my moniker. A compartment in its side opens and dispenses the thin paper square. Wordlessly, I take it. The drone flies away. I put the chet on my tongue and allow it to melt. Closing the door, I lean against it and immediately begin to relax. The panic subsides to a faraway feeling of mild angst, but the chet makes me feel sluggish and drowsy.

Walking back to the drawing room, I sit on the soft sofa. My shoulders round forward. The room spins a little. Slowly, I lie down, rest my head on a velvety throw pillow, and pull my feet up. Closing my eyes, I try not to think of anything. Not the Gates of Dawn. Not the war. Not my insane family. Not the brat named Grisholm. And especially not the one person I worry may already be dead. *Hawthorne.*

Clang, clang, clang, clang, clang—Phoenix's rapidly shifting steps bang on the floor directly in front of me. I open my eyes to see its glowing red ones just inches from my face. It's night. Only one small lamp on the side table lights the apartment. I must have fallen asleep. I rub my eyes and raise my head from the pillow. Suddenly, fingernails dig into my scalp, yanking me up by my hair. A meaty arm around my neck chokes me in a brutal stranglehold. The arm moves. A dagger at my throat cuts into my skin.

Phoenix's vacuum arm whines to life. The mechadome points its cannon-barrel-shaped limb at whomever is behind me. My hair whirls and rips toward it. The vacuum arm grows longer. The man's hand yanks free from my neck, the powerful suction from Phoenix pulling it away. Grunts of pain and frustration come from behind me. The assailant lets go of his knife, which disappears inside Phoenix's arm. A hatch blows the weapon out of a round chamber in the robot's upper back, and the knife sticks into the wall.

Phoenix's extended vacuum arm locks on to my attacker's wrist and sucks the large man's forearm to the round metal opening. Phoenix's vacuum retracts, jerking the man forward. He lets go of me, wrenched by his arm, falling to his knees and sliding toward Phoenix's feet as the vacuum shaft continues to shorten. The crunching of bones is barely discernable over Phoenix's loud whirring.

The man struggles, but it's no use. In one grotesque motion, his forearm folds in half and disappears inside the vacuum. Harrowing screams bleat from behind the man's dark mask. The powerful suction dislocates the assassin's arm as he feebly punches his free hand against Phoenix's metal limb and bellows in agony.

A shadow crosses my peripheral vision, and I lurch off the cushion just in time to avoid a fusionmag pulse to the head. The pulse strikes the man on the floor, exploding his brains all over Phoenix's iron fasteners. Most of the blood vaporizes in the heat.

I land on the floor beside Phoenix and brace for the next fusionmag shot, but Phoenix reverses his arm-cannon, spewing out pieces of the dismembered limb at the second assailant, knocking the fusionmag from his hand.

While the second assassin scrambles to pick up his weapon, I dive to the wall and force the knife blade from it. Twisting, I hurl the weapon just as the second assailant rises to aim the fusionmag at me. The knife sticks in his Adam's apple, and he reels backward. His gun bounces toward me as he hits the rug. I tumble to it near the side of the sofa. He twitches on the floor, blood spurting from his throat as he dies.

On my knees, I reach for the fallen weapon. Another pulse flashes before my eyes, and I flinch, expecting to feel it burn them right out of my head, but Phoenix's stout body lurches in front of me. The pulse connects with the mechadome, making a sizzling sound that quickly dies out, probably because Phoenix is lined with lead, the worst conductor of fusion energy in this room. The little robot stomps from foot to foot, its infrared eyes glaring at a third intruder standing by the balcony door.

My hand closes around the grip of the fallen fusionmag. Lifting the weapon, I fire a shot. The glowing pulse strikes the third man in the shoulder where I intended it. I want him alive. He pitches to the side. Wounded, the man spins and escapes over the balcony railing.

I'm on my feet, sprinting to the balustrade. Reaching it, I peek over the edge. One floor below me, the third assassin stumbles away, holding what's left of his shoulder, disappearing behind a hedgerow of the rose garden.

I grip the line, secured to the railing of the balcony, that he used to leave. Clutching the fusionmag in one hand, I wrap the line around my forearm and step over the barrier. The line stretches like elastic, setting me down on the ground with minimal impact. Disengaging from it, I run in the direction of the escaping man.

Salt air and the sound of crashing waves greet me at the end of the formal garden. The ocean is ahead, at the bottom of a perilous cliff. The stairway to the beach is in another direction. This is a dead end. I push on, seeing movement in the darkness. The assassin runs toward the edge of the cliff. I contemplate killing him from here, but then I won't be able to question him, so I run as fast as I can, expecting him to slow down. Instead, he reaches the cliff's edge and jumps.

"Roselle!" a harsh voice snarls behind me. A strong arm captures my legs. I fall forward, hitting the grassy terrain hard. We slide almost to the brink of the cliff. The man above me flips me over, glaring at me in the moonlight, and I stare up at the Star-Fated soldier who invades my dreams almost every night.

"Reykin," I whisper, stunned. "What are you doing here?"

Chapter 3
Star at Midnight

Reykin lets go of me, shoving himself up to his feet.

He moves to the cliff's edge and gazes down. I join him there. Below, the swirling ocean waves crash over jagged rocks. In the darkness, it's impossible to see if the assassin survived.

Reykin's clean-shaven jaw tightens in anger. He runs his hand through his thick dark hair, smoothing it back into place. "Were you going to follow him over?" he demands. I just stare at him. I haven't seen him since I left his home in the Fate of Stars and sailed away on a rusted cargo ship. He's just as handsome as I remember—all hard angles and savage intensity. "Were you?" he asks, latching on to my upper arms.

I knock his hands away. "What are you doing here?"

"I'm protecting our asset from her ruthless family." He moves away and scuffles our dewy imprints in the lawn, covering our tracks.

"How did you even know I was out here?"

"I hacked your mechadome."

"You what—how?"

"Kinjin uploaded a program into your Class 5Z. I took over from there."

"So . . . *you* woke me up?"

"You're welcome," he replies angrily, grasping my chin and turning it sharply, making me look up at him. "Never mention my brother's name again. To anyone! Do you understand?"

Guilt makes me hesitate for a second, then I bash his hand away with my own. "I was just trying to find him for you," I reply with a scowl.

"Don't," he orders. His impossibly bright aquamarine eyes are discernable even in the moonlight. He leans nearer. "You're hurt," he says, his tone softened. He reaches for my throat.

I push his hand away again. My fingertips go to my neck, exploring my injury. The assassin's knife cut me. "It's nothing. A nick."

Which probably would've been a big, gaping hole if Reykin hadn't hacked my mechadome. Reykin leans in. His scent triggers something I don't expect, a feeling of safety. He saved me once from the worst beating of my life, and I want to cuddle up to his side and have him comfort me now.

Which is confusing. I take care of myself.

"Let me see it," Reykin says.

"No," I reply, backing a step away.

"Why not?" he asks mulishly. Typical firstborn, used to getting his own way.

"Because you're a horrible medic. I still have a star on my palm to prove it." I shove my right palm in his direction. He takes my hand in his and rubs his thumb over the small, raised star scar—a leftover from when his fusionblade hilt seared his family crest into my hand on the battlefield where we first met. The gesture is unmistakably tender. His shooting star moniker casts a golden glow between us. "How did you get into the Halo Palace undiscovered?" I ask. As part of the rebellion, a secret Gates of Dawn officer, Reykin risks being eviscerated by the Fates Republic government if they find out what side he's truly on. But first they'd torture him to find out what he knows, and he knows plenty.

"I'm a guest," Reykin replies, dropping my hand abruptly. He turns away and heads toward the formal garden. His broad back is clad only in an undershirt, and he wears gray pants that qualify as sleepwear. His feet are bare.

"Whose guest?" I blurt out, following him.

"Grisholm's guest."

"Grisholm?" I hiss. "How do you know him?"

"Go back to your apartment. I disabled the night owl bots out here, but that won't go unnoticed for long." He points to a tree where an all-too-real-looking owl clings to the bark, unmoving. "We're fortunate Grisholm doesn't allow roaming maginots in his area of the Palace."

"Doesn't he have maginots?"

"No, the automated wolfhounds tended to kill his late-night female guests, so he banned them. I want you to alert Iono security to the break-in in your apartment tonight. Mention nothing about me to them."

"How do you know Grisholm?" I don't like being surprised or kept out of any plan they might be hatching, especially if that plan involves me as the "asset."

He keeps walking, weaving around hedges in the garden. "Now is not the time for explanations."

I know he's right, but I need to know one thing. "The program I uploaded into the maginot," I ask breathlessly, following him, "did it work?"

Reykin pauses and faces me. "Of course it worked. We're saving thirdborns every day." A burst of fear, and maybe relief, turns my belly to ice and weakens my knees. He doesn't seem to notice. "Stay alert. Those assassins may have found you because you ordered a chet. Maybe they saw where it was delivered and followed it to you. Or your mother has her own spies here. Either way, never use the Atoms at the Halo Palace for anything. I don't trust them. If you need more chets, tell me. I'll get them for you." He turns and walks away again.

This time I don't follow him. Shame over my weakness today makes my cheeks burn. I should be able to control my fear without using chets. Putting my hands on my knees, I take a few deep breaths to try to calm my heart, which bludgeons my sternum. Slowly, with Reykin gone, my anxiety subsides. I straighten, find my way back inside, and alert the first guard I find to the horrific homicide that took place in my room.

I surrender the fusionmag. Two Iono guards conduct me to the underground security level of the Halo Palace. The subterranean inter-rogation room, devoid of everything except a metallic table bolted to the floor and a few stiff chairs, is as sterile as it is spare. Bright lights shine down from the ceiling, heightening my fear of exposure as a spy. The two guards, both women, listen with skeptical expressions as I report the murder attempt on my life. After asking me very few ques-tions, they leave to investigate. The door closes behind them. I test the door. It's locked. I'm confined to the room. I return to the metal chair and sit. It's cool down here. I notice I neglected to put on shoes dur-ing the chaos. My feet are grass-stained. Alone in a small interrogation room, I stare at my dirty toes.

Hours later, I'm virtually in the same position, seated at the small table, when the door opens and an Exo officer enters. She's probably in her early thirties, fit, with a firstborn sword moniker shining golden from the back of her left hand.

"Roselle St. Sismode," she says, pulling out a metal chair across from me and taking a seat.

"It's Roselle Sword," I reply.

"How about just Roselle?" she asks with a small smile. "I'm Vaughna Jenns. I'm in charge of this investigation." She sets a metallic mug of what smells like coffee on the table in front of her and pushes it in my direction. "Thirsty?"

I am, but she's a Sword. She could be working for my mother and brother. "No. Thank you." I give her a polite smile.

"I can take a sip of it first, if you're worried." She leans back in her chair.

I pretend I don't know what she means. "Did you locate the man that dove into the sea?"

"We recovered two bodies from your apartment, but as for a third, that one seems to have gotten away."

I cross my arms, wishing I'd followed the killer off the cliff. Not knowing for sure if my brother ordered the strike stirs intense fear within me. If it wasn't by Gabriel's order, then I have more to worry about than the power struggle with family. I've committed treason for the Gates of Dawn. I've made an enemy of Grisholm by usurping Malcolm Burton's position in the Halo Palace. I've done things in the name of my Fate as a secondborn soldier that could lead to retribution. I'm also a high-profile figure in the Salloway Munitions Conglomerate—it's face. "What Fate were they from?"

"We don't know. Their monikers were removed."

"Let me see the bodies. Maybe I'll recognize them without their masks." She complies, using her moniker's holographic screens to show me the bodies in my apartment. They're both young—my age or younger. I don't recognize either man and exhale in frustration. "They're not familiar."

Firstborn Jenns extinguishes the images. "Can you think of a reason why someone would want to kill you?" she asks with a straight face.

"We're at war. I'm a Sword."

"You're in the Halo Palace. The Virtue—or his heir—would make for a better target than you."

"Find the third assassin, and we'll have our answers," I reply.

She purses her lips. Perhaps she expects some kind of theory from me? She must know that if I were to accuse my mother or brother of plotting my death, I could be convicted of treason. I'm secondborn. I don't have the right to make any unsubstantiated claims or statements against firstborns—especially not The Sword.

She sighs. Lifting her left hand, she touches the light of her golden holographic sword. The moniker opens a holographic screen, and she retrieves the statement I gave to the Iono officers hours before. "So, this is your story. Three men entered your apartment to murder you. You killed two of them—"

"No, the first was shot by the second. The second I stabbed in the neck with the first's knife."

"Quite right. And the third, you . . ."

"Shot in the shoulder."

"Where did you get the weapon?"

"The second assassin dropped it when I stabbed him."

"With the first one's knife?" she asks. I nod. "And you were able to shoot the third . . ."

"In the shoulder," we say in unison.

"That's quite a feat," Firstborn Jenns says. "Three against one, and you were unharmed except for a small cut on your neck?"

"My mechadome helped."

She snorts skeptically. The door behind her opens. Dune enters, making the small room feel tiny. Firstborn Jenns jumps to her feet, nearly spilling the coffee. "Commander Kodaline."

"Firstborn." Dune acknowledges her with a slight nod. "The questioning is finished for this evening. If you have anything more, you'll submit it to me." He turns to me. I don't move. Fear and devotion hover just behind my serene mask.

"Yes. Of course," Firstborn Jenns acquiesces. She's clearly intimidated, but if I had to guess, it's more by his presence—the raw power in him—than by his position.

"Roselle, please join me," Dune orders.

I rise from the chair, sore from not having moved in hours, and leave the room with him. We walk the bland corridors of the security floor side by side. Dune shows me to a lift. Unlike the others, its walls are made of glass. It takes us upward within a shaft gilded in gold leaf. The air feels thinner, but mostly from the awkwardness of spending my entire life with him, only to have been kept apart for more than a year now, unable to tell him about all the devastating events I encountered as a soldier. An invisible wall divides us. He's a stranger I've known all my life—a spy. I don't know what was real between us and what wasn't. I feel a mix of emotions—hope, desperation, fear, betrayal, and despair. I struggle to contain it all.

To give the illusion of being unaffected, I focus on the mundane. His hair is pulled back in a tight knot, making him appear younger than his thirty-nine years. Earlier today, he was wearing an Exo uniform—a promotion from the Iono uniform he wore as my mentor at the Sword Palace. Now his formal attire is of Sword aristocracy. He could rival my father, Kennet, in elegance.

He notices my puzzled expression. "I was at a Secondborn Pre-Trial event hosted by a tremendous bore when I was pulled away."

"You look nice." I glance away from him, hoping my hero worship isn't apparent in my tone. "Who was the bore?"

"Firstborn Harkness Ambersol," he replies. "Have you met him? I don't recall."

"No, but I've heard of him." If Harkness had been to the Sword Palace, I wasn't introduced to him. He's firstborn and I'm secondborn. I was kept away from most social gatherings at the Sword residence for that reason. "Isn't Harkness next in line for the position of The Sword, should either Gabriel or I be unable to claim the honor?"

"He is. Your friend was there as well. He asked me about you."

"Which friend? I have so many," I lie. I have two—Hawthorne and Clifton. Maybe Reykin. Maybe none. I can't decide. They all come with strings.

"Exo Salloway. He asked me to tell you that he misses you."

"Was Clifton holding on to the arm of the loveliest Diamond-Fated starlet in the room when he told you that?" My smile is ironic, imaging the handsome Exo Sword with his movie-star good looks.

"He was quite alone this evening and adamant that I deliver his message." A definite frown accompanies Dune's answer. A year ago, I would've been devastated by any inkling of my mentor's disapproval. Now I'm surprised to find that I'm somewhat annoyed. Clifton has done more for me than I can repay.

"I miss him, too," I reply, wanting to see Dune's reaction. His frown deepens.

The transparent elevator suddenly exits the opaque shaft and travels through the open air toward the golden halo-shaped crown that hovers over the rest of the Palace. The night sky is glorious with glowing stars. For several moments, all I can think about is how beautifully decadent the city of Purity is at night. From the skyscrapers that hover far off the ground, to those that spiral and change their shapes before my eyes, the city shimmers with opulent extravagance.

The elevator enters the golden circlet of the Halo Palace, and the view cuts off. When the doors open, we enter a magnificent foyer. A grand staircase climbs to a golden balustrade lined mezzanine. More than ten military-grade death drones hover about this lavish room. Several Iono guards in crisp gray uniforms stand like statues at equal intervals in the foyer. "That staircase leads to Fabian and Adora's private residence," Dune says, referring to The Virtue and his wife. I peer up. Exo guards in black uniforms stand at intervals along the mezzanine's curved walls. All of them have fusion rifles. Dune must have cleared my moniker for the visit, because our presence goes unchallenged.

Golden columns support gilded architraves on both levels. Between the pillars, on the mezzanine's landing wall beyond, hang portraits of The Virtue and his sublime spouse. Adora's green eyes, wondrous and cold, cast a gaze of emerald ice upon Dune and me. Her long blond hair gently moves on the portrait's visual screen, held in place by her halo crown—a circlet of pure gold. The difference between the two royal figures is such to make them worlds apart. Where Fabian is dark, Adora is light. His mouth is ruthless. Hers is supple. His face is hard angles. Hers is rounded softness.

Dune and I don't climb the exquisite staircase. Instead, we turn and head for an adjacent corridor, our shadows stretching beneath the everwatchful gazes of our sovereigns until we're out of the foyer.

Dune's gait is gentle, the pace of a panther whose tail caresses the confines of his cage. He leads me to his private apartments. I'm impressed by the beauty of his drawing room, everything masculine and high tech. I approach an arching glass wall with godlike views of the city beyond the expansive grounds. The world almost makes sense from this altitude.

"Privacy mode," Dune says.

I huff in disappointment as shutters of thick steel close over the wall, severing my connection with the outside world. Doors close and latch. A pinging high-intensity frequency bursts to life and ascends in pitch until I can no longer hear it.

Dune stands near a luxurious tungsten and black-velvet sofa. Large chairs of the same shiny metal and matte fabric face it. He gestures toward one. I settle into it and feel small by comparison. He lifts a silver orb from a glass bowl on the low table between us, holding it in his palm. It levitates and hovers in the air. Light erupts from the device, shining out in spidery legs that expand into an iridescent bubble around us.

The orb slowly descends into the bowl. It settles among the other spheres, still emitting the light. "We are secure," Dune says. "You can speak freely. Not even our monikers' transmitters can penetrate the whisper orb."

"Thank you for seeing me, Commander Kodaline," I murmur.

"No need to thank me, or to call me 'Commander.' I'm not your mentor anymore. We both know I'm neither firstborn nor secondborn."

"What shall I call you?"

"Dune."

"Is that your real name?" I'm surprised to hear the hurt in my own voice.

"Yes."

I once thought I knew everything there was to know about this man, but I know very little. "Your last name isn't Kodaline. It's Leon."

"You met my brother Daltrey."

"Does one really *meet* Daltrey Leon, or is he more like something that happens to you? Like an airship crash. I brought him the monikers that Flannigan and I stole from Census. He accepted them and then left me little choice but to infiltrate the Sword industrial systems for the Gates of Dawn."

"He does have a way about him. He sees your potential."

"Daltrey is your *real* firstborn brother, is he not?" I ask. Dune resembles the leader of the Gates of Dawn.

"He is. I had an older sister, Kendall, but she was murdered not long after her Transition by a firstborn from the city where she worked."

"I'm sorry."

"As am I."

"Where was her post?"

"In the Fate of Virtues. She had a brilliant mind. She was training to be an energy engineer."

"What happened?"

"She was raped by a man whose father controlled the energy contracts for the region. She became pregnant with his firstborn. He didn't want anyone to know, so he strangled her."

I should be shocked, but I'm not. "Was he punished?" I ask. Usually only secondborns suffer the consequences of any crime perpetrated against them by firstborns, especially the crime of rape.

"Not by Census. He paid a fine to the Fate of Stars, and they let him go."

I shiver, seeing the intensity in Dune's eyes. He has made pain his companion. I've always felt it, but I didn't know why. "You avenged her." It's not a question. He's patient and precise—dark and powerful.

"I tortured my sister's murderer, and then I tied his rotting corpse to the trunk of a tree in front of his parent's estate in Lenity." Pain isn't just Dune's companion, it's his lover.

"He was Virtue-Fated?" Lenity is a wealthy district not far from here.

"He was Star-Fated but living in Virtues."

"Was it enough?" As a soldier, I know once the inertia of passivity is broken, crossing the line of violence has its own momentum. Revenge doesn't have a master. It is a master.

"His death will never be enough. This Republic that allows first-borns to commit atrocities with little or no repercussions—that enslaves us—will end." The caged-animal look is back, darkening his features. It's unnerving. Dune's usually so careful, so controlled. He has never spoken to me like this before, as if I'm his peer.

"It's not your fault—what happened to her," I say quietly.

"Isn't it?" His tone is harsh. "You saved your secondborn friend from a similar atrocity."

"It wasn't the same thing. I was lucky."

"Was it luck or was it you being brave, daring to act despite the consequences?"

"I don't know."

"Nor do I." He paces behind the long sofa, within the whisper orb's confines.

I clutch the arm of the chair to keep myself from going to him. He wouldn't want that. I clear my throat. "Daltrey is the oldest in your family, then Kendall, and then Walther? That makes you technically fourthborn—thirdborn now that your sister is gone."

"Walther is older than me, but only by minutes. We're fraternal twins."

Twins are rare. If a second pregnancy results in twins, one fetus is terminated and delicately removed or left to be absorbed by the other. With a first pregnancy, the parents can choose to keep both twins, but one must be secondborn, and eventually given to the government on its Transition Day. "How did Walther become a secondborn Sword?"

"Walther and I have been a secret since our birth. Census would've executed us both, and our mother for hiding the pregnancy, but my parents were wealthy and made sacrifices to keep us alive." His parents were more than wealthy. The Leons are the Second Family in the Fate of Stars. They would inherit the title of "The Star" if the current First Family's heirs in Stars, the Vukes, were unable to claim the title. In other words, if they were dead. If Aksel Vuke and his two children were to die, Daltrey rules his Fate as The Star.

"What sort of sacrifices?" I ask.

"Some firstborns in the Fate of Swords find the secondborn laws particularly brutal. Secondborn Swords aren't just ripped away from their families, they're often slaughtered by war or they die due to the extreme hardship of being raised as soldiers. Some firstborn Swords are unwilling to sacrifice their own child to that kind of brutality."

"But . . . they have no choice. The law requires them to have a second child to fulfill their duty to the Fates. If they don't, they lose everything."

"In Walther's case," Dune explains, "his adoptive Sword mother pretended to be pregnant. When my mother gave birth to us, my family paid a physician to assert live Sword-Fated births. The physician forged all the DNA screenings necessary to provide sword monikers for me and Walther. Walther's adoptive family claimed him as their secondborn son so that they wouldn't have to have another child of their own and give it up. In exchange, they receive Walther's earnings as a secondborn Sword soldier and keep their positions in the Sword hierarchy. There's no love there. Walther is a means to an end."

"How did your Star-Fated family manage to keep all this a secret?"

"Walther's adoptive family took him into their home as an infant and gave him to a mentor to raise. He lived with them in their house. He was brought to a few of their Sword family gatherings when he was a very young child, but when he became old enough to train in the art of war, he was sent back to Stars, to my real family, per their agreement. We were five years old when I was reunited with my twin brother and began training with my father and Daltrey. We come from a long line of warriors, spanning from a time when there were no Fates or laws to decide who or what a person should be. Our mistake was not training Kendall as well."

"I've always believed you to be firstborn."

"I was more fortunate than Walther. My adoptive family couldn't have children. They tried for years and failed. The Kodalines are Sword aristocracy. They would've lost their titles and their wealth if they couldn't produce a firstborn. They were desperate for a child. My adoptive mother, Corrine, and my adoptive father, Quinton, were eager for the illegal adoption, even knowing they'd be executed if it were ever discovered. They love me as if I'm their own child. They missed me when I was at my Star family home. They demanded visitations. I spent time in both Fates. Then they adopted another child in the same way—a secondborn girl named Surrey. My younger sister came from a Star family as well. She was the Star's thirdborn child and would've been killed otherwise. The Gates of Dawn began as a secret movement to save thirdborns from Census. It grew from there into the network it is today."

"What happened to your Sword sister?"

"Surrey was killed just after she Transitioned at an outpost in Darkshire. Friendly fire, they said. Our adoptive mother cried for days."

"Were you close to Surrey?"

"Surrey felt more like a sister to me than Kendall. We spent more time together. She had no business being a soldier. It wasn't in her nature." Another note of regret. Maybe another reason why my training was always so brutally rigid? Every lesson, Dune stressed that mastery meant life or death.

"How did you come to know The Virtue?" I ask.

"When I was eighteen, I was sent to Virtues to be an Iono guard at the Halo Palace. It was an honor for my Sword-Fated family. I was one of the Halo Palace's most proficient fighters. The Virtue noticed. Not long after, Clarity Bowie sent me to the Sword Palace to be your mentor."

"You're a firstborn aristocrat. Why did you take the job? You don't have to work."

"Before he died, my real Star-Fated father was an aristocratic advisor to The Virtue. He used his influence to plant the seed that I be sent to you to protect the future of the sovereignty of the Fate of Virtues."

"You had plans for me even then?"

"Not plans exactly. We had scenarios. If we could train you from infancy, we'd have another angle of attack."

"Why not Gabriel? Why not train him?"

"You know the answer to that."

"Mother."

"Yes. Your mother only saw him. She never saw you. I could train you any way I saw fit, and she rarely interfered. I could teach you to be strong and decent."

"Do the Kodalines know your loyalties lie with the Gates of Dawn?"

"No." He frowns. "It would kill them to know."

"If you can pay physicians for monikers, then you don't need the stolen monikers I delivered to the Fate of Stars."

He waves his hand dismissively. "Those physicians no longer exist. They've been routed by Census, one by one. I've been fortunate to have maintained my identity—my moniker wasn't a copycat. When Census converted to the new monikers, my device appeared legitimate, so I was issued a new upgraded version after mine was rendered useless. Other thirdborns with copycats were discovered and executed. You saved lives by bringing the new monikers to us."

"Only a few." Most of their spies in the field were executed last year.

"You'll save thousands from Census agents. All our attempts to reverse engineer the new monikers were failures, but because of you, our agents have access to the Fate of Sword's industrial systems. We can create new profiles—new identities for thirdborns to avoid being sense-lessly slaughtered. Soon, we'll locate the schematics and encryptions for the new monikers and duplicate them. You've done far more for the resistance in a short time than anyone could've imagined."

His words don't bring me comfort, not really. They make me feel torn. Sword soldiers are fighting the rebellion—the Gates of Dawn—as I sit here in a literal palace. My regiment is still in active combat. Conspiring with the Gates of Dawn makes me a Fate traitor. When I help them save thirdborns, I'm helping the very people my secondborn regiment is fighting against. I'm choosing to save one side from being murdered while neglecting to do the same for the other side. My side. Secondborn Swords die every day in this war. My people. *Where is their peace? Who will save them?*

"Was it worth it?" I ask, my voice taut.

Dune stops pacing. His entire focus is on me. He arches an eyebrow. "Was what worth it?"

"Killing all those people with your Fusion Snuff Pulse. Was it worth it?" The bitterness in my voice is clear. My eyes fill with tears.

"Daltrey didn't tell you?"

"Tell me what?"

"The attack against Swords on your Transition Day wasn't us."

"What do you mean? I was there. I saw . . ." I growl, trying to keep the tears in my eyes at bay. My fingernails dig into the soft fabric of the chair.

"It wasn't the Gates of Dawn."

"But even Daltrey said—"

"Daltrey was probably trying to protect you, Roselle. He told me you were fragile when they found you. You were beaten almost to death and barely able to move. He didn't want to add to it."

"What are you saying?"

"Those soldiers—the ones dressed like the Gates of Dawn—that wasn't us. Those were Swords dressed as Gates of Dawn—Admiral Dresden's special death squad, your mother's people. Her spies uncovered our technology, the Fusion Snuff Pulse, and she used it, attempting to kill you on your Transition Day and make it look like an enemy strike."

I shake my head in denial. "No! They had on uniforms. They had masks." A tear slips from my eye. "She wouldn't do that! She wouldn't risk her firstborns like that—her reputation—"

"She would—for Gabriel, she would. They knew our protocol. They knew our route. They knew everything. If they'd been Gates of Dawn, explain how they got into Swords."

"You let them in!" I accuse. "You told them where and when to attack us!"

"I would never risk you in that way. Those ships could've easily killed us—we barely survived. You saw my face, Roselle. You saw me." I did see him. He was surprised. He wasn't expecting what happened that day. A part of me believes him—the other part of me feels murdered by what it means, left bleeding beneath the broken ships.

"Gabriel knew," I mutter numbly, putting it all together. "He sent Hawthorne to find out if my mother had killed me." Hawthorne had been told to search for me and make sure the Gates of Dawn didn't take me, but really, that was just a cover so that no one would know The Sword did this to her own people—so she could murder her own daughter.

"Deep down, you've always known it was her," he replies, "and you'll survive it."

"Will I?" I ask in the same kind of shell shock that I'd felt that day.

Dune squats down in front of me, using his large thumbs to wipe away the few traitorous tears that escape. "I'm your family. You're more my daughter than you've ever been hers."

"Did you ever love her?" I wipe my cheeks with my sleeve, relieved when no more tears fall.

"No, I never loved your mother, but I know you do, even as unworthy of that love as she is." He stands and goes to the bar, still within the whisper orb's sound bubble. A holographic menu appears at a wave of his hand. A fat tumbler rises from the surface of the bar. Ice clinks inside the glass.

"Why were you with my mother if you never cared for her?" I watch him pour water over the ice from the pitcher beside the tumbler.

He turns and faces me. "I was her lover so that I could exert influence over her, to make sure that no harm came to you. She was more afraid of you than she was of anyone. The more powerful you became, the more she feared you and The Virtue."

"Why have you brought me here?"

He walks to me and hands me the glass. I accept it, taking a sip. He sits on the tufted sofa. "The Virtue knows he has to protect you if they're to have any future."

My tears are gone now. "I know your endgame, Dune," I reply, setting the glass down on the low table between us. "You want the complete destruction of the Fates. That's what the Gates of Dawn desires. Why not kill The Virtue yourself and have your way?"

"Killing one man or two will do nothing. The regime keeps going—"

"Unless you kill it from within."

"You can bring us peace, Roselle—an end to the barbaric society we live in."

"What if I can't? What if I don't want the job?"

"Unacceptable," he growls. His eyes pierce me with a predatory stare, just like they used to when I'd forgotten some lesson he'd taught me.

"What about Harkness Ambersol?" I ask. "From what I've heard, he'll kill it from the inside by sheer incompetence." This kind of insolence is new territory for me. I've never spoken to Dune like this in my life, but I find I don't care what he thinks of my tone.

"You jest," he replies, "but you hold the lives of every secondborn and thirdborn in your hands. For Harkness to be in a position of power, you'd have to die, and *that* is completely out of the question."

"There has to be another way."

"You think I want this for you? I tried with everything in my power not to destroy the sweetness in you. If there's another way, I don't know it." His definitiveness scares me. He always seemed to know every angle of every situation.

"You're talking about the destruction of the Fates Republic."

"I'm talking about a new world order—one that doesn't tolerate Census agents or government-owned slaves." Fear so strong it makes my knees weak courses through me. He means a world without Transition Days, without people like Agent Crow. I'm afraid of wanting that world, because it's not real, and allowing myself to hope for such a place could crush me. Dune reads my fear. His voice is gentle when he says, "For now, you'll be Grisholm's mentor. You can handle that. I'll take care of the rest."

"What about Reykin? Did you know he's here and he hijacked my mechadome?"

"I know. He briefed me before I came to find you. He's protection for you. Cooperate with him. He's here to help you."

"He's annoying," I mutter.

"Is that why you saved him on the battlefield? Because he annoyed you?"

"I couldn't kill him like they wanted me to—like a coward would kill."

"So, you saved him instead. That's why you're the one who will change our future."

"I love my brother," I blurt out.

"I'll do everything in my power to save Gabriel, but he'll never be The Sword. He'll have to accept that."

"He'll never accept it."

"Then that's on him. Do you want me to call a medical drone for your neck?"

I touch my throat, where my blood has mostly dried. "The assassin shouldn't have tried to slit my throat. He should've just stabbed me from behind—thrust his knife through my nape."

"You wouldn't have made that mistake," he replies.

"I should've killed the third one."

"No, taking him alive was optimal. You would've followed him into the water had Reykin not stopped you?"

"Of course."

This brings a small smile of approval to Dune's lips. "Reykin was right to stop you," he says. "You cannot take risks like that. Your life is very important."

Dune and I talk late into the night. He asks me questions about the past year. He's especially interested in Clifton Salloway and the Rose Garden Society. I don't seem to know anything more about the Sword secret society than what Dune does already, but I'm not sure, because he isn't as forthcoming with his information about the Rose Gardeners as I am.

"You haven't spoken much about Hawthorne," Dune says.

"We're friends," I reply with a shrug. I feel very protective of Hawthorne. Members of the Gates of Dawn have been watching us—Daltrey admitted as much.

"He helped you when you needed him."

"That's how it is when you're a secondborn soldier. We have each other's backs."

"But he's firstborn now."

I don't like what he's implying. "You're basically firstborn, Dune, but you're still loyal to thirdborns."

"Be cautious with Hawthorne. The lifestyle of a firstborn of the aristocracy is seductive. The longer he's a part of it, the more he may get to like it."

Dune's words anger me, not because he's wrong, but because he's right, and in direct opposition to what my heart wants. The thought of not being able to trust Hawthorne again tangles with the love I feel for him and puts me in an even fouler mood.

"I'd like to speak to Hawthorne," I say.

"That's not possible now. Trust me, it's better this way."

My hands form angry fists, and I rise from my seat abruptly. "If you'll excuse me, the evening has caught up to me, and I wish to rest now."

"Of course. Forgive me for keeping you so long."

I wave my hand, dismissing his apology. "I missed you, and I wanted to see you."

"I'll make time for you whenever you need me, Roselle." Dune lifts the whisper orb from the table. The iridescent bubble around us bursts. "I'll walk you to your apartment."

"I can manage it on my own."

"I know you can handle yourself, but I'd feel better if you weren't alone."

"I insist. I'm not a little girl anymore."

I'm out of step with our new relationship. Dune wants us to pull the pin on this world and watch it explode. He's willing to risk everything for change. I'm worried about who will be left standing.

Disappointment shows in his eyes. "A lot has happened in a year, hasn't it? At least allow me to walk you to the lift." I nod. Dune escorts me to the opulent foyer. "Rest for a day, Roselle. Grisholm's training can wait."

"I'm sure he'll be thrilled to hear that."

I retreat into the glass elevator car. When I look back at Dune, there's sadness in his eyes, just like on the day we were forced to part. This man, no matter what he says to the contrary, will always be my mentor—or much more than that. Before the doors close between us, I lurch out of the elevator and into his arms. He squeezes me tightly, resting his chin on the top of my head.

"You're my father, Dune," I whisper so only he can hear me. He acknowledges my words with an even tighter hug. When he lets go, I enter the elevator and descend from the halo.

Chapter 4
Phantom Star

It takes me a while to find my way back to my apartment from the glass lift. I get confused and lose my way. All the small conveniences of my moniker, such as navigation maps, become huge irritations the moment I no longer have access to them. I finally end up asking an Iono guard for help. He summons a mechanized domestic to lead me to my corridor. The tall, lanky android with its holographic humanoid face and features is foreign to me. We never used them at the Sword Palace. My mother never trusted them, calling them a "security liability." She barely tolerated the maginots. I see her point. If the enemy were to infiltrate automated soldiers, an entire army could be turned in a single moment. If the automated soldiers themselves gained a greater awareness of "self," the result could be the same.

My apartment's corridor is cordoned off and crammed with Iono guards who have probably been here since just after I reported the attack. One of the guards behind the barrier lets me through when he recognizes my face. Hovering stingers are positioned on either side of the door of my apartment. As I near them, they don't react to me.

My moniker is scanned, gaining me entry. Inside the apartment, a swarm of Exo guards investigates the crime scene. Among them is Firstborn Jenns. She's on the balcony outside, staring out into the garden below. A couple of Census agents are also there, recording their findings using databases accessed through their monikers. They were probably called because the corpses didn't have monikers. I stay as far away from them as possible without appearing to.

A team of Exos and drone cameras documents the scene. They've already removed the bodies. Now they're pawing through everything in the apartment, but it doesn't bother me. I don't have any personal items here because I was taken from the Fate of Swords during the middle of the night and not allowed to pack. Everything I have has been provided by The Virtue.

I lean against a wall near the entrance to the drawing room and watch the activity. An hour later, the investigation winds down. Exos and Census agents trickle out until only Firstborn Jenns and a few of her people remain. She comes in from the balcony and secures the door. "The assailants' DNA profiles aren't in any of our databases. It's as if they don't exist. Census was called, and they'll be handling that aspect of the investigation. Expect questions from them."

Dread over speaking to a Census agent makes my stomach clench. "Who do you expect is involved?"

"All signs point to Gates of Dawn." I know she's wrong, but I refrain from saying as much because I have no evidence to the contrary. "We'll post stingers in the corridor and by your balcony for now. Extra Iono patrols will remain in the garden, but don't expect that to last. Grisholm doesn't like a large security presence. He cherishes his privacy."

"I'll be fine," I reply. "Thank you for your help, Firstborn Jenns."

"Call me Vaughna. If you need me, contact me on my moniker."

"I can't. Mine has been restricted."

She points at Phoenix. "Then send that little guy to find me."

I don't bother to tell her that it would take Phoenix a long time just to walk down the corridor. I simply nod. Firstborn Jenns and the rest of the investigators collect their equipment in hovering transporters and exit the apartment. A small army of mechadomes cleans up the blood from the fallen assassins. Phoenix's iron exterior is scrubbed and buffed by a particularly advanced domestic robot. When they're finally finished, my apartment is even cleaner than it was the day I arrived. The last mechadome out closes my apartment door.

Alone, I deflate a little. It's past dawn. The sun is bright. Phoenix toddles over from the drawing room toward me. I squat down and run my hand over its head. "You look better, Phee," I whisper, my voice a little shaky. Its rudimentary mouth curves up.

I find my fusionblade where I left it upstairs in the bedroom. My own investigation of the lower floor doesn't uncover any monitoring devices left behind. On the balcony outside my apartment, the two hovering stingers guard the entrance. I use privacy mode to turn all the windows and glass doors opaque.

Hunger drives me to the kitchen. I order a meal via the commissary unit located on the wall. When it arrives on a golden salver, I find that I'm afraid to taste it, worried that it's poisoned. Tears well up in my eyes. Phoenix lumbers in, the top of its head barely reaching the surface of the table. Lifting its vacuum arm, it delicately sucks in a few bits of pasta from the side of my plate. Humming and churning noises ensue. Words written in red laser appear in the lenses of its eyes, detailing a list of ingredients. I study it for a second, not understanding. Then I realize that Phoenix has analyzed my meal on a molecular level. Nothing about the list appears lethal. Its eyes return to glowing red.

"You're sure this is okay to eat?" I ask in a soft tone.

Its lenses move up and down in a nod-like gesture. I lift my fork, taking a small bite, and then a much larger one when I don't notice anything unusual about the flavor. Shoveling the food into my mouth, I finish the entire portion in a few more bites, hardly tasting it at all. We repeat the process for several more dishes and beverages, until I have a small food baby in my belly and eater's remorse.

"Are you Phee?" I ask, setting my fork aside. The burly mechadome's eyes move side to side. "Are you—" Using its right hand, the one that's like a claw, it lifts my hand and points to the small star on my palm. *Reykin*. I stiffen. "I'm going to bed," I murmur. "You should do the same."

Leaving the kitchen, I trudge to the stairs and start to climb them. Behind me, Phoenix's feet clang against the floor. I pause, turning around to find the small bot running into the bottom step, trying to follow me upstairs. It points to the sofa, clearly wanting me to sleep there. "No," I reply. "I'm sleeping in my bed."

More clanging sets my teeth on edge, but I ignore it. I take a quick shower and change into sleepwear that I can fight in if need be. The first-aid kit in my bathroom has liquid stitches and bandages. I use the salve to sterilize and glue my frayed skin together, and a bandage to cover the wound on my neck. Returning to my bedroom, I climb onto the enormous mattress. I grip the silver hilt of my Halo Palace–issued fusionblade and, with supreme effort, try to keep my eyes open.

A murderous nightmare leaves me breathless. I'm jerked awake by something brushing up against my arm. In my right hand, my fusionblade ignites, and I strike, but it's met by an equally strong dual-blade, the X16 model I helped design. The energy of our blades growls where they meet, spitting and sizzling in protest. "It's me," Reykin hisses between clenched teeth. The golden glow of the blade makes him look like a statue of an ancient deity—maybe even Tyburn himself. "You're having a bad dream."

My eyes narrow, and I look around from my half-reclined position on my bed. My bedroom is the same as before, except the fat chair that's usually by the window has been moved to the corner. It has a small blanket draped over the arm and a large indention in the cushion.

I withdraw my fusionblade and power it off. Reykin does the same. The soft light beside my bed illuminates when I touch its base. "What are you doing here?" I demand. Everything is hazy and my voice sounds groggy, even though I have adrenaline coursing through me. My nightmare was particularly horrific—my mother's soldiers were destroying the city of Purity to get to me.

Reykin retreats to the chair, lifting it and moving it back where it was. His hair is sticking up on one side, and his dark, expensive trousers are wrinkled. The broad expanse of his back is completely bare. He turns, and I see a large handprint on the side of his cheek.

My eyes widen. "You slept here!"

"You have bad dreams," Reykin grunts.

"So?" I ask defensively. It's none of his business.

"So you sounded like you were being hurt."

"I wasn't." I rub the sleep from my eyes and sit up straighter, shifting my legs over the side of the bed and setting my feet on the floor.

"How was I to know?" His lip curls in a snarl. "You refused to sleep on the sofa. I couldn't *see* you. Phoenix can't get up the stairs." He stretches his long arms over his head to work out a kink in his shoulder. His body is even more toned than those of most of the Sword soldiers in my unit. He's perfect, except for a long, faint scar from his shoulder to his abdomen.

"Are you insane? You can't be found in my room."

"I know." He exhales deeply in frustration. "I'm going to have to stay until tonight when things become quieter. I'll sneak out then."

"I can defend myself."

"Unless you sleep through the attack. You didn't even hear me enter your room."

"I'm in more danger with you here! If someone were to find you in my quarters, it's not you they'll punish, it's me. You're *firstborn*." My tone implies all the malice I'm beginning to feel for all firstborns.

"Do what I tell you next time, and I won't have to come looking for you!" Reykin snatches up his discarded shirt. I lift my chin, realizing I've been staring at his bare chest.

"Your shoulder healed well," I mutter.

He has his arms through his sleeves, the material gathered at his elbows, ready to pull it over his head. Instead, he lowers his arms and glances at his thin scar. His irritation cools. "The med drone you called on the battlefield mended my bones and cauterized my skin. It sterilized the wound and inoculated me against infection. It hurt like being branded by a fusionblade when I woke up in the back of the cargo ship that transported me back to a Star base."

"You didn't have the scar removed." He could easily have done it. He's a wealthy, aristocratic Star—a landowner and a prominent member of the community that provides power and energy to the Fates. A Winterstrom.

He shrugs into his shirt. "No. I didn't."

"Why not?"

He folds the small blanket, placing it on the arm of the chair. "It's a reminder."

"A reminder of what?" He doesn't answer. I sigh. "How did you get past the stingers outside? Did you use lead to cover your moniker?" If he has more, I want some. I haven't yet fashioned a block for my moniker, and I need to be able to travel freely around without being tracked by The Virtue or anyone else.

"These aren't like Sword stingers. These are Virtues stingers—equipped with an arsenal of elite caliber weapons. *Your* leader saves all the best technology for himself. You can't just rely on a lead shield over your moniker. They have infrared."

"So, how'd you do it?"

"I created an orb that allows me to cloak my temperature—used with the lead shield over my moniker, stingers can't ping me or sense me." He pulls a small device from his pocket and hands it to me. It's a silver sphere the size of a walnut.

"What do you call it?" The orb is icy to the touch. The cool sensation travels across my skin on contact. In seconds, I'm practically hypothermic.

"Nothing yet, I just made it."

"You just made it?" I ask, agog. "How did you know it would work?"

"I didn't." He snatches it back from me, powering it off and returning it to his pocket. "But you were crying."

"I was *crying*?" I feel sweaty. I need his device back so I can get rid of my blush.

"I thought someone was hurting you," he replies gruffly. He looks away.

"I think you should call it a 'phantom orb,'" I mutter, trying to change the subject. "Can you make me one?"

"No." He scowls, turning and leaving.

I follow him.

Reykin switches on the lights with a holographic board in the hall. In the drawing room, the iridescent glow of a whisper orb draws my attention the moment I cross the threshold. The orb sits silently on the low table, its bubble spanning the entire apartment. Reykin set up a perimeter to hide me in.

"Why won't you give me a phantom orb?" I ask as I catch up to him in the foyer.

"Because you'll use it. You're supposed to be Grisholm's mentor. You're not to go snooping around the Halo Palace. You're not to do anything out of the norm. End of story." He finds Phoenix inside the niche in the foyer wall, connected to a recharge station. He squats down and disengages the unit.

I talk to his back. "Maybe I don't want it for here. Maybe I can use it to go back to Swords . . . see if I can get a secret meeting with my brother."

Reykin lifts the heavy mechadome. Turning, he brushes past me. "Your brother will kill you. Didn't you learn that last night? Or even last week? You're not leaving Virtues. That's final."

"You don't know that Gabriel had anything to do with what happened last night."

"Don't lie to yourself."

"If he did, it's because he's afraid of—"

"Gabriel should be afraid. I'll kill him if he comes near you again." He sets the fat bot on the table in the formal dining area.

"My brother—"

"Doesn't love you. He wants you dead." He lifts a silver case from a chair and places it on the table next to Phoenix.

"You don't understand!"

Reykin rounds on me, his expression furious. "What am I missing?" he demands.

I place my hand over my heart and whisper past the aching lump in my throat. "I told you before. I *love* him. I feel for my brother what you felt for your little brother before they killed him. Gabriel didn't take Radix's life. He didn't do that to you. Census did that. The Fates Republic did that. You're condemning Gabriel for wanting to live—the same as I want to live."

Reykin's hand closes around the nape of my neck, gathering me to him. My cheek rests against his chest, and I stare at his bicep where it strains against his sleeve. I choke back tears, refusing to cry in front of him ever again. I'm surprised by his embrace, but at the same time I'm not. Because we've saved each other's lives in the most harrowing of situations, I have a very visceral connection to him. A trust beyond what's rational. "That's not why I want Gabriel dead," Reykin says softly. "I want him dead, Roselle, because he'd rather kill you to save himself and his dying way of life than change and grow stronger to protect you. We're never going to see eye to eye on this."

I pull away from him. "No, we won't."

Reykin sighs. "Do you want to help me make some upgrades to Phoenix?"

"Aren't you afraid Grisholm will wonder where you are?"

"I left word for the Firstborn Commander that I was going into the city to visit some establishments and wouldn't be back until tomorrow." He faces the table and removes fasteners from Phoenix's hull.

"What kind of establishments keep you out all night?" I murmur, mostly to myself. I pick up a tool and ease a fastener from Phoenix's side.

"For a soldier, you're very naïve," he replies, but there's a look of relief on his face.

"I'm not naïve," I reply with a sniff. "I work with arms dealers and the underbelly of Swords society. Are you talking about some kind of betting establishment?"

"No," he replies. "I'm talking about a pleasure house."

"Oh." My spine straightens. "Do you visit them often?" I want to bash him over the head with the fastener extractor in my hand.

"No, it's just a cover." I don't know whether I believe him. My frown says as much. He becomes angry again. "Those places offer the rape of secondborns who have no choice. If you know anything about me, know that! What do you think I'm doing here?"

"Okay. I'm sorry," I reply. "What exactly are you doing here?"

"I'm trying to change the world." He's as intense as Dune. I could drown in the depths of his eyes.

"Is *that* all?" I ask with a small conciliatory smile. "I thought you were here to make sure I do everything you tell me to do." I'm overwhelmed by the firstborn Star and his plan of the future. I even find it mildly amusing because it's so insane. His ambitions are in direct opposition to how I was raised—where conformity to the rules of the Fates Republic is paramount. He expects me to just switch my thinking and my loyalties to fit into whatever vision he sees this rebellion taking.

"Making sure you do everything I tell you to do is just a bonus," he replies. He's not joking. He's enjoying the power he has over me. One whisper from him in the right person's ear, and I'm dead. He could turn me in anonymously to be executed for treason.

A rusted bolt slips from my fingers and clatters on the table. I reach for it, my fingers shaky. "What would you do . . . if I stopped helping you? Would you turn me in?"

He picks up the bolt, circling it between his fingers. "I would never turn you in, Roselle." He gazes into my eyes. "You know too much. I'd kill you myself. You're too big a liability for me to leave your death in the hands of the Fates Republic."

"I'm hard to kill."

"Then I hope it never comes to that."

He hands me the bolt. "Do you want to learn how to install weaponry in a Class 5Z Mechanized Sanitation Unit?" He holds up some parts from a disassembled hydrogen cannon.

"Yeah."

We spend the next few hours upgrading Grisholm's prank mechadome with several degrees of firepower. Midway through the upgrades, I order us some coffee from the automated food and beverage dispensary unit located on the wall in my kitchen. At the formal dining table turned workshop, we stand over Phee, sipping the steaming brew after Reykin uses Phoenix's programs to test it for poison. The firstborn Star explains that he installed technology in my mechadome that will allow him to see through Phoenix's eyes like real cameras and receive a regular video feed instead of just infrared images.

I frown. "I'm not so sure I completely love that upgrade," I mutter, leaning my hip against the table edge.

"Why?" Reykin truly looks puzzled.

"Umm . . . I'll have no privacy. You'll see everything."

He shakes his head. "Would you rather be dissected on your sofa?" His eyes are blue smoldering flames. "I thought they were going to slit your throat last night. I didn't know if Phoenix had the arsenal to stop them." He points to the balcony. "If you hadn't woken up . . ." I stop listening, his voice just a noise. My throat tightens with the horrifying memory of fingernails dragging against my scalp. Panic seizes me with cold claws. My heart contracts painfully and then rages in accelerated flares. My skin instantly becomes clammy—I'm dizzy . . .

"Are you okay?" Reykin scowls and reaches out to touch my elbow. I yank it from him and back up a step, bumping into a chair and knocking over my coffee. It spills onto the floor. I hurry to the stairs, climbing them with my arm on the wall for support. In my bedroom, I retreat to the bathroom and close the door.

"Shower," I croak. The water in the glass enclosure turns on, but I don't get in. I want the sound to cover the panting that leaves me feeling as if I might pass out. At the sink, I whisper, "Cold water," and splash some on my face. My vision blurs. I clutch the enameled edge of the sink, lowering myself to the floor. Steam fills the room.

Reykin taps on the door. "Roselle?" His voice is low. I can't catch my breath enough to tell him to go away. The door opens. I start to rise, but my world tilts, and I slide back down the wall. My hands go to my forehead. I'm trembling. *Am I dying?*

Reykin kneels in front of me. "I'm sorry I said that." His voice is soft and low. He strokes my hair. "You're okay. I'm not going to let anyone hurt you again. I promise."

I still can't breathe.

From his pocket, Reykin pulls out a silver case like the cigar case Clifton uses. Inside, it's different, though, with a secret compartment behind the narrow green cigars. From it, Reykin takes out a chet. He tears off a corner of it. "Stick out your tongue," he orders. "I'm only giving you a little. You can't take a full one again. You're too small. It'll wipe you out." He places the small piece of chet on my tongue, where it melts.

Reykin sits down and puts his arm around me. I lean my cheek against his chest. After a few minutes, I can take a full breath again.

"Better?" He squeezes my shoulder.

I lift my cheek. "I need a shower." Reykin helps me up. I'm weak, as if I just sprinted for miles. I shake off his hands, not meeting his eyes. "I'm okay now. You can . . ." I nod my head toward the bathroom door.

"Oh. Okay. You're sure?" He hovers closer to me.

"Yes," I growl.

"You don't want me to stay and help you into the shower?" I glare at him. "What?" he scoffs. "I've seen you naked before, Roselle. Who do you think bathed you after I found you beaten half to death?"

"Out!" I point to the door. He stuffs his hands in his pockets.

After he leaves the bathroom, I take a long shower, trying to wash away the scent of fear. I'm relieved to find my bedroom empty when I exit the bathroom. I select a dove-gray lounging outfit and dress quickly in the closet. I towel-dry my hair and braid it in one thick plait. The sound of voices leads me to the den, where Diamond-Fated anchors on a visual screen report on preparations for the Secondborn Trials.

It's dark in here with all the windows turned opaque. Reykin sits on the couch against the wall, his long arms resting on his thighs, his hands clasped, scanning the images in front of him as if he's searching for someone. I lean against the frame of the doorway. The sharp planes of his face have a blue tint from the light of the visual screen.

The scene cuts from the secondborn candidates registering for The Trials. Reykin eases his back against the charcoal suede of the tufted couch. His hands absently rub the tops of his thighs.

I enter the den. "What are you watching?" I ask, sitting beside him on the couch.

"Pre-trials."

"Why? You can't possibly like them."

"I don't." He gestures to the moving images in front of us. "Ransom has skills. He's brilliant and he's not half-bad with a fusionblade."

"You expect to see your brother register as a competitor?"

His worried gaze shifts back to the screen. "Like I said, Ransom's brilliant. He knows the odds of winning this travesty are slim, and he knows that, even if he were to survive it, he wouldn't come out with his soul intact."

"You're assuming he got to keep his soul after his Transition."

Reykin winces. "You kept yours."

"Did I? I don't know if that's true." I'm different now. I'm not sure I'd make all the same choices I once did.

"You know you did. You saved me on the battlefield when you could've killed me." He picks up my hand, rubbing his thumb tenderly over my scar.

"Fat lot of good it did me," I tease him. "You're worried he's like you. You'd risk everything not to be their slave."

"I'm hoping he's not like me—or maybe I'm hoping he's exactly like me. I don't know," Reykin growls. He lets go of my hand and rubs his face where the shadow of a beard is forming. "I just want to see him again."

"I hope you do." I rest my back against the soft cushions and pull my feet up next to me, leaning near him. He smells like lemongrass and a soft hint of cologne, the scent I remember from his bed in Stars. The piece of chet relaxes me—not to the point of sleep but enough that my head feels heavy.

"How long has it been going on?" He pretends interest in statistics about would-be competitors on the screen.

"What?" I feign ignorance.

"Your panic attacks."

I shrug. "I'm fine now."

"How long?"

I sigh. "On and off for a while. Never as bad as what you just witnessed. I've always kept it from blowing up. The chet I took yesterday—the one that almost got me killed—was my first. I didn't know I shouldn't take that much."

"How have you avoided a full-blown panic until today? Done anything dangerous to trigger adrenaline and combat the panic?"

I stare at his profile. "How did you know?"

He turns to me with eyes that could pull me out to sea. "Adrenaline doesn't always work. You think I was carrying those chets around for you?"

"Oh." Something about his admission makes me feel better. We're more alike than either of us wants to acknowledge. I know where I stand with him. He doesn't lie to me. He tells me exactly what he'll do if I don't go along with the Gates of Dawn's plans. No guessing. We're friendly for now, but that ends if I ever decide that his cause isn't for me. Reykin, Daltrey, and Dune make more and more sense the longer I'm around them. *What if I were in a position of power? Could I make the kind of changes that would save secondborns? If so, isn't that worth the fight? Or is that the chet talking?*

The price of power is my brother's life, at the very least. Many more people would have to die for Dune and Reykin to attain the influential positions they would need to topple the Fates Republic. The most likely outcome of the plot to destroy the Fates Republic is that we'll all be tortured and killed for treason. I don't care about any of it now, though, and *I know* that's the chet talking.

"Are you hungry?" I ask.

"Very," he admits.

"Me, too. Did you know that I can order anything I want here and they'll send it to me? Anything. I don't even need merits. I can have as many crellas as I want."

"Do you like crellas?"

"I love them," I admit, and then whisper, "I don't even know most of the food items on the food dispensary's menu."

He smiles. It might be the first time I've ever seen him smile. I feel like I ate an entire chet. "What don't you know?" His dark eyebrow raises in a cunning arch.

"What's 'foie gras'?"

He stifles a chuckle. "It's duck liver or goose liver."

I wrinkle my nose. "It sounds gross. Do you like it?"

"No. It has a peculiar aftertaste."

"If I'm stuck with you until tonight," I say, "I'm going to make you my official translator." I rise and walk toward the kitchen. Over my shoulder, I ask, "Coming?"

He catches up, his hand brushing past mine, though he doesn't seem to notice. "First, let's put Phoenix back together. He can be our official taste tester."

The theoretical joy of a food fest just lost some of its appeal, but I try to shrug off the sense of dread at the thought of being intentionally poisoned.

Phoenix is still lying inoperable on the table. Reykin opens the case he carries in his pocket. He extracts a star-shaped programmer and inserts it into one of Phoenix's ports. The star whirls until it resembles a sun. When it winds down, I ask, "What was that?"

"That was a stockpile of malevolence," he says with a smug smirk. He motions for me to help him, and together, Reykin and I reassemble the mechadome.

After lifting it from the table and rebooting it, Reykin gives it a series of voice commands through his moniker. He tells it to terminate the vases on the bureau, and Phoenix waddles over to them, lifts its vacuum arm, and emits short bursts of air that topple over each small urn one at a time. Shards of glass scatter on the floor.

"Um . . . I liked those," I mutter.

"I'll buy you new ones," Reykin replies, just like a privileged first-born who has no idea of the value of things like that.

"They're not exactly mine."

Reykin orders the bot to suck up the pieces. The mechadome performs each order without a hitch, but its hover mode is still broken. "I can't test its new weapons in here. We'll have to do it later."

"Good. I'm running out of vases."

"Phoenix," Reykin says, "go to the kitchen." The mechadome trundles away. "After you," Reykin says, gesturing me forward.

I go to the command center in the kitchen, where we peruse the food dispensary's menu. Reykin explains several dishes to me, some of which I order, like the puff pastries in the shape of swans and the pan-seared whitefish in truffle butter sauce. Others, like the snails sautéed in their shells and the fried beef tongue, I want to mark so that I never accidentally order them. Reykin carefully feeds a small bit of each delivered dish to Phoenix as they arrive.

With two fully laden platters that would make an epicure jealous, we move to the den and set them on the low graphite table in front of the sofa. The lights are dim, and the visual screen is muted. Sitting cross-legged on the soft carpet, I pass Reykin a plate, silverware, and a napkin. He sits on the floor across from me.

He piles food on our plates. I almost die of happiness at the bite of cheese-encrusted potatoes that he insists I taste from his fork. He leans forward and feeds it to me. "That might be my favorite thing ever," I murmur.

"I told you," he replies, a smug grin on his lips.

"We would've killed for even a small pouch of this at the Stone Forest Base."

"You didn't have food like this?"

I give an unladylike snort. "Uh, no. We had nothing like this."

"Did you ever go hungry?"

"Sometimes. In combat, when rations ran low and the supply carriers were shot down." We both know that it was his side who shot them down. Rebels. Gates of Dawn. The enemy. I can see he's thinking the same thing. "You know who'd like this the most?" I ask.

He shakes his head.

"Edgerton. That man can *eat*. It doesn't matter what. He's just hungry all the time." I set my fork down. "Are Edgerton and Hammon okay?"

Reykin nods. "They're—"

I hold up my palm. "Don't tell me where they are. They're safer if I don't know."

"They're like family to you, aren't they?"

I think of the two Sword soldiers who showed me the ropes when I first arrived at the Stone Forest Base. "No. They're better than family."

"They're doing well. Hammon is healthy—experiencing a normal pregnancy."

Tears cloud my eyes, but I force them back. Swallowing hard, I nod.

Reykin wearily scrubs his face with his palms. "Edgerton is a problem, though."

My eyes narrow. "Why?"

He drops his hands and looks at me. "He's too 'mountain,' for lack of a better term. He doesn't blend in well. When he opens his mouth, you know where he's from."

"Can you teach him to hide it better?"

"Mags is doing what she can. If anyone can help him, it's her." I nod, thinking of Reykin's enigmatic secondborn assistant. I must look worried because he says, "There's nothing more you can do for them now. Our network will take care of your friends."

I flop back, stretching out on the carpet. "I know."

Reykin crawls around to my side of the table, lying down beside me. He turns toward me, resting on his side. I do the same, meeting his gaze. The weariness of being awake for so long shows on his face. I wait for him to say something. He doesn't, he just stares back, his eyelids drooping.

I whisper, "You never told me how you know Grisholm."

Reykin's eyes open again, and he yawns. "My father sent me to the best schools in Purity. Grisholm and I were in some of the same circles. He is younger than me. He used to follow me around because I was the best fusionblade fighter, thanks to Daltrey's instruction on my time off. Grisholm has a fascination with weapons—and a serious obsession with betting, especially on the Secondborn Trials. Grisholm always tries to get me to help him figure out who'll be the winner. He even offered me a seat on his council in exchange for my insight."

"His Halo Council?" I ask.

"Mmmhmm," he answers with a deep murmur. His eyes droop again.

"Are you going to take his offer?"

"Mmmhmm."

"Does Grisholm ever win when he bets on The Trials?"

"Yes." Reykin closes his eyes. His breathing becomes heavier.

"Will it be hard for you to betray him?" I ask, but Reykin is already asleep.

Chapter 5
Ebb Tide

He's not going to show.

I lie in the center of the sparring circle staring up at the intricate golden ceiling of Grisholm's training facility. Lifting my hand, I stare at my moniker's timekeeper. Grisholm is officially three hours late for his scheduled training. I think it's safe to say he's never coming. He has been a no-show to every single session I've scheduled for him in the past few days.

I rise to my feet and climb the golden steps to the balcony. Nothing stirs here but the breeze from the sea. I wander out onto the shimmering terrace. The stone is veined with gold, glinting in the morning sun. The blue sky—uncluttered by airships, which are restricted from flying near the Halo Palace—still holds the warmth of summer here, even as we have slipped into autumn.

The view overlooks the stone stairs that wind through the jagged cliff to the water below. I pull off my protective wrist shields and hauberk setting them aside. My sleeveless under-armor top and lightweight leggings are warm enough for a jog along the shore. Descending the uneven steps to the sandy beach, I discard my footwear. My toes sink into the white powdery grit. I stroll to the water. It's always a shock, the coolness of the sea as it settles around my ankles. I remember my first view of the ocean with Hawthorne and wonder what he's doing right now—if he's all right. If he's alive. My heart burns from the agony of not knowing.

I turn my gaze toward the cliff again. Lavish white silken tents topped with streaming golden pennants stand ready along the shore, erected on the off chance that one of the firstborn residents of the Palace will need to use them. None of them does. I'm alone—the only visitor.

Secondborn Stone-Fated attendants stand near the tents to cater to firstborn royalty. I lift my hand to acknowledge them. Their heads lean together in suspicion, trying to figure out why Secondborn Roselle St. Sismode is in the Fate of Virtues when she should be off fighting the Gates of Dawn. I've been treated like an extreme outsider by all the secondborns I've encountered since I arrived. No one speaks to me. It's as if they fear me, but why I can only guess.

I jog along the shore in the direction I haven't explored yet. The tide is ebbing. It's peaceful, and I hardly break a sweat in the thirty minutes it takes to reach the end of the inlet. Rounding the high cliff wall of the cove, I slow to a halt. Ahead, tall stone spires reach toward the sky from a small island in the middle of the sea. Waves crash around the jagged rocks and slate-colored stone walls. The retreating water uncovers a sandbar that leads to the arching gates of the medieval fortress. I'm captivated by the triangular white flags on the forbidding parapets, each pennant adorned with a silver halo.

The arching mouth of the castle is open. Heavy doors with a sea-foam patina stand wide. A slow procession of women emerges from the yawning maw of the castle. They travel toward the shore along a small strip of sand. At the center of the parade, a young blond woman in a flowy white dress wades gracefully through the shallow surf, holding her long skirt in her hand, exposing her ankles to the sunlight.

Death literally hovers over her in the form of ten black, bat-winged death drones. The drones cast cold shadows onto the sand and water around her. Seagulls fall silent as they near, scattering in the presence of the drones.

A team of secondborns scurries around the beach. Stone-Fated workers set up tents and awnings and direct a hovering easel into place. A half-executed oil painting adorns the canvas in a palette of bright hues. Paintbrushes of various sizes levitate next to the easel. Secondborns with the white roiling wave monikers of the Fate of Seas amble around, digging up clams and throwing out nets and woven traps.

Before I can circumvent the party, the young woman in the white dress drops her hem, allowing water and sand to soak it as she hurries to me. The death drones follow her. "Roselle St. Sismode!" she gushes. "I'd heard rumors that you'd come to Virtues!"

Recognition dawns abruptly. It's Balmora, a younger version of her mother, Adora. "Hello, Secondborn Commander," I reply with a deep nod of my head.

Balmora Virtue, formerly Wenn-Bowie before her Transition, is hardly ever photographed or shown on the visual screen. As the spare heir to the title of The Virtue, she's kept from the public eye so as not to be a distraction to the true heir. Her secondborn Virtue-Fated attendants move away from us to a discrete distance, but their eyes and ears are all tuned to our conversation. Based on their upscale attire and silver halo monikers, I'd guess they're secondborns of other prominent families in Virtues—all but one of them, a secondborn Stone-Fated girl around the age of twelve. She hovers near Balmora.

"How long has it been since I last saw you at the Sword Palace?" Balmora asks.

"I was ten, so nine years ago?" I ask.

"That sounds about right. I was eleven, I believe."

"I'm surprised you remember me."

Her eyes grow wide. "I remember you quite vividly, Roselle! How could I forget? You smashed a clock over Grisholm's head! I also see you almost every day on the visual screen, running through a barrage of explosions or shooting at your enemies." She holds up her hand with her thumb up and two fingers out in the shape of a fusionmag, popping off rounds. Her pouty mouth curls into a snarl. She isn't mocking me, it's more like admiration.

"That isn't real. Those are just Salloway Munitions ads."

"Yeah, but you got to meet Firstborn Derek Burgeon!"

My brow wrinkles. "I'm sorry, who?"

"The soldier . . . the one who lifts you up at the end of that one ad and carries you to the waiting airship." She wraps her arms around herself in an embrace.

I remember the ad. It depicted a scenario very much like Hawthorne's rescue of me from the battlefield in Stars. "I didn't catch that Diamond's name," I reply.

"If I were that close to Diamond Derek, I would definitely remember his name." She holds her hand to her heart with a dreamy expression.

I frown. "He . . . he's okay. It's just . . . it wasn't real." The real Derek, if put into a situation with megaton bombs exploding in actual combat, would probably wet himself and never leave the airship. He'd be cringing in the corner beneath his artificial helmet of hair products, crying and sucking his thumb. It's men like Hawthorne and Reykin— who repeatedly dive into danger despite the threat to their own lives— that I find attractive. More than attractive. Irresistible.

"Do you think he'll visit you here?"

"Who?"

She rolls her eyes. "Derek!"

"No."

"That's a shame. I was hoping you'd introduce me to him." She pushes out her lower lip.

"Sorry, Secondborn Commander."

She waves her hand. "Please, call me Balmora! 'Secondborn Commander' is so formal." Her grin stretches wide, showing her perfect teeth. "When did you arrive?" Her fingers catch her windswept hair from her cheek, tucking the long blond strands behind her ear.

"A little over a week ago."

"Why are you here?" she blurts out. "No one knows. It's the most delicious question on everyone's lips." She moves forward and links her arm in mine with a familiarity that I cannot fathom. We've only met that one other time. Back then, Balmora had been more interested in Gabriel than me.

One of the death drones breaks formation and veers closer to me. Turning its harrowing gun barrels in my direction, its initiating whine sends my hand to the hilt of my fusionblade. "Step away from the Secondborn Commander," it warns in a rumbling robotic tone. I can see my reflection and Balmora's on the drone's veneer. My fingertips slowly ease the hilt from the leather sheath secured to my thigh.

"Stand down!" Balmora orders her security drone with a wave of her arm, as if swatting away a nagging insect. "This is my friend, Roselle St. Sismode." The drone takes a moment to process her words before it powers down and shifts away to join the others in formation. "Now then, let's go for a walk," Balmora continues, holding on tighter to my arm.

I relax my grip on my fusionblade, replacing it in its sheath. We stroll the shore together. The young girl trails behind us. Balmora seems not to notice. "Don't mind my sentinels," she says. "I rarely have visitors. The drones are unaccustomed to new faces."

I glance again at her "sentinels." They aren't Sword stingers, like the ones that guard Grisholm. Stingers are meant to defend. Death drones are meant to kill. It's their only job. I wonder if they're protecting Balmora, or if they're her prison guards, ready to kill her if she tries to slip away.

"Do you live there?" I nod my head in the direction of the stone fortress amid the waves.

Balmora's smile fades as her gaze goes to the enormous structure surrounded by water. "The Sea Fortress? It's the Secondborn Commander's residence," she counters with a sharp note of bitterness. "Where else would I live?"

"It's lovely." It's something from a fairy tale. The water is clear enough to see the coral reefs. Diamond patterns dance on the weathered stone. The spires are topped with silver tiles that sparkle in the sunlight.

"It is, but it's also very lonely." She sighs with the kind of melancholy I remember from my days living at the Sword Palace. But I had no companions. She has several. The gaggle of females follows us, whispering behind their hands. Balmora tightens her grip on my arm. "They're not good company," she hisses. "They're no better than spies. One must watch everything one says around them. And anyway, they're boring. The only one I can trust is Quincy." Balmora indicates the freckle-faced twelve-year-old behind us. "You'll have to visit me while you're a resident of my father's home. Which reminds me, you haven't yet told me why you're here."

She holds her breath while she waits for me to answer. It gives me pause.

"I . . . I'm to assume Firstborn Malcolm Burton's position as Grisholm's mentor."

Her expression turns incredulous. "*You* are going to instruct *Grisholm* in the art of warfare?" She giggles and tries to smother it with her hand.

"Yes."

"And how is he taking that?" she asks, wiping a stray mirthful tear from the corner of her eye.

"Not well," I reply, straight-faced.

"I should think not! His overinflated ego won't stand for a secondborn telling him anything, let alone a young woman half his size."

"His ego is in for a beating, then."

She snorts. "And my father knows about this?"

"He's the one who gave me the job."

"If only I could be around to see that," she says wistfully.

"Come to Grisholm's sparring facility tomorrow and see for yourself. I could teach you both at the same time—if he ever shows up for training."

She gives me a side-eyed look. "You're not serious?"

"Why not?"

Her cheeks puff out as she exhales. "I can think of a few reasons. First, I'm not allowed inside The Virtue's Palace, or even beyond this beach, without his invitation. Second, I'm not allowed anywhere near Grisholm. And third, I'm forbidden by law to train in the art of war unless I become Firstborn Commander."

"You're confined there?" I cast my eyes out to the Sea Fortress once more.

"You see that stone formation ahead?" she asks me, gesturing to jagged rocks on the beach. "That's the farthest I can go without creating chaos among the Exo and Iono guards on the estate."

She's their prisoner. We're not so different, she and I, secondborns to the two most powerful Clarities in the world. But unlike me, Balmora's family wants her alive, in case something happens to Grisholm. Mine wants me dead so there will be no alternative to Gabriel.

"What do you do here all day?" I ask. "Do you have a job of some sort?"

She shakes her head. "I have no duties and few interactions with anyone, apart from my staff and the occasional visitor. But now that you're here, you can be my special friend and come for tea and tell me about all the things you're doing out there in the world." I'd hardly call the Halo Palace "the world." It's more like the most privileged island in the world. "Please say you'll come!"

"I'll come when I can," I reply.

On the walk back, she chats nonstop about her visit to the Sword Palace when we were children—her memories of me and of Gabriel. It's clear that she has romanticized that time, talking about Gabriel as if he's the most heroic person she has ever met. I try not to become irritated. I'm not really mad at her. I'm mad at our parents and society for turning the chivalrous boy into a bitter man. When we near her easel, she shows me her oil painting. To my untrained eye, it's exquisite, the exact likeness of the castle in the sea before us. "This is beautiful, Balmora. You're an artist."

"I'm not allowed to be an artist," she replies, her lips pouting. But I know my compliment has made her happy because her mood changes quickly, and she pounces on my arm once more. "You have to let me paint your portrait! I won't take no for an answer."

"But I—"

"I said I won't take 'no' for an answer!"

"I don't know the first thing about sitting still."

"No. You wouldn't, would you?" She giggles. "We'll figure something out."

She needles me until I say yes, and I spend the next few hours watching her paint the castle. She teaches me about perspective, using a focal point to determine the angles and lines. It's fascinating. I use focal points to target and kill. She uses them to capture and create.

We have a small picnic together, set up by her secondborn staff on the beach under a luxurious awning with tables and chairs and linens. We sit apart from the other secondborn women, who talk quietly among themselves about the upcoming Secondborn Trials and their favorite Diamond-Fated actors. I pick at my food, afraid to try anything not tested by Phoenix first. I only eat the finger foods from the same plates as Balmora, even when she tries to offer me things she's not eating. A part of me feels stupid and paranoid. Another part of me knows everyone is a potential enemy.

Balmora grills me about life at the Sword Palace, and especially about Gabriel. She listens to my tales recollecting his childhood games and acts of chivalry. These are the only stories I can give her, because after the age of eleven, I hardly ever saw him. She laps them up like the pastry cream on her fingertips.

"Do you want some advice?" Balmora asks as she wipes her hands with her napkin. She has a smile much like her mother's, though more sublimely impish than wickedly beautiful.

"I don't know. Depends on what we're talking about." I set my napkin aside.

"My brother hates to be embarrassed above all else. If you want him to do what you tell him, that's your leverage."

I think about it for a moment. "Thanks."

The tide is fully out now, and the sea castle is completely exposed. The sun is scorching. It's so much warmer here than in Swords. By this time of year, we'd be issued heat-regulated armor. I should wear a bathing suit the next time I come to the beach.

The dishes are just being cleared by mechadomes when combat airships suddenly fly by overhead. The teacups tremble on their saucers. I shield my eyes and track them. They're new, heavily armored troop carriers. By the look of them, they have multiple types of guided missiles and advanced combat weaponry. The Salloway Munitions signature is in every sophisticated line of the airships. Clifton is nothing if not meticulous when it comes to his products, and I would know his designs anywhere.

"What is it?" Balmora asks.

Several more fly over in combat formation. "We should get off the beach," I warn as I get to my feet.

"Why?" Balmora asks. She doesn't seem the least bit alarmed.

"Something's happening. Something's not right."

The death drones blare and move into a tighter formation, herding the secondborn women into a circle around us. Some scream and

71

overturn their chairs, skittering to get away from the drones. I remain calm. In a few seconds, the noise cuts off. Some of the women are crying.

Airships with arsenals pointed away from the beach hover above the water in defensive positions. They appear to be protecting the Halo Palace and the Sea Fortress. On both sides of the beach, guards uniformed in black and gray swarm onto the sand, moving in our direction, fusion rifles resting just below their shoulders. They don't have their weapons trained on us, so I know we're not the targets. They scan the water and the cliff's edges through the scopes on their tactical weapons. A death drone breaks formation and flies menacingly close to Balmora. In its robotic voice, it orders, "Secondborn Commander, return to your residence for lockdown."

"Why? What's going on?" Balmora retorts with a scathing look. She's not frightened, not like her attendants.

The first wave of Exo guards from the Halo Palace makes it to us. The highest-ranking officer steps to me. With his forearm raised to his mouth, he speaks into his moniker. "Secondborn Commander secure. We've also located Secondborn Roselle Sword."

The holographic soldier projected from his moniker says, "Commander Kodaline's orders are to protect Roselle Sword and bring her to the safe area."

The firstborn Sword Exo frowns. "What about the Secondborn Commander?"

"Secondborn Commander will be shown to her residence by her security detail."

The lead soldier nods, ends the communication, and drops his forearm. "Roselle Sword, you're to come with us," he states. Balmora's death drones surround her and her entourage, aggressively prodding the secondborn Virtue-Fated women to retreat to the sea castle. Something's wrong. Balmora is the most important secondborn here, isn't she? And yet they're more concerned about securing me than her. Of course, the orders did come from Dune, but it's still counterintuitive.

"Promise you'll come visit me!" Balmora calls in a desperate plea as the drones urge her away. I give her a quick nod so she'll stop resisting and return to her home. She smiles and turns away, moving at an unhurried pace across the sandbar toward her towering fortress of stone.

Chapter 6
Crow Sights Carrion

A horde of security personnel forms a wall, cutting me off from Balmora. I've no choice but to go with the soldiers back to the Halo Palace. We run across the sand toward shelter on the clifftop. The stone stairs are just ahead, but we don't use them. A concealed elevator in the face of the rock opens behind the colorful tents. The head Exo and ten of his detail all cram into the elegant lift, with me at the center. The rest of the unit falls back and waits. The doors close, and we rocket up to the main level of the Halo Palace.

We emerge from the marble belly of the giant sea god statue. Its head and beard resemble an ancient mariner's, and its torso merges into the tail of a merman. A downward-thrusting trident is in his grip, frozen as if just before slaying us all.

I'm escorted to Grisholm's private residence. Cutting through his seaside garden sanctuary next to the formal rose garden, we enter the arching doorways into a labyrinth of indoor bathing pools and bubbling spas. The walls and floors are tiled in mosaics of gold and lapis. Vaulted ceilings and archways are supported by columns carved with mythical sea creatures. The soldiers' footsteps echo through the bathing chambers. Diamond patterns of light reflect off the water in waves.

We come upon a hall with a glass-domed ceiling. It features the largest, deepest pool at its center. To one side, smaller hot pools bubble and flow together, forming a river with waterfalls. A golden walkway made to resemble shells separates the steaming water from the enormous, cooler pool. Exotic plants and flowers infuse the room with intoxicating scents.

On the other side of the domed hall, posh furniture arranged in clusters circumscribes a lounging area. The floor is glass. Water flows beneath it. A bar of pure glass gleams near the far wall, a massive aquarium, in which vibrantly glowing jellyfish undulate in the calm water. Lighted glass shelves occupy each side. High-end bottles of alcohol line the pristine shelves. Lighted from behind, the bottles smolder with a unique fire.

Seated around a circular table by the bar are Grisholm and six of his entourage. The Firstborn Commander is appropriately attired in a dark-purple swimsuit with a loose shirt, unbuttoned to expose his tanned chest. His companions, all male except for one female, are similarly dressed. Cards are strewn about the table. Sweating bar glasses, with colorful liquors and ice cubes infused with gold-leaf shavings, chill on frosted stone coasters. Blue, green, red, and yellow plumes of cigar smoke hover in the air.

Among the firstborns at the table, the bare-chested one in the black bathing suit catches my eye. He's fitter and more handsome than the others. His dark hair is wet and slicked back, and his eyes rival the sublime aquamarine of the pool. The moment Reykin spots me, his shoulders lower, and he eases back against his chair with a look of relief. The expression vanishes almost immediately behind a green puff of smoke he exhales.

When he sees me with the guards, Grisholm's eyebrows lower, slashing together. "They managed to find you alive, Roselle. I was giving odds on it, after the events of a few nights ago. They weren't very good odds." He sets his cards facedown on the onyx table and gets to his feet. To the leader of the Exo guards, he says, "You're dismissed."

The Exo team leader walks forward, pointing his fusion rifle down and away from the heir to the Fate. "We have orders to stay with the secondborn Sword and keep her safe."

"Safe from what?" I ask. "What's happening?"

Grisholm scowls in derision, scoffing at my ignorance. "Didn't you hear? Rasmussen Keating was found dead." Grisholm snorts rudely. "You don't know who the Keatings are, do you, Roselle?"

"They're the Second Family of Virtues," I reply. "Firstborn Rasmussen Keating is third in line to the title of The Virtue, just behind you and Balmora. I just . . . How did he die?"

"He was murdered," Grisholm replies. "Why do you think there are guards everywhere?"

His disdain eats at me a little, and my pulse leaps. "How? By whom?"

"If we knew that, none of us would be on lockdown—we'd be out at the Secondborn Trials training camps, evaluating the stock."

His crudeness makes me want to cut his lips off with my sword. I don't touch the hilt of it, lest I'm tempted to follow through with the urge. I mutter, "How tedious for you."

Grisholm stares at the guards. "You'll leave this hall—secure the baths from outside. We don't need you hovering."

The jaw of the Exos' leader tightens. "I'm under orders to remain with Secondborn Roselle Sword."

"Whose orders?"

"Commander Kodaline's."

"Ah, what a surprise," Grisholm says. "She'll be fine. She can probably slaughter all of us." His eyes drift to Reykin. "Not him, though." Grisholm points at the Star across the table. "He can cut her into a pile of flesh in less than sixty seconds."

I want to refute that claim, but I remain silent. I haven't sparred with Reykin. We have no way of knowing who is better.

"I wouldn't dream of it," Reykin retorts with a pirate smile, holding up his hands in a show of humorous surrender. "I might fix her a drink, though."

"Wait outside!" Grisholm orders the Exos between gritted teeth. When they don't move immediately, he roars, *"Now!"* I turn to go with them, but Grisholm growls, "You stay." The lead Exo and his armed men retreat from the sweltering hall.

The scrawny, ferret-faced firstborn next to Reykin punches him in the arm. Reykin doesn't seem to notice, but the other firstborn immediately regrets it, rubbing his knuckles with his other hand. "How come your parents let you train in weapons with a mentor? Didn't they like you?" the weaseling man asks.

Reykin's smile never falters, but his eyes turn cold. "You forget, Simont. My parents had more than one backup for me. I think they loved my thirdborn brother best." The bitterness in his tone is thick. Radix was really fifthborn, and Reykin loved him.

"They got theirs, ol' man," Grisholm says in a soft, conciliatory tone. "Census brought justice and gave you back your dignity."

The aqua light in Reykin's eyes dims. There's darkness, and then there are the things that inhabit darkness. Reykin's one of those things. I know how he really feels about his murdered brother and parents. It led him to the battlefield in Stars—to slaughter as many Swords as he could until they took his life. But he didn't die, because I wouldn't let him. His anger toward his family is a mask he wears to keep his position and protect his other younger brothers. He's a star floating in the abyss, and a part of me wants to save him from it.

Reykin gracefully rises from his seat in a slow uncoiling of muscle and sinew. "I don't believe we've met. I'm Reykin Winterstrom." The other firstborns' laughter sets my teeth on edge. They think he's mocking me. No other firstborn here would think to stand for a second-born. His outstretched hand is an invitation. I straighten my shoulders. Moving forward, I take his hand. He lifts mine to his lips, kissing the back of it. A small shiver slips through me.

"Roselle Sword," I murmur with a small curtsy. His fingers linger on mine a bit too long. I pull my hand back.

The firstborn man next to Grisholm clears his throat. Pushing his chair out, he slaps the tops of his thighs with his hands. "Why don't you come sit here, Roselle?"

The crowd erupts in laughter again, but it's quickly silenced by Reykin's frown. "You should be thanking her for her service, Charon."

"Oh, I'd like to thank her for her service," the Moon-Fated man replies, leering at me. He can't be older than twenty. If he were a sec-ondborn Sword, I'd simply punch him in the teeth, but these aren't secondborns. Retaliation is ill-advised.

Reykin holds out his chair. The harmony of his skin over defined muscles is distracting. "You can have my seat." I frown. I want to say no. He should probably be ignoring me, but maybe this is better. I don't know that I can hide the intimacy between us, so establishing an acquaintance could conceal our true relationship. "Thank you," I reply and take a step in his direction.

"No one sits here without a suit," Grisholm drawls with a smug smile. "Even this *highborn* secondborn." He mocks with an oxymoron.

Reykin takes it in stride. "There's a wardrobe closet just over there, Roselle. You can change while I order you a drink."

"Get me one, too," the redheaded woman next to Grisholm says.

"What do you want, Cindra?" Reykin asks.

"Something lethal," she replies with a wide grin. Her ice cubes clink together as she raises what's left of the last drink to her full lips. She watches me over the rim of her glass. Condensation drips onto her skin, sliding down the valley between the sides of her ruby-colored bikini top. She wipes it away with her finger. Her moniker resembles a carbon atom. Lights representing protons and electrons orbit over her hand.

Reykin nods. He touches his holographic shooting star. A command screen projects from it. He locates a bar menu and orders drinks. Flying mechadomes rise into the air by the bar, selecting bottles of alcohol and setting them on the glass in front of the automated bartender.

I drift away in the direction of the wardrobe closet. Entering it, I lock the door behind me. Facing the holographic mirror, I touch the menu on the side. My reflection wears the first bathing suit on the list—a tiny black bikini. I swipe it away. The next one is white and even more revealing. I scoff. After swiping twenty more to the side, it's clear that the only suits in this program are meant for style rather than function—possibly for Grisholm's special late-night "friends." I settle for a shimmering metallic-silver bikini top with matching bottoms and a graphite wrap skirt.

The ensemble arrives in a silver box. Inside, the outfit is wrapped in delicate, lavender-scented tissue paper and tied with a graphite-colored satin ribbon. I lift the package from the box that ferried it through the air-driven conveyor in the wall, toss my clothes in, and send them back into the chute to be laundered.

Once suited up, I adjust my fusionblade's sheath so that it wraps around my right thigh. Slipping the hilt of the sword into the black straps, I leave the wardrobe. Four of Grisholm's friends grin as I approach. Grisholm, seated at the onyx table, scowls at me from head to toe. Reykin's face darkens with a frown of disapproval. Cindra raises an appraising eyebrow. My fingers twitch near my fusionblade.

A hovering drone delivers a tumbler to the table in front of Reykin. A slice of lemon floats in the center of clear liquid and gold-leaf ice cubes. As I join him, he stands and holds out his chair. I settle in opposite Grisholm. Reykin pulls another chair away from a nearby table and squeezes it in between me and the ferret-faced man, making Simont scoot over. Reykin seats himself close to my side.

On the other side is a firstborn with a blond cowlick in front. His belly pushes down a rather loud, maize-colored swimsuit as he leans toward me. He extends his hand in a way that leaves me wondering if I should kiss its sun moniker or slap it away. I choose to do neither. His cheeks turn ruddy at the slight. "Ahem." He clears his throat, dropping his hand. "Allow me to introduce myself. I'm—"

"Shove off, Milken," the firstborn next to him says as he strokes his dark beard. The light from his aqua cresting-wave moniker makes it look as if one could surf his hairy chin. "She'll never be interested in you."

If Milken's bluster is any indication, then he's genuinely offended. "I'm a firstborn heir to the most powerful growing operations in the Fate of Suns! Why wouldn't a secondborn be interested in me?"

The bearded man leans back in his chair, propping an elbow on the backrest. The wave of his Seas moniker crashes over and over. "I heard a rumor that she's not going to be secondborn for long." His appraising eyes make me feel more naked than the locker room in my air-barracks ever did, but I try to hide it. "She's going to be The Sword one day, and your plantations won't mean a thing when she's in control of all of our armies."

Milken's soft cheeks puff out. "She'll always have the secondborn taint on her, though. That never goes away."

"True," Reykin agrees. "A secondborn will always be inferior." His knee nudges mine beneath the table—an apology. I step on his toes with my bare heel, grinding them as hard as I can. He stifles a small grunt and edges his foot from beneath mine.

I almost need to bite my tongue to keep from cursing Milken out. "Thank you, gentlemen, for your concern for my brother's well-being, but he's in good health and liable to outlive all of you."

"Gabriel is as good as dead," Grisholm replies with an amused look. "It's time that everyone at this table knows it, especially you, Roselle. These are my closest advisors, part of my Halo Council, except for Reykin, of course. But he'll be added soon enough. You'll be called upon to advise us when you're not presiding over the Sword Heritage Council. My father has already anointed you. Now it's just a matter of killing your brother." He says it as if he has accepted the truth of it. My stomach churns. I was counting on turning him into an ally on this one issue.

"I know you and Gabriel were never friends, Grisholm," I acknowledge, "but he's firstborn. He'd stand by your side and defend you—no matter what."

Grisholm lifts an eyebrow. "You always surprise me, Roselle."

That's not difficult, I think. *You never see anything coming.*

"A plot is brewing," Grisholm continues. For a moment, fear runs rampant through me. *Does he know of my involvement with the Gates of Dawn?*

"Please do elaborate," I reply.

"Initial reports say Rasmussen's death is assassination," Grisholm says.

"Do you suspect his brother Orwell?" Reykin asks.

"It's the logical choice," Grisholm replies. "Secondborns murder us all the time for power. It's in their nature." I want to pull my hair out. It isn't nature. Most secondborns accept their fates, no matter how unjust. "I'm bringing in an expert to get us answers."

Grisholm tries to hide his grin, and my stomach tightens in dread. He scrapes the cards together in front of him and forms a stack. Choosing two from the top, he positions one against another. When he pulls his hands back, they remain standing. Carefully, he sets another one against them. "My specialist should be here any moment to meet with us."

The others at the table casually converse about the Secondborn Trials galas planned every night for the next few weeks until the Opening Ceremonies. I listen as Cindra details the glowing electron-inspired dress she had made for an Atom-themed party she's attending this evening. Dune has already advised me that I'm to attend the Gods and Goddesses Ball tonight at a Sword social club, to be hosted by an aristocrat named Firstborn Shelling. Speculation is high as to whether the parties will go on as planned, despite Rasmussen's murder.

I lift my glass to my lips and take a small sip. It's mostly water with a little bit of alcohol. It won't get me intoxicated. I nearly curse under my breath after I swallow it. I need a bit of the courage that alcohol could provide. Reykin is trying to keep me sharp, but a part of me longs for oblivion.

The clipped sound of sharp-heeled boots rings in the lofty room, pulling my attention away from Grisholm and his house of cards. I set my glass back down on the table. A solitary man approaches us from the entryway. His blond, slicked-back hair is neatly trimmed. The long black coat that he normally wears is absent, shed for the warm weather of Virtues. His crisp white dress shirt and tight black slacks I remember from when I first met him at the Stone Forest Base in Swords. When he sees me, Agent Crow's lips stretch across his steely front teeth in a possessive smile. My hand unconsciously goes to the hilt of my fusionblade.

Bile rises in my throat. Inky-black death-tally notches line his temples and neck. His hands are clasped behind his back, and yet I feel as if he has a dagger pressed to my throat. I dare not look at Reykin beside me for fear of giving something away—a thought, a connection, anything that might unmask us both. Agent Crow tears his blue eyes away from me and greets Grisholm. "Firstborn Commander," he says. His deep voice sends chills down my spine. "I've been briefed by your undersecretary regarding the death of Firstborn Keating. May I offer you my condolences?"

"No," Grisholm says. "No condolences necessary. I thought Rasmussen was a pathetic weakling who would ruin Virtues if given it to rule. I don't really care if someone wipes out his entire family. What I care about is *why* he was killed. That's the reason I sent for you, Agent Crow. I have it on good authority that you are relentless in your pursuit of justice." Grisholm's eyes flutter to me, and I can only hope that he cannot hear the rampaging thumps of my heart. A ferocious smile curves his lips. He knows my history with Agent Crow—knows of this man's obsession with me.

"You suspect it was something other than an inheritance issue?" Agent Crow asks.

"I wouldn't rule that out." Grisholm sets another card against the growing house of cards. "But it could be something much more sinister."

"You believe someone covets the title of 'Firstborn Commander,' by chance?" Crow's eyes shift from Grisholm to me, as if they cannot stay away. His voracious stare takes in my every detail. My mind flashes with images of Agnes Moon, Hawthorne's ex-girlfriend, who helped gain my release from the underground cell where Agent Crow had planned to kill me. Grisholm had sent Agent Crow a gift basket of soaps on my behalf once I was freed. Agent Crow used them to bludgeon Agnes to death.

My eyes move between Grisholm and the Census agent. Grisholm sets another card up. Its balance is precise, the angle correct. I suddenly feel buried in a cell with no way out.

They continue to talk about the murder of Rasmussen Keating, neither knowing many of the details, but I'm no longer listening.

A thigh nudges mine. I pretend I don't feel it. I can't look at Reykin. Agent Crow will know. He'll see. A part of me believes I'm being irrational. The cold-hearted Crow who drowned his own sister to gain his firstborn status couldn't possibly know anything about Reykin, but I stare straight ahead just the same.

Without looking up from his house of cards, Grisholm asks, "What do you need to start your investigation?"

"I'll need security access to all of your systems," Agent Crow replies.

"That won't be possible, but I can grant you limited access to systems that lie outside the Halo Palace."

Agent Crow's eyes smolder, but Grisholm doesn't see it because his attention is on setting the next card. "We can start outside the Halo Palace, if you wish," Crow says. "I'm particularly interested in tracking the movements of Sword monikers."

"Why Swords?" I ask.

"Swords are the second-best killers in the Fates." Agent Crow believes the best to be Census agents, like himself, hunters tracking down thirdborns and terrorizing them before killing them. I disagree. Swords fight other soldiers who have weapons. Census kills unarmed people without the power to fight back. "And Swords have the most to gain from the death of Rasmussen."

"Not true," I reply. "His Virtue-Fated brother has the most to gain. The next in line after that is—"

"Kennet Abjorn," the agent states. "Your father."

"He's not Sword-Fated."

"I know. He's a Virtue, but he's your mother's husband—the Fated Sword."

"My mother wouldn't lift a finger to help my father, especially if it were to obtain a position of power above hers."

"What about you, Roselle? You're not above suspicion."

Grisholm snorts. "Someone just tried to have her killed a few nights ago. I think it's safe to say she's not involved in this plot."

"With all due respect, you're assuming whoever attempted to kill Roselle is the same person who murdered Firstborn Keating," Agent Crow replies. "They're separate incidents. I'd like to speak with Roselle Sword about the details of the so-called failed attempt on her life."

"I don't answer questions, Agent Crow, unless I have—" I stop. I was about to say "Dune present," but I don't want him anywhere near this Census agent. Agent Crow's eyebrows rise as he waits for me to finish. "—my family fusionblade back." I couldn't care less about the weapon. It means nothing to me now, but I know it's a trophy for Agent Crow—one he's unwilling to part with. But it has the desired effect of throwing Agent Crow off, and giving me a reason not to be alone with him.

"I cannot accommodate your request," he says, "but you may come and visit it whenever you wish." He touches its hilt on his hip. Etched upon the hilt is the St. Sismode crest. Roses and vines entwine along its length. Agent Crow's possession of it used to be salt in a wound, but it's only a symbol of bad blood for me now. "And I don't need permission to talk to you."

Reykin yawns, stretching his arms with an obnoxious groan. With the unmistakable tone of firstborn privilege, he says, "If I have to sit here for another second and listen to the boring details of your investigation, I might die." He slaps his palms against the top of the onyx table. The impressive house of cards comes crashing down, prompting Grisholm to hiss and scowl at him. "Last one into the pool has to be my slave for a day."

All around me, chairs slide away from the table. The Firstborns fight tooth and nail to get to the water. Arms flail. Elbows fly. Palms cover faces and shove them in opposing directions. Grisholm is first in the pool, cannonballing with the biggest splash I've ever seen. The others follow with ungraceful twists and harrowing belly flops. I'm as surprised as Agent Crow at the lack of decorum among this so-called elite. They act like children. Frivolous children.

Reykin snatches me from my seat with little effort. I clutch him around the shoulders, afraid he'll drop me. His strong fingers grip my thigh. Sweeping me up, he rests me against his abdomen as he runs to the water's edge. The last thing I see before Reykin tosses me like a coin into a wishing well is Agent Crow's homicidal expression over Reykin's scarred shoulder. The Census agent's favorite prey is snatched away once more.

I plunge into the cool water and sink down. The whoosh of Reykin entering the water just next to me pulls me toward him. As the bubbles clear, his dark hair waves hello to me. Concern lines his fuzzy expression. I press my index finger to my lips, and then I run it across my neck like I'm slitting my own throat. When I point upward to the pool deck, Reykin nods. Everyone else is at the surface, treading water. Agent Crow appears at the edge of the pool above, casting a shark-shaped shadow over us.

I kick to the surface. Reykin emerges just after me. Grisholm splashes me in the face. "You were the last one in! You have to be Reykin's slave for a day!"

"That shouldn't be too difficult," I reply, unwrapping my skirt and tossing the sodden fabric to the side of the pool so that it splashes Agent Crow's boots. "I can train him at your sparring circle. If we go in the morning, I can cut him in half with my fusionblade and have the rest of my day to myself."

Reykin chuckles. "Show me the blood I'll bleed," the roguish firstborn replies. He glances at Grisholm beside me. "You up for this, Grisholm?" His tone is a challenge. "Between the two of us, we can defeat this tiny Sword and then make her evaluate the stock with us. She can probably help us separate the secondborn winner from all the losers."

Grisholm arches an eyebrow at me, as if he's just seeing me for the first time. "Maybe you're right. Tomorrow we'll see what she knows."

The sinister voice of my nightmares interrupts. "Firstborn Commander, might I take my leave now so that I may begin my investigation?" Agent Crow gives Reykin a lip-curling scowl. My belly quivers at the sight of his steely teeth.

Grisholm makes a shooing gesture with his hand, dismissing Agent Crow. "Yes, yes. Go and report back." The death-tally notches by Agent Crow's eyes are the feathers of a black bird, twitching before flight. Whatever he's planning, it's coming soon.

Chapter 7
The Gods Table

When I return to my apartment, I'm met outside the door by the cold, assessing look of a secondborn Diamond-Fated attendant. I was supposed to meet Crystal here over two hours ago to get ready for the Gods and Goddesses Ball. Dune arranged for her help because I have no one else, Phoenix being utterly incapable of helping me dress for a costume party. Crystal's disapproving frown makes me remember that I'm still in my silver bikini, with only a long towel wrapped around my waist. I look like a layabout.

"I'm sorry I'm late," I apologize. The sole of her dangerously sharp high-heeled shoe taps against the marble floor in decisive clicks. She's a slight woman in her early sixties. Her silvery hair is pulled back in a severe knot, but it doesn't hide her beauty. "I was on lockdown at the—"

"I'm secondborn. No explanations necessary for wasting my time." Apparently, Crystal is a master at the passive-aggressive arts. My cheeks heat with a blush.

"Can I help you with your things?" I ask. Over her thin arm is a black garment bag. Under it is a long box. Clutched in her other milky-white hand is the black handle of a large black case. The case hovers above the ground. Judging by her small frame and the enormity of the bulky coffin-like box, I doubt she could carry it. The stress lines around her mouth pucker in disapproval.

"I'm capable of performing my duties," comes her clipped response. "Please hurry, we have less time now."

I've selected a non-goddess character to impersonate this evening. After Dune informed me of the invitation to the ball and assigned Crystal to help, I explained to her via hologram that I wanted to go as Roselyn. She's not technically a goddess. She was Tyburn's lover. I first saw Roselyn's image on the side of the Tyburn Fountain, the monument to the God of the West Wind. Roselyn points to the door that ultimately leads inside the Sword Palace grounds. Hawthorne kissed me in that fountain. I can still feel it. All the costume entails is a crown of roses and a skimpy gown. Done.

I close the door behind Crystal. Phoenix's clanging footsteps ring in the hall. He greets us with the bright-red glow of his eyes. Crystal's already severe disdain turns to scorn at the sight of Phoenix.

"What is that creature?" she asks, recoiling.

"My mechadome. It's harmless." I'm pretty sure that it's Phoenix, and not Reykin, greeting me now, because I left Reykin in the bathhouse with Grisholm and the others. I'll have to watch the mechadome to see if it gets clingy. The minute that happens, I'll know Reykin is at the controls.

"Where would you like to work?" I ask.

Crystal gives Phoenix a wide berth as she passes. She stops in the drawing room, her black coffin case still hovering by her side. "This will do." She lets go of the black handle and touches her blue-diamond moniker. The crate opens and unfolds, becoming a vanity with a mirror and studio lights. Crystal hangs the garment bag on a hook on its side and sets the long box beside it. She lifts an ornate, gold-leaf-encrusted chair from near the bureau and places it in front of the vanity. "Please, sit."

After I do, she opens a drawer that contains ropes of thorny vines and small red roses in various stages, from buds to full bloom. She pulls on gloves with polymer protectors on the fingertips and palms and immediately goes to work on my hair, creating a halo effect with a crown. She braids thorny vines into the full length of the long hair in the back, weaving the rosebuds and blooms into the thorns and around the crown. It's a decidedly un-Roselyn-like look. Tyburn's lover was soft, with flowing hair. This is very warrior-like. This reminds me of—

I stand up just as Crystal is about to place another rosebud. Opening the garment bag on the hook, I spread it wide. Instead of a flowy medieval peasant gown, I find an ancient warrior-goddess ensemble consisting of a fawn-colored leather halter that will barely cover my breasts. It laces in the back but leaves the shoulders and midriff bare. Low-rise leather pants of the same hue and a primitive cut hang behind it, and a tight vest of brown suede with a brown fur mantle hangs behind that.

"What is this?"

"Your attire for this evening." Crystal eyes it with approval.

"This isn't what we discussed."

"No. It's not."

"Why did you change it?"

"Your name is Roselle. You should be the Goddess of War, your namesake."

"I don't want to be the Goddess of War. I want to be—"

"Tyburn's lover." Crystal's austere posture takes on an even more rigid mien. "Why would you be subservient to a god when you could be the goddess who presides over him?"

I blink. I have no good answer, except to say, "That's not the point."

"It's exactly the point. But it wasn't me who changed your request, it was Commander Kodaline, so you should bring it up with him if you have a problem with it. Now, if there's nothing further, I'd like to continue my work."

I want to argue, but I know that she's just following instructions, so I relent. I sit back down, and she releases a small, handheld drone into the air. The drone flies in close, airbrushing makeup onto my face.

It draws an intricate vine of inky thorns on the side, beginning above my eyebrow and drawing sharp points near my eye and over my cheek and jaw. Continuing down my throat and over my shoulder, the thorns grow down my arm and wrap around my right index finger.

Crystal directs me to stand. The drone inks more thorny vines down the side of my abdomen. When it's finished, the little drone flies back to Crystal's hand, and she returns it to a drawer in the vanity. The makeup dries instantly.

With Crystal's help, I dress as the Goddess Roselle. She ties the bodice laces, and I take care of the rest. Reaching for the box, she extracts long mocha-hued suede boots. The boots are lined at the tops with brown fur and reach to just below my knees. The leather pants tuck into them. Without the suede and the fur mantle of the vest, my thorny braids would slice my skin to ribbons.

Crystal pulls out an iron belt with sharp, rose-shaped throwing stars attached to it. "Careful," she warns as I take it, "those roses detach. The petals have razor-sharp edges."

I arch an eyebrow. "Why?"

She gestures to my fusionblade, which sits on a nearby chair. "You can't take that with you." Fear threatens to bury me, but I try not to show it. "Dune told me of your need to defend yourself, given the recent attempt on your life. We came up with these as a compromise. You'll need these also." From the box, she extracts iron bracers, the kind that archers used to wear. Clamping them on my wrists, she says, "Turn the rose counterclockwise."

I turn the intricate iron rose on the left bracer. A dagger ejects from inside the hollow sheath and locks into place above my palm. I grip its handle. It's stiff and hard to wield, but useful. I turn the rose clockwise, and it disappears inside the bracer.

Crystal steps back and appraises me with a critical eye.

"What do you think?" I ask.

"It needs one last thing." From the bottom drawer of the vanity, she takes out an iron crown with nine sharp, sword-shaped points. She asks me to sit, and then she sets it on top of my head, positioning it so that it's wreathed by my halo of hair, thorns, and roses. I gaze in the mirror. The image is unmistakably powerful. "I'd fight with Roselle—die for her and what she represents," Crystal murmurs. "I wouldn't lift a finger to help Roselyn. Decide who you are, so I know if it's worth risking my life for you."

"You're—"

"An old woman who is tired of the way things are." She turns from me and touches her moniker. The vanity folds away again, back into a hovering case. She hands me goggles with rose-colored lenses. "Now, let me tell you about the bracer on your right wrist . . ."

The waning sun is blocked by tall, intricate marvels of architecture that are the hallmark of the city of Purity. Each building is more impressive than the last. My reflection in the elegant hovercar's window shines with streetlamp eyes. The image of the iron crown upon my head slices the growing darkness and twinkles, mirroring the lights outside. Lounging beside me in the back seat, Dune is the heart of darkness in his God of Dawn outfit. His boots are ebony. The dark-black fabric of his trouser legs tucks inside them, lightening to a softer shade toward his waist. His shirt is an even fainter shade of black, turning to gold as it reaches his shoulders. A golden, lionlike fur mantle covers his shoulders. His cape attaches to it, gold on the inside, and night turning to golden sun on the outside.

Our hovercar comes to a stop as we queue up for the extravagant costume gala. A slow-moving line of expensive vehicles leads to an enormous hovering glass building with seven towers jutting up from it. A frosty veneer decorates the massive structure, which appears to balance on the head of a thin needle point above the calm, glass-like surface of a deep lake, resembling a floating crystalline formation. A brilliant, burning pink sunset presides. The water beneath reflects the building in the fuchsia sky, the mirrored image like an alternate universe.

The building has only one way in from the ground level, a hauntingly beautiful transparent bridge that reminds me of ice shards frozen in a winter gale. Our hovercar stops in front of the wide bridge. Ushers dressed as fantastical snow people stand on either side of the glacial-looking supports. Frost-covered hair and skin shimmer in the glowing lights of the streetlamps. The ushers have the torsos of men and women, but the lower halves of their bodies are encased in films of faux ice, blurring them.

A particularly tall iceman opens my door and reaches to help me out. The brown mountain range of his secondborn moniker hovers above the back of his hand. I grip his fingers and step into the night air. His eyes fall on my silver sword moniker, widening before moving up to my face.

"I can assure you I was invited," I murmur.

His smile is anything but icy. "Of course. You're Roselle St. Sismode."

"I'm Roselle Sword," I correct him.

A warm breeze blows. I had been expecting wintriness.

"You look like Roselle, the Goddess of War, to me."

I glance down at myself and laugh self-effacingly. "Only for tonight."

His smile fades. "Let us hope not."

Dune emerges to stand beside me. The golden fur mantle covering his shoulders makes him appear even stronger—lionhearted. The attendant's eyes travel up Commander Kodaline's powerful build, and then the secondborn says, "My master, Hail, the God of Ice and Flurry, welcomes you to his social club."

This is all a bit silly, but I play along. "Thank you."

Dune simply nods.

"Please," the usher continues, "allow me to escort you to the doors." His arm sweeps in the direction of the bridge.

"That won't be necessary," Dune says, taking my arm in his. We walk to the north-facing bridge. Firstborns, mostly Swords, garbed in costumes ranging from the ridiculous to the sublime, stroll near us, all moving in the direction of the shimmering ice fortress.

The bridge is a marvel of design, with a long arch that doesn't appear to have any support between its two ends. Beneath us, the water is so clear and deep that it's not hard to imagine that we're the ones walking upside down in a different world. Before us, enchanting snow-flake-shaped doors roll open.

Pairs of Diamond-Fated secondborns greet us inside the doors. One young woman is garbed in a tight, icy bodice. Her counterpart wears a fiery red ensemble, her skin licked with decorative flames. The one with the short blue bob and snowflake-patterned skin scans my moniker with a handheld device. "You have a VIP all-access pass! Are you ready for a seat at the Gods Table?"

"Or are the depths of the Underworld more to your liking?" her redheaded counterpart asks.

Dune's eyebrows slash together, and his demeanor becomes stern. "We're here to see the host," he replies with an air of authority.

"Of course," the blue one says, all business now. "You'll need these to reach the Gods Table at the summit. You'll find the God of Ice and Flurry there." She points up before handing us both a set of hover-discs. The round, metallic pieces are each about two inches in diameter. Lifting my boot, I press one to my sole. It latches onto the stiff leather. I do the same with the other foot. The hover mode engages and lifts me several inches off the floor. I can access the controls of the hoverdiscs through my moniker because they're attached to me, and therefore not blocked. We walk forward, only we don't touch the ground.

"Rise and fall in the recommended channels, or you're liable to get hurt," the red one warns us.

I gaze back over my shoulder to watch the greeters fawn over the next arrival—a decadent, bare-chested god with a very lethal-looking white snake wrapped around his broad shoulders. The fiery greeter directs him to the left and over to a dark ballroom, where a sinister fog and a flare of hellfire creeps over the threshold. He sees me watching him and sends me a sultry air-kiss.

Ahead is a winter palace. Icy fog covers a glass floor. Costumed firstborns use it like an ice rink, only their feet never touch the surface. Above the rink, a holographic field displays a scene from last year's Secondborn Trials, where several of the contestants from different Fates were forced to cross an icy lake. Some tried to tread where the ice was too thin and fell through. Others waited too long for the ice to harden, dying of hypothermia before reaching the other side, freezing solid during the night. A group that constructed primitive sleds to distribute their weight did well. Others assembled hoverdiscs to accomplish the crossing. The ingenuity of the various competitors is astounding, but watching the losers makes my belly ache.

Dune and I move away from the rink. We find a channel, essentially a dedicated path leading upward. The building has tiers of floors, but in the middle, there's open air up to the ceiling. As we rise through the channel, we pass an ice wall with firstborn Swords clinging to its surface, using glacial pickaxes and cliff boots with hoverdiscs to make the climb a breeze. A holographic field in the cliff depicts three-dimensional secondborns in a challenge in last year's Secondborn Trials. The contestants were required to climb a treacherous mountain to obtain golden ration tickets that could be used to purchase food supplies.

My mood sours as I watch the footage. Cyborg mountain lions pounce on Sun-Fated secondborns who couldn't climb fast enough. Their bodies are torn apart in the most horrific ways. The drone cameras cut away to a Moon-Fated team. The climb up is simply too much for one. He calls something to his partner before letting go of the ledge. My heart pounds, watching his body free-fall into the mist below. His partner chooses not to continue the climb, letting go as well and falling to her death. The terror of that moment must have been excruciating. I shudder.

Dune whispers in my ear, "Remember all of the things you'll no longer tolerate when you have the power to change them."

We reach the top of the tallest tower and power off our hoverdiscs, preferring to walk on solid ground. Security is tight here. Firstborn Exos and secondborn Sword soldiers stand in position all around the penthouse level of the tallest tower. Stingers hover in legions. Dune and I are subjected to a battery of security checkpoints, including body scans for high-tech weaponry. I wait for a soldier to balk at my belt of razor-sharp roses or the bracers on my wrists. No one does. *Do they consider these weapons merely decorative?*

Ahead, large golden gates representing the entrance to the Kingdom of the Gods lie open, awaiting the chosen few. This is the gallery level. Dimly lit, it gives an impressive view of the ballroom below. The gilded railing is shaped like a horseshoe and decorated with ancient deities. At the far end, opposite me, is a wall of glass windows, providing a view of the cloudless night sky.

The gods on this level are nefarious at best. I can't help thinking, as I observe them frivolously spilling their cocktails and grinding on each other, that they've been the ruin of secondborns. Some are swathed in latex and lace, others are bathed in cosmic fog and little else, each paying tribute to different gods and goddesses from recorded history.

Below us, down a sparkling glass staircase, is the ballroom's main floor. In the center of the room is the Gods Table, an elevated, Gothic-columned platform where the elite of the Sword aristocracy have gathered to play games of chance. Bright lights stream from it. Elaborate gilded tables, shiny with animated holographic figurines resembling secondborn competitors from all the Fates, do battle in different gaming scenarios. On the dance floor surrounding the Gods Table, couples sway to driving music performed by a Diamond-Fated man resembling the God of Thunder. The glass ceiling above him is an awning against the sky.

A gray-bearded firstborn with a wide mouth, dressed as the God of the Sea, stands at the top of the stairs, announcing arriving socialites. His salt-laden eyebrows weigh heavily over the creases of his eyes, which scrutinize me. "The tide has swept in a prize." The deep rumble of his voice is amplified and echoes around us. He opens his fist, and out swim tiny, holographic porpoises that disappear after sailing by. He leers at my cleavage. I could kill him with the trident in his hand. That thought makes me smile.

"I'm no one's prize," I reply, passing him and descending the glass steps.

"Roselle, the Goddess of War!" he bellows behind me. His gravelly voice carries, coinciding with the final chords of the God of Thunder's song.

His announcement of Dune is lost in the collective gasp from the crowd. Nearly everyone on the floor, and in the gallery, turns to us. I'd give anything to be the Goddess of Peace at this moment. War is easy to perpetuate. Peace, on the other hand, is nearly impossible. It will be hard-won, if it's achieved at all.

The crowd in front of me parts. Thankfully, the music starts again, so I'm not subjected to the hissing whispers of the revelers. A mixture of hostility, pointed stares, and open admiration pummels my invisible armor. I lift my chin. Dune takes my wrist. We thread through the firstborns on the dance floor. A watery moat and glistening fountains wind around the Gods Table, separating it from the dancers. To reach the table, we cross a small arched bridge and climb a short flight of stone steps. Passing between Gothic stone columns, we emerge on the other side of a glittering, transparent sound barrier. The music from the God of Thunder fades, replaced by high-pitched voices and cheering from firstborns crowded around gaming tables.

Within the chaos and revelry of the blinking lights, I find Clifton. He has taken a position at the far end of this exclusive club. Seated amid a table of gamers, he's engaged in a rousing match of Pyramid Conspiracy. I know the card game well. The arms dealer himself taught me how to play it. It's a game at which he particularly excels, and he loves this diversion, but by the way his eyes drift over me, I get the sense that cards are the furthest thing from his mind.

Clifton sets his hand aside, opting out of the match in which he has a substantial bet placed. The officiator takes the stack of chips away without a word. Clifton gets to his feet, lifting his shiny cigar case from the table. He opens it and extracts a thin blue cigar. Putting it to his lips, he lights the end with a flame from the case. Blue smoke rises into the air. He snaps the case closed, rubbing the pad of his thumb on the smooth metal surface. The rigid set of his shoulders relaxes.

His normal blond whiplash of bangs is swept back into a knot at his crown. He's dressed as Cassius, the ancient Lord of Raze and Ruin, with a golden sickle attached to a wide leather belt over a rustic kilt. Thick leather straps crisscross his otherwise bare chest. At the center, where the leathers meet, a gold circle glints. Etched into the thick metal is the face of a rose. A long rust-colored cape hangs from his broad shoulders. With the face of a film star, he reminds me more of a sun god than a harbinger of annihilation.

I can't help the smile that forms on my lips. Clifton's sultry green eyes pass over me, their golden flecks shining. I stop in front of him. He leans over to the table, crushes out the blue cigar, straightens, and reaches out, teasing a small rosebud from my hair. Stroking the delicate flower, he brings it to his nose and inhales its scent. The gesture is surprisingly intimate. "I've been worried about you," he says softly, as if no one else is around.

"I'm okay," I reply. "I'm bored, actually. I have very little to do now that I've been working for Grisholm."

"That isn't what I heard. I heard there was an attempt on your life." His eyes drift accusingly to Dune's, pure malice seething in them. "No one's protecting you."

"She has my protection," Dune replies with polite menace.

Thinly veiled hostility marks Clifton's tone. "Those assassins should never have gotten to her." He rarely loses his cool, and the rage that contorts his normally playful expression surprises me.

I try to reassure him. "I don't need protection, Clifton. I'm a secondborn Sword. You know this." I look around to see who else is listening, and my eyes fall on Valdi Kingfisher, seated at the table next to where Clifton had been. I recognize him as the bookmaker we sold arms to earlier in the year. I know his last name probably isn't Kingfisher. At Salloway Munitions, we replaced last names with bird names to protect clients' anonymity. Valdi's powerfully built, with a thick red scar that runs from his temple to his cheek. The brutal-looking man at the table rises and grins.

Clifton swings his hand in the direction of the firstborn Sword. "Roselle, may I introduce Valdi Shelling, your host for this evening."

I pretend not to know him. "I'm pleased to meet you, Firstborn Shelling. Thank you for your kind invitation."

His lips twitch with repressed amusement. "It is my honor." He takes my hand in his and kisses the back of it, an unlikely welcome for a secondborn. It makes me uncomfortable. Others might draw the wrong conclusions. I tug my fingers from his.

"You have a lovely social club." The word "club" seems wrong. "Glass palace" is probably more fitting.

"Thank you. Most of the guests at the Gods Table are members of the Rose Garden Society. It's usually not like this. The theme is my wife's doing." He gestures toward a young firstborn woman attired in a sparkling silver gown with icicles dripping from it. Her delicate hand rests on the arm of the rugged-looking God of Rain and shines with a golden sword moniker. The stormy deity holds a pair of dice and puts them to her mouth, and she blows on them with a sensual purse of her lips. Wintry snowflakes emerge from between them, a clever trick. The rain god brings the dice to his own lips and kisses them before shaking his fist and tossing them across the table. Tiny storm clouds follow the dice, raining as they tumble and bounce across the table. "The Snow Queen has outdone herself tonight," Valdi continues. He says it with a sour note, watching his wife fawn over the rain god at her side. "Take my advice, Salloway, don't wait too long to settle down. All the good ones will be taken."

Clifton gazes at me with surprising heat. "Oh, I intend to leave nothing to chance when it comes to that."

Dune moves nearer to me, his annoyance plain. "Do you always make your wishes aloud, Salloway?" he asks.

Clifton's laugh is humorless. "I do when it's warranted. So, you're the God of Dawn?"

"The dawn to end all nights."

"Does she know what you're selling?" Clifton asks with a nod in my direction.

"What am I selling?"

Clifton leans in. His pointed finger touches Dune's chest. "You're peddling the end of the world."

"I could say the same of you. Does Roselle know about the Rose Garden Society's end game?" Dune asks.

"What's to know?" Clifton asks. "We're but a group bent on making the world a more beautiful place, one garden at a time."

"The more you sell, the more you're bought," Dune replies.

Clifton's expression turns stormy. "You cannot protect her like I can."

"Roselle has a destiny," Dune says. "If you're smart, you'll be a part of it. If not, you'll be a casualty of it."

Valdi moves between Dune and Clifton, separating the two. "I suggest privacy for a discussion such as this," he says. He scans the room and waves his meaty hand in the air. A secondborn Stone hurries forward. "Show these gentlemen to my private retreat." The servant nods and gestures to Clifton and Dune to follow him.

Reluctantly, Clifton nods. He faces me. "I'll find you when we're finished."

"It sounds as if you plan to discuss my future," I say. "Don't you think I should be present for that?"

Clifton finds my hand and squeezes it. "You should enjoy the party."

Around me flutters a garish display of excess. I know there are secondborns who at this very moment shiver in battlefield bunkers, while here, firstborns are packed in every corner of the dance floor, dry-ice fog blowing on them to keep them cool. "I don't like parties."

He cracks a smile. Strong fingers cup my chin. "No, you're far too serious. I'll teach you how to have fun. I promise."

Turning from me, Clifton and Dune follow the secondborn Stone. I stare broodingly after them until they disappear in the crowd and out onto one of the rooftop terraces at the back of the Palace. I consider following them to see if I can eavesdrop on their conversation, but I'm distracted by the amplified voice of the God of the Sea.

"Roban, the God of Retribution!"

I turn to see my father at the top of the staircase.

Chapter 8
No Way To Slow

A soft billow of black mist floats around my father, Kennet Abjorn, God of Retribution.

He gazes down at the packed crowd as if he were born to rule them. Elegant black eel skin covers him, and thick wolf fur adorns the mantle of the black cape covering his wide shoulders. His hair is dark and slicked back, different than how he normally wears it, but nothing disguises that he's the Fated Sword—my father. Ebony ram's horns protrude from either side of his head. Three women dressed as vengeful night spirits accompany him, curving themselves around him. His Virtue-Fated moniker shines against the cheek of the woman his hand rests against.

There's no possibility of his spotting me in the crowd. Heavy agony stabs my chest. The last time I saw him was at my former home, the Sword Palace, the night they tried to kill me. *Was he a part of the decision to murder me?*

His presence tests my heart's mettle. My father turns and makes his way along the gallery, mingling with throngs of costumed revelers. I take a step in the direction of the stairs, but Valdi's hand on my upper arm makes me pause.

"You need to go to Clifton. Now."

"Why?"

Valdi motions to his security. Armed Sword guards materialize from the crowd. "Because your father wasn't invited tonight."

Confusion crosses my face. "You mean he's crashing your party?"

"I mean I don't know why he's here."

"Maybe he wants to see me."

"Perhaps," Valdi replies skeptically. He nods, and the armed guards close in on us.

"I'll go ask him why he's here," I insist.

Valdi's grip tightens on my arm. "Clifton wants—"

"I'm going to speak to my father!" I shake him off me. Valdi's Sword security tries to block my path to the stairs, but I change direction and make my way to one of the long Sword banners attached to the metal framework of the glass ceiling. Climbing the fabric like a rope, I reach the gallery level. The crowd beneath me cheers, as if I'm a performing monkey, here to entertain them. Swinging my legs, I gain enough momentum to hurtle over the gallery's glass railing. Applause erupts around me. I ignore it.

My mind races. If my father wasn't invited by the host, then who invited him? Chills slip down my spine. *What will I say to him?* Our last encounter was filled with bitterness. Still, I need to talk to him.

Weaving my way through the people in the gallery, I pass large rooms with more gaming tables, others offering strange cuisine, and still others that are completely nefarious. I scan each room for my father. Nothing.

I turn the corner into a new hallway, which is domed like a tunnel. The walls and ceiling project wintry scenes. Holographic snow falls around me. The rooms along this corridor are much smaller than the others—virtual rooms. I pause at one, activating a program that transforms it into a salacious dungeon. I back away and pass another with an open door. A few steps past it, I'm captured around the waist and dragged back into the room. The door slams. My cheek is pressed to the wall by a hand that covers my mouth.

I throw my elbow back and simultaneously attempt to use my heel to crush my assailant's shin. The man behind me avoids both strikes. He whispers, "Is that any way to say hello?"

My eyes widen. A small squeak slips from me. He loosens his hand on my mouth, and I turn in his arms.

"*Hawthorne!*" I whisper. Storm-cloud eyes meet mine. His sandy hair is hidden beneath an ancient golden helmet. The faceplate has eye slits angled in a fierce scowl. The gold nose guard comes to a sharp point. Cheek protection follows the contours of his chiseled face. A golden half-moon shape adorns the crest of his helmet, slicing through the center of it, deathhawk style. Only his full lips are exposed.

He's dressed as Tyburn, the God of the West Wind. A crimson cape hangs from his powerful shoulders. His chest is encased in a hard brown leather hauberk. A warrior's leather skirt stops at his midthighs, showing his powerful legs in tall leather sandals. His bare arms are cuffed with golden circlets that highlight the sheer enormity of his biceps. A round golden shield is strapped to his back, covering the crimson cape. He sheds the shield, setting it beside us.

My knees weaken. He doesn't wait for me to catch my breath. Strong lips cover mine in a searing kiss. His large, calloused hands glide over my shoulders to my neck. The contact sends shock waves of sensation straight through my belly. My lips part. I exhale. Hawthorne's tongue infiltrates my mouth. I lean into him. My fingers splay over his hard chest. My heart pounds. Blood floods my cheeks, turning them rosy and hot.

"I found you," he murmurs.

His fingers slip to my nape. Sharp thorns from the vines in my hair dig into the backs of his hands. He hisses, but he doesn't pull away. I break our kiss, taking one of his hands in mine. His blood drips in tears from the scrapes. My thumb runs over the top of it, wiping at his wounds.

"The thorns cut you," I murmur.

"Worth it," he growls. Hawthorne leans down and kisses me again.

"I was afraid you were dead," I whisper. Tears brighten my eyes. I'm having a hard time containing my emotions.

"I'm devoted to you, Roselle," he whispers, "and you know it."

In this moment, I could believe he's a god with supernatural powers, capable of destroying all my enemies. His hands move down my back and cup my butt. He lifts me in his arms. My legs encircle his narrow waist, and he presses my back against the wall. His hard torso rocks against me. Heat bursts in my core. Every nerve in my body strains to get closer to him. I want to snatch his golden helmet from his head so that I can see his face. My back brushes against a control panel on the wall, and the lights dim. The walls and ceiling become an ominous, darkening sky. Storm clouds gather on the horizon.

"Where have you been?" Hawthorne groans, like he's in agony, but he continues to ravage my mouth. A rumble of thunder reverberates. The deep sound penetrates my soul. Brilliant flashes of lightning ripple through the landscape, turning it white, and then gold, and then gray. Gusts blow across a field of barley, the stalks bowing in the wind. "I couldn't find you," he says, breathing the words.

"Halo Palace," I whisper. The silver moniker on the back of my hand shines against the gold of Hawthorne's helmet. I wrap my arms around his nape. His lips slip to my neck. I gasp softly. He groans, and the vibration fills me with fire. Hawthorne forces me harder against the wall. A thrilling ache of longing shudders inside me.

"I've dreamt of kissing your skin," he murmurs, trailing his mouth over my flesh. "It's all I dream about." His lips find the hollow of my neck. He's the moon, and I'm a wolf willing to howl and commit mayhem to possess it. Hawthorne's hand grips me, and my eyes close, feeling the warmth of his touch to my marrow.

Amy A. Bartol

My head falls forward. The iron sword points of my crown battle with the golden, sickle-shaped blade of his helmet. He lifts his chin, finding my lips again, covering them with his. Opening my eyes, I reach for his helmet, sliding my fingers on either side of its dome. I lift it, pull it from his hair, and let it fall to the floor with a loud clang. My fingers tremble when I cup his face. He gazes into my eyes.

"I walked the beach in Swords where I last saw you," he says, "hoping to find you, even when I knew you weren't there. I thought I'd die without you. I'll give anything to be with you—my firstborn title, my wealth, my soul, all of it." I lean forward and kiss him. He groans again, as if I've stabbed him in the chest.

"I missed you, too. What are we going to do, Hawthorne?"

He hugs me to his chest. "Whatever it takes. I need you. Life without you is—"

A harrowing scream resonates through the rumble of thunder in the holographic room. At first, I convince myself that I imagined it. But then more shrieks and cries bellow from beyond the corridor. Hawthorne goes rigid in my arms. He reaches past my shoulder, cutting off the storm-effect sounds. My legs unwind from him, and my feet slip to the ground. He turns toward the closed door, listening. The ring of fusionmag pulses rises above a cacophony of panicked shouts.

Hawthorne snatches up his helmet and settles it back on his head. He lifts his shield. The gold reflects the dim light of the storm-clouded room. He pauses by the door.

I stop behind him. "Do you have a weapon?" I ask, while easing an iron rose from the belt around my waist. The points of the petals curve like claws.

Hawthorne crouches down on one knee and flips his shield over. The underside has a wide grip that unlatches, revealing a golden dagger hidden within. "When do you know me *not* to have a weapon?" He grasps the hilt of the blade and extracts it from the shield before latching

106

the handle back into place. He holds the shield in one hand and the dagger in the other. Using the shield, he nudges the door open a crack.

I squat down behind him. Lifting the iron rose to my hair, I cut the vine that holds my crown secure to my head and then ease the circlet from its bed of thorns and roses. The iron crown is heavy in my fist. I wish I could cut out the rest of the vines, but they're woven into the braids.

Movement—the sound of pounding feet. A woman dressed in black runs past the door, crying and stumbling. Blood and brain matter mottle her hair. Streaks of red and pieces of flesh, presumably not her own, dot the black eel skin of her costume.

Recognizing her as one of the women who came in with my father, I bound up and leap over Hawthorne, pulling the door wide. Fusionmag pulses rip past my cheek, singeing a piece of my hair. I recoil. The bullet connects with the back of the woman's head, blowing her brains out through her face. Her body crumples.

I turn to see who fired. A ghoulish man, dressed in all black with raven wings, aims his fusionmag at me. His face is covered by a black leather mask, but his lips are exposed in a sinister smile. He utters a single word: "Roselle."

He pulls the trigger. Hawthorne lurches in front of me, holding up his golden shield. The metal dents in and sizzles. Hawthorne flinches and shouts in pain.

I shift to Hawthorne's side, draw my arm back, and throw an iron rose. It embeds in the forehead of the dark-clad God of Death, slicing through his skull and exposing the inside of his cranium. I throw two more, hitting his cheeks. He falls backward from the force, bouncing onto the floor. Holographic snowflakes shower down but never reach his body.

"Incoming!" Hawthorne shouts. He maneuvers around me with his shield in front of him. Another round of fusion pulses career against it. He pushes me back into the room, closing the door.

We crouch down. Hawthorne points. I nod and take the position he indicated, hugging the wall across from him. We wait. Fusionmag blasts shatter holes in the door. A gunman pushes it open, and Hawthorne stabs his dagger into one of his knees. The black-clad figure falls forward. I swing my crown down at him, slicing his arm. The iron blades cut through his muscles and the tendons, slicing his flesh to the bone. He screams in agony, drops the fusionmag, and writhes on the ground.

A second gunman at the threshold fires at Hawthorne, who protects himself with his shield. I dive for the fusionmag the first assassin dropped. Rolling with it, I aim at the man in the doorway and pull the trigger. The pulse caves his face in.

"They're all dressed like Vinsin, the God of Death," I mutter to Hawthorne. "Who sent you?" I demand of the writhing man beside me.

Hawthorne crawls forward and claims the fusionmag from the dead gunman in the doorway. He gets to his feet and peeks around the corner. Chilling screams come from the main ballroom.

The Death God at my feet is bleeding out fast. The hue of his skin is ghostly white. Lifting my boot, I kick him hard in the side. "Who sent you?"

The assassin smiles at me, his teeth smeared with blood. "You're gonna die," he croons in a singsong voice. He bites down on a white tablet in his mouth. The cyanide goes to work immediately. His eyes roll back in his head, and froth trickles from the sides of his mouth. The rest of his body twitches.

I look at his left hand. No moniker shines from it to indicate his Fate. But there aren't any marks there. It's like he never had one.

"We gotta move," Hawthorne urges, taking my arm and hauling me to my feet.

"My father!" I whisper-shout. "I was following him."

"Which way did he go?" Hawthorne mouths.

I point in the opposite direction from the main ballroom. He nods, and we both peek out into the corridor. Golden fusionmag blasts light up the gallery entrance. Beyond the railing is the ballroom and the Gods Table one level below. Hawthorne strips his crimson cape from his shoulders and wraps it around his singed forearm before lifting the shield once more.

He silently signals me to move away from the sound of the massacre. He steps out into the corridor with his shield arm held up and his fusionmag pointed in the direction of the main ballroom. I fall into place behind him. Threading my left arm through the circle of my crown, I let the iron hang on my wrist like a very large bracelet. I place my left hand on Hawthorne's shoulder. In my right hand, my fusionmag points away from him, protecting Hawthorne's back. Together we inch away from the ballroom, one tentative footstep at a time.

We pass several more rooms. Each time, I swing my weapon toward them, only to find them empty. The snowy scene on the wall of the corridor has a streak of blood spattered across it. I tap Hawthorne on the shoulder with the barrel of my fusionmag. He slows his pace. I pivot my gun in the direction of the room on my right.

A Death God runs into the winter corridor from the gallery. Hawthorne fires and picks the target off with one shot. The assassin crumbles onto the floor. Distracted, I miss the target at my side until almost the last second. The Death God seizes my arm, wrenching the hand that holds the fusionmag. My other hand slips from Hawthorne's shoulder. The iron crown slides into my palm. The Death God almost pries the fusionmag from me, but I swing the crown, slicing his jugular vein. He falls onto me, clutching my forearm, attempting to hold himself up while his blood gushes out.

I slide the crown back on my wrist, clutch the dying man to me, and use him as a shield. The Death God behind him shoots his accomplice several times in the back, struggling to hit me. I position my fusionmag under the now-dead man's armpit and fire pulses into his partner. The hit man falls back, his head in pieces. I shrug off my human shield, letting him fall to the ground.

I peer into the room. It's a bloody mess of body parts. A strange sound chokes from me. Beyond the dead assassin on the floor is the body of my father and two of the women he arrived with. They're in pieces. Kennet's tongue has been cut out and placed in his hand. The ram's horns are twisted into his head for real. His eyes have been plucked out.

Two more Death Gods infiltrate the winter corridor. Hawthorne picks them off. He looks past me into the room and swears softly. "Don't look," he whispers. My shoulders round. I'm rooted in place. "We can't help him. He's gone. Move! Put your hand on my shoulder."

This isn't happening.

"Put your hand on my shoulder!" Hawthorne repeats.

I put my hand on his shoulder. Hawthorne takes another step backward, nudging me to do the same. A fusionmag pulse strikes the front to his shield. He swears again and returns fire, hitting one of the handful of Death Gods at the mouth of the winter corridor.

Something inside me clicks.

I maneuver around Hawthorne and his shield, raising my fusion-mag. Squeezing the trigger in rapid succession, I strike each enemy in front of me with a shot to the head.

"Roselle!" Hawthorne howls.

I sprint toward the gallery. Behind me, Hawthorne's feet pound as he tries to keep up. "They're looking for you, Roselle. They'll kill everyone until they find you."

"Well, here I am!" I snarl as I rush into the gallery.

Then I stop, overlooking the ballroom and the Gods Table. Carnage everywhere. A crush of firstborns is trying to move up the glass stairs. The gallery is lined with Death Gods firing into the mob. The black-clad devils are swarming the Gods Table as well. The door to the balcony where I last saw Clifton and Dune has been barricaded against the horde.

I pick off a handful of Death Gods without even trying. Another one rushes at me from the side. I swing my iron crown, slashing his face and blinding him. I cross my arm over my abdomen and shoot him in the chest. Blood spatters the wall.

Touching my moniker, I engage the hoverdiscs on the soles on my boots. Skating forward as if on ice, I gain momentum. With my arm out straight, I shoot every Death God in my path. In my peripheral vision, a black-clad figure, the feathers of his raven wings stretched wide, flies right into me, knocking me over the gallery railing. The hoverdiscs thwart our fall as the winged assassin seizes me around my waist and lifts his gun to my temple. Before he can fire, I throw my head back, breaking his nose. I trigger the bracer on my left arm, and the blade thrusts out. I stab downward, cutting open his thigh. He lets go, but his hoverpack keeps him airborne.

I touch my moniker, and my hoverdiscs turn off. My hair whips past my face as I fall toward the ballroom floor. I reengage the hoverdiscs just inches from the glass tiles. Lifting my fusionmag, I aim at the dark-winged god above me, shooting him out of the air. When he hits the ballroom floor, he doesn't move.

A horde of Death Gods on this level does battle with a few of Valdi's security personnel. Bodies litter the ground all around me. From the pocket of my leather costume, I extract the rose-colored goggles Crystal gave me and set them on the bridge of my nose. Lifting my right arm, I twist the rose-shaped emblem on the bracer. Red powder sprays out in a sprawling crimson cloud that billows like a shifting sandstorm. The dust swirls, blinding the Death Gods and everyone else in its path. Blood-red tears—the hallmark of the Goddess of War—weep from my victims' eyes.

I stride through my hunched-over enemies, blowing holes in their heads. When I reach the far end of the ballroom, a Death God, standing by the wall of glass, holds up a grenade. Crying tears of blood, he pushes the detonator down with his thumb. Rapid flashes of light pulse from it, warning of impending destruction.

First yellow. I engage my hoverdiscs and skate toward him.

Then orange. From somewhere above me in the gallery, Hawthorne calls my name.

Then red. I plow into the Death God and hug him to me, knocking us both through the window and out into the night sky. Jagged shards of glass scatter around us like a thousand stars, cutting us both. He lets go of the grenade, which falls from his fingers. Silently, I brace myself, counting the seconds to detonation. And then—*boom.*

Fire blows out in every direction. The wind from the explosion push us upward. The Death God clings to me, screaming. As he hugs me, I clutch the fabric covering his chest, holding him like a shield from the impact of the grenade. His body blocks the shrapnel and keeps the flames from engulfing me. Metal riddles his back, but I remain mostly unscathed. His grip loosens, and I let go of him. He falls from me into the black cloud, disappearing from my sight.

I begin to fall as well. I try to gain control of the hoverdiscs on the soles of my feet, only to realize that one has been ripped from my boot. The other one can't keep me aloft on its own. I lose altitude, slowly at first, but as I fall into the choking black cloud of smoke, I gain speed. I can't see anything except for the lights below me, growing closer by the second. I dial up the power of the hoverdisc, which slows me down some, but it won't matter when I hit the ground at this velocity. I'm going too fast.

Bracing myself, I shut my eyes.

I'd forgotten about the lake, and the shock of hitting the water is overwhelming. My entire body feels as if it will break apart. Water fills my lungs.

I can't breathe! I'm unable to tell which way is up in the darkness.

On the verge of blacking out, I feel someone tug a fistful of my hair. An arm encircles my waist. I'm listless. Water gushes into my nostrils.

It hardly registers when I break the plane of the surface. "Roselle," Hawthorne growls in my ear, "breathe!"

Brutally strong arms around my waist. Something presses beneath my sternum, thrusting upward several times. Water leaves my lungs, flowing from my nose and mouth. I cough and gasp. Hawthorne's arms shift. One crosses my chest, and Hawthorne drags us through the water with sidestrokes and scissor kicks.

We reach the shore. Hawthorne wades with me to a low wall. He yanks my limp body from the lake. Sitting on the stone edge, me on his lap, he tries to catch his breath.

Roses hang in my face. He snatches them from my hair and tosses them away. My goggles are gone—washed away at the bottom of the lake. Touching my cheek, Hawthorne pats it lightly. "Don't die," he whispers hoarsely.

I open my eyes. Water drips from Hawthorne's chin onto my chest. He lost his helmet at some point. The thorns in my hair dig painfully into my back. My hand struggles to reach his. I touch his skin, and my silver holographic sword entwines with his gold one before my fingers slip limply from him. He lifts me in his arms and carries me over the wall and into the night.

Chapter 9
Something Left Behind

The inside of Hawthorne's chrome airship has that new-craft smell.

Quietly shivering, I feel my lips tremble. Water drips from my hair, sliding down my shoulders and arms. Droplets of red blood from scratches and cuts from broken glass and thorns stain the creamy leather of the copilot's seat. Hawthorne leans into the cockpit, fawning over me. He grasps the straps of the seat, securing them over my shoulders. The thorns in my hair dig into my skin. I wince.

Hawthorne scowls. "Who put these vines in your hair? It's completely asinine!" He tugs my bristly braids from behind my back, laying my hair over the seat back. I don't answer him because the violence of my chattering teeth won't allow it. "I left you in the hands of a bunch of sadists."

He opens a compartment next to me. Inside is a small aerosol device containing CR-40, a topical polymer. He shakes the can and coats the skin of my left hand with the chemical. The silver sword of my moniker dims, and then goes dark.

I reach up and touch his cheek, finding it almost hot compared to my icy fingers. He's cut up, too. Bruises are forming on his jaw and chin, and under one eye. His bottom lip is swelling. Seared skin on his forearm is red and angry. His hand envelops mine for a moment, and the fierceness of his stare warms me. Then, he straightens and closes my door.

Hawthorne comes around the airship, touches a fingerprint panel, and the pilot's door lifts. He seats himself, and the door glides down, locking in place. The engines fire with serious growls that only erupt from a premium airship with power-upgrade modifications. He must have spent a fortune on it.

As if reading my mind, Hawthorne mutters, "I didn't buy this. It was a gift from my parents—or maybe not a 'gift'—maybe a bribe."

He doesn't bother to spray his own hand with the CR-40 but tosses it behind his seat. The golden glow of his holographic sword shines between us. Reaching over, Hawthorne touches a light on a holographic cockpit board. Heat radiates from a vent in front of me. I lean forward, extending my juddering fingertips to it. We lift off into the night sky. The windscreen in front of us modifies, illuminating the terrain, making it discernable as if everything is bathed in the first blush of morning light. He flies the airship away from the chaos of the social club. The heat warms me, and I stop shivering so hard.

"A bribe?"

Hawthorne's expression turns brooding. "What do you do when the son you sent away at ten suddenly returns and holds your future in his hands?" he asks.

"You're loved, Hawthorne."

He gives me a side-eyed look. "They don't love me."

"No . . . I do."

He turns to me. "I love you, too, Roselle, so maybe you can understand how I felt when I saw you throw yourself off a building, clutching a man who held an incendiary device. You could've vaporized before my eyes."

"They killed my father." I can hardly say it without choking. Kennet didn't love me. I know that. But now he never will. I lost my chance. My heart feels puncture, as if it's being forced through the narrow space between my ribs. I didn't know how much I was holding out hope that he'd one day love me, until this moment. "Someone had to stop those soldiers from killing everyone. I could, so I did."

"If you love me, like I love you, you won't do anything like that again."

I look away. "I can't promise you that. I'm secondborn—"

"You think I care that you're secondborn?" he snarls, and then clenches his teeth. "The only person I care about *is you*."

"I'm still a soldier. It's my job to—"

"You're so much more than a soldier—just promise me you won't do anything reckless like that again. Everything is about to change. The Rose Garden Society has an agenda, and you're at the top of it. You know as well as I do what Salloway is planning. After tonight, it won't just be Gabriel's death they call for—Salloway and his cronies will up their timeline."

"What do you mean by that?"

"Who do you think had your father killed tonight?" he asks with a note of cynicism that was never there when he was secondborn. "I would've thought it was the Rose Garden Society. Don't get me wrong, they wanted Kennet dead. But Kennet wasn't just executed, Roselle. He was tortured. Someone hated him enough to make it extremely painful. It wasn't just political. It was personal."

"Mother," I say. A lot of people had a motive to kill my father, but no one hated him like my mother did. Kennet would have inherited the title of The Virtue before I would. Dune and the Gates of Dawn want me to rule. I'm closer now that my father is dead, but the viciousness of Kennet's murder is not their style. They would've simply put a fusion pulse in his head. Mother sent the Death Gods to brutalize my father. If they'd caught me, would they have tortured me as well?

"Othala hasn't been able to get to you at the Halo Palace, so she changed her line of attack," Hawthorne says. "If she becomes The Virtue, she'd rule everything. Now that your father is dead, she's one step closer to her goal. That's bad for the Rose Gardeners. They need you to become the firstborn heir to The Sword before your mother has a chance to become The Virtue, or you're as good as dead. If she eliminates all the other heirs to the title, then everyone bows down to Othala, and she saves her son."

"My mother would then become The Virtue, and Gabriel would become The Sword. I'd still be a threat to Gabriel, so they'd get rid of me. Then Gabriel will inherit the title of The Virtue when my mother dies."

Hawthorne's expression is grim. "But Othala can't save Gabriel. He's the only one who can do that, but he won't. No one needs to kill him; he's doing that all by himself. He's completely psychotic now that he's mixing Rush with Five Hundred."

I cringe. A painful ache squeezes my heart. Separately, the drugs Hawthorne is talking about are dangerous. Together, they're lethal. "Something can be done. Gabriel—"

"Doesn't care about anything except getting high and killing you."

In a broken whisper, I ask, "How are you still alive, Hawthorne?" The night I left him, he'd betrayed my brother, a death sentence in the Fate of Swords, especially if Gabriel is as sick as he says.

"I don't know," Hawthorne admits. He sighs, as if he's trying to sort it out. "Your family doesn't know what we did the night you escaped. Everything was erased."

"Erased? How?"

"The security logs were all compromised. Not one drone camera, security camera, satellite, or maginot recorded us. Not on the Sword Palace grounds, or in the streets of the city, or even near your apartment. Every file was corrupted—they're all blank. Tracking in the city of Forge was wiped out—a total blackout. Gabriel and Othala suspect The Virtue is behind it."

My eyebrows pull together. The only explanation is that once the malware I uploaded into the maginot infiltrated the industrial systems,

Reykin took over and covered our tracks. That must have been risky. He could've let Hawthorne burn for what he did that night. It would've been smarter where the Gates of Dawn are concerned. No one would suspect a breach. Maybe Reykin's program is such a ghost that it doesn't matter?

"What are you thinking about?" Hawthorne asks.

"I was wondering how that's possible."

"I've wondered the same thing. At first I thought Gabriel was playing me, but then it became clear that he truly doesn't know what happened that night."

"What did you tell him?"

"I told him you slipped away. I followed you and the maginot, but you were able to escape to your apartment, where you were met by The Virtue and taken away."

I stare out the side window. "They still believe you'd murder me if given the chance?"

"I don't know—maybe. Things changed after that night. Gabriel has become more and more deranged. I'm his first lieutenant. I run the Heritage Council now, but we haven't met in days because there's no point—no information is coming from the Sword Palace. Gabriel doesn't leave its walls—for his own protection—and no one's allowed to see him."

"Is anyone getting him help?" I ask.

"The only person who isn't terrified of Gabriel is your mother, and I think she's in denial. She's like a lioness. I don't believe the Rose Garden Society saw tonight's attack coming. Salloway would never have put you in danger like that if he had."

Neither would Dune, I think. "Have you spoken to Clifton?"

Hawthorne grunts. "You think Salloway talks to me?" The derision in his tone is telling. "He'd never let me near you if he could help it."

My brow wrinkles in confusion. "But you were at the party tonight. Surely Clifton would have made certain that you weren't on the guest list if that were the case."

"I didn't have an invitation. I snuck in tonight—came in through the roof. I had to try to see you." He puts the airship on autopilot. Reaching up, he unclasps his chest armor and opens the side, exposing a gravitizer inside the breastplate. We employ these antigravity mechanisms in combat jumpsuits. They use a magnetic force to repel themselves from the molten core of the planet and slow the descent during airship jumps. That explains how Hawthorne survived the fall from the building and his plunge into the water to rescue me. "I was locating a quiet place in the social club where I could bring you to talk, and then I was going to find you when you walked by."

"I was following my father." I realize that I might have been able to save Kennet if I hadn't been distracted by Hawthorne.

He reads my face. "I'm glad I stopped you. They might have killed you, too."

"Did you see Dune or Clifton during the mayhem in the ballroom?"

"No. I was only watching you," he replies. A grudging tone of admiration enters his voice. "You destroyed them all, Roselle. They didn't even stand a chance. I could hardly take my eyes off you."

"Even when I temporarily blinded everyone?"

"I was on the gallery level. Your red cloud didn't make it up there to the end of the gallery. I watched you shoot every single target. Then you stopped my heart, throwing yourself on the grenade. After the glass blew in from the explosion, I saw you fall. I ran along the balcony and dove through a window after you."

"That was brave of you," I murmur.

"Brave." Hawthorne laughs self-effacingly. "It was self-preservation, Roselle. I'm lost without you." I reach my hand out to his. He takes it and holds it. "I've been to the Halo Palace a handful of times, hoping you were there, demanding they let me see you."

My eyes widen. "No one told me."

"I figured as much when your mentor informed me that I should move on with my life."

"Dune said that?" I shift in my seat. My side aches, making it hard to breathe. I can't find a comfortable position.

"Yeah. He said, 'Secondborns don't have the luxury of friends,' as if I have no clue what it's like to be secondborn. As if I don't understand the dehumanization and subjugation, being treated like a piece of meat! Then he gave orders not to let me back in the Halo Palace without an invitation."

Anger swells in my heart. All this time, I've been worrying that Hawthorne was dead. Dune could've easily assuaged my fear, but that didn't fit into his agenda.

No longer surrounded by skyscrapers and the bright lights of the city, I wonder for the first time where Hawthorne is taking me. The night travels by. I don't care where we go. I just want to keep flying and never look back. I wonder if there's any place in the world to hide with Hawthorne. It's too hard to be without him, every night lonesome and long.

The aircraft slows and descends, passing over a tall wall that has a fusion-powered security dome. As we near the energy field, a hole develops, allowing Hawthorne's airship to enter before it closes behind us. We circle a sprawling estate centered amid pastoral grounds. The house itself is old and majestic, made of stone and glass with cathedral peaks. "You live here?" I ask.

The airship sets down on a hoverpad adjacent to the formal entrance of the mansion. "It's my family home in Virtues. This is Lenity; we're just outside of Purity." An illuminated path leads through a formal garden to the stone steps of the house.

Lenity is the sister city of Purity, but I don't see a city. I just see land and lakes in every direction. Hawthorne powers down the engines. My mouth hangs open a little in awe. "This is quite a change from the air-barracks. It must keep you busy."

"The secondborn staff runs the place. I have very little to do." Opening his door, he climbs out, pulls his armor from his chest, and sets it aside on the ground. He closes his door and walks around to my side, unlatching my door and offering me his hand. I take it. As he pulls me up, I wince. My ribs feel cracked. My hand goes to my side. "Are you okay?" Hawthorne asks, concern etched in the lines on his face.

"One of the Death Gods slammed me into the railing. I think I cracked a rib—hitting the water like a brick didn't help."

"Can you walk?"

I nod. "Yes. It just hurts." I limp forward. My boots squish with water.

"Hold on." Hawthorne bends down and pulls my boots off, leaving them on the ground. The powerful muscles of his side look a little like shark gills. He straightens, and I get to see him in just a leather war skirt and sandals. My heart beats harder. My cheeks feel flushed. "Better?" he asks. I nod. He takes my arm gingerly, hugging me to his side with his arm around my waist for support.

We follow the illuminated path through the gardens. "Tell me about your house," I urge, trying to think about anything other than the ache in my side.

"The original house was a gift to my great, great—I don't even know how many 'greats'—grandfather, from The Virtue of a few hundred years ago for some act of bravery. My father went on and on about it when I told him I was coming here to get away from Forge for a while."

"What act of bravery?"

"I don't know. I wasn't listening."

"Hawthorne," I chide him.

Hawthorne's expression turns stormy. "My father didn't care what happened to me for the past ten years, and now he wants my attention?" His jaw tightens. "Now he wants me to care how we got a pile of stone and mortar—like it means something? It doesn't. It's all just stuff—possessions. You and I never needed any of this—we had each other."

All this time that I've been struggling with the loss of him, he's been doing the same *and* trying to adjust to a life and a family that never wanted him. "You're right. They can have only what you want to give them and nothing more." We take a few more steps. "But"—Hawthorne slows—"I'm not sure they're entirely to blame. They didn't make the laws."

He resumes a faster pace. "No. They just follow them unquestioningly."

The front of the house is a gigantic open archway with no doors. A security field of soft golden light shines down from the keystone. Up-lighting from the base of the structure makes it look like some monster about to swallow us whole in the moonlight. I'm able to pass through the security field with Hawthorne because of his moniker. Had I been alone, it may not have allowed me access.

On the other side of the entryway, the floor is made of rough black slate with fossilized pyrite swords embedded in the stone. The foyer branches off in several directions, taking different paths. The ceilings are a couple of stories high with a gallery and a clerestory above the nave-like entrance. Skylights glow with moonlight.

It's obvious that the exterior walls were once made of ornate stone, but some have been replaced by invisible, open-air security fields so that the outside merges with the inside, a connection with nature. It's fascinatingly beautiful, and so different from where we come from, Hawthorne and me. We lived in a windowless, tree-shaped fortress and air-barracks, hardly ever seeing the outside unless we were fighting or mobilizing. Now his house is literally a part of the landscape.

A sleepy-looking secondborn with a brown mountain range moniker enters the foyer. He stops short when he sees us. His hand moves to the side of his head in an "oh dear" gesture. "Sir?" he says.

"Send a medical drone to my quarters, Ashbee," Hawthorne orders.

"Would you like a tray as well?" Ashbee inquires, eyeing the smudges our dirty feet have left on the slate floor.

"Yes. Thank you. Just send it with a mechadome and go back to bed."

"Very good, sir. Will our guest be staying for the evening?"

"Good night, Ashbee," Hawthorne replies.

Hawthorne takes me to his quarters at the back of the house on the main floor. His bedroom is nearly barren, except for a very large bed and a couple of large wingback chairs. There are only three "solid" walls. A fourth side is open to the outdoors. The seating stands in front of this nonexistent fourth wall. Without the lights on, it's easy to see outside. The view of the lake is gorgeous in the moonlight.

"Someone stole your wall," I murmur.

Hawthorne snorts with laughter. "There's a wall. It's an invisible security field. You can't walk through it unless you have my moniker or you're touching me. It allows in the breeze but keeps out the bugs." A warm wind blows in off the lake outside. In the distance looms a wilderness of trees. I hear their leaves rustling and the sound of the frogs and insects chirping. I'm unaccustomed to it, but it appeals to me on a visceral level. "Low light," Hawthorne orders. Dim illumination pushes away the darkness.

Hawthorne shows me to the attached bathing area. An array of automated white candles flames to life as we enter. At the far end of the chamber, a huge claw-footed tub sits on a floor of limestone. The outside wall has been removed here as well, replaced by an invisible security field. Smooth river stones and stepping stones lead to a walled garden beyond. Flowering trees and topiaries offer some privacy, but the starry night is perfectly unobscured.

Hawthorne lets go of me. I lean against a stone countertop by a sink while he goes to the tub. It has a spout on either end. One is for water, and the other, to my surprise, is for ice. He turns them both on. Cold water streams from the tap. Ice is dispensed and floats on the surface. "I prefer hot water," I say with a frown.

He glances at me over his shoulder. "This is better for your ribs. I'll give you some anti-inflammatory tablets and a bone refortification injection, but nothing works like ice." He trails his hand in the frigid water.

"That looks like pure torture," I reply.

A small smile tugs at his lips. "It's a far cry from the showers in Tritium 101." I think of the air-barracks where we shared a locker room, when he was mine. It seems like another lifetime, wholly disconnected from this one.

Behind me, the medical drone hovers in the doorway. Its long bullet-shaped body is just narrow enough to fit through the wide doorway. Soundlessly, it creeps into the room. Hawthorne programs it to scan me from head to toe. Because it's a private device, it doesn't need to interface with my moniker.

Its readouts indicate that two of my ribs are, indeed, fractured, and I have multiple contusions riddling my body. Two syringes of medication are injected into my side, followed by a pain reliever. An anti-inflammatory is next, followed by skin regeneration therapy. After the drone is finished with me, Hawthorne allows it to tend to his injuries. He gets a spray of skin regenerator and a laser seal on the worst of his cuts and burns, then a bandage that covers his entire forearm.

"I can wrap your ribs after you soak in the ice. Do you need help?" he asks.

I try to reach my arms back to unlace my leather halter. I wince. "Yes. I need help," I admit.

"First things first," Hawthorne says. Retrieving scissors from a drawer, he gently lifts my hair and begins the arduous task of unbraiding it and cutting out the thorny vines. When he's finished, he sets the scissors aside. Warm fingers brush my wavy hair away from my back and over my shoulder so he can get to the laces of my halter top. Slowly, he unties the strings. Heat flushes my cheeks at his touch. With the laces undone, the small scrap of leather covering my breasts falls away.

His hands encircle my waist from behind, unfastening my belt. The iron strap clangs against the floor. The leather of my pants is torn in several places, but it clings to me like a second skin. Strong fingers grasp the waistband on either side of my hips, tugging my pants down so I don't have to bend. Hawthorne crouches behind me, easing them past my thighs and ankles. I step out of them.

Rising, Hawthorne stands behind me once more. Gently, he pulls my naked form against him, while his head bends to my throat. His lips are a whisper as he kisses my neck for a moment, and then his hand slides to my elbow, urging me toward the tub.

Goose bumps immediately break out on my flesh when I step into the water. "Hawthorne, *this* is completely sadistic."

He chuckles and squeezes my elbow. "I promise I'll warm you up when it's over." I lower myself into the water and hug my knees. After a minute, I force myself to lie back and rest against the slope of the tub. Hawthorne mumbles, "I'll get you a robe."

He leaves. The CR-40 begins to dissolve and peel from my hand. My silver moniker shines up, a sword slicing through the water. The crown-like shadow at the top of the sword appears to be riding on a cube of ice.

Hawthorne returns. My eyes devour him. He's still shirtless, but he has changed from his Tyburn costume into a pair of long black pants. They hang loose on his hips, showing a deep V of rippling muscles. The sight of him should be enough to melt all the ice in this bath, but I continue to shiver.

The pain is nearly unbearable. My lips must be bluer than when he pulled me from the lake. I sit forward, my hands gripping the edge of the bath. "Had enough?" Hawthorne asks. I nod, my teeth rattling. He unfolds a black silk robe and holds it out for me. I climb over the edge of the tub. Water drips off me onto the floor. His arms embrace me, threading mine through the robe's sleeves, which are way too long.

"Is this y-your r-robe?" I ask, trying to stifle a frigid tremor.

"Yes."

"Are y-you aware that you h-have m-monster arms?" I let the fabric dangle to illustrate my point.

He grins. "No, I wasn't aware of that."

"They're g-goonish." I scrunch the fabric up so that my hands emerge. "I f-feel b-bad for y-you."

"Maybe you have T. rex arms. Have you thought of that?"

"No one has m-mentioned it b-before."

"I never wanted to bring it up. Can you sit on the edge of the tub?" he asks.

I nod, my teeth still chattering, and sit down with my back as straight as possible. From his pocket, Hawthorne extracts a bandage and a roll of medical tape. He kneels in front of me. Using a towel, he dries my chest and abdomen before wrapping the bandage around my rib cage and then binding it tight with the tape.

"This is old-fashioned," I murmur. "They have laser fusion for broken ribs."

Hawthorne grimaces. "I hate that surgery. I'd rather tape them. In my opinion, this hurts less. We used to do this instead of the invasive procedure at the Base. It takes longer to heal, though." He pauses and his gaze meets mine. "I can't do that surgery here. My medical drone isn't equipped. I'd have to take you to a medical facility. Do you want me to?"

I frown. "No, they'll separate us."

"They're going to do that anyway, Roselle. We'll have to submit to questioning at some point, but I'm hoping to avoid it for as long as possible."

"I've had the laser-fusion procedure done a few times. You're right; it hurts like someone is soldering your guts. I'd rather you tape them instead."

Hawthorne nods and resumes the work of bandaging my ribs. When he's finished, he pulls the sides of the robe closed and ties the belt. His hands take mine, and he helps me to my feet. His fingers feel hot. The robe is too long. I look down at my hidden feet and the pool of fabric on the floor. "Giant," I whisper.

His hands let go of mine. He cups my face and leans down to brush my lips with a tender kiss. "*Your* giant," he whispers.

"Yes, *my* giant." I deepen the kiss, even though my side aches unceasingly.

Sensing my pain, Hawthorne pulls away and takes one of my hands. We walk to his room. A tea urn, cups, and a tiered tray laden with petite sandwiches rest atop a hovering cart.

Hawthorne pours me a cup and offers it on a saucer. I ignore the saucer, lifting the delicate porcelain in my frigid grasp. It's piping hot. I take a small sip, feeling its warmth all the way to my belly. He pours another cup for himself. We both devour the finger food, standing over the tray like heathens. A yawn escapes me.

Hawthorne takes my empty cup. With a hand on my back, he leads me to his bed. Gingerly, I climb in. I try to lie on my back, but it's intolerable, so I turn onto my left side. There isn't a comfortable position. "Do you want another pain reliever?" he asks. I nod. He gives me a tablet and some water. I swallow it and then lie back. Hawthorne settles in next to me, spooning me, careful to rest his arm on my hip instead of my ribs. The heat radiating from him is irresistible. I press my back firmly against his chest. He kisses my hair.

What we're doing is a crime, a punishable offense. A secondborn in the same bed as a firstborn is even more taboo than two secondborns being caught together. Unless it's a sanctioned encounter in a pleasure house—regulated, restricted to a one-time event, with no relationship or offspring resulting—it's a violation of law. But this is intimacy. The deadliest crime. The penalty for me is much more severe than it would be for him. He'd pay a fine. I'd pay the price. The danger suits me. I thread my fingers through his.

"Missed you," I whisper.

"I don't sleep well without you. I keep reaching for you, but you're never there."

"I'm here now."

"We need a plan."

"I know." I try to focus on the problem, to come up with a plan that allows me to stay with Hawthorne, but his snuggling is like a lullaby, and I can't even find a way to stay awake.

Pressure on my side brings me up from a deep sleep. I want to ignore it, but the hand squeezes tighter. Pain brings my eyebrows together. I whimper. It's hard to breath without my whole side aching. I open my eyes. It's near dawn. The horizon is a bruising of light, blocked by a dark silhouette. I lift my head from the pillow, my vision blurs from exhaustion. Blinking a few times, my eyes focus.

Reykin is seated in one of the wingback chairs, blotting out the view of the lake. A tight black shirt and military-style pants highlight his formidable figure. I almost don't see the black fusionmag resting on his lap. The golden light of his shooting-star moniker hides beneath a black leather glove. I haven't seen him seethe with anger like this since I first encountered him on the battlefield. "Get your clothes," he says.

Hawthorne, still spooning me, whispers in my ear, "Don't move." His hand on my hip is no longer heavy, but tense, poised.

"What are you doing here?" I ask Reykin. Fear wends its way through me. He clutches the weapon in his lap threateningly.

"I came to rescue you," he says with the menacing ring of hard-fought patience.

"Rescue me?" My groggy mind stutters. It takes me a second to remember last night.

"Get. Your. Clothes." Reykin doesn't raise his voice, but it feels like he slapped me. I tense with a sick dread that he'll hurt Hawthorne if I don't obey him.

"Who are you?" Hawthorne snarls. "How did you get past my security?"

Reykin doesn't answer him but continues to stare at me with barely controlled rage. I mutter, "It's complicated, Hawthorne." I raise myself up on my elbow and wince. My fingers go to my sore ribs, holding them, hoping to stave off the pain. It does little. I turn to Reykin. "Put your gun away."

"You'll be lucky if I don't shoot him," he replies. "Now get dressed. We're leaving."

"Hawthorne saved my life last night."

"So you slept with him." It's not a question; it's an accusation.

The rumble of Hawthorne's deep voice contains its own barely restrained fury. "Who is this, Roselle?"

My eyes narrow at Reykin. I shift, moving my feet to the floor and sitting up with difficulty. My hair falls in my face. I bend at the waist, hoping to gain some relief, but it doesn't help, so I straighten.

"Who are you?" Hawthorne roars at Reykin.

Instead of answering, Reykin asks him, "Did you tell her that you're engaged?"

My gasp feels like a knife through the ribs, straight into my heart. Hawthorne's jaw is rigid. I try to meet his eyes, but he won't look at me. "I'm not engaged," he denies.

"Oh no?" Reykin asks. "I just imagined that announcement this week in *The Sword Social*?"

I know the firstborn Star is telling the truth. He doesn't lie to me.

"I didn't agree to it." Resentment is thick in Hawthorne's tone. "My parents made that marriage contract without my consent. Fauna

Kinwrig was my brother Flint's fiancée. They think I have a moral obligation to fulfill that promise to her."

Reykin's blue eyes are unwavering. "That will be a difficult contract to break. The Kinwrigs are powerful. I'm sure they like the sound of Fauna Trugrave just a little too much, given what comes with the name."

"Hard to break, but not impossible."

"Do you know what would happen to Roselle, a secondborn, if she were found like this in your bed? They'd whip the skin off her back—and that's just the beginning. And do you know what would happen to you?" He pauses. "Nothing. You'd get to live on and marry Firstborn Kinwrig."

I get to my feet, unable to sit any longer. My ribs are aching, and my heart is breaking. I clutch my side and move toward the bathroom.

"Roselle!" Hawthorne calls.

"Don't move," Reykin orders him, raising the barrel of the fusionmag.

I enter the bathroom and close the door. My clothes are still on the limestone floor near the bath. Gathering them, I shrug the leather top over my bandaged ribs, pain stabbing in my side. Cold sweat breaks out on my brow. I refuse to call Reykin to help me. I don't even know if he would. Instead, I reach behind me, holding my breath against the agony, and tie the laces myself. The pants are a little easier to manage. I don't have my boots, but I'm not sure I could put them on anyway.

Glancing in the mirror, I'm not surprised to see deep-blue and -purple bruises on my shoulders and arms. Cuts from shattered glass and thorns still mar my skin, despite the round of skin regeneration therapy. In short, I'm a mess.

I rummage in a drawer near the sink, finding toothpaste. I rub some on the tip of my finger and clean my teeth. When I'm done, I use a smear of toothpaste to write the coordinates of my Halo Palace apartment on the mirror.

Both Hawthorne and Reykin are on their feet, sizing each other up, when I exit the bathroom. "Let's go," I order Reykin, holding my side. His eyes widen in surprise. I don't think he realized the extent of my injuries. The black robe had covered a multitude of wounds. Now they're a billboard on my skin.

"Roselle," Hawthorne growls between clenched teeth. He doesn't understand what's happening here.

"It's okay, Hawthorne." I try to give him a reassuring smile. "He won't hurt me. He'll take me back to the Halo Palace where I'll be protected. You don't have to worry."

"Who is *he*!" Hawthorne demands.

"If I tell you, he'll kill you. Trust me, Hawthorne, it's better this way. I'll see you soon."

Hawthorne is visibly shaking with rage. He points at Reykin. "If you hurt her, I'll rip your heart out."

"It's already gone," Reykin retorts. The belligerent firstborn Star gestures to the door. We pass through to a small garden and into the shadows of a coming dawn.

Chapter 10
The Nature of Dawn

I hold my stinging ribs, silently cursing Reykin.

Speckled with stones, moss, and prickly things, a path winds through the majestic trees and shrubbery. The stones dig into my bare feet. Reykin trails behind me. My pace is slow because every step hurts. He touches my elbow. I ease my arm away from him, even though I could use the support. We trudge along the path, and every few steps Reykin glances behind us, maybe expecting to see Hawthorne. He won't. Hawthorne is stealth itself. He won't try anything, though, not with Reykin training his fusionmag on me.

We make it to the tree line near the lake. Just inside the copse, a black airship rests beneath a small pile of fir boughs. Reykin pulls them off the concealed airship. The sun hasn't broken the horizon, but the gray shadows are pushing back. Reykin opens the copilot door for me. I hold my breath, carefully climbing onto the seat. He closes my door and rounds the airship.

Once inside the two-seater aircraft, Reykin tucks his fusionmag into the black holster on the side of his chest. He spares little time getting us into the air. We fly low, skimming just above the leafy canopy, avoiding detection. The set of his jaw tells me I'm in dangerous territory with him. I'm confused about why, but I'm unwilling to ask. Nor will I explain myself to him. It's time he learns that he doesn't own me.

"Have you ever thought about the nature of dawn?" I ask. Reykin doesn't answer. "I have. When you're a soldier, you think about those things, especially because you hardly ever see the sunrise unless you're in battle." He doesn't look at me, but he's listening. "I've heard it said that dawn is the light, asking the night for permission to exist."

Reykin snorts rudely.

"I agree," I reply, watching the sun break the plane of the horizon. "I don't subscribe to that either. I believe dawn is the violent over-throw of night. But night is always still there—just on the periphery—waiting . . . and at the end of the day, it comes to claim us all."

"I thought you were dead!" Reykin shouts. My fingers curls on the armrest in reaction to his violent outburst. "Witnesses saw you push a man through a window at the top of the building. Sea-Fated divers are dragging the lake beneath the social club searching for your body."

"People think I'm dead?" I ask.

"No one survives that fall!"

"I had hoverdiscs on. One of them continued to work. How did you find me?"

"I infiltrated the secure access at the Halo Palace and located your moniker tracking . . . and then I waited. At first there was nothing. You were just gone. But then, I got a ping. It faded in and out, but it was there. The readings were bizarre: spotty location, alarming health read-outs, hypothermia, distress. I was sure you were alive, but being tortured."

"My ribs are broken. I soaked in a bath of ice water last night. If you think that I derived any pleasure from it, I invite you to try it. I'll even break your ribs for you."

He makes a growling sound that raises the fine hairs on my arms. "I thought you and Trugrave . . ."

"I know what you thought, and it's none of your business!" I retort.

"It is my business! I can't hide you like I hid your friend Hammon. Most people know you on sight."

"Don't try to shame me, Reykin. You spent the whole night and an entire day in my apartment alone with me. You're a firstborn. It's the same thing."

"That was different!"

"How was it different?" I ask.

"It just was. I wasn't in your bed with you all night. Dune wasn't standing by the social club's lake, demanding it be drained."

I cringe. "Does he know I'm alive?"

"He doesn't know for sure yet," Reykin admits.

"You knew I was alive when my moniker showed the coordinates of Hawthorne's home," I press. "Why didn't you tell him then?"

He ignores my question. "Tell me, why is Hawthorne still alive? Your brother didn't kill him. Maybe your new firstborn Sword changed his mind and decided your brother and mother were the safer side?"

"Hawthorne would never do that."

"Desperate people do desperate things," Reykin replies.

"He's alive because of you," I murmur. Reykin's eyes narrow. "I know it was you who saved him. You erased every trace of our escape from the Sword Palace that night."

"I did that for you, not for him."

"That was dangerous. It could've alerted them to the fact we'd infiltrated their systems."

"They'll never find anything."

"Do you think my family are the ones behind the attack last night?"

"Yes."

"Is there evidence in any of their communications? Something we can use?"

Reykin frowns. "I don't know. I need to dig in and search for it, and that will take a while, but I know a few things. It wasn't Gates of

Dawn who attacked last night, and I'd rule out the Rose Garden Society, seeing as how quite a few of them are dead now. They wouldn't shoot up their social club. Media outlets have already been calling it the 'Rose Goddess Massacre.'"

"Why 'Rose Goddess'? Why not 'Rose Garden'?"

"They've been interviewing survivors all evening. The accounts of you defending Sword-Fated firstborns is becoming legendary. Complete idiots who attended other balls, like the one Grisholm and I were at last evening, are actually upset that they weren't at your party to see the Goddess of War smote the Gates of Dawn." I give him a side-eyed look. He stares at me derisively. "You didn't think The Virtue would call out your mother, did you? The Gates of Dawn are a good scapegoat. It makes the continued conflict more palatable and you more of a heroine. The Virtue is biding his time. This attack binds Salloway closer to him. Their common enemy is proving to be a many-headed dragon."

I gaze out the window at the landscape flying by. Large tracts of land stretch as far as I can see. It's so green, the kind of green that you never see in the city. Horses startle and run from our low-flying airship.

I watch for a long time. Reykin communicates with Dune, letting my ex-mentor know that he found me. When the messaging between them ends, the silence grows.

"I want to see my father," I murmur.

Reykin's face changes. He loses some of his anger. The struggle in his eyes is real. "Roselle . . . I don't know how to tell you this, so I'm just going to say it. Your father was murdered last night."

"I know. I saw him. I killed his murderers." I think the shock of what happened last night is finally wearing off. My hands are trembling, and my throat aches with emotion I refuse to show. "He wanted to be buried in Virtues—beside his parents. He told me that. He said, 'Don't let them entomb me in that Sword whorehouse.' We were at my grandfather's funeral. He was drunk, of course, but he made me swear not to let his body rot in the Sword Mausoleum."

"He was the Fated Sword. Your mother is expected to hold his body in state and inter him in that shrine."

I grit my teeth. "He didn't want to be there. It's insanity to give his body to his murderers. Do you know what they did to him?"

"No."

"They cut out his tongue. They literally made him hold his tongue."

"You can't stop what they'll do with his body. You won't even be allowed at his funeral."

He's right. Transitioned secondborns are rarely allowed to attend the funeral of a parent. In Swords, it's usually because we die before our parents. But if that doesn't happen, the surviving secondborn isn't welcome at the funeral because it makes the rest of the family uncomfortable, and maybe a little afraid for the firstborn. "This is an insane world, Reykin."

"I know."

"I still need to see him. I need to say good-bye."

"Your father was a cruel man."

"Still."

Reykin sighs. "I'll see what I can do to find out where his body is."

We fly in silence to the gorgeous city of Purity, though I hardly see any of it because I'm lost in thought. "Reykin?"

"Yes."

"Can I ask you a question . . . about your family?" I glance at him. He nods. "After Census murdered them, did they allow you to bury them?"

He stiffens. "No," he replies softly. "My mother and brother were dragged through the streets of our town, and then left in the square to rot. I wasn't allowed to move them. My father was killed trying to defend them. They set his body on fire."

"I'm sorry," I whisper, holding back tears. I can't cry. Not now.

"I shouldn't have yelled at you. I'm sorry."

"It's okay. It's actually normal. After a battle, one or two fights between Sword soldiers usually break out. Someone will accuse someone else of being reckless or thoughtless. They'll usually brawl. It's a reaction to fear. Fear turns to anger, and they need to put it somewhere, or they'll turn it inward. It's probably healthier to vent it. You were afraid I was dead. When you found out I wasn't, your fear turned to anger. You know what that means, right?"

"No," Reykin replies.

"It means you care about me."

He turns on me, his stare cold, devoid of emotion. "You've got it wrong. I care about no one. The only thing I want is revenge. You're a means to an end, Roselle. I need you to help me topple a government. As soon as we accomplish that, I'll have no more use for you."

I'm not sure why his words destroy me like they do. The heat of embarrassment floods my cheeks. "You may not care about me, but you care about your brothers. I can see it on your face when you talk about them."

"Not in the way you think. My heart is gone, Roselle."

"I think it's the opposite. I think you carry around all their hearts now."

"You don't know what you're talking about," he growls. "Just do your job so I don't have to kill you."

His words are a punch in my stomach. "Now who's the cruel man?"

"Did I hurt your feelings?" he asks with derision.

I refuse to answer him.

We're stopped by security at the Halo Palace gates. The airship hovers by the barriers as we wait for clearance. Our arrival causes an uproar. Drone cameras and beat reporters who lurk near the grounds converge on the airship, beating on the glass and yelling questions that are too muffled to make out. The guards draw their weapons on the raucous crowd, pushing them back. Our vehicle is quickly scanned and searched. An Exo guard says, "You're both required to report immediately to the Upper Halo pad 985. Do you need coordinates for the dock?"

"No," Reykin replies. The airship flies forward and into the sprawling landscape of the Halo Palace grounds. We gain altitude, lifting toward the golden halo-shaped crown. The sea beside us is magnificent. White flags and pointed spires from Balmora's Sea Fortress are visible as we climb higher, and the castle is surrounded by the crystal-blue high tide.

Reykin's tone is gruff as he says, "I was hoping to avoid this until later." He scrutinizes me. The frown on his face indicates I'm a disaster. "Just tell them what happened last night. You have nothing to hide."

I don't look at him, but I lift my arms and fight the urge to weave my hair into a thick plait. "So, you *do* believe that nothing happened between Hawthorne and me."

"You can hardly breathe. Whatever happened last night, it wasn't much fun."

"How do I explain how you found me?"

"You had Hawthorne contact me on your behalf because you're supposed to be my slave for the day."

I snort with derision. "I'd never do that. I'd contact Dune first."

"Then lie. Or maybe you can say that you asked Hawthorne to contact me because I *care* about you."

My heart aches. "Don't make me regret saving your life, Reykin."

He lands the airship on a golden platform. Once it's secure, a wide hangar opens. The platform moves, swinging sideways, bringing us inside the hangar. The doors close, and Dune emerges from an interior doorway ahead of us. His face is lined with fatigue.

Exiting the vehicle on my own, I walk to meet Dune. He watches me, his gaze missing nothing. His eyes shift to Reykin. "Thank you." Dune's deep voice resonates in the hangar. Reykin simply nods. "How bad is it?" Dune asks me. His concern is muted. Injury is part of secondborn Sword life. It's unavoidable.

"No worse than most of our training days," I reply with the same detachment.

"I'll have my physician examine you," Dune says.

"It's unnecessary," I reply.

Dune frowns. "You're required to answer questions from The Virtue about last night."

I want to lash out at Dune for not allowing me some time to recover before subjecting me to an inquiry. The lack of empathy for me after what I've been through is appalling, though I expected it. I nod and force my anger down.

Dune ushers me into the corridor. Reykin trails us. I'm led to the Grand Foyer near the air elevators. Security has doubled. Everyone is scanned, even Dune, which makes me want to laugh. He wouldn't need a weapon to kill The Virtue.

The portraits of Fabian Bowie and his wife, Adora, stare at us as we ascend the stairs. I need to hold on to the railing, and my progress is slow. Reykin tries to take my elbow, but I snatch it away.

Dune sees the exchange and frowns. I don't care what he thinks. I want nothing more than to return to my room and be left alone. I feel empty and torn. My mother and brother tried to kill me again last night. They murdered my father. Hawthorne will marry a firstborn named Fauna. She'll have his children, no matter what he says to the contrary. He'll give his second child to the Fate of Swords. Nothing will ever change. Tears well up in my eyes, but I force them back, hoping my numbness lasts just a little longer. I might fall apart if it doesn't.

At the top of the stairs, a sophisticated reception area shines with ethereal light. Dune is immediately surrounded by The Virtue's staff. I'm relieved. I walk away from them to the wall of windows and gaze out at the view of Purity. I cross my arms over my middle, holding myself. People I don't know hover around me. They also work for The Virtue. A lovely Diamond-Fated secondborn scurries to my side. Her violet hair is in a tight twist. Dewdrop indigo lights flash on her eyelashes. "Hi, I'm Glisten, an assistant to The Virtue. How are you feeling?" Her eyes move from mine as she peeks at the rest of me. Her smile slips a little, but when her eyes meet mine again, she brightens with even more fake cheer. "Is there anything I can get you?" she asks with enthusiasm.

"No," I reply.

Reykin hovers near us. "She'll take a sweater, slippers, some water, and a chet."

"No, she won't," I growl.

"Yes, she will. Have you got all that, Glisten?" Reykin's smile is devastatingly handsome. It annoys me.

Glisten is absolutely enthralled. "Of course. What size slippers?"

I glower at her.

"Right," she says, backing away with her finger pointing behind her. "I'll just go look it up." Glisten hurries away to do Reykin's bidding.

"If she only knew the real you, Reykin, and not your playboy persona, she'd run away."

"Only you know the real me," he replies.

"What are we waiting for?"

"I heard someone say Grisholm is on his way up."

"Why are you still here?" I ask.

"I'm required to be here. And anyway, you're my slave for the day, remember? We firstborns take that power very seriously."

"'Slave for a day' only counts when it's firstborn to firstborn. I'm secondborn. I'm a slave all the time."

"Finally," he whispers. "Get mad, Roselle. Let the rage and injustice of what they've made you sink in. Together, we'll destroy them all."

"Oh, it's sinking in. Just like my claws in your face if you don't leave me alone." I'm too exhausted to be tactful.

"What's this about claws?" Grisholm asks behind us. The first-born golden boy is swathed in light from the window. Reykin turns to greet him.

"Roselle is angry at me," Reykin says, "because I won't let her out of being my slave for a day. I might have to postpone it, though, otherwise I'll feel cheated. She's restricted to the Palace for the briefing and she has to see a physician."

Grisholm grunts. "I'm not allowed out right now either. I don't understand why we can't just go to the trial grounds and watch the secondborn training camps. Roselle already decimated the attackers." He looks at me with surprising admiration.

Reykin snorts in agreement, playing along. "Is it true they didn't have monikers?" he asks.

"I didn't see any monikers," I reply. "Some of it is a blur."

Glisten returns with an armload of items. "I have a few choices for sweaters," she says, holding them up. Reykin reaches out and takes a long cream-colored one. Shaking it out, he holds it for me. It's more like a coat that clasps in the front, sensor-controlled with a small apparatus on the sleeve to regulate the temperature.

Surprised by Reykin's gesture, I pause for a moment. Slowly, I turn and thread my arms through the sleeves. Reykin's nearness floods my senses. His scent surrounds me. I turn back, and he's already reaching for the clasps, securing the ones to cover my abdomen and leaving the ones below my waist undone. I touch my hair, smoothing it, self-conscious about what I must look like.

Glisten hands me matching slippers. I drop them and shove my feet into them without bending down. The fit is perfect, and that annoys me, too. These people know entirely too much about me. That's part of their strength—information is the key to their power. Their data scientists are as lethal with information as I am with a sword.

"Water," the assistant says, passing me the glass with ice. "And chets." She holds up a packet with maybe twenty inside. The value of this in my air-barracks back on the Base would be stunning.

"Thank you." I accept the chets, resisting the urge to take a whole one now, and drop them in the pocket of my sweater for later, when I can better afford to be dull. Right now, I need my wits.

Clifton's deep voice greets the liaison at the entrance to the reception area. He looks immediately to me, cuts off the man in front of him with his hand, and walks in my direction. "Roselle." He says my name with such relief that I feel as if he cares. Large hands reach out for me and hug me. It's shocking that he's embracing me in a setting like this. He's firstborn. I'm secondborn. The intimacy is taboo. It's also causing excruciating pain in my ribs.

"Clifton," I whimper and exhale.

Reykin puts his hand on Clifton's shoulder and shoves him away from me. "Don't touch her." Clifton looks at the hand on his shoulder, then their eyes lock. The arms dealer isn't used to anyone coming between us, and he doesn't like it. Not one bit. "She's injured," Reykin adds.

Clifton throws Reykin a murderous glare. It was a trying night for him. Many of his friends and associates were murdered. He's probably still adjusting to the shock.

"I'll be better in a day," I explain gently.

Clifton's expression softens. "I'm sorry. I've been worried about you. I thought you died last night." Real sorrow shines in his eyes. I want to fall back into his arms. He's not emotionally bereft like all the other people here. It makes me almost forget he's dangerous. Almost.

Clifton still has an agenda, and I'm a huge part of it.

"Excuse me, sir," a Star assistant interrupts Clifton. "I was told that you have the surveillance footage?"

Clifton nods. He lifts his hand and unlocks his sword-shaped moniker. His eyes open menus made of holographic energy. "Where do I send it?" The man indicates his moniker. Clifton nods and initiates the transfer. Dropping his arm, he says to me, "You haven't introduced me to your friend."

"Firstborn Clifton Salloway," I begin, "may I introduce Firstborn Reykin Winterstrom."

"Winterstrom," Clifton says, "I don't believe we've met."

"We haven't," Reykin says.

Clifton gazes at his left hand. "You're a Star. How do you know my Roselle?"

"*Your* Roselle?"

"I'm her commanding officer."

"She's an advisor to the Halo Council, of which I'm a member," Reykin replies with an entitled firstborn air he has perfected.

Suddenly The Virtue storms in, lifts a vase of irises from a mirrored side table, and throws it against the glass wall. It shatters into pieces. A ripple of flinches moves through the assembled assistants, but I'm used to the tides of war. Breaking glass merely gets my attention.

"Every unapproved secondborn *out*!" The Virtue bellows.

Secondborns claw each other in their haste to leave. Glisten is among the wiliest, leading the way. I don't move. After the mass exodus, only an intimate number of secondborns and a slightly larger number of firstborns remain. Some I've met before, like Valdi Shelling. Others I don't even recognize—except maybe the one in the corner, staring at me.

"How could you let this happen in Virtues? In *my* city!" The Virtue rages at Dune. Dune remains silent, unruffled. "And *you*!" The Virtue points at Clifton. "You should have seen this coming!"

Clifton begins making his apologies and shifting the subject to the plan for upgrading security features around the city. "With the massive wartime technology my team is developing . . ."

My eyes return to the firstborn in the corner. He's still watching me. This older man seems so familiar. I don't know why. My head tilts.

He smiles at my who-are-you gesture, and then recognition dawns—I should say, *Gates of* Dawns.

Adrenaline crashes into my bloodstream. He's Sword Commander Walther Petes. Dune's fraternal twin brother. Here, in the Halo Palace. It must be him. My eyes go to his moniker, expecting to see a silver secondborn sword, but it's gold. He's a firstborn Sword.

He has the same build as Dune, with the same chiseled bone structure and the same full-lipped smile. His hair is a warm chestnut color. He wears it short—military length. His nose is different from Dune's. This man's nose has been broken a few times and never repaired. He's clean-shaven. I try to see the color of his eyes, but he's too far away.

"And *you*!" The Virtue rages on, his finger jabbing at me. "How are *you* still alive after you fell from the top of the Sword social club?"

"I'm hard to kill," I reply.

His eyes flare. He glances from my face to Dune's, and then back. "You're 'hard to kill.' That's your answer?"

"Yes."

A rumble of surprised laughter shakes his shoulders. "She's hard to kill," he roars, laughing furiously and looking over everyone in the room. Others join him tentatively. His rage-filled gaze returns to me. "So am I. If I find that you were a part of this, I will rip your throat out."

I nod once, not looking away.

Clifton intervenes. "I brought the security footage from the social club. We can review it now."

"Show it," The Virtue barks. Clifton nods to the secondborn Star behind us. The security shutters lower over the transparent wall, blotting out the sun. Soft lighting illuminates the room. The security doors close, imprisoning us inside.

The Virtue remains standing, but others find seats. Grisholm gets Reykin's attention and indicates a chair for him. I choose not to sit with them, drifting to the back of the room near the wall of flowing water and its tranquil pattering sound. Clifton takes a position on one side of me. Maybe he's already seen the footage, and he was present for the event, but he doesn't watch when the holographic images of the main ballroom, the gallery level, and the Gods Table take shape. The noise of the party is clamorous. I tense, waiting for the mayhem.

A warm hand brushes mine with a gentle stroke against my smallest finger. I glance up at Clifton's face, a mask of remorse. Impulsively, I latch on to his hand for the briefest of moments, squeeze it, and then let it go.

The holographic recording flares with light. Death Gods invaded the club through a rooftop terrace entrance in pairs. More than likely, they used gravitizers, which means they had extensive military training. The assassins trickle in and blend with the revelers, taking up positions near doors, exits, security drones, and the club's private security.

Hawthorne and the Death Gods entered the building in the same way. That bothers me, although it makes strategic sense. It's how I would enter if I wanted to get in and weren't invited.

"Why aren't the drones picking them up?" The Virtue bellows.

"Pause," Clifton orders. The footage stills. "They didn't have monikers."

"The drones should have alerted us to that."

"We believe they used a device that reflects the moniker closest to them. At such proximity, the drones cannot discern there are multiple people. It fools them into believing the person has simply moved." From the pocket of his trousers, he holds up a black cuff bracelet with a flat, square chip embedded in it. "We recovered these from the bodies of the attackers. We've never encountered this type of technology before. My engineers are pulling them apart as we speak. We should know more soon."

"Do you suspect Burton?"

"I do," Clifton replies without reservation.

"Resume!" The Virtue orders, his hands clenched into fists.

My holographic image enters the social club. I can hardly watch. The burn of adrenaline, of knowing what lies ahead, sickens me. I want to reach into her world of light and warn her—tell her to save her father—but I can't. The sound transports me back to that living nightmare. Panic seizes. My vision blurs. I'm gasping. No one notices. They're all riveted by the footage. Then the carnage begins.

Reaching into my sweater pocket, I take out the packet of chets. The cellophane wrapper crinkles loudly beneath the recorded screams of a violent massacre. My shaking fingers have a difficult time tearing open the seal. Walther eases the packet from my grasp, deftly opening it and offering me a small white stamp in his palm. I don't take it all. Instead, I rip off a corner piece and put it in my mouth. Dune's brother stuffs the rest of the chet back into the cellophane and slips them into my pocket. Slowly, my breathing eases, though everything still has a faraway perspective.

My holographic image enters the gallery, sparking cheers from some of the group assembled here. The firstborns are enjoying this, as if it were some form of entertainment. I stifle a snort of derision.

"Who is that Sword?" The Virtue shouts.

"Pause," Clifton orders. "That's Hawthorne Trugrave. He's a newly Transitioned firstborn. You remember him—he was at the Sword Palace the night you acquired Roselle."

Acquired. Have I been acquired? Is that what they're calling my internment here?

"Get him here!" The Virtue barks.

"Of course," Clifton replies. "Resume." He sends a message with his moniker.

Under the influence of the chet, I analyze the Goddess Roselle before me. She's possessed, eviscerating her enemies with the vengeance of a wrathful deity. Ruthlessly, she hunts them. The fusionmag is an extension of her will. With Tyburn behind her, shielding her back, she's the north, south, and east winds.

The men watching shout thunderously and applaud when Roselle slices open the leg of the flying Death God with her dagger. Her fall to the ballroom floor elicits gasps. More cheers roar as she targets the flying assassin and shoots him out of the air. But when she dons goggles and spews a billowing cloud of red dust into the ballroom, the firstborns jump to their feet, clapping uproariously at the wholesale slaughter of assassins, as if she's some favored competitor in the Secondborn Trials.

I am unable to look away. I feel nothing when the war goddess tackles the bomb-wielding assassin, crashing with him through the window and out into the night sky. The grenade explodes. All the glass blows inward, shooting shards toward the surveillance cameras. The firstborns raise their arms to their faces and gasp.

The holographic footage ends. Whoops of laughter seize the group. Grisholm is one of the most riotous, as if he's been on a thrill ride and can't stop talking about the experience. He turns to Reykin, chatting boisterously. Reykin glances over his shoulder at me. His expression is grim. I look away.

The Virtue calls Clifton back to the front of the room. He and Dune brief Fabian Bowie and his advisors on their preliminary findings about the massacre.

I'm barely listening.

"You were brave," Walther says. I meet his eyes. They're jade colored, not sand.

"It wasn't bravery," I reply. "It was rage—a Sword-Fated threnody."

"Remind me not to upset you."

"I'll do that, Walther."

His smile is one of pure pleasure. For a moment, it soothes the ache in my chest.

Dune says, "I'd like to introduce Firstborn Walther Petes." He gestures in our direction. "He's a newly Transitioned firstborn, a former secondborn commanding officer at the Twilight Forest Base in Swords. His brother, Fergusson Petes, was among the casualties at the club last night. He flew in this morning to assume his new position as a military consultant to The Virtue."

"Please excuse me, Roselle," Walther says, turning and making his way to the front. He calls for the holographic footage to be replayed and begins to dissect the crime, pointing out all the crucial elements The Virtue hadn't noticed.

As I analyze the players before me, questions take shape in my mind. I'm no longer so certain that my mother and brother perpetrated this crime. For one thing, they weren't the only ones who had strong motives. Fergusson Petes was at the social club. His death not only elevated Dune's twin brother to firstborn, but it also afforded Dune the opportunity to infiltrate The Virtue's trusted advisory panel with yet another Gates of Dawn operative.

Clifton explains the device that mirrors monikers. The accusation that it may be Burton's technology certainly plays in his favor, but is it enough of a reason to make him shoot up a Sword social club? Maybe not, but the plan to install Salloway security technology everywhere throughout the city of Purity—that is. A plan like that allows Clifton to control the capital, especially when The Virtue no longer trusts the Sword military.

My mind reels with all the possible political motivations for last night's slaughter. The problem is that neither the Rose Gardeners nor the Gates of Dawn wants me dead. Maybe they knew I could handle myself if given the proper motivation? Killing my father wouldn't only motivate me, it would get them both one step closer to making me the most powerful person in the world.

Reykin nudges Grisholm. The Firstborn Commander rises from his seat. Approaching The Virtue, he leans down and whispers in his father's ear. The Virtue glances at me absently. He gives a dismissive wave of his hand and then turns back to the briefing. Grisholm nods to Reykin, who makes his way to me. "You're cleared to leave and seek medical attention," he says. "I'll accompany you." He holds my upper arm in a tight grip. I can't pull away without making a scene.

I walk with him to the exit. Reykin scans his moniker, opening the security doors. Together we descend the stairs and pass by the mob of assembled guards. Neither of us speaks as we wait for the air elevator. A car arrives, and the glass doors open. A single passenger steps forward. My knees weaken.

"Hawthorne!" I say in a hushed tone.

Hawthorne's eyes widen. He looks at Reykin's hand on my arm and then to his face. With an instant snarl, Hawthorne swings his fist, connecting with Reykin's jaw. A lesser man would hit the ground, but Reykin doesn't fold. He strikes back, thumping Hawthorne in the throat with the heel of his hand. Wheezing and reeling, Hawthorne stumbles sideways. Reykin kicks him in the side. Hawthorne lurches forward and tackles Reykin. They crash hard onto the marble floor. Exo guards surround them and pull them apart.

"Enough!" I shout. I wait for them to stop struggling against the guards. "Let them go," I order the security team. "They both have important business with The Virtue. Firstborn Trugrave was summoned here." But I'm secondborn and have no authority. I'm completely ignored.

A female guard scans Hawthorne's and Reykin's monikers. She nods to the other guards. Both men are tentatively released, but burly Exos surround them. Drones circle, their weapons trained on the pair. The female guard turns to Reykin. "Do you want to press charges, Firstborn Winterstrom?"

Hawthorne jerks in my direction. His eyes burrow into me. He recognizes the name as the Winterstrom crest seared into my palm. "Reykin," I say in my sweetest tone, "can you decide on that later? I missed breakfast, and I was hoping you'd join me. I know you like ham and eggs."

Hawthorne's aggressive posture slowly eases. He understood that I meant our friends, Hammon and Edgerton. Reykin straightens his black sleeve, pulling down on the cuff. "Anything for you, Roselle." From his pocket, he takes out a small square of cloth and dabs the blood from the corner of his mouth. He turns to the female guard. "Let him go. Trugrave has a meeting with The Virtue, and I have an appointment for brunch."

Reykin joins me by the air lift. We enter the elevator car together. I don't turn to see Hawthorne's expression as I leave. I can't bear it. He knows now that I've been hiding how I got my scar, and what it means. If he doesn't already suspect that I'm a Fate traitor, he will soon.

Chapter 11
The Promise of Dawn

The air elevator descends. Tears brighten my eyes. My body begins to tremble.

"He won't talk," I whisper. "You control the lives of the people he loves."

"Shh," Reykin replies.

Our eyes meet. Fear drives through my heart. "Don't do anything. Please."

He stares ahead at the city skyline as we descend into the main Palace, toward the medical facility on one of the subterranean floors.

Upon arrival, I find that the Atom physicians on duty have been expecting me. I'm ushered into a private room, where a male technician cuts my taped bandages away. He provides me with a white bodysuit with cutouts that expose my ribs. After donning the flimsy garment, I'm joined by a team of physicians. I expect Reykin to leave, but he doesn't. He presides over the medical team, scrutinizing every device. My ribs are scanned. Knowing what's ahead, I want to forgo it, but Reykin convinces me to submit to the bone fusion and skin regeneration procedure. I lie down on the table beneath the white lights and looming laser arm.

A secondborn female technician enters and takes a seat behind the laser's control panel. The rest of the Atom-Fated medical team leaves. Reykin sits beside me. The laser emits a nauseating whine as it boots up.

"I hate this part," I murmur.

Reykin lifts his chin toward the technician. "Give her something for pain."

"She's secondborn," the woman replies. "Pain relief isn't protocol in noncombat situations."

"How much to circumvent protocol?" he asks.

The technician looks around. "A hundred merits."

"Done."

She slides from her seat and leaves the room.

"You're going to make me soft," I murmur.

"I'll risk it this one time."

In minutes, she's back with a cylindrical tank. "I can't give her the regulated drugs—they track them—but this will do the trick. It'll make her happy and sleepy. It's a little old-fashioned but effective." She threads tubes over my ears and into my nostrils, instructing me to breathe deeply. I do. A heady rush of euphoria softens my pain. I smile broadly and giggle.

Reykin matches my smile with his own. "What's so funny?" he asks.

"Nothing. My life is utter hell." I sigh, and then laugh harder.

The technician winks at him before reclaiming her seat at the controls. The laser moves, emitting a precise beam. I don't care. I feel like I'm floating. "I didn't know this could be painless," I say. "No one ever told me when I had this done before."

Reykin frowns. "Dune was probably trying to prepare you for the life of a Transitioned soldier."

"Nothing could prepare me for that." I laugh lightheartedly, even though I mean every word.

The laser moves around, fusing cracks in my bones. My skin and muscle will be repaired after the bone is set. The smell is atrocious, but even that doesn't matter.

Reykin leans near my ear. "Roselle, what do you want?"

"Want?" I smile dreamily. "I don't know. What do you want?" *He's silly. No one ever asks me that.*

"You can tell me. What's your greatest ambition?" His aquamarine eyes shine like light on water.

"Middle age," I mutter with more giggles. The room spins. I close my eyes.

"What else?" Reykin touches my arm. I open my eyes again.

"A puppy," I whisper. "I've always wanted a puppy. Isn't that a strange word? Pup-pee . . . pup . . . pee . . ."

"Anything else?" A faraway voice asks, distracting me.

"Hawthorne . . . not to hate me." My eyelids are too heavy to keep open. "Someone . . . who will . . . sticketh . . ." I feel him take my hand.

Someone squeezes my shoulder. I open my eyes, squinting and tearing up in the white lights. Turning my head, I find Reykin beside me. "How do you feel?" he asks.

"Thirsty," I reply, sitting up and rubbing my eyes.

Reykin hands me a small cup of water. I take it and drink it all in one long swallow. He takes the empty cup and thrusts an armload of clothes at me. "Get dressed. We don't have a lot of time."

"For what?" I look down at myself. All my bruising is gone. My skin is smooth.

"I found your father's body. They're going to transport him to Swords soon. We have to hurry."

In stunned silence, I rise and change into slacks and a loose-fitting top. Reykin turns his back and waits by the door. I don't know whose clothes these are, but they're comfortable. My ribs no longer ache. I can breathe deeply, without pain. Bending isn't a problem either. I slip on the shoes Reykin left on the chair.

He opens the door and waits for me to pass through. "This way." He directs me to a stairwell at the back of the medical facility. Descending several flights, we stop at a red hatch-like door. Reykin uses his moniker to infiltrate a program into the Halo Palace's operating system. In seconds, the hatch pops open. I pass through.

The corridor is cold and empty, but when voices sound from the junction up ahead, Reykin jerks my elbow and pulls me to a nearby doorway. We flatten against the wall. I glare at him. "Didn't you clear this?"

"Not exactly." His jaw tightens. "There wasn't time. They're shipping him to Swords in a couple of hours. It was now or never. I don't know the state of his body, Roselle."

The corridor quiets. Reykin grasps my hand. Our fingers thread. We hurry to the last door on the end. Checking his moniker, he says, "This is it." He unlatches the door and opens it.

The morgue contains long steel tables with shiny surfaces. Long hoses hang from the ceiling like tentacle arms of a monstrous sea creature. Fluid congeals inside a swollen sack suspended from above. The air reeks of it. And of death. I hold my fingers to my nose. Reykin closes the door behind us.

No one attends the bodies. Every table has a corpse on it. Most of them are Sword socialites still in their god or goddess costumes. A few are assassins. I pause by one of the Death Gods. He doesn't have a moniker. It was either cut out and repaired extremely well, or he never had one?

I scan the room for my father. At the far end of the morgue, high above one of the tables, a levitating transporter pod waits to be lowered over a supine corpse. I move toward it, weaving through victims, trying not to look at them. I shudder when I see it's him, and a small gasp escapes me. His pieces have been fused back together. Someone took their time with him, cleaning him up and dressing him in a plain white outfit.

His eyelids are closed. He looks peaceful. Streaks of tears drip from my chin, spattering on the metal table. Reaching out, I touch his hair, smoothing it back. I don't ever remember touching it before. *Did he ever hold me? Did my chubby baby hands ever touch his face?*

"I can't change this," I whisper. "I can't fix anything."

"No, you can't change this," Reykin replies, "but you can change the world, Roselle—the future."

"Why bother? No one's worth it."

"You're worth it. Do it for you." I wipe my chin and cheeks with the back of my sleeve, sniffling. "Do you want a moment alone?" he asks gently. I nod, and he walks away to give me some time.

When he comes back, I know it's time to go.

I dry the tears from my cheeks with the backs of my sleeves. "I'm ready."

Reykin slips the pinkie ring from my father's hand. It has an embossed golden halo on it. The ring has been in his family for generations. Kennet loved to wear it because it's Virtue-Fated, not Sword-Fated.

"Here," Reykin says, "take this."

"What are you doing? Put that back!" I whisper-shout. "It's Gabriel's now."

"Gabriel has everything—a palace full of your father's things. What do you have? Fused ribs?"

"I don't want it." I move toward the door.

"Maybe not, but if you take it, that means your mother won't get it. You can bury it wherever he asked you to take him, as a symbolic gesture."

I pause. "Is that what you did?"

"I buried all their favorite things together."

Turning toward Reykin, I hold out my hand. He drops the ring in my palm.

Suddenly a door swings open. Reykin and I both crouch to the floor like criminals. I peek from between the tables and see a pair of black boots. A voice says, "It wasn't easy extracting the horns from Kennet Abjorn's cranium. Whoever did it must've really wanted him to keep them."

The voice of Agent Crow barks with laughter. "If you asked most people," he replies, "they would swear the horns of The Sword's husband were real!"

This elicits more cackles from them both.

"I had the room secured for your visit," the technician says. "No other personnel have attended the bodies but me."

"Show me all the corpses without monikers," Agent Crow orders.

They walk from assassin to assassin. As they move, Reykin and I crawl along the ground, trying to make it back to the door unseen. My heart thumps in my chest when Agent Crow pauses at a table a few feet from us. I hold my breath.

"They don't appear to have had monikers, wouldn't you agree?" he asks.

"That is my conclusions as well!" the technician says proudly. "It's astounding."

"Quite," Agent Crow agrees.

They wander toward my father, and Reykin and I scurry for the open door. In the empty corridor, I get to my feet and hug the wall. Reykin is beside me in seconds, breathing hard. We hurry up the hall, exiting the morgue the way we came in.

"That Census agent is everywhere," Reykin mutters.

"You have no idea," I reply with a shudder.

After backtracking through the medical center, I breathe easier. We take another air lift. My father's ring is heavy in my fist. "You're on lockdown until further notice," Reykin orders softly. "Don't even think about leaving the Palace grounds." I don't answer him.

The elevator doors open. "They didn't have monikers," I mumble. "What does that mean?"

Reykin's expression is grim. "I don't know." He follows me out of the lift.

"I know my way from here."

"Get used to me, Roselle. I'm not going anywhere."

When we get to my apartment, I find a half dozen security stingers hovering around by it. I glare at Reykin, but he merely shrugs.

Once inside, I close the door immediately. Phoenix's clanging steps ring out in the foyer. I smile, despite everything, and kneel to greet it. "Hey, I missed you, Phee. I have something important. Can you hold it for me?" The mechadome's red lenses nod. I hold up my father's ring. Phoenix lifts its vacuum arm and sucks the ring out of my palm. It disappears inside the squat bot. "Thank you."

Reykin is already in the den after securing the apartment with his whisper orb. He sits on the sofa, leans his head back, and closes his eyes. I cross my arms and rest against the doorframe. "No one touches Hawthorne."

Reykin doesn't open his eyes. "Not your decision," he replies, his jaw tight.

"It is if you ever want my help with anything in the future."

"We have your friends."

My eyes narrow. "We'd all risk our lives for Hawthorne—and he'd do the same for us—so he won't talk. Tell them what I just said. Make Dune and Daltrey understand that this point is nonnegotiable. You kill him, I kill all of you."

Reykin opens his eyes and lifts his head. "They're going to want to use him."

When Hawthorne was secondborn, he hated the way things were. Now that he's firstborn, I don't know what he'll do. He says he loves me, but he'll think that joining the Gates of Dawn is treason. This is going against everything we were raised to believe. Breaking that kind of indoctrination doesn't happen overnight—if ever. "I'll see what I can do to explain things to him, but I can't promise anything. He has fought against the Gates of Dawn in active combat. It'll feel like he's betraying the soldiers he commanded."

"Tell him his life depends on it—no—tell him *your* life depends on it."

"Does it?" I ask.

"All of ours do, Roselle."

My plan to sneak into Hawthorne's room shouldn't terrify me, but it does. Under the cover of darkness, I pad softly out onto my balcony. Scaling the ornate stonework of the building, I climb several stories to a ledge wide enough to walk on. My footsteps don't make much noise as I hurry across the outside of the Halo Palace. The balmy breeze carries the scent of roses from the garden below. I'm turning frosty from the phantom orb in my pocket, which masks my body temperature from the stingers. The swatch of lead covering my moniker does the rest.

Having memorized the route, I'm almost 100 percent certain that the balcony below me is Hawthorne's newly issued suite, granted to him while he answers questions about the attack against the social club. He has a sea view, like me, but on the other side of Grisholm's residence.

I scale down and pry open the glass panel doors. No lights are on, but my night-vision glasses compensate. For a moment, I worry that I have the wrong apartment, but then I recognize the Trugrave crest on the fusionblade locked in the weapons vault in the wall. My heart races. He should have his sword with him. I could be an assassin.

I tread softly up the stairs. At the top of the landing, something doesn't feel right. I pause and listen. The soft sounds of sleep-breathing rasps from the other side of the bedroom door. Gently, I ease it open. It's dark. Hawthorne is burrowed under his blanket. Moving forward, I just about make it to his bed when a lamp turns on. My hands go up to shield my eyes as the night-vision glasses adjust.

I lower my arms, my heart beats like that of a leveret's before a coyote. Hawthorne is seated in the chair in the corner with a fusionmag in his hand. He's dressed all in black, like me. Devastation ravages his face. He raises a remote and cuts the fake sleep sounds coming from the area near the bed.

"I prayed it wouldn't be you," Hawthorne says sorrowfully. "I figured Winterstrom would try to do it himself."

"What are you talking about?" I whisper. I take a step in his direction. He holds the fusionmag a little higher.

"How were you going to do it?" Hawthorne asks, choking on emotion.

"Do what?"

"Kill me."

"I could never!" I say in a rush. "How could you think that? I'm here to talk. I swear! I'm unarmed." I hold up my hands and turn around slowly.

"What's in your pocket?" he asks suspiciously. I reach in slowly and pull out two orbs. "This is a phantom orb. It masks me from the stingers." I hold up the other. "This is a whisper orb. It forms a perimeter around us so we can't be overheard." I trigger the whisper orb, and an iridescent bubble billows outward.

"Set them on the floor." He motions with the fusionmag.

I do, slowly.

"You came here to talk?" he snarls. "So, talk." The pained look of having been betrayed etches every line of his face.

It breaks me. I feel a tear slip from my eye and wipe it away. "Hawthorne—" I struggle for the right words.

"Are you . . . are you a Fate traitor?" Sadness frays his voice.

I move a step closer. He holds the fusionmag a little higher. I stop. "It's not what it seems, Hawthorne."

"What is it, then?" he asks bitterly.

"Have you ever let yourself think that maybe every Fates Republic secondborn is on the wrong side?"

"Never!" Rage transforms his face. "Were you in the same war as me? Didn't you see them sending us back in body bags?"

"Yes, I saw! I also saw the Gates of Dawn body bags, and the way we slaughtered their wounded without mercy. And for what? So the Fates Republic can tear us away from our families, enslave us, and send us off to die while they attend balls and soirées and watch us kill each other in sadistic games they create in the name of entertainment? I'm tired of being on the wrong side, Hawthorne. I can't justify what they're doing anymore."

"I don't even know you, do I?" he seethes.

"You know me," I reply with a note of desperation. "And you know your friends—the ones who love you unconditionally. They're Fate traitors, too."

"Because of you," he accuses.

"I did what I had to do to save their lives. I'm not going to apologize for it."

"How long?" he demands.

"How long, what?"

"How long have you been the enemy?"

"I'm not your enemy!" I insist. "I made a deal for Edgerton's and Hammon's lives. You were gone. No one else could help them. But there was no going back after that . . . I just didn't know it until now."

"How does Winterstrom play into all of this?"

"I can't tell you."

"You can't or you won't?"

"I won't."

"He's firstborn," Hawthorne says. "How do you know that you can trust him?"

"He has plenty of reasons to hate the Fates Republic."

"It's not too late, Roselle. Whatever you're mixed up in, we can get you out. Salloway will help—I'm sure of it."

"Don't involve him. Please, Hawthorne. He's more dangerous than you know."

"He wants you to rule Swords. Once you do, you can make the kind of changes that matter."

"You want me to be The Sword?"

"I want you to *live!*" he retorts. "The Rose Gardeners will make you the Clarity of our Fate. You'll be powerful."

"You want us to live as *firstborns* while our friends are hunted by Census? Let's say I agree to all of that. One day we'll have to give our secondborn child to a system that will brutalize her until the day she dies. Now who's the traitor? We'd be betraying our child like our parents betrayed us. We've been brainwashed for so long that it's hard to see the truth, Hawthorne, but once you do, you can't unsee it. Anything less than freedom for all secondborns is unacceptable. Anything less than life for thirdborns is murder. When you accept that, you won't be able to go blindly along with the Fates Republic anymore—you'd rather die for freedom than live one more day without it."

"You *will* die if you keep this up, Roselle."

"It's only treason if I lose." I take a step in his direction, and when he doesn't shoot, I take another, and another, until I'm close enough to reach for the fusionmag. "I'm still the woman you shared a million kisses with." I touch the cool metal of the barrel. "It's still me."

Hawthorne groans, relinquishing his weapon. "If you're going to kill me, do it fast."

In seconds, I disassemble the fusionmag and set the pieces on the side table. I stare down into his eyes. His hand lifts to the back of my neck. He pulls me nearer until my lips meet his in a ferocious, all-consuming kiss.

"Why are you doing this?" he asks.

"Because it's right—like you and I are right. We can save them, Hawthorne—this isn't unfaithfulness to Sword secondborns. It's loyalty. We can change their lives for the better. Don't decide now. Just think about it. I'm only asking you to continue to protect Hammon, Edgerton, and me with your silence."

Hawthorne pulls me down to him. I straddle his hips. His hand cups my jaw. His thumb traces my cheek. His sorrow burns away in the heat of his desire. The yearning that always accompanies his touch destroys my resolve. As his thumb slides over my bottom lip, I shiver, craving more. I wish he could hold me until I die.

My hands slip under his shirt, feeling his muscles beneath my fingertips. I push away the black fabric. He grasps the hem, lifting it off over his head and dropping it on the floor. The sight of him makes me long to be his again. I wish he were still secondborn. I know I shouldn't, but I do. He was mine then. I want him back.

His hands thread through my hair, pulling it from its knot. The strands unfurl around my shoulders and down my back. His expression turns fiercer, and he tugs off my eyewear. With his hands under my thighs he picks me up. I wrap legs around his waist and my wrists around his neck, drawing his mouth to mine. We kiss as he carries me to his bed and sets me down. My back touches the blankets. His knee digs into the mattress beside my hip. Long fingers splay in my hair. Firm lips hover above me.

Inching up my black shirt, Hawthorne pulls it over my head and tosses it haphazardly on the floor. "How are your ribs?" he asks. His eyes move with his fingers, stroking a path down my skin, gently touching the ones that were broken. It's both sensual and ticklish. Gasping softly, I suck in my bottom lip to keep from giggling. A rush of desire overtakes me. "Did I hurt you?"

"No." I breathe the word, but I don't know if it's true. I ache for him to keep touching me—to never stop. "I'm okay now. I had them repaired."

His lips travel with whisper-softness over my ribs, his warm breath against my cool skin. I inhale sharply. His finger hooks in the fabric of my black bra—the valley between the cups where the clasp lies. "If I'm not mistaken, this isn't military issue," he murmurs. His fingertips rim the edges of the fabric.

Heat pours through me. My skin flushes. "They gave me girl clothes."

"Oh, I noticed." His finger deftly unclasps my bra.

His shadow of a beard skims against my breast. His mouth latches on to my hardened nipple. I arch up against his lips, my eyes closing, my mouth opening. His tongue flicks, and my ache intensifies to a burning need. I grip his arm, digging into his muscle. "Hawthorne," I whisper harshly.

"I missed your voice." He growls low against me, kissing the valley between my breasts. "The raspy way you say my name when you want me. It rushes under my skin."

"I always want you."

"You're all that matters to me," Hawthorne confesses. That, too, is an act of treason. He rests his forehead against my belly and sighs. "This isn't how I saw this night ending."

"Hawthorne, this is how I want every night with you to end."

He closes his eyes. "I love you, Roselle."

"Maybe it's okay . . . maybe just this one time . . ."

Hawthorne opens his eyes and shakes his head. "We can't, Roselle. They'd murder you. I won't risk it. We shouldn't even be doing this—especially here. Just kissing could get you flayed. I'm so weak around you." He gets off the bed, finds my shirt, and hands it to me. I reclasp my bra and slip my shirt on.

He sits beside me and then lies back against the mattress, staring up at the ceiling. I rest my cheek on his chest, listening to his heartbeat slow. He wraps his arms around me. I know I need to go. Dawn is coming. I try to sit up, but his arms tighten.

"Hawthorne," I whisper.

He kisses my hair. "I know," he replies, but his arms don't loosen.

"How long are you staying at the Halo Palace?"

"I have to leave first thing in the morning."

"Why?" I apply a bit more pressure, and he relents, easing his grip on me. I rise on my elbow so I can see his face. He reaches for my hair, tucking strands of it back behind my ear.

"They already know what happened at the social club," he says. "It was captured by the surveillance drones. They just wanted to know why I was there."

"Do they know about us?"

"Not in the winter corridor—just in the gallery and ballroom. Salloway told them that the snowy hallway isn't monitored because it's private, and the members like it that way. But you only had to watch us together in the gallery to see my devotion to you."

My voice softens, "You jumped after me, even when you thought I might already be dead."

"Yeah. It's pretty clear I'm in love with you."

"And I love you, Hawthorne, but . . ." I think for a moment. "How did you explain being there?"

"I told them I came there to see you because we were secondborn friends."

"How did The Virtue take that?"

Hawthorne exhales deeply. "He didn't like it—said I was firstborn now and I ought to know better than to try to maintain friendships with secondborns. Then he gave me another honorary title and a small piece of land in the Fate of Seas for my 'bravery' at the social club, and told me I'm not allowed to see you anymore. Then he wished me well with my engagement." Hawthorne's jaw ticks with tension.

My throat tightens. Now there's no hope in appealing to The Virtue to break the marriage contract between Hawthorne and Fauna. "Will I see you again?"

"Seeing you again is the only thing that will occupy my mind," he says, "until I find a way."

"I hope it's soon. I have to go," I whisper. "Good-bye, Hawthorne." My own devastation is almost more than I can bear. I kiss his cheek, get to my feet, and retrieve the orbs and night-vision glasses. Shoving the orbs in my pocket, I put on the glasses and move toward the door. I tug on the handle, but Hawthorne's hand reaches past my shoulder and holds the door closed.

"I'll never talk," he whispers. "Your secret is safe, but you knew that already. I have to think about everything else."

A shiver slides through me. I lean back against him, feeling the strength in his powerful body. I turn around and meet his eyes. He leans down and kisses me with a yearning that threatens to destroy us both. When he lifts his lips from mine, I murmur, "Thank you, Hawthorne," and then slip out the way I came.

Chapter 12
Lullaby of Insomnia

I'm confined to the Halo Palace.

It's even worse than prior to the attack. Now I'm followed everywhere by hovering Virtue stingers for my "protection," just like Grisholm. And like Grisholm, I'm restricted to the Firstborn Commander's private residence. Security has been reinforced with increased Exo presence and heightened technology provided by Salloway Munitions. Huge mechanized weapons were airlifted and placed on the cliff outside my balcony, just beyond the garden. The guns can track and shoot just about anything out of the sky without much trouble. They can do the same to people.

Reykin hasn't visited me in a couple of days, even though he can. I told him that Hawthorne agreed to stay silent and to think about helping us. I thought Reykin would be happy to hear that, but he didn't take the news well. Instead, he stomped around my apartment, giving me the silent treatment while working on Phoenix's hover mode. I was too tired to argue with the firstborn Star, but Phoenix doesn't clang anymore. It silently glides everywhere it goes.

Reykin left shortly after dawn the morning I'd returned from speaking to Hawthorne in his room. He'd mumbled an excuse about discussing everything that's happened with Dune and Daltrey. I haven't seen him since. Not that *he* hasn't seen *me*. Through Phoenix, he can surveil me anytime he wants, although I think I can tell now when Phoenix is in auto mode and when the mechadome is Reykin-possessed. It's a subtle changeover. Phoenix doesn't "watch" me in the literal sense. It sort of just keeps track of me. But Reykin-possessed Phoenix is a stalker. Like now. It's just parked in front of me, staring, as I lie on the sofa in the den. I'd throw a blanket over its head, but it will just pull it off, so it doesn't seem worth the effort.

With my cheek against the seat cushion, I stare blankly at a vapid holographic announcer describing how to get the most from my next virtual vacation. Yawning, I couldn't care less. I'm so tired, but I can't sleep. Not much anyway. Only a few hours, and then I'm awake—panicking about whether Hawthorne will change his mind and decide he never wants to see me again, or maybe the Gates of Dawn will conclude that it's safer to kill Hawthorne, or a hundred other equally terrifying scenarios. It's exhausting. So I just watch virtual access, hoping for something so boring it forces me to sleep.

I search through what's on. The face and profile of an Atom-Fated man flashes inside my den, while anchors from a news organization flitter about in excitement. Along with the man's image are a description and a short bio of his physical traits. "Before we go to our live coverage in Swords," the commentator says, "we have a Secondborn Deserter Bulletin in effect for the Purity area of Virtues." I sit up, recognizing the morgue director Reykin and I encountered a few days ago. His sandy, wiry hair and goonish leer are unmistakable. "Cranston Atom, master mortician, has failed to report for duty in over twenty-four hours. If you know the whereabouts of Cranston Atom, you're asked to contact your local Census agency."

Before I have time to process the implications of the missing secondborn, his image is gone, replaced by the soaring city skyline of Forge, where citizens are lining the streets, waving blue flags adorned with a golden sword in the center of each. The female newscaster smiles somberly. "We're just about ready to witness the procession coming down the Avenue of Swords," she says in a hushed tone, "on their way to the memorial where they will lay to rest a cultural icon, the Fated Sword. It's a sad day for the Clarity of Swords, the Firstborn Sword, and all their Fate. As you can see, mourners line the streets, hoping to get one last glimpse of the Fated Sword before his interment in Killian Abbey." The anchor is firstborn. It's customary for only firstborns to cover such prestigious events. She peers directly into the drone camera's lens. "The Fated Sword is, of course, the father of Firstborn Gabriel St. Sismode and his arguably more famous younger sister, Secondborn Roselle Sword."

Wisps of her dark hair blow in the cold air. The tip of her nose is red. White plumes of breath show as she continues. "I'm standing in front of one of the largest tributes to a secondborn ever erected." She gestures with her hand. The drone camera pans to a skyscraper behind her. On the side of it, a holographic image plays the footage of me tackling the Death God and shattering through the glass wall of the Sword social club. My stomach twists in a knot. I know what that is. It's propaganda designed to undermine Gabriel and his inherent position. Most people won't understand that they're being influenced, but my mother will. The drones turn back to the newscaster and the Avenue of Swords.

Slowly, I lie back down. My cheek rests against the cushion. I stare at the funeral procession playing out in front of me. I want to feel nothing, but a wave of crushing sorrow hits me. Tears leak out of the corners of my eyes, but I don't bother to wipe them away. I just sob.

The channel changes on its own. It stops on a cuisine program. Rows and rows of crellas line the case at a bakery in the Fate of Suns. With the handheld remote, I turn the hologram back to the funeral. The three-dimensional image of my mother and brother leaving the Sword Palace scurries across the den. I can hardly make out their shapes behind their Vicolt's tinted windows.

The image changes again, to some sort of dance recital. I glare at my mechadome. "Reykin, stop!"

Reykin-possessed Phoenix shakes its lenses—no.

"Yes!" I yell. I can't remember ever being this angry in my life. I try to turn it back, but the entire virtual-access unit completely dies. Frantically, I point the remote at the receiver. Nothing happens. I turn and glare at Reykin-possessed Phoenix. "I hate you!"

Getting up from the couch, I storm out of the room, and then out of the apartment. Stingers flank me as I run down the corridor to the nearest exit. The bright sunlight is a shock after hours of being inside with the privacy shutters drawn. Wiping at my cheeks, I try to hide my hot tears from the Sun-Fated secondborns I pass in the garden.

Before I know it, I'm down the stone steps and onto the beach. I jog along the shoreline, trying to outrun my demons. When I get to the bend, I find Balmora, once again staring off at her sea castle. She's in front of a hovering easel, painting the structure as if her life depends on it. Beside her, the little twelve-year-old girl watches her.

Balmora lowers her brush and looks at me. Her smile is big and toothy, until she reads the look on my face. She sees my limp hair and lounging attire. "Roselle," she says, "what's wrong? What's happened?" She reaches out and touches my arm.

"Do you have virtual access in your residence?"

"Yes."

"Can I see it?"

"Of course!" She sets aside her paintbrush and locks her arm in mine. The nearest death drone begins to wail and hover nearer. "Oh, hush!" she exclaims, waving it away. It silences and settles back to hover at a distance. She walks with me across the sandbar toward the gigantic doors of her Sea Fortress. Her attendants scramble to gather up her belongings behind us. "Are you okay?" she asks.

"No," I reply honestly, trying to hold back tears. "They're memorializing my father today, and my visual access is broken."

"Oh," she replies in a sympathetic tone. "I hadn't known that you two were close."

"We weren't." My toes sink into the damp sand, leaving a trail of footprints.

"And yet, you're upset," she says, puzzled.

"I'd hoped that someday things would be different between us."

"Oh," she says softly, "and it wasn't because he was a narcissist?"

"Did you know Kennet?"

"No. My father always said yours was a narcissist. I sort of envied you for that."

"What?" I sniffle. "Why?"

"Well, mine's a tyrant, so yours didn't sound so bad," she replies with a wink. Despite everything, I feel myself smile. As we walk, Balmora chats about the architectural features of her castle, pointing out each of the nine spires that represent the nine Fates. Seagulls perch and gossip overhead. We pass through the enormous portico, and the shade of it feels several degrees cooler, the damp air heavier. An inner courtyard lies within the high stone walls. The sun finds us once more as we walk across the lawn. The ever-present sound of the waves follows us until we climb the steps and enter the royal stone edifice. Dimness greets us. It takes a second for my eyes to adjust.

The ceiling is high in the foyer. Exposed wooden beams are draped with colorful banners from all the Fates. Sunlight dots the floor from high windows. Ancient painted portraits of past secondborn commanders are everywhere. It's like going back in time.

"You have a beautiful home," I murmur.

She looks around with a critical eye. "There are some days that I think I'll go mad if I have to stay here one more second." Her honestly is surprising. "I sometimes wonder if I'd have been better off born into a lowly Fate of Seas family in a fishing village somewhere. At least then I'd be allowed to sail away. Go places. See things firsthand." She gazes at me. "But we can't change our Fate, can we?" The way she says it, it sounds more like a challenge than a certainty. "Come, my media room is this way."

We pass through a glass sunroom and into a round room with a grand balcony that overlooks the sea. Balmora stops. "Quincy," she says to the girl, who is still following us, "make sure no one comes in. I want privacy." The freckled girl nods solemnly and stands guard outside. Balmora closes the doors. She goes to the airy balcony, drawing the curtains, shutting off the stone terrace. The beautiful white fabric waves in the breeze.

Using her silver halo-shaped moniker, she dims the lights and turns on her virtual access to holographic mode. Rapidly changing the station, Balmora pauses on one showing nothing but holographic smoke-filled gloom. Dust obscures the visual, but the audio is something else entirely. Screams of chaos swirl from the audio feed. Balmora turns to me, shocked. "What's happening?"

I shake my head in confusion. "I don't know. Try another channel."

Balmora changes it. It's the same, except firstborns with red-rimmed eyes and golden sword monikers are emerging from the smoke with their hands over their noses and mouths. "Is that Swords?" Balmora asks, with a catch in her voice.

"Try another station!" I demand.

The next one is similar, but an announcer is saying, "An explosion, or what we believe was an explosion, has occurred in the city of Forge, where the Fated Sword was being memorialized today on his way to Killian Abbey."

"Swords has been attacked," I say to Balmora, though I hardly recognize the voice as mine.

"It's unclear how many casualties there are," the announcer continues, "and whether The Sword or Firstborn Gabriel St. Sismode were harmed in the incident that some are now calling an attack."

Balmora reaches out impulsively and takes my hand in a death grip. She's biting her bottom lip, holding back tears. She studies my left hand, and a look of relief crosses her face. My moniker still shines silver. My brother is alive.

Balmora wipes away a tear. "Who would do this?" she demands.

It could be any number of factions. Retribution from the Rose Gardeners for the social club. The Virtue's response to my mother's bid for power. The Gates of Dawn. Then I think about Reykin. *Did he know? Is that why he didn't want me to watch, or was he just trying to protect me from more sorrow?*

I sink into a silk lounge chair. Another massacre.

Balmora joins me on the long cushion, still holding my left hand. Her eyes keep darting to it. The announcers are at a loss for what to say. No one knows exactly what happened, except that an explosion went off along the route to the memorial.

Footsteps approach Balmora's room. A few of her secondborn attendants storm in, young women in elegant sundresses with flushed faces. Quincy seems flustered, wringing her hands. *"Get out! All of you!"* Balmora screams. Their retreat is hasty, and they close the double doors behind them in a flurry.

Neither of us speaks. Time is strange. Sometimes it doesn't exist. The two of us stare, waiting for the clouds of smoke to clear enough for us to see the damage. I think I experience every kind of emotion there is to feel. Survival guilt threatens to choke me. None of this would be happening if I'd died on my Transition Day. Another part of me exults in supreme satisfaction that my mother's attack against me is being avenged. A part of me died that day, and I've never fully mourned its loss. Shame and disloyalty tangle with the realization that I truly, deeply want my mother dead.

The smoke finally dissipates, uncovering horrific carnage. In a replay of the events leading up to the attack, a glass hearse hovers down the avenue. Nothing appears to move toward the vehicle. Then it explodes outward. Whatever weapon was used, it was inside the vehicle—the vehicle that carried my father's corpse.

The Vicolt carrying my mother and my brother mysteriously drops back right before the explosion. The recording doesn't show what happened to them, but I think I already know. It was staged. They knew it would explode. Whatever just happened, it was a political move to further my mother's agenda. And it was personal. She'd rather kill innocent bystanders than allow Kennet inside the St. Sismode tomb.

"My family is fine," I say numbly.

"How do you know?" Balmora asks.

"I just do."

We continue to watch the aftermath of the attack for almost an hour. A feminine voice at the door rouses me from the holographic nightmare. "Roselle, there's a man here to see you." It's Quincy. "He's not allowed to enter, so he requested that someone come and fetch you before he levels the building." The sun outside is setting. I've been here for hours.

"Who is it?" I ask in a daze.

"Firstborn Clifton Salloway."

"Tell him to go away," Balmora orders.

I lurch to my feet and take a step toward the door. "It's okay. I need to see him."

"When are you coming back?" Balmora asks, gripping tighter to my left hand, unwilling to let me leave. Her hair is in disarray, ribbons hanging limply on her shoulders. Her eyes dart to my moniker.

The stingers in the room react. Their weapons power up noisily. Balmora lets go of my hand when the lethal barrels turn toward her. "Don't!"

I get between one of the stingers and her, and it moves off. "Balmora, I'll come back soon," I say, trying to keep my emotions in check—trying not to fall apart. Impulsively, I turn and hug her. "I promise."

I untangle myself from her and hurry to the door, past the attendant, and through the sunroom made of glass. My stingers trail me. In the hallway, everyone who lives and works in the Sea Fortress seems to be standing around and gossiping. They fall silent when I appear. "Where is Firstborn Salloway?" I ask. An elderly secondborn with a white roiling wave moniker on her hand points.

"Thank you," I manage to say, continuing outside and across the courtyard.

Clifton leans against the portico with his arms folded over his chest, glowering at the Exo guards and death drones hovering nearby. When he sees me, he straightens. My unshed tears blur his features, so I can't tell what he's thinking. I want to say his name, but my throat tightens. When I reach him, he catches me in his arms, hugging me.

"Roselle," he says softly, like he's addressing a tiny kitten. "I came as soon as I could." He takes off his jacket, wraps it around my shoulders, and hugs me again.

"How did you know where to find me?"

"Bribes," he whispers.

I laugh and choke on tears at the same time. His arms shift from my back to my waist. We turn toward the shore. The tide has come in, and the sandbar is covered with water. Clifton's Verringer undulates in the nearby cove, resembling a beautiful swan with its wings up. "I brought an extra pair of hoverdiscs for you, but you don't have shoes. No matter. I'll carry you." He reaches under my knees and lifts me with almost no effort. My arms circle his neck, and I lay my head on his shoulder. The stingers don't react at all.

Clifton treads out onto the water, walking just above the surface. "Why were you at Balmora's?" he asks calmly. I shrug and bury my face against his neck. If I speak, I'll sob. He seems to understand. "I need to talk to you, but you don't have to say anything, just listen. I'm going to take you to my airship, all right?"

I nod. The breeze mists us. Fish swim beneath the surface, some with tiger stripes, some speckled gray and white. The hum of the airship keeps the birds away. I stare toward the shore. Exo guards gather there, pointing at us. The stingers aren't reacting, though. They trail us like faithful hounds.

The door opens upward as we near the Verringer. "Stinger R0517 and R6492, remain where you are," Clifton orders.

To my surprise, they heed his order, halting and hovering above the waves. He carries me over the threshold, and the door closes behind us. Clifton finally sets me down near a fat lounge chair in the airship's great room. He takes a seat and leans toward me.

"Do you know what just happened?" he asks, concern etched in his face.

I pull his warm jacket tighter around me. "You mean the explosion in Swords?"

He nods.

"Yes, I saw the replay."

"Then you know it wasn't us, right?" He's anxious.

I swallow down some of my emotion. "I know more than that—I know it was my mother. She's probably in her office right now, rehearsing the speech she prepared days ago, condemning the Gates of Dawn for the attack. I doubt she'll be able to shed a real tear, though. Emotion has always been difficult for her."

Clifton leans back in his chair, studying me. "Your military acumen is exceptional."

"Maybe. Or maybe I just know Othala."

"Things cannot continue the way they are now," he warns. "You know this."

"I know. Someone has to stop my mother. She doesn't care about her people, just her power."

Clifton glances at the windows behind me. He swears softly. I look over my shoulder to see Exo soldiers manning boats. "I came to reassure you. The Virtue has you under his thumb now, but it won't be for long."

My eyes meet his. "What are you planning?"

"It's better you don't know," he replies.

"You have control over the stingers following me." It's a fact, not a question.

"Who do you think made them? The first rule for anything I create is an indefinite moratorium against harming me. The second is a built-in assurance that it follows *all* my orders."

Something about that makes me smile. He really is quite brilliant. "The Virtue doesn't see you coming, does he?"

"No," he replies. "I will take care of you, Roselle. You won't be a prisoner here much longer."

"It's hard to know who to trust," I say, almost to myself.

"You can trust me." Clifton is dangerous, but I'm determined to be dangerous, too. "My concern right now is for your welfare. You've been lucky up until now. You defeated your assassins. I want to make sure that trend continues. To that end, we've developed a new fabric we're calling 'Copperscale.' It's a defensive material. I want you to use it. From now on, all your clothing will be provided by Salloway Munitions. I'll clear it with the Halo Palace until we can make other arrangements."

"Defensive, how?" I ask.

"We created a textile that acts like armor. It conducts energy away from the wearer, but the fabric is lightweight, and to all outward appearances, you won't look to be wearing anything out of the ordinary. We'll reinforce whatever normal fabric you choose with it. The jacket you're wearing now is made from Copperscale. Here, let me show you." He uses his moniker to pull up a holographic display. Footage shows lab demonstrations of tactical munitions being fired at a secondborn test subject wearing what looks like ordinary street clothes. Although the subject survives a fusionmag pulse at close range, he is lifted off his feet and propelled backward several yards.

"Please tell me you gave him hazard pay," I murmur.

"He volunteered," Clifton replies, "but, yes, he was well compensated. It's not perfect. You'd be hurt by a direct fusionmag pulse, but it won't kill you." I run my hand over the sleeve of the jacket. It's a little coarse, but the inside is lined with cashmere, which makes up for it. "We can line the inside of your clothing with Copperscale and use a different fabric as outerwear, if that suits you better."

"This jacket won't protect from a head shot, Clifton, unless . . ." I drape the garment over my head like a veil. When I pull it back, I find him grinning.

"We'll have to learn how to duck," he says.

Outside, boats draw up to the Verringer. Someone pounds on the metal door, and the sound echoes through the airship. Clifton growls in anger. I want so badly to be able to talk to him about everything I know, including the Gates of Dawn. I need the Rose Gardeners and the Gates of Dawn to agree to coexist. *Can I build a bridge between them? Can the Rose Gardeners change?*

"The mortician is missing," I murmur.

"I'm sorry, the what is missing?"

"The master mortician who worked on my father's body and prepared him for burial. He went missing . . . and then my father's hearse blew up."

"You think this mortician had something to do with it?" he asks.

"I don't know, but Agent Crow was with him. I saw them together. It means something. I just don't know what."

More thumps on the door. Clifton clenches his jaw. "You're not to go around asking questions about it. I'll look into it. Do nothing."

"If Census agents are involved, this is bigger than the vendetta between my mother and my father, bigger than the Rose Gardeners. This is an alliance between Census and the Sword." The thought horrifies me, and it seems to have the same effect on Clifton.

"I'm serious, Roselle. Not a word to anyone. I'll make inquiries."

I was afraid before. Now I'm terrified. I nod in agreement. Impulsively, Clifton leans forward, kisses my forehead, and takes both my hands in his. "You'll be safe. I'll make sure of it." He rubs his thumbs over my skin. It reassures me. He's shelter.

He rises from his seat and moves to the door. Opening it, he swears at the waiting security outside. An argument breaks out between the lead Exo guard and Clifton. I rise from the chair, walk to the entrance, and lay my hand on Clifton's arm. "Firstborn Salloway, thank you for the tour of your Verringer. It's really quite lovely. I believe you should definitely make those changes to the Dual-Blade X16 that we discussed."

I try to hand him back his jacket. "Keep it," he says, still scowling at the guards.

I step into the boat, Clifton's coat securely around me, and settle between two well-armed Exos. The stingers follow us when we pull away from the airship. I stuff my hands in the pockets and find Clifton's cigar case. I pull it from his pocket, and I'm about to ask to go back so I can give it to him, but we've almost made shore, and the Verringer is already in the air. I climb out of the boat and make my way back to my apartment amid a swarm of bodyguards.

I pat Phoenix's head on my way in. Settling onto the sofa in the den, I stare up at the ceiling. Phoenix parks itself in front of me, so I know it's Reykin. "Phee, can you get me a crella from the commissary?" The mechadome leaves the room. I shove my hand into the pocket of the jacket and pull out the cigar case. Thin brown cigars, the kind with the scent of roses, lie in a neat row. I check for a secret compartment and find one with a thumbprint scanner. Testing it, I'm surprised when it opens for me.

A small holographic screen projects up from the case. Clifton's face, made of blue light, is grinning at me. "Hello," he murmurs. "Do you like your new communicator?"

"You could've just given it to me," I reply.

"Where's the fun in that? I had a bet with my technicians. I said you'd find it in under an hour."

I rise from the sofa and carry the communicator with me to the door. Closing the door, I lock it and return to my seat. From inside a compartment of the cigar case, I lift a metallic bracelet and examine it. It's a device that I've seen once before at the briefing after the attack on the Sword social club. It's the mirroring technology that reflects whatever moniker it's closest to. Right now, it's showing my moniker, without my crown-shaped birthmark. Clifton notices the device and says, "We're calling that a 'looking-glass moniker.' We're working on reverse engineering it, but that one is an original; we found it on one of the assassins you killed."

"Why are you giving it to me, Clifton?"

"There may come a time that you'll want to, shall we say, 'part company' with The Virtue," he says. "Should that time come, I'd like you to have all the tools you need to take your leave. You'll find codes inside your cigar case that will allow you to take control of your Halo stingers, just like I did today."

It's just like Clifton to be a few steps ahead of everyone else.

"Tell me about the rest, Clifton."

Chapter 13
The Bottom of the Sea

Reykin wears black. I wear white. We spar with fusionblades, and I imagine it's like watching someone sparring with a shadow. We tangle and fold in on each other. Our swords are dialed down to their lowest training setting, but if they weren't, neither of us would survive. As it is, skin regeneration treatments are required after each interaction in Grisholm's sparring circle. We savage each other. I've taken to using protective eyewear when I fight him because he has nearly cut my eyes out on a few occasions. He dons eyewear, too, for the same reason. Neither of us has yet to win a duel.

Grisholm snorts, watching us. "The sexual tension in here is savage. Find a way to be together so I don't have to be subjected to your mating dance every day." He takes a sip of water, still breathing hard from the training I put him through. He's slowly getting better with his fusionblade. It's been a month since I began training him, and I'm just now losing some of my worry that he'll chop off his own leg.

Reykin pauses and scowls at Grisholm. "She's secondborn." His tone contains no small amount of disgust. I murder him with my eyes.

Grisholm takes another sip of water. "Hey, I know, it's slumming, but I do see the attraction." A backhanded compliment, the best I can hope for, though it still makes me want to skewer him with my sword.

Instead, I walk away, toward Grisholm's spa, to get my burns treated. They trail behind me.

The sophisticated spa area is just down the hall from the main pool. Its tranquility comes from rough black tile on three of the walls. There isn't a fourth wall. It's just an opening with an indoor-outdoor pool and pool deck providing a stunning view of the sea. Ocean breezes stir large potted palms. Atom-Fated secondborn technicians wait for us at hovering medical tables.

I change into an emerald bathing suit and join the Firstborn Commander and Reykin. Grisholm is lying facedown on one table while an attractive female secondborn works on the burns I gave him across his back and calves. Reykin, bare chested and attired in a black swimsuit, sits on the opposite table, holding his forearms up to his female attendant. I take the middle table. My attendant is a tall, leggy female, too. Grisholm selects them. Like Reykin, my arms need attention, but nothing else.

"We're still on for tonight," Grisholm says. "You're not going to back out on me, are you, Winterstrom?"

"No," Reykin replies. "I'm still in."

"And you're coming, too, right, Roselle?"

I sigh heavily. "Do I have a choice?"

"No," they both say in unison.

"You're my slave," Reykin says. "We need you to assess the competitors."

"Then I'll be at your stupid Secondborn Pre-Trial event."

"You make it sound horrible," Grisholm replies with a chuckle, "but it'll be fun."

"It is horrible," I retort, "if you're on the other side of it, Grisholm. Are you sure your father said it's okay for us to go?"

The Virtue only just agreed to let The Trials move forward. I'd hoped that when Clarity Bowie postponed the Secondborn Trials, it would be indefinitely. It's only been two weeks since the chaos of my father's funeral. The Virtue declared a state of mourning, and second-borns slated to be in The Trials were shipped back to their Fates to resume their duties. Now, apparently, they're all coming back to compete. Well, most. Some of the Swords have gone into active duty or died fighting the Gates of Dawn.

"Of course I'm sure!" Grisholm replies. "And I'll wager that, by the end of the evening, you'll place a bet on someone, Roselle."

"I bet I won't."

Grisholm hisses at his attendant. "Are you using a wire brush to scour my skin? Why don't you try numbing it first!"

"Stop being a baby," Reykin replies with a smirk. "You don't hear Roselle crying about her burns."

"That's because she has no feelings," Grisholm replies. "I'm convinced she's a cyborg."

"Is that true, Roselle?" Reykin asks with a condescending grin. "Are you a cyborg?"

For some reason, his question stings. Maybe it's because it's only one of a handful of words he's said to me in the past two weeks. He has kept his distance from me since the night I last saw Hawthorne. Reykin and I see each other almost every day, at training or in council meetings, but he never comes to my apartment anymore—at least, I don't think he does. I've awoken a few times and thought I heard the door close. And sometimes, I think I smell his scent when I wake up, or see the indention of his shape in the chair by my bed, but I can't be sure.

"Sometimes I wish I was," I reply, "but I can assure you that I do think for myself, and my heart is my own."

As soon as my skin is repaired, I slide off the table and go to the tranquil pool. I wade down the stone steps, plunge beneath the surface, and swim underwater to the far end. When I emerge, I'm in the sunlight, squinting. I lean my arms on the stone deck of the pool. A shadow falls over me, and I gaze up directly into Agent Crow's killer stare.

"Did you miss me?" he asks, crouching. He's the most dressed down I've ever seen him, in rolled-up casual pants and a short-sleeved cotton shirt. "I came to see you." He smiles, his steel teeth glinting in the sunlight.

"I don't want to see you."

His icy eyes turn colder. "Last time I checked, you're still second-born. I don't need your permission."

Grisholm and Reykin wander out onto the pool deck toward us. "Census," Grisholm says, "do you have information for me?"

"There's been an interesting development that I thought you might not be aware of," Crow says.

"Oh?"

"It's been reported that the Second Family of Virtues, the Keatings, have suddenly misplaced their newly minted firstborn heir, Orwell. It's such a shame. Firstborn Rasmussen Keating is murdered. Now his brother is missing. The Keatings will lose their position as Second Family of Virtues. They might even find themselves having to leave Virtues altogether because they no longer have an heir to guarantee their position in society."

"How long has Orwell been gone?" Grisholm asks.

"A week or more," Agent Crow replies.

"Well, find him."

"There's a high probability that he's already dead. No one is getting any feedback from his moniker. I'd like your permission to question Roselle regarding the matter."

"Why do you want to question her?" Reykin asks. His voice is calm, but there's tension in his body language. "She's not the next in line for the title. Her mother and her brother are."

Agent Crow frowns. He doesn't like his authority questioned. "I would like to ascertain what, if anything, she knows about the disappearance."

Reykin crosses his arms over his chest. "How can she possibly know anything when she's been here on lockdown for the past two weeks?"

"People go missing all the time," I interject. "Why, just a couple of weeks ago, I saw that a secondborn went missing from this very palace. What was his name? Cramer . . . Clarkston . . . Cranston—that's it, Cranston Atom. He was a mortician, I believe. You wouldn't happen to know anything about *his* disappearance, would you, Agent Crow?"

Agent Crow looks like he'd like to drown me in the pool. "Who did you say?"

"Cranston Atom," I repeat. "It'd be interesting to find out who was the last person to see him alive. I bet someone like him kept records of his appointments. The question that keeps swirling around in my mind is: 'Why would anyone want to hurt a mortician?' What could he possibly know that would threaten anyone?"

"Maybe he's a deserter." Agent Crow's voice is deadly calm.

"A man like that—in love with his job—I don't think so," I insist. "I think he knew something that someone wanted to keep secret."

"You have quite an imagination," Agent Crow hisses. "Secondborns desert all the time. He'll probably show up in the Gates of Dawn body count. A defector."

"I wonder, if he does, will he have a moniker?"

A bead of sweat slides down Agent Crow's cheek. His fingers twitch to where his fusionblade should be, but it's not there. He had to relinquish it before he entered Grisholm's private domain—a new security measure that was recently mandated.

"You might have made a good Census agent, Roselle," Agent Crow says with a chilling look.

"Probably not. There's just one person I'd enjoy killing, Agent Crow, but he isn't thirdborn."

Reykin steps between me and Agent Crow. "I believe you have the wrong St. Sismode," he says. "If you're attempting to uncover information on the disappearance of Orwell Virtue, you should start with Othala and Gabriel St. Sismode."

"This is the second time you've come between me and this second-born," Agent Crow seethes.

"Listen, ol' man," Grisholm says. "I like your style—it's creepy, and that works for a man like you." He slaps Agent Crow on the back. "But Winterstrom's right. You got the wrong St. Sismode. I can vouch for her. She's been here on lockdown for weeks. We're so bored that any one of us might kill Orwell if he shows his face here, just for fun, but he hasn't, and we didn't. So go to the Sword Palace, ask those same questions about Orwell, and then report back to me." Grisholm cuffs him on the shoulder.

He turns and winks at me, completely missing the glowering look from Agent Crow. "Very well, Firstborn Commander," Crow caves. "I will return with a full report soon."

Grisholm is already walking away. He puts up his hand in a dismissive gesture. Reykin doesn't move until Agent Crow disappears down the garden path, then he turns, glowers at me, and sits down on the pool deck, putting his legs into the water. "What was that all about? Who is Cranston Atom?"

"The mortician we encountered on our trip to the morgue. He has been missing for two weeks."

"You didn't bother to tell me?" he grumbles and then looks in Grisholm's direction. The firstborn has returned to the table and is now receiving a massage.

"You haven't exactly been talking to me, so no, I didn't bother to tell you."

"I've been busy!"

"Okay. Do you have time to talk about it now?"

"What do you know?"

"You saw Crow's face when I said the part about the mortician's moniker."

"He reached for a weapon that wasn't there."

"He's ready to kill to keep a secret."

"What secret?"

"I don't know, but Census and my mother are working together. He came to see if the Halo Palace's guard is down. He wants to take me from here."

"You think he's aligned with your mother?"

"I have no proof, but yes. I've thought it since my father's funeral."

"Why haven't you said anything?" His grip on the rim of the pool turns his knuckles a shade lighter. His handsome face is more forbidding than usual.

"Like you said, you've been busy."

"I'm never too busy to discuss something as important as this," he growls.

Quincy, the young secondborn attendant from Balmora's Sea Fortress, enters the private sanctuary, clad in a summer dress. Her feet are covered in sand. She's met at the door by a member of Grisholm's staff, who turns and points to me in the pool.

Quincy nods and approaches us. "Roselle Sword, Secondborn Commander requests the pleasure of your company for lunch at her residence today at noon."

Since my father's funeral, I've been spending more and more time with Balmora. She's kind and easy to talk to, even when she's painting the same landscape over and over. It's borderline obsessive-compulsive, but I try not to judge. I do a lot of things most people would find insane, just to keep my panic at bay. Her paintings don't hurt anyone.

"Tell her I'll be there at noon," I reply, "but I can only stay a short time. I have an appointment with the Firstborn Commander this afternoon."

"Very good." Quincy sighs with relief and walks away.

"You shouldn't grow attached to her," Reykin says.

Heaviness settle on my chest as I climb out of the pool. "I could say the same to you about Grisholm."

"Don't be late for our appointment," Grisholm calls to me as I leave.

Balmora is in her private drawing room when I arrive. Inside the lofty, round tower room, scores of paintings of the same seascape, her secondborn Sea Fortress, hang everywhere: big murals on the walls, small miniatures on the tables.

The moment she looks at me, I know there's something terribly wrong.

"Everyone leave us!" she bellows in a fine rendition of her father, The Virtue. Her attendants scurry away, closing the doors behind them. The death drones remain hovering near the doors. So do my Virtue stingers.

Balmora opens her palm, revealing a whisper orb. She clicks the device, and an iridescent bubble forms around us. The hovering machines seem not to notice. She motions for me to come closer. I do, and she pulls me into a hug. Her blond hair smells like sunshine.

"I need to ask you for something, but I'm afraid," she whispers.

"What is it?" I whisper, too, though I know I don't have to be quiet.

"Please tell me I wasn't wrong—during the attack on your father's funeral procession, you were afraid—afraid for Gabriel."

I nod. "He's not well, but that doesn't mean he can't get better."

"Your brother needs help," she insists, "and you're the only one I can trust. I know where he is."

"He's in Swords, right?"

"No. He left Swords after your father's funeral. He couldn't stand it anymore. He's in Virtues."

My hands move to her upper arms. "He can't be here. If your father finds out, he's dead!"

"Don't you think I know that?" Her eyes narrow to slits. "I'm desperate to protect him from my father. I need you to find him for me and bring him here. I'll hide him until we can figure out how to help him."

"Why would you protect him?" I ask suspiciously. I know I'm not getting the whole picture here.

"Because we're in love." I stare at her, not sure if she's being honest or delusional. "You don't believe me?" she asks. "I'm not making it up." She lifts a small gilt-frame miniature of her Sea Fortress and shoves it into my hand. "Look at that!"

"I've seen a hundred of them," I say softly, trying not to provoke her.

"No, I mean really look at it!" she insists.

I stare at it, trying to see whatever it is in it that she wants me to see. My eyes blur. A gasp hitches my breath, and my heart begins to race. I turn the painting upside down. The negative space forms a profile of Gabriel. The water is his face. The fortress is his neck and torso. My lips part. My head snaps up, and I glance at every landscape in the room. They reveal themselves to be portraits of my brother. Now that I see it, it's as obvious as a six-fingered hand.

"He gave me this," she says, pulling a necklace from beneath the fabric of her white sundress. A ring hangs from the golden chain. It's one of Gabriel's Sword-Fated rings, very old, small enough to fit on a child's finger. "When Gabriel becomes The Sword, he's going to change everything. He's going to marry me. We've been planning it since we were children." Her voice grows frayed and raw. Tears fill her eyes. "It's always been Gabriel and me. Who do you think he visited when he came here? Grisholm? Fat chance!" Scorn twists her face. "It was me. He loves *me*."

I hug her to me as she sobs. "Shh . . . I believe you."

She sniffles. "You do?"

"Yes. What do you want me to do?"

"My father isn't the only one with spies, Roselle. I've been able to locate Gabriel, but no one is willing to bring your brother here."

"Why not?"

"It would be treason. My father will kill them if he finds out."

"Where is he, Balmora?"

"You'll get him and bring him here?" Her eyes are both pleading and suspicious.

"Will he come with me?" I ask. "The last time I saw him, he was certain that I wanted him dead."

"Make him come with you," she replies desperately.

"Where is he, Balmora?" I ask again.

Pure fear shows in her eyes. She wants to tell me, but she's terrified of what I'll do with the information. This is her battle. I can't fight it, so I wait silently. Desperation wins out.

"He's at Club Faraway. He has a private room under the name Firstborn Solomon—" She falters. "Solomon—"

"Solomon Sunday," I murmur.

"That's right. How did you know?"

"When Gabriel and I were really young—six and seven—we used to play 'swords' with sticks whenever no one was around to scold us. He'd let me be the heroine, Fabriana Friday"—a tear slips from my eye, and my chin wobbles—"and he'd be the villain, Solomon Sunday." I wipe the tear away. "I'll find him, and I'll bring him here if I can. I promise."

"I have an underground network of people who will help," Balmora says, relieved. She takes the miniature from me and sets it back on the table. Next to it rests a small box, which she picks it up and hands to me. "Inside is an old wrist communicator. With the new monikers, these have become obsolete, but they're perfect for modified communication on frequencies that no one seems to be paying attention to. I've established a private one for you and me. Whatever you need, I'll get it for you."

"I need to know how your network operates."

Chapter 14
Secondborn Network

The secondborn training camps are set amid agrarian and sylvan landscapes between Purity and Lenity. Only the training and pre-trials are held on solid ground. The Secondborn Trials will take place on one of the nine landmasses suspended in the air a half mile up. These hovering islands are marvels of engineering; some are as big as thirty miles across. They contain vegetation and water sources, with wildlife created specifically for whatever challenge each island is to host. Lakes, valleys, mountains, plains, and deserts comprise the terrain, along with horrific hidden quagmires and automated deathtraps. A single crown-shaped colosseum levitates in the center, above the floating islands. Made of glass and steel, the Silver Halo hosts the opening and closing ceremonies.

Shadows from the floating behemoths above us blot out large areas of sunlight on the training fields below, like a shadow of doom over the secondborns competitors. To compensate, mounted light grids shine down from beneath the floating structures, but the additional light the floating islands provide is much dimmer than direct sunlight.

The training fields are sectioned into fan-shaped areas designated by number, and they meet around a circle reserved for the enjoyment of firstborns. The only secondborns allowed in are those who work there or are accompanied by a firstborn of the aristocracy, like I am.

Reykin offers me his hand as I climb out of his two-seater airship. My Halo stingers hover outside, having followed Reykin's vehicle to the training grounds. Along with Reykin, the two stingers comprise my security team, and they're the only reason I was granted permission to leave the Halo Palace without Exo guards in tow.

Grisholm isn't so lucky. His airship lands next to ours. Fifteen Exo guards and a handful of Halo stingers alight from his vehicle and the several surrounding it. The Exos, thankfully, are not my problem.

The levitating hoverpad gives us an aerial view of the training facilities that stretch out before us for miles. Weapons training is in the section nearest to where we're standing. Pyrotechnics is farther afield, identifiable by the mushroom-shaped dirt clouds in the distance. Obstacle courses are to the east and west. Special-operations pavilions freckle the terrain. The most curious courses hide under dome enclosures, presumably to regulate temperature. One contains a mountain range, the other a desert.

Dressed in stylish training fatigues as if he'll be participating, Grisholm bounces boisterously toward us, throwing his arms wide. "Welcome to the ultimate test of champions!" He grasps me by the upper arms. "I wish I were you, Roselle! Getting to experience it all for the first time! What I wouldn't give!" He grins like a madman.

"I wish you could be me, too," I murmur. *And experience everything a secondborn goes through.*

Reykin puts his hand on Grisholm's shoulder, pulling him off me. "Who do you want to look at first?"

"I don't know! There are so many! I'll have to consult my brackets." He touches his golden halo, activating the moniker.

The firstborns herd me toward a line of waiting hoverbikes. I've never driven one, so I ride with Reykin. He mounts the hovering beast. It reminds me of him, black from fender to fender like his brooding personality. Sleek and forward leaning, clearly fast and agile. When Reykin starts the cycle, it purrs. He touches the throttle, and it growls, deep, vibrating the ground where I stand. It feels as dangerous as the man himself.

Grisholm's cycle is pure gold—shiny and overstated. Our security force has silver cycles. Some jet off ahead of us to secure the route. Others fan out to our sides and behind us.

Reykin gives me a side-eyed look. "Do you plan on walking, or are you going to get on?"

I straddle the seat behind him, glad that I wore a black jacket, tight white shirt, black leggings, and tall black boots. My feet rest on pegs behind me, forcing me to lean forward, my knees hugging Reykin's thighs. I place my hands on my own thighs rather than touch his.

"Put your arms around my waist," Reykin orders over his shoulder, "or you'll fall, and I'll have to scrape you off the ground."

"I'd never fall," I scoff. "I have excellent balance." It sounds like a boast, but it's true.

"You lean a little to the right when you hold your fusionblade at a seventy-degree angle," Reykin prods.

My gaze should melt his back, but it doesn't. "That's because I have to compensate for the crooked elbow on your weak left arm."

Reykin chuckles. "My elbow is perfect, and I will arm-wrestle you with my left arm anytime you say. Now hold my waist, and try not to fall off."

I slip my arms around him. He's solid muscle. When he leans back unexpectedly, the soft fabric of his shirt brushes my cheek. The scent of him is disturbing. I want to rest against his back and inhale deeper. I grit my teeth.

"Ready?" he asks.

"Of course."

We jet forward, going from zero to two hundred miles an hour in seconds. If I weren't holding on to him, I'd be broken. As it is, a small backrest rose behind me and caught some of the force. My arms cinch tighter to Reykin's waist, and I mold my chest against his back. I can feel him chuckling.

I settle in. My arms loosen a bit. The hovercycle is exquisite for an adrenaline junkie like me. Wind whips through my hair. All I can think about is going faster. Security trails us, and so do my Halo stingers, as we take a lap around the perimeter of a fan-shaped training field. The obstacle course is mostly wooded, about fifteen miles in circumference. Perilous paths through the trees jet off from the firstborn observatory track that we cruise. Massive redwoods tower above our heads. Sunlight filters through the branches as we fly by makeshift shanties constructed of pine boughs, thatches of limbs, and toppled tree trunks.

Secondborns in the contest aren't living off the land yet, but they're learning how. Exposure and dehydration will kill around 20 percent of the contestants in the first couple of weeks. It's an agonizing way to die. The truth is that, even though they're the property of the government, most of them wouldn't know how to exist without it. They're institutionalized.

Reykin increases our altitude and slows the hovercycle. We arrive at a hoverpad outside an observatory in Flabellate One, part of the elaborate, interconnected set of tree forts high in the canopy. Grisholm is the first one off his bike, heading straight for the rope bridges to the main treetop fortress. Reykin stays with me, walking by my side. I look around, growing more and more annoyed. The observatory is really an adult playground, where firstborns can be pampered by Stone-Fated secondborn domestics while they watch the participants of the trials struggle to hone their survival skills.

Beside the observatory, with its aerial views of the clearing below, Sword-Fated secondborn commanders who will not be competing in The Trials give live demonstrations. Targeting games are set up high in the canopies so firstborns can test their own skills with various weapons.

When a firstborn's aim strays, live ammunition finds its way down to the fields where the secondborns train.

Grisholm beckons us to the central observation deck. "Tourists!" he growls, shunning the other activities with a scornful sneer. "You're ruining the sport!" he shouts at the nearest firstborns with their hunting crossbows and grenade-tipped arrowheads. The security team starts to manhandle the firstborns, and they scurry off to a different target, leaving us alone on the observation deck.

The hovering platform is made of a lightweight material with the look of wood. It blends in with the surroundings. The open face is guarded by an invisible, restrictive energy field that allows air flow but prevents anyone from falling off the edge and plummeting to a horrifying death. Grisholm passes out enhanced telescopic eyewear, and I'm able to observe the combatants on the field below us as if I'm standing right above them.

He points out his favorites. He has a surprising understanding of their skill sets and knows details down to their vitamin supplements. One combatant is his particular favorite—a man by the name of MacGregor Sword. He's a redheaded twenty-three-year-old man of epic proportions. I note that MacGregor holds back from aggressive training today. I mention as much to Grisholm.

"It's strategy," Grisholm says with assurance. "He doesn't want others to know how skilled he is."

"It's pain, Grisholm," I reply, "not strategy. He likely has a hamstring tear. See the back of his left leg? Notice how the muscle looks lumpy? It's going to pop soon, and he'll be useless until it's fixed. He's probably taking all kinds of medications to numb it. Look at the way he's clenching his jaw and favoring his other leg. An injury like that is excruciating and takes a few days to recover from, once the muscle is reconstructed. He only has a few days left until the Opening Ceremonies. It may not be enough time, and that's if he has the merits to get it repaired. But he can't back out, can he? Once he committed, he's in whether he wants to be or not." That part I say with no small amount of scorn.

Grisholm must think my scorn is for MacGregor, because he says, "What a scam artist! I bet the odds makers are counting on him keeping his mouth shut about his injury so they can capitalize on it."

"Why would he reveal it?" Reykin asks sarcastically. His eyes look right through Grisholm. "It would let his adversaries know how to attack him effectively."

"Well, you both need to keep it to yourselves," Grisholm demands. "Uncovering the winner is only a small part of this. There are other bets along the way—like who won't survive certain challenges."

"Is there a way out of this for him, Grisholm?" I ask. MacGregor probably enlisted in The Trials when he was healthy. Now he'll likely be killed in a gruesome exhibition.

"He chose this. He must live with it. Come to think of it, he has to die with it, too," Grisholm quips.

Violence touches every part of my life. It's unavoidable. It's in every breath I take. Watching the competitors train, I begin to loathe myself for not using all my resources to put an end to it. They might have chosen to enroll in the Secondborn Trials, as Grisholm says, but doing so is a suicide note to the world: *You've brought my spirit to its knees, and now you may rip apart my body as well.* Some probably believe they have a chance, but most know they don't. They just want their pain to end.

Grisholm logs everything I say on his moniker. After we exhaust this field of competitors, Grisholm is anxious to move on. Mounting the hovercycles, we fly to the next section, staying close to the ground as we ride. I rest my cheek against Reykin's back. We pass a small lake, and the air suddenly gets cooler. Passing meadows, the wind grows sweet with lush flowering plants. I'm disappointed when we get to Flabellate Two. I'd rather keep riding, bumping over pockets of air, letting the tension of this world ebb.

Flabellate Two is hauntingly similar. After it, we tour the other sections until the sun sets and the competitors are excused to scrounge for meals. Grisholm suggests we take a break and find some food ourselves. Mounting the hovercycles once more, we fly to the center of the training matrix.

The fan-shaped training fields encircle the Trial Village. Reykin slows the hoverbike as we near the epicenter for firstborns and the media, a wooded glade filled with fantastical architecture and surrounded by gleaming walls of fusion energy. Round orbs of light float above and cast a glow over the bustling crowds. Security is tight here at the enormous arching stone portico to the modern-medieval village. Armed Exos stop us at the entrance. As part of Grisholm's entourage, we're waved through, but others—those not high enough on the aristocratic ladder—are turned away.

Grisholm and Reykin park their vehicles. Reykin's hand drops from the throttle. His fingers skim the outside of my thigh. The gesture is possessive, even if it's brief. He climbs off the bike and extends his hand to me. This suddenly feels very intimate. I'm not sure why. He's told me that he doesn't care about me. I should listen. Reykin always means every word he utters, but it's confusing nonetheless. I decline his help and climb off on my own.

A cool wind blows through the trees, rustling the needle leaves. A gorgeous starry night peeks through the redwood canopy. Paved paths lined with wrought-iron lampposts branch in several directions. I pull my jacket closer around me.

"Are you cold?" Reykin asks. His dark hair is windswept, but no less attractive for that.

I shake my head. "No. I'm fine."

A festival atmosphere prevails. Dressed for clubbing, the throng around us is jovial, thrill seeking. I've never been in a crowd this happy before. Firstborns are dance-walking, moving to the beat of live instruments. Glitter tints the women's hair and skin in vibrant colors, with small holographic fireworks displays bursting around them like crowning laurels. Strings of holographic bluebirds fly around the heads of others. Some men sport holographic angel wings that flutter with white light. Others carry miniature holographic monsters that sit reaper-like on their shoulders and lurch out at passing women, whose screams mix giddy fascination with surprised terror.

Unsettled by the strangeness of it all, I reach for my fusionblade, but I don't have one on me. I feel exposed. Reykin's hand brushes mine as we walk. He seems closer than normal. I can still feel his shape against me, and I wonder if he feels mine. The paved path forces us closer still as we follow Grisholm, surrounded by his security force.

I recognize a famous face as it passes—Firstborn Gerard Hampton, a Diamond-Fated actor who plays a secondborn Sword in a popular drama. He's with a Virtue-Fated firstborn woman I don't recognize. He recognizes me, though. He says my name and gives me a soldier's salute as we pass. It makes me want to crush him. He's clueless about what it's like to be secondborn.

We see more film stars and musicians. Some are working, but most are here as spectators. Everyone steps to the side for the heir to the Fate of Virtues, and they whisper about us behind their hands after we pass.

Drone cameras and news crews occupy live-coverage booths, and roaming commentators narrate the ongoing action for a worldwide audience. The carnival atmosphere extends to the vendors. Salloway Munitions Conglomerate has a multilevel, interactive showroom in the Trial Village, prominently featuring the latest in advanced domestic weaponry for the private sector. The featured weapon is the new Culprit-44, complete with neon-tinted energy filters that render hydrogen rounds in a variety of rainbow colors. My holographic image runs through the mock battlefield on the outside of the Salloway showroom, acrobatically maneuvering and destroying fake enemies. My cheeks feel hot as I watch it. Reykin gently squeezes my waist, but I pull away. I don't need his sympathy. I do what I do to survive. In that, I regret nothing.

We keep walking. Around every bend is a fanciful bronze water fountain composed of statues of victorious secondborn competitors. Most are depicted in their final challenge along with the loser at the defining moment of victory. One stands before us with his bronze fist entwined in the hair of a severed head, holding it aloft. Glorious? Maybe. Gruesome? Definitely. I'm glad that we don't linger.

We come to a restaurant in the shape of a spike of barley several stories high. Made of gold-painted steel and gold-tinted glass, each barleycorn on the stalk boasts a private room with its own chef, Grisholm informs us. We're escorted to the golden elevator and taken up to a tear-shaped private room. An exquisite table is prepared on the edge of a balcony. The smell of fresh-baked bread surrounds us. Reykin helps me off with my jacket, handing it to a waiter. He pulls out my chair for me. I sit beside him, across from Grisholm. Beer and wine are served in abundance. Appetizers on wooden trays litter the table. Meats and cheeses melt in my mouth, and I think about how much Hammon and Edgerton would love this place.

Grisholm, Reykin, and I enjoy a quiet meal together with our security team discretely hanging back in strategic positions. Grisholm does most of the talking, discussing the champions while he devours a rare steak and a half a loaf of bread.

Reykin watches me. The candlelight of the table casts a certain smolder in his eyes, like light from the setting sun on water. Shadows play upon his black hair and the angular planes of his face. He looks dangerous.

The communicator hidden on my upper arm keeps softly vibrating, alerting me to Balmora's attempts to contact me. Placing my napkin on the table, I murmur, "Gentlemen, please excuse me." I rise, and Reykin does, too.

Grisholm settles back in his seat. "May I remind you that she's secondborn?" he teases.

I follow the corridor to the bathroom. My Halo stingers scan it before allowing me in alone. Once inside, I lock the door. From inside my sleeve, I pull down the wrist communicator, its face shining with blue light, and contact Balmora.

"You're at the Barleycorn?" Balmora's holographic image says as soon as she answers. She's tracking me.

"I am."

"I've arranged for your transport to Club Faraway. Your contact is Secondborn Franklin Star. He's a drone operator for the *Daily Diamond*. He'll take you there in less than an hour. You have to meet him at the news hovervan."

"You're kidding?" I ask, frustrated. "I'm surrounded by Grisholm and his security."

"You're going to have to lose them." Her voice is brittle with anxiety.

I exhale deeply. "Where's the hovervan?"

"Sending you the coordinates now."

I study the holographic map. It isn't far. The problem is losing my entourage, getting there alone, and trying not to be recognized along the way. "I'm going to need a weapon—fusionblade, preferably."

"I'll see what I can do," Balmora says.

"I'll be in touch with you after I make contact." I end the transmission and push the communicator back into my upper sleeve.

Returning to the table, I find the men ready to leave. Grisholm, in particular, is anxious to get to the betting houses. He goes over his potential wagers with me while I don my jacket and Reykin pays the bill.

In the elevator, Reykin's hand presses the small of my back. Possessive. I wonder about it until we reach the ground floor. Grisholm insists that we go to the Neon Bible, the high-end bookmaking establishment a few doors away. The indoor-outdoor betting house thumps with action. As we approach the entrance, Reykin turns to Grisholm, saying, "I have to check on something. Keep an eye on the secondborn for me."

Annoyed, Grisholm sputters, "Can't it wait? I want to get my brackets set before I'm locked out of the odds for the evening!"

"I'll be just a minute. There's a weapon at Salloway's that I've had my eye on for months. Just watch her for me."

Grisholm gives me a scowl, as if I'm some sort of child thrust upon him. "Fine, but be quick," he growls. "I'm not placing bets for you."

Reykin walks away with a secretive look on his face. Getting away just became immensely easier. Grisholm and I continue into the Neon Bible. The crush of people inside is harrowing. Firstborns grind against one another on tiered dance floors. Some dance above the crowd using hoverdiscs. We're shown to a higher, more private deck several levels up. The music here is muted, but I can still watch the action below from the railing. All the men on this floor are in evening attire. Very few women are about. My attention is drawn to the dangerous men in the room, most with fusionblades and fusionmags from Salloway's arsenals.

Grisholm begins greeting the men. I recognize Valdi Shelling's associate, Pedar. I know him as Firstborn Albatross, the Sword-Fated man who groped me during an arms deal with Clifton almost a year ago. He appears to be the proprietor of the Neon Bible.

Pedar notices me almost immediately. Although he's a smaller man than Valdi, he still cuts a brutally large figure. His dark hair is slicked back and well oiled. In his late thirties, he looks like he could bend steel with his bare hands. So it's ironic when he has the same reaction I did upon seeing him—the strong man cringes a little. I nod to him in acknowledgment of the awkwardness.

Pedar turns to the nearest member of his staff and says, "Get our guests anything they want, on the house."

Grisholm practically cackles. He rubs his hands together in anticipation and orders a "Death Defier." When the drink arrives, it's black, with swirls of milky-white liquid resembling a skull and crossbones. Grisholm stirs it with a long spoon and drinks it in one gulp. He wheezes a little, handing the glass and spoon back to the waiter, and walks toward the nearby holographic displays running commentary on the competitors in The Trials.

His security entourage follows. Pedar's gray eyes catch mine again. He approaches and says quietly, "I never had the opportunity to apologize to you. I was gravely out of line."

I lift my chin a notch, meeting his gaze. "All will be forgiven if you do me a small favor."

He smiles slowly. "You have but to ask."

"I need to slip away for a moment to run an errand. No one with me can know I've gone until I'm away. A firstborn Star will join us shortly. I need him to receive a private message." Pedar eyes the two hovering Halo stingers behind me with a dubious look. "Don't worry about them," I tell him. "They're not a problem."

Pedar's eyebrows rise, but he says nothing. He lifts his hand, and another burly man comes forward and listens as Pedar whispers something in his ear. The man nods, turn to yet another man farther away, and says, "Get Christof."

A ten-year-old secondborn boy is brought forward. He's a Sword, made from Pedar's mold. Dark hair hangs in his face, and he has broad shoulders already. The young secondborn comes forward and stops in front of Pedar. Pedar leans down and whispers something in the boy's ear. He nods, sizing me up. "Ready?" he asks.

"We'll distract the Exos for you," Pedar says. "You will be taken out the back way." He makes no move toward me, maybe having learned his lesson from our previous encounter. Then he nods his head, and suddenly a fight breaks out on the dance floor below. People brawling and throwing punches. The noise and chaos is deafening. Everyone rushes to the railings to watch. Grisholm is enthralled.

"Thank you, Pedar," I murmur. "All is forgiven."

Christof Sword moves toward the back of the club, with me on his heels. We escape through a secret door in the wall and down some back stairs. My Halo stringers still follow me closely. When we get to the bottom of the stairs, Christof dismisses the guards on duty there. They turn and go, as if he's the boss. He opens the door that leads outside.

I turn to the hovering black hardware behind us and rattle off the stinger code that Clifton gave me. "R0517 and R6492, return to the Halo Palace." They hesitate. My heart beats hard in my chest. The boy beside me watches the heavily armed stingers with suspicion. Then, as if they finally recognize the command, they fly past us, out into the night sky, and disappear into the darkness.

With the machines gone, it feels as if a weight has been lifted from me. From the hollowed-out heel of my boot, I extract a black fingerless glove and a small piece of lead. I cover my moniker with them. The silver sword goes dark. I take out the looking-glass moniker and turn it on before slipping the bracelet onto my wrist. It reflects Christof's moniker beside me. He watches everything I do.

"What's your message, and who do I give it to?" he asks.

"Find Reykin Winterstrom," I reply, and then describe him. "He'll come to the Neon Bible. Tell him to cover for me. Tell him I will meet him back at the Halo Palace tonight."

"That's all?"

"Yes."

"The boss says you need cover to blend in," Christof mutters.

"I do," I reply. I use the hood of my jacket, pulling it over my hair and as low on my forehead as I can.

"This way," Christof says, taking my hand. It's strange, being led around by a ten-year-old boy who acts like a thirty-year-old man. Not that I expected him to act like a child. He's not firstborn.

"Are you Pedar's son?" I ask as we maneuver through the frolicking crowd, which grows louder and bawdier by the minute. I try to keep my chin down.

"Might be," he replies with a stoic expression, "but he ain't sayin', and I ain't askin'. The one they says was my father is dead—killed by the Gates of Dawn . . . but I heard he was just someone who couldn't pay what he owed." I wonder about how Pedar operates. If someone fell into debt with the firstborn Sword, that person might have to do whatever was demanded of him to get out of it—maybe even marry and pretend his wife's children are his. Christof bears such a resemblance to Pedar that I could see that.

We approach a street vendor selling holographic masks. They shine and blink on a hovering wire rack in the front of the pavilion. The vender takes one look at Christof, recognition dawns, and he quickly looks the other way, as if he's afraid of the boy. I stare at the masks on display. Some mimic wildlife—elephants with long gray trunks made of light, swine with triangular ears and round snouts, wolves with long muzzles and sharp teeth. Others suggest eerie monsters with viper fangs, or mouthless beasts. Christof choses a black panther mask with black triangular ears, long whiskers, and yellow eyes. He hands it to me. "That's you for sure," he says. "A cat."

Lifting it to my face, I pull the strap over my hair and tug my cowl down once more. Unable to help myself, I touch his cheek. "You take care, Christof."

"You, too, St. Sismode." Why he chooses to call me by my old last name, I don't know, but I have no time to wonder. I set a brisk pace to the news hovervan before Franklin Star leaves without me.

The news van has a big, bold blue holographic iris surrounding a black pupil on its side. Every few seconds, the eyelid blinks and the iris changes color. Beside the eye, a sandy-haired secondborn paces, consulting his shooting star–shaped moniker. Crowds of people jostle past him on their way to different party venues. Sidling up to the secondborn, I murmur, "Franklin?"

A scared scowl crosses his face, and his glasses go askew when he jolts. He rearranges them on his nose. Grasping his heart, he tries to see me beyond the hologram of my mask. "Who sent you?" he whispers. His thin body leans closer to me.

"Balmora," I reply.

He looks around, deciding whether we're being watched. Finding no one, Franklin gestures to the side with his head, motioning to the hovervan's sliding side panel. He ushers me inside and closes the door. In the dark, the smell of stale beer assaults me. My eyes adjust to the dimness. One side of the van is a command center. The other has metal racks bolted to the floor. Inside mesh bins, drone cameras lie charging, their green-spotted lens eyes seeming to stare into my soul. A workstation is next to the drones. It has a couple seats, folded away. I sit down on the dingy steel floor toward the rear of the vehicle.

Franklin gets into the driver's seat. Over his shoulder he says, "If we get caught, I'd appreciate you saying that you stowed away in here without me knowing."

"Sure, Franklin," I agree.

"Keep your head down." He starts the hovervan. With a low rumble and a sway of the hulking van, we're off. Wires on hooks jumble around. Equipment I have no name for rubs against other equipment I have no name for. I lie on the cold, dingy floor and stare up. Moonlight glints through the dirty window.

We're not stopped or checked as we exit the Trial Village. No one seems overly concerned that we're leaving. Franklin attempts to make small talk, but beyond confirming that I want to go to Club Faraway, I ignore his questions. After a few minutes, he gives up and focuses on the route.

It's not until this moment that I allow myself to unleash what I've stuffed down deep inside since agreeing to do this. Goose bumps prickle over my skin. Fear grabs me by the throat. This could be a setup. Even if it's not, I'm not optimistic that I'll make it out of this alive. I'm about to storm into a drug den and attempt to kidnap my firstborn brother, the heir to the deadliest Fate in the world. I could paint this as a selfless act—wax poetic about how noble it is to save Gabriel and reunite him with the love of his life—but that's not why I'm doing it. If I'm being honest with myself, I'm terrified of Gabriel dying and forcing me to take his place. Othala will never forgive me. *Not that I care,* I tell myself, even as shame burns my cheeks.

But there's more to it than that. If Gabriel dies, and I become first-born, I'll be something I've come to despise. If I'm required to take over, there are no guarantees that I won't be worse than Gabriel. I'm significantly more vicious, and I know this about myself. If I became firstborn, any faction seeking to destroy me or attempting to wrestle away my power would be met with ruthless retaliation . . . just like my mother's. Othala and I will never again be on the same side. The problem is, if I can't maintain power, the odds of me descending into some nightmarish prison of Othala's or Bowie's or even Crow's making is high. If Othala is aligned with Crow, I can include soul-crushing torture.

But the final reason that I welcome this fight tonight is because it may be my one shot at having a family again. I had love, a makeshift family, but I've lost it, and there's a gaping hole in my heart where it used to be. I need to be honest with myself. Hawthorne isn't coming back. He's going to go on with his life—his *firstborn* life. He would've contacted me by now if he planned to be a part of the rebellion—or to see me. It's been weeks. He knows where I am. He also knows the odds are against our fixing anything. We have a better chance of making things worse.

Saving Gabriel could be my only shot at happiness. If Balmora, the secondborn of the Fate of Virtues, and Gabriel, the firstborn of the Fate of Swords, can unite and fight for change, then maybe there's a better world ahead for all of us. Maybe together, they can bring us peace.

Chapter 15
The Consolation of Oblivion

Franklin stops the hovervan on the street corner one block from Club Faraway. Before I even close the door, he speeds away. Taking off the cat mask, I toss it into a garbage receptacle. The streets aren't very crowded in downtown Purity. The upscale metropolitan area is more office building than residential.

Slowly, I follow the navigation on my wrist communicator. "I'm approaching the club," I whisper into the device. "Have you located a weapon?"

"Go look under the bench in front of the mechadome clinic," Balmora replies through the communicator.

I spot the hovering bench in front of a mechadome storefront. Different types of bots are on display. None of them resemble Phoenix. Attached to the bottom of the seat bench, I find a generic fusionblade, tear it away from the adhesive, and strap the thigh sheath to my right leg.

"Got it," I mutter into the communicator.

"Good. You're clear to go."

"Copy."

I tighten the belt of the long black jacket that Clifton's team made for me. My hand smooths down the Copperscale. I hope it's as good as

Clifton claims, or I'm dead. The navigation points to a posh, fin-shaped skyscraper. The outside of the slender building resembles gray shark skin. It's intriguing without being overt. Club Faraway is nestled on the corner, next to other elegant facades of what appear to be average-looking office buildings.

The drug lair doesn't overtly advertise. No signs. No patrons milling around outside. Balconies speckle the side of the building, reminiscent of an elegant hotel. The rooftop has a penthouse at the peak of the dorsal fin. At street level, glass doors filled with undulating blue water blur the view inside. Pushing one open, I take a cautious step in. The door closes behind me. Bright light from the ceiling and the floor make it hard to see. Security traps me in the vestibule between the outer and inner doors. I'm in a faux tank, the walls all filled with water, blurring everything on the outside. "This is a weapons-free zone," an automated feminine voice sounds. "Please check all weapon in the receptacle."

A silver cylindrical apparatus rises from the floor, and a round chute opens inside it. My heart sinks. I have to give up my weapon if I want to get in. I consider leaving, but if I do, I'll always ask what-if. Reluctantly, I pull the fusionblade from the sheath on my thigh and deposit it in the receptacle. The weapon disappears, and an orange plastic disc emerges. I place it in my pocket. The bright light fades. The doors slide open.

The pristine lobby is dimly lit. The floor shines with wavering aquamarine light, like sunshine filtering through water. Softly lit chandeliers barely push back the shadows. Clusters of dark velvet chairs with high seat backs float above the floor. I gaze around for elevators, hallways, or other attached rooms. There aren't any. For a drug club, it isn't attracting any customers.

Soft instrumental music plays. A woman with thick dark glasses sits in the corner facing the door. Her hair is white, with blunt-cut bangs in the front. A fat tumbler of amber liquid rests on the table beside her. A rose-colored cigar sends a curl of fragrant pink smoke up from her ashtray. A glove masks her moniker. On the opposite side of the

Traitor Born

room sits a thin, well-built man. He's hollow-cheeked, and dressed as if for the opera, drinking a wine spritzer. I don't judge: wine spritzers are delicious.

A clerk—middle-aged, a Virtue-Fated secondborn with slicked-back hair and a dark suit with a high collar—stands at a blue wave-shaped desk at the back of the room. The wall behind it is a shark tank. Holographic screens in the desk cast hieroglyphic symbols up onto the clerk's face.

"Hello and welcome to Club Faraway." The secondborn smiles. His teeth glint. His glittering diamond ascot pin twinkles. "Do you have a reservation or are you here to meet a party?"

"A party," I say. "Solomon Sunday."

His nostrils flare, and his finger hesitates on the virtual screen. He has been expecting me.

"Firstborn Sunday is—" His eyes widen in terror. I duck. The clerk's neck and jaw explode from a fusionmag shot, spattering brain matter onto the tank behind him. I don't look back but jump over the desk. A second fusionmag blast strikes me in the back between my shoulder blades. Judging by the angle, the shot had to have come from the wine spritzer man. The Copperscale of my coat absorbs part of it, but the impact is like being hit by a speeding hovercraft. I slam into the shark tank and slide to the floor. The clerk's corpse twitches beneath me. I wheeze. My lungs feel turned inside out. Flecks of the clerk's blood mar his diamond tiepin. I pluck the tiepin from the cloth.

Footsteps draw nearer. Ignoring the pain, I lurch up and throw the tiepin at the man who shot me. The needle and diamond slice into his pupil. Wine Spritzer screams and holds his hand to his bloody eye. I reach across the desk, grasp his other hand, and turn his fusionmag. We shoot at the white-haired assassin stalking toward us, but she dives to the floor. I twist the fusionmag in Wine Spritzer's hand again and shoot him through the chin with it, blowing off the top of his head. As he crumbles, I tear the weapon from his hand.

209

The woman on the floor fires again. The pulse hits my right bicep. My jacket absorbs most of the pulse, but it still knocks me off my feet. My fingers go numb. I can't hold on to the fusionmag, and it drops to the floor and slides. Straightening, I reach for it with my left hand. The woman walks around the desk, and her perfect cherry lips gape open when she sees I'm not dead. My fusion pulse blows her shattered heart out of her chest. She flies backward and hits the ground, bouncing.

I stagger to my feet as the numbness in my arm gives way to aching tingles. It still works, but it aches like hell. Moving my fingers to get the feeling back into them, I search Wine Spritzer with my other hand. A spade-like knife is concealed in a leg sheath. He was waiting for me. Whoever planted the assassins in the lobby knew I was coming—or someone like me. I remove his glove. No moniker—but a scar where it used to be.

I move to the woman. Her hair is a wig, and when I pull it away, she's bald. Gruesome scars cover her scalp. I pluck the dark glasses from her face. Brown eyes with a silver tint stare up, unseeing. I don her glasses and wig, stuffing my long brown strands beneath it. I untie her rose-colored scarf, wrap it around my throat and the lower half of my face, and remove her glove. She doesn't have a moniker either—it was cut out. I take her fusionmag and shove it in my pocket. Back at the clerk's desk, I use the spade knife to cut out his secondborn moniker, stuffing it inside my glove so that it shines through the mesh.

Then I use the holographic screens above the desk to find Gabriel. He's registered in the penthouse suite. I do another search. Solomon Sunday is registered to a suite on the eighth floor—the Euphoria Room. Maybe it wasn't Balmora who set me up. Maybe Gabriel *is* here after all. Maybe my mother knew someone might come to kill him, now that he's in Virtues, and set a trap here and in the penthouse.

The wall behind me slides sideways. Straightening in surprise, I realize that the wall was merely a holographic illusion. An entryway to a drug den lies open. Everything inside is red. Huge, round, ruby-colored lanterns hang from the ceiling. It's like a multilevel casino, but instead of gaming tables and machines, there are tall transparent cylinders containing bodies. The bodies are suspended behind the glass. Some are alone in their tubes and simply float like dreamy fetuses in wombs. Others are suspended together in massive glass cylinders, entangling each other in orgies of passion. Decadent crimson furniture surrounds some of the glass tubes, occupied by firstborns watching the haze of smoke and naked bodies.

People walk the floor like zombies, with pallid skin and unbalanced gaits. A Virtue-Fated firstborn with bloodshot eyes stops in his tracks next to me. He's stooped and unsteady on his feet. "Is this real?" he asks.

"No," I reply, making my way into the red-poppy haze. The wall slides shut behind me, hiding the lobby. Serpentine clouds of red smoke hang in the air. The scent spins my head in lazy circles, even through my scarf. Red banners hang, curling and floating, from beams above, blooming like poppies—opening and closing, opening and closing.

A young boy, maybe eight, takes my hand. Wordlessly he leads me to a jewel-red counter where a secondborn—wearing a mask with a painted poppy over her nose and mouth—dispenses a menagerie of mind-altering substances from behind glass. Holographic menus display on the glass.

"Do you have aerosol?" I ask the Moon-Fated attendant. "Something that will make me sleepy?"

She languidly twists pieces of her garnet-colored hair around her finger. "Of course. Hazy Daze-99." She holds up a cylindrical can and depresses a button on top of it. The aerosol mists in a short burst. The arch of it forms a rainbow. It doesn't seem to affect her. "How many?"

"Everything you have and a mask like yours."

Her eyes bug out. "Do you want that on a hovercart?"

"Yes."

"Scan your moniker," she says.

I scan the clerk's moniker as she loads a few dozen aerosols into a hovercart. The cart passes through to me.

"Do you know where the lifts are?" I ask the little secondborn boy at my side. He nods, calls the lift with his moniker, and tugs my hand. As we walk to the lift, I ask, "What's your name?"

He shrugs lethargically. I make a mental note to come back for him when I have the power to change his life by rescuing him from this awful place.

I enter the lift alone and wait for the doors to close. Then, opening the lid of the hovercart, I take out several cans and place them on the floor. I slip the mask over my nose and mouth and wrap it with the scarf. I lift a can and spray the cameras in the elevator, puncture several other cans in the hovercart, and close the lid.

The dial on the hovercart is set to "Follow Mode." I reset it to "Propel Mode." The hovercart hits the doors and grinds against them. Positioning the clerk's moniker beneath the scanner, I select the eighth floor. The elevator rises. I lean back into the corner where the walls of the elevator meet. I lift one foot and place it on one wall. My other foot pushes against the other wall. With my feet on each of the two corner walls, I use the leverage to scale them and press myself against the ceiling near the doors. When the car stops and opens, armed guards are waiting, their fusionmags drawn. The hovercart idles forward. One of the guards opens it. An aerosol cloud wafts out. Their shoulders round, and their arms grow heavy. Thumps resound as the guards topple over.

Someone calls, "What is it?"

I drop down from the ceiling.

A guard glances at me and smiles dopily. "Adreana," he murmurs. He must think I'm the female assassin from the lobby. He slumps against the wall and slides down it.

Sounds of pounding feet grow near. I puncture more cans and toss them into the hallway. Billowing fog fills the air. Feet slow. Bodies hit the floor. When the fog clears, I peek my head out and draw it back fast. A dozen guards sit limply against the walls—some lie on the floor, weapons fallen haphazardly beside them. It's rainbow fields forever out there.

Following the trail of bodies, I reach the door at the end of the corridor. No sounds come from the other side. Pulling out my fusionmag, I aim it at the door, and then, on second thought, I hide the weapon behind my back, and knock. The door opens partway. "You're supposed to be in the lobby," a tall, burly man says. I kick in the door. He stumbles back, drawing his fusionmag. I shoot him in the chest. His colleagues are gathered around a virtual screen watching a pre-trial training session. They draw weapons. I lift my fusionmag and pull the trigger in rapid succession. Bodies twist and fall like discarded puppets. I should feel bad, but I don't. If I were here to kill Gabriel, they wouldn't have stopped me because they were too busy entertaining themselves.

I bar the door and cautiously creep to the main apartment. It's empty. In the master bedroom, I find Gabriel alone, passed out on the bed. His dark hair is in disarray. Cadaverous eyes rimmed in dark circles sit atop his hollowed cheeks. His elegant silk shirt is open, revealing his sunken chest. His rolled-up sleeves reveal scabs and bruises. He trembles. He's either done too much or not enough.

I tug the scarf and mask from my face. "Gabriel," I whisper. Tears prickle my eyes. I touch his shoulder and try to rouse him. He finally opens his eyes and squints at me.

"Who are you?" he whispers.

I pull off the white wig and glasses. "Fabriana Friday," I murmur through my tears.

"Are you here . . . to save . . . the world?" he asks weakly. It's something he would've said when we were kids.

"I'm here to rescue you, Solomon Sunday." I touch his hair. It's brittle. He doesn't reply, just continues to tremble.

I speak into the wrist communicator. "I have him, Balmora. I need a superfast airship."

"You're getting a delivery hover." Balmora's voice rings through the wrist communicator. "Creamy Crellas. Side alley—below your position. Can you get there now?"

"We'll get there."

The extra glove and leaded swatch I brought with me slide easily over Gabriel's left hand, blotting out his moniker. I roll my brother onto his side, and then reach for his belt, sliding it from the loops of his trousers. Undoing my own belt, I hook them together. I thread the long belt behind Gabriel's waist. Lying next to him like a spoon, so that my back is pressed against his chest, I secure the belt around my waist so he's strapped to my back. Reaching behind me, I lift his arms and hoist them over my shoulders. The bruises on my back and chest ache. So does my arm, but I ignore the pain.

When I stand, Gabriel comes with me, his dead weight distributed to my shoulders and back. Hunching over, I carry him to the empty balcony. We inch out onto it, and then I lean Gabriel against the wall, holding him there with my back against his chest. I pluck the clerk's moniker from my glove and drop it on the balcony. I peel back the glove covering my moniker, and menus spring up from the silver sword. I may not be able to communicate with it, but I can activate the hoverdiscs on the bottoms of my boots. I program them for rapid descent and smooth my glove over my moniker again. I clutch Gabriel's arms. He isn't very heavy, but it's awkward to move with him on my back. Disregarding gracefulness, I climb over the railing of the balcony and leap off.

The cool wind whistling past my ears deadens the shouts from the henchmen on the rooftop. They don't shoot, probably because Gabriel is shielding me. A few of them jump from the peak of the dorsal fin. My brother doesn't move. He's barely conscious.

Near the ground, the hoverdiscs activate and slow our fall. When I halt just above the sidewalk, inertia makes it feel as if my kneecaps will explode. Wincing, I look around for the alley. Sinister figures using gravitizers land on the avenue behind us. Black-clad, they hold rifles that could blow holes through Gabriel and me. But none of them fires. They pause, speaking into their monikers. I use my hoverdiscs to skate in the opposite direction.

They pursue us, but they're on foot, so they fall behind. Rounding a corner, I nearly run into a hovering delivery craft idling in the alleyway. Animated characters made to look like crellas dance in a three-dimensional display of jouncing revelry around the perimeter of the hovertruck. Crella creatures bathe in chocolate streams that morph into showers of glaze and sprinkles.

For a second, I think I must have been sprayed by Hazy Daze-99, because this is my biggest fantasy, but then a man with a thick unibrow and a double chin calls to me through the window of the hovertruck: "Get in." He points his thumb to the rear of the vehicle. The truck lurches forward, picking up speed as it moves through the alley.

"No!" I whimper. The back door of the craft slides open. I force my legs to move, skating behind it, my thighs burning. The holographic crella creatures wave banners and march next to me. Clenching my teeth, I lurch for the opening. As we dive through the doorway, the driver triggers the hatch, and it falls closed, hiding us within.

Small lights near the floor illuminate the inside of the hovertruck. Steel racks of ice-cream-filled crellas line the walls to the ceiling. In the truck's crisp refrigeration, I lay on the floor beside Gabriel, our breath huffing in white wisps. I can't tell if my brother shakes from the cold or from detoxification. The belts cut into my flesh. Unhooking the clasp, I free us from them. Gabriel tumbles away, curling into a ball on the floor.

"Gabriel, are you okay?" I ask.

"Where . . . am I?" he whispers.

"You're in a hovertruck. I'm taking you to Balmora." His forearms are so thin it makes me want to cry.

"Should let me die," he says between clenched teeth.

My heart throbs painfully. "I'm not letting you die." Peeling off my jacket, I lay it over him. We take a corner, and Gabriel rolls across the floor. I lift his head, stabilizing him against my shoulder. In my other hand, I hold a fusionmag pointed at the back of the hovertruck, in case the guards catch up to us.

I don't remember the last time I was this close to my brother. Maybe when he stopped my mother from killing me on my Transition Day? That's how it goes, though. The Fates Republic won't allow us to be a family, using propaganda and their stupid hysteria-eliciting rhetoric to sow suspicion between siblings—casting doubt over secondborns' intentions. Anger heats my face. A tear slips over my lashes. They should've left us alone as kids—let us be each other's friend. Everybody always pointed out his golden sword instead, like it was *the* reason for him not to love me. But Gabriel loved me anyway, and it destroyed him. I can see that now.

Tears like I've never allowed myself course down my face. The Fates Republic keeps selling us the biggest lie of all—that we're nothing to each other. Enemies. Now we're all just liars.

My wrist communicator lights up. Wiping tears and snot, I take a few seconds to answer it.

"Do you have him? Is he okay?" Balmora's voice trembles.

I take a deep breath and exhale. "I have him. He's not okay. He's sick and frail."

"Just get him here," she says with a shaky voice.

Soon the hovervan comes to a stop. I wipe my face on my sleeve again and train the fusionmag on the door. It slides open. "Let's get this over with," Double Chin says. "I'm late for my rounds." He ignores my weapon and waves me out. "Move. We have a delivery barge ready to take you to Balmora at the Sea Fortress."

Two more men with silver sun monikers flank him. One of the men has scars on his face from burns that went untreated. Lowering the fusionmag, I allow the three bakers to help me with Gabriel. They hoist him up and carry him out. I take my jacket and hop down. We're on the waterfront. Tall white lights push back the darkness along the length of the pier. Sea air pushes at my hair. The bakers unload tall steel containers from the back of the hovertruck. Two are empty. "Get in," the one with the burn scars grunts. The other two bakers are already loading Gabriel inside a separate case.

Harrowing fear blows through me. I'll be at their mercy if I get inside.

The burned one reads my dubious expression. "You think we want you dead?" he asks. He's missing a few teeth and smells like bread. I shrug. "We don't want Grisholm to be The Virtue. We want one of us—a secondborn. We got nothin' against you. You're secondborn . . . and anyway, Balmora says you're not to be harmed." My options are limited, so I swallow my fear and step inside the hovering steel case. "You're going to have to give me your weapons and wrist communicator. The security scanners near the Halo Palace might pick 'em up." Reluctantly, I hand over my communicator and all the arms I've collected.

"Now lift your shirt," he says.

I stiffen. "Why?"

"I have to put this on you." He holds up a clear plastic swatch with silver wires running through it.

"What is that?"

"It mutes your heart so no one can tell that anything inside the box is alive. The case will hide your body heat." I lift my shirt, and he attaches the adhesive swatch over my heart. "Paddy, you got some of 'em calico crellas?"

The one with the oblong face and a beatdown expression nods and walks to the cab of the truck. He returns and hands a small satchel to his partner. The baker offers it to me. Inside, a couple of pastries sit wrapped in wax paper. "For the brave one," he says, and then shuts the door, locking me inside. Darkness and a delicious fresh-baked crella scent assault me. The case floats forward amid muffled shouts. Unwrapping a crella, I bite into it, and I'm overtaken by the taste of cinnamon-flavored sunlight. *I should've been born into the Fate of Suns. If this is a last meal, it's a good one, maybe the best one.*

When the case finally opens, maybe an hour later, I inhale large gasps of fresh air and squint against the lamplight. I'm in a room that resembles the exposed belly of an ancient sea vessel. An enormous chandelier made of coral and sea glass hangs from wooden rafters. Its lights resemble white tapers, but they're actually fusion energy.

Quincy holds the door for me. I brace my arm against the side of the case. My knees ache, but I rise and step down out of the crate. I stand inside a palatial bedroom with an archway to a stone terrace.

Balmora's melodic voice says, "You're in the Fate of Seas' tower."

Gabriel is sprawled on the floor with his head cradled in her lap. She strokes his damp hair. My brother has been sick. Bile clings to his lips, which are a frightening shade of blue.

"We need to get him to a bed." Balmora's pleading eyes stare up at me.

I kneel on one knee and hitch Gabriel's arm around my shoulders. Balmora does the same on his other side. We lift him up and drag him. His black boots skim across the carpet, kicking up dust motes.

The bed isn't as musty. Its ornate frame is carved from real wood, which hasn't been done much for centuries. It's a pirate's bed, or, at least, that's what it seems like. Its four massive posts are carved dragonheads resembling mastheads from sea ships that no longer exist. Someone has recently changed the bedding, and dustcloths have been removed from the furniture and left in a heap in the corner. We hoist Gabriel onto the mattress and rest his head against the plump pillows.

"Where are your drones?" I ask Balmora.

"Outside my bedroom in The Virtue's tower." She fusses over Gabriel, pulling his boots off, removing his shirt.

"Why aren't they with you?"

"I had a Star-Fated secondborn infiltrate them. A coded voice command from me will trick the drones into thinking I'm in my bedroom. Another will make them believe I'm in the gallery, and another that I'm in the media room. The Exos who monitor me have grown bored and often just rely on the drones to keep track of me. And my attendants are afraid of me, so when I tell them I want to be alone, they're happy to leave me to myself."

"How do you go anywhere in this place without being seen?"

She looks at me with an appraising stare. "My father's brother, Edward, the last secondborn commander, taught me the secrets of the Sea Fortress before he died. We lived here together for years, my uncle and me. He introduced me to the network of spies who helped you tonight."

"I thought you had developed it on your own."

Balmora's laughter contains little humor. "This network has existed for hundreds of years—passed on from secondborn to secondborn. You wouldn't know about it, of course. We always lack Swords, because secondborn Swords within a family are rarely able to communicate with one another. Take your uncle, Bazzle, your mother's brother. He was killed at eighteen, only a few weeks after his Transition. He could hardly pass any information to you. You weren't even born. And the secondborn workers in the Sword Palace are terrified of your mother. They're not a good resource for our network. The risk of discovery is too great. It's not like that with other Fates. We live much longer than secondborn Swords. We work together, sometimes live together."

"Census doesn't know about it?" I ask.

"Census infiltrates our network from time to time. We recently had a whole branch of our operatives sheared away in the Fate of Moons. Some were murdered. Some destroyed themselves to protect others. We're nearly blind there. Same within the Fates of Stars and Atoms. They've sided with the Gates of Dawn and cut us off, but we continue to groom operatives—individual Star- and Atom-Fated secondborns who reside outside their fatedoms will sometimes work with us. In Virtues, I have hundreds of secondborns of all Fates who have sworn loyalty to me."

"What we need right now is a physician for Gabriel," I urge.

"He'll have one. An Atom will be here soon."

Quincy brings a bowl of water from the bathroom. Setting it on the table next to the bed, she wrings out a small cloth and hands it to Balmora, who uses it to bathe Gabriel.

My brother opens his eyes when she washes his face. "Where am I?" he whispers.

"Safe with me," Balmora assures him.

He lifts his shaking hand, touching hers. "Told you not to come . . . too late . . . should've . . . let me die." His voice is raspy and slurred.

"You're not allowed to die," Balmora scolds in her bossiest tone. "Do you hear me?"

"I can't stop her . . ."

"Who, Gabriel?" I ask, coming closer to the bed. "Who can't you stop?" I'm worried that he means me. "I don't want to hurt you."

"I can't," Gabriel whispers. His eyes are now bleeding from their corners. "Only you can. Too many zeros."

Is he delusional? Am I just part of his hallucination?

"Who is *she*?" I ask him. "Mother? Are you talking about The Sword, Gabriel?"

"Gabriel's dead." His smile is tragic. "Only Solomon Sunday's left."

"You're Gabriel," I whisper.

"Gabriel's dead!" he shouts, his voice higher but not actually louder. *"Just let us die!"* He struggles to sit up, but he's too weak. Balmora holds him down. His eyes flutter shut, and he pants for breath.

"You should go," Balmora says to me anxiously. "You're upsetting him, and I can't have Exos looking for you here. I'll have Quincy show you the secret way out. Don't come back unless I call for you." Pearls of sweat shine on her upper lip.

Gabriel is still trembling, covered in sweat. I desperately want to stay with him, but I know I'd only put him in more danger. "Balmora, you'll keep me updated on how he is?" I ask.

"As best I can," she replies, rising from the bed to hug me. We cling to each other for a few moments, and then she lets me go. "Thank you for bringing him to me. Quincy, help Roselle get back to shore. Use the sea gate, and make sure no one sees her leave."

Quincy nods. "It's this way."

She leads me to the stone balcony, where the wind tosses my hair, pushing it into my face. Stone griffins, frozen in midpounce, stare at me from above. Quincy climbs the protruding mortar of the tower like a monkey and pulls on the stone snout of the griffin, wrenching it to the side. A stone wall beside the tall column opens, showing the outline of a doorway. Quincy climbs down and pushes against the wall, and the opening grows larger. She disappears inside. I follow her. Her small fusion-powered light pushes back the darkness inside, allowing me to see past her into a cramped hallway about three feet wide and maybe seven feet high.

"Push the door closed," Quincy says.

I lean against it until it locks in place. Quincy turns away and walks farther into the stone hallway, a spiraling ramp down the outer wall of the tower. It's a dizzying journey. The walls are dry and rough, but the air is damp and has a faint scent of rotten fish that gets stronger during the long descent. At sea level, other passageways branch off. Quincy stops and turns, whispering, "This leads to the main hallway. Security for the fortress is nearby." She puts her fingers to her lips.

I nod. We tiptoe farther down the spiraling stone ramp. The air grow damper. Sea urchins encrust the walls. At the bottom is a small landing and a deep pool of water.

"The sea gate is down there." Quincy points to the dark depths.

"You mean, underwater?" The last thing I want to do tonight is get wet.

She nods and walks to a round wheel with handholds. Turning the wheel activates a pulley system, which raises an iron gate, drawing it up from the water. "Are you a good swimmer?" Quincy asks.

"Decent," I reply, tugging off my boots.

Quincy opens a wooden box and pulls out a device that looks like a small torpedo with handlebars. She set it down on the stone floor. Opening the front of it, she places my boots inside. "Anything else you don't want to get wet?" she asks. I shrug off my jacket and hand it to her. She folds it and places it neatly in the torpedo. "This mask goes over your eyes and nose so you'll be able to breathe. There's a dim headlight that I've programmed to extinguish when you get close to shore. When you get to the beach, press this button to open the hatch. Remove your things, then press this button, and the underwater propulsion device will return to the fortress."

"Anything else?" I ask.

"Watch out for sharks."

My insides quail at the thought.

The mask sits tight against my face, and the air activates before I ease into the water holding the propulsion device with both hands. Sinking beneath the surface, the mask illuminates the opening to the sea ahead. The right handlebar has the throttle grip. Turning it slowly, I ease away from the stone fortress.

The water is cold, but it's not unbearable. My legs drift as I circumvent rocks and reefs. Beautiful coral is alive with sea plants that sway in the current. As I near the Halo Palace, the water becomes shallower, and my chest and thighs bump against the sand. I let go of the throttle, and the waves push me gently toward the shore. I stand up and wade forward until I'm only waist deep. I collect my boots and coat from the niche, holding them above the water with one hand, then take off the mask and drop it inside before closing the compartment. Following Quincy's instructions, I press the button, and the vehicle submerges and jets away.

Chapter 16
Carry these Bones

When I enter the foyer, my apartment is quiet and dark. Phoenix doesn't waddle in to greet me. I drop my boots by the door and wait, but it doesn't come. Maybe its hover mode malfunctioned? I take one tentative step, and then another. "Phee?" I slip off my jacket and leave it on the small table. I have sand all over myself. I need to shower and sleep.

Walking out of the foyer, I slow my steps. The lights don't come on automatically in the drawing room. The shutters are closed. "Lights," I order. Nothing happens. I fumble for the lamp I know is on the small bureau near me. I touch it, and the soft glow barely pushes back the shadows. I move to the other lamp near it, but the shadow of a figure on the sofa in the drawing room captures my attention.

Reykin.

Seated on the middle cushion, the Star is hunched over, his elbows resting on his thighs, his head bowed, his hands gripping the back of his skull. I take a few steps toward him. "Reykin?"

He lifts his chin and drops his hands. His expression is a mixture of rage and relief. Dressed to kill, literally, he wears black everything—his moniker covered by his lead-lined glove—the outfit of someone ready to do murder. A shadow of a bruise mars his jaw. The muscles of his arms twitch. In a sword fight, we're equals. In hand-to-hand combat, I might not fare as well. Icy chills run down my spine. "Where have you been?" he asks in a low snarl.

"I . . ." I haven't thought this part through. He can't know about Gabriel and Balmora. He'll kill my brother.

"Is that a hard question?" His lip holds a sneer.

"Yes." I hate hearing the quiver in my voice.

"Well, let's start with where you weren't. Maybe that's easier. You weren't in the Neon Bible with Grisholm."

"No," I reply breathlessly, "I wasn't."

He leans forward and reaches for a fat tumbler of amber liquor. Lifting the rim of the glass to his lips, he drinks all of it in one swallow. He sets it down and seizes a nearly empty diamond-shaped bottle, splashing more alcohol into his tumbler. "If that child you sent to me with your message hadn't delivered it when he did, I would've killed Grisholm."

"Why?" My stomach twists with dread. I put out my hand and steady myself against the seat back of a chair.

"My first impulse was that he arranged your kidnapping. I thought he let your mother's killers take you. Do you know what that feels like?" Reykin's jaw flexes. He looks as if he's ready to throttle me.

"It should feel like nothing. You said you don't have a heart—that you don't *care* about me." The rawness of my emotions chokes me. I blink away tears. *Why does this man affect me so?* "You should be more concerned about Grisholm being assassinated by my mother than about what I'm doing. I can handle myself."

Reykin throws the glass against the wall. It shatters. "Haven't you figured it out yet?" He rises from his seat, seething. "You're the most important person. You. Not that ridiculous excuse for a man who thinks he should be the ruler of the world!"

"Tell me you didn't hurt Grisholm!" My knees grow weak.

"No. I left him at the Neon Bible. I told him that I found you but you were ill and I had to take you home. In essence, I lied for you. Nobody knows you were gone. I fixed it, like I always do!"

Anxiety like I've never known passes through me. I'm not a fan of Grisholm, but it's not that. If Reykin were to kill Grisholm, he'd be hunted down like no other man in the history of the world. He may not care about me, but apparently, I care about him . . . enough to feel the crushing force of panic building.

I wring my hands to try to get them to stop trembling. My breathing becomes heavier. Cold sweat develops on my skin. Reykin continues to rant at me, but I can hardly hear him over the pounding of blood in my ears.

I turn away and, in a daze, hurry from the sitting room to the den where I put some chets away for an occasion such as this. It's dark when I enter. I stumble to the box on the table. Its clear wrapper crinkles when I try to unwrap one. The walls spin. I knock over the box. *Why is this happening?*

I didn't feel an ounce of panic when I was fighting my way through a club full of assassins, but that was different. I was in control. It's the things I can't control, like Reykin, that turn me into a panting, shaking mess of heighted emotion.

"I need . . ." I can't breathe.

Reykin stands in the doorway. The light in the room responds to his presence. Lamps turn on. He must have messed with it to irritate me. The room responds to him but not me. Without Reykin—if I'm alone—I'll be in the dark.

My hands become fists as I attempt to catch my breath. Reykin approaches me with his hand out warily, as if I might startle and run. "I . . . need . . ." I try to force myself to breathe slower, but I can't.

He takes the chets from my fumbling fingers. Tearing off a piece of one, he holds it out to me, but when I reach for it, he pulls it back.

"Why should I give you this?" he asks. "You left me to panic for hours with no relief."

A flare of anger spikes. Dizziness turns to tunnel vision. Full-blown, merciless fear catapults my heart into a frenzy. I'm dying. My nails bite into my palms.

Reykin swears softly. His fingers press the small piece of a chet to my lips. I take it into my mouth, and it melts on my tongue. My heart feels like someone is punching it.

He touches my sleeve, smoothing his hand over my arm. I cringe at the ache it brings. I must be one enormous bruise from head to toe. I've compartmentalized my physical pain, and now an awareness of it roars to the forefront of my mind. The chet steadily dulls it, but I'm beyond sore in the places where I was shot.

Reykin pummels me with a dark and brooding stare. I don't want to see his pity. He must think I'm weak and stupid. Why it matters to me what he thinks, I don't know. He's not my friend. He's barely my ally. His arm goes around my middle, tugging me to him. My back rests against his formidable chest. My head is heavy. He sweeps my damp hair away from my neck, baring my nape.

"Shh," he whispers softly, soothing rather than scolding. The scent of whatever he was drinking mixes with his normal scent. It's sweet, and I turn toward his lips. His cheek skims the sensitive part of my throat. His hand brushes back my hair again. He pulls me to the sofa and tugs me down next to him, holding me to his chest. He covers me with the charcoal-colored cashmere blanket. My cheek rests against his neck. When normal breathing returns, I don't move. Exhausted, I lie limply against Reykin's side.

"I'm sorry," he murmurs, grasping the bridge of his nose with his fingers, as if his head hurts and he can't find relief.

The palm of his other hand rests on my side, one of the only places I'm not bruised beneath my white shirt. The crest of his knuckles is scabbing over. "Who have you been fighting?" I ask. My voice is hoarse.

He lifts his hand, studying it. "Where do you think I went when I couldn't find you?"

I wince. "I wasn't with Hawthorne."

"I know."

"Did you hurt him?"

"He's alive," Reykin replies grudgingly.

"What did you do?"

"We had a conversation—mostly with our fists. We stopped trying to beat each other senseless when it became obvious that neither one of us knew where you were."

"What did you two talk about?"

"That's between us."

"Did he say anything about joining our fight?" My voice is weak.

"No. We didn't talk about that. My only concern was finding you." When I don't say anything, he sighs. "Whose side are you on, Roselle?"

"My side."

"Were you with Salloway—the Rose Gardeners?" he asks. He sounds jealous.

"No."

"Then where were you?"

"Nowhere."

"You have to tell me. I'm going to lose my patience if you don't."

"Then lose it," I reply. "I'm not afraid of you."

"I think I'm the *only* person you're afraid of."

"Why would I be afraid of you?"

"Because you *care* about me," he says scornfully.

"That would make me stupid, Reykin."

"You care about what I think of you, and what I might do, and what might happen to me."

"You're delusional."

"Am I? I don't see you panicking around anyone else."

"That's because you're not paying attention."

"I couldn't be more attentive."

"How was I able to get away from you at the trial grounds, then, if you were so attentive?"

I sit up. His hand reaches out to stay me, but I'm beyond ready to end this conversation. "Do you know where I was," he asks, "when you slipped away at the training grounds?"

I pause. "I take it you didn't go to Salloway's."

"I went to see a different vendor." He lifts his hand and gazes at his moniker. In a few seconds, Phoenix glides into the den with a very playful puppy trailing behind it. The tiny beast has a black nose, floppy ears, and white fur with black- and chestnut-colored spots. It leaps and bounds after the mechadome. Phoenix stops in front of us. Reykin stoops and scoops up the furry, wiggling puppy, whose tiny tail wags as he licks Reykin's face and softly whines.

"Here." Reykin places the adorable creature into my arms. The puppy immediately tries to shower my face with kisses. "He's yours," Reykin says gruffly. "I bought him for you *before* you did your disappearing act. I know secondborns aren't allowed pets, but I'll claim he's mine."

I'm unable to speak for a few moments. Every ounce of anger flows out of me. "You got me a puppy?" I lower the long-eared face-licker away from my chin.

"You said you wanted one."

"When did I say that?" I ask breathlessly. I hold the incredibly soft fur baby to my chest and snuggle my cheek to the top of his head. The puppy begins chewing on my hair.

"You told me when the technician was fixing your ribs. Do you like him? He's a beagle."

"He's mine?" I whisper with a tight voice. My throat suddenly hurts.

"Yes." Reykin's voice is soft. "I was hoping he'd help with your anxiety."

"Thank you," I whisper. I lift my face and accept more kisses from the excited hound.

"What are you going to name him?"

"I don't know," I murmur, my eyes blurring with tears. "He's perfect."

A smile develops on Reykin's lips, but only for an instant. Then it's gone, and his stern, forbidding stare is back. It makes me want to see him smile again. "What about Cudgel," Reykin asks, "since he's beating me with his tail?"

"Rogue," I murmur and rest against Reykin once more.

"Rogue." Reykin reaches over and pets the little hellion. "Welcome to the family, little brother."

The puppy puts its front paws on my heart, trying to climb up me. I wince as a sharp pain stabs through me.

"What's wrong?" Reykin asks.

"Nothing," I grunt, trying to shift Rogue in my arms so that he won't stomp on my bruised chest again. My face twists in pain. Reykin takes Rogue from me and sets the rambunctious creature on the carpet. The tiny hound attacks Phoenix playfully.

Reykin reaches his hand out, trying to grasp the hem of my shirt. I block his arm with my forearm. He scowls and reaches out again, saying, "Let me see."

"I'm fine."

"Then let me see," he replies, "or I'll pin you down and look. Your choice."

"Pfft, like you could," I retort. He moves as if I've just thrown down a challenge. Leaning away, I thrust up my arms to block him, which aggravates my wounds. "Okay! I'll show you, but only if you agree not to overreact." His glare could melt ice. "Okay," I relent, "so maybe you don't have the stoic gene. Just try to remain calm." He nods and stares at the hem of my shirt. "Is that an 'okay'?" I ask.

"Roselle!"

I sigh heavily. Grasping the hem of my dirty white shirt, I lift it over my head, peeling it off. Above my bra, a dark contusion, shaped like an enormous ink drop, spiders across my skin to my collarbone. Another one covers my bicep.

"What did that?" Reykin reaches to touch me. Gently, he traces the raised welt.

"Fusionmag." I watch as his long finger traces the wound.

"Fusionmag? How are you alive?" I'm not sure that he believes me.

"I have a really good tailor."

His angry scowl returns. "What does that even mean?" he demands.

His fingers soothe my abraded flesh, causing goose bumps to break out. I shiver. "It means Clifton Salloway made me clothes with fabric that repels fusionmag and other energy pulses." I sweep my hair over my shoulder and show him my back. "How bad is this one?"

Reykin sucks air between his teeth. "Who did this to you?"

"It's not what *they* did to me. It's what *I* did to them."

"You went to speak to your *brother*!" he snarls. Reykin is so intuitive, it's almost scary. I should keep in mind how similar we are. I slip my shirt back on and pull my hair from beneath the collar, letting it spill over my shoulders once more. I shift and face him.

"I went to speak to Gabriel, but it was a setup. Assassins were waiting for me. I think Othala sent them." It's not a lie. They *were* waiting for me, and it *was* a setup. The fact that I was still successful in my goal of kidnapping Gabriel and bringing him to the Sea Fortress doesn't have to be mentioned. "The assassins are dead, though."

"And your brother?" he asks.

"I wasn't able to talk to him like I wanted." Again, not exactly a lie, just not the truth.

"Of all the stupid, irresponsible—"

"Don't tell me that if you found Ransom, you wouldn't try to speak to him."

Reykin covers his face with his hands and scrubs it in exasperation. "Uhh," he groans, "you know that's not the same thing! My brother isn't trying to kill me."

"Why are you so angry? I'm here—I didn't die."

Reykin removes his hands. "There are so many reasons why I'm livid right now, I can't even name them all. And you're *not* fine. You're beaten up. Maybe I'm tired of seeing you hurt."

"You leave bruises on me all the time," I point out. It's true, but it's unfair, and I know it.

"That's different! That's training! I'm making sure you never lose your edge—that anyone who comes at you, you can destroy."

"I know," I murmur. "I'm sorry. I didn't mean that. I'm just exhausted." The puppy attacks my toes, trying to pull off my damp sock. I reach down and lift him in my arms. "Thank you for Rogue." I lean back against Reykin's chest, petting my beagle's floppy ears.

After a few minutes, Reykin's anger ebbs. His chest softens beneath my cheek. The next thing I know, I'm being lowered into my bed. I must have fallen asleep. The blanket settles over me, and Reykin begins to back away.

"Reykin, are you leaving?"

"No. Go to sleep."

Bombardment by puppy kisses might be the sweetest way to wake up. I've only spent a few days with Rogue, but I'm hopelessly in love with him. I help him off my bed and hurry to change so that I can take him out to the garden. Outside, my Halo stingers wander with Rogue and me around the topiary bushes and shade trees. The secondborn Suns stop supervising the pruning drones to kneel and greet my curious puppy. Having been a pariah most of my life, I appreciate the sudden chattiness and ease with which the secondborn gardeners speak to me.

I feel different, like maybe there's more to life than horror, violence, and lethal power struggles. I think what I'm feeling is hope. It scares me.

I wander near the cliff. The wind whips my hair. Rogue, in my arms, nips at it. The tide's going out, which means I can visit the Sea Fortress and maybe see my brother. I'm anxious for news of how he's doing. Balmora hasn't sent me any messages since our last meeting. I keep telling myself that she's under a lot of stress, taking care of Gabriel. He was in an awful state the last time I saw him. I wish I could help her.

I set Rogue down, and we wander back toward the rows of roses and shrubbery. "Do you want to get some breakfast?" I ask him. He wags his tail, puts his two front paws on my shin, and begins whining. "Oh, you want me to pick you up again, do you?" I reach down and scoop him up.

As I straighten, Reykin rounds the hedgerow near me. I grin. "Good morning! To what do we owe the honor of your presence?" I ask, trying to sound surprised. I'm not. Ever since Reykin gave me Rogue, he's been with me just about every waking minute. I'm not sure if it's by his own volition, or if he's been ordered to stay with me, but he sticketh closer than a brother to me now. Closer than mine ever did anyway.

The corners of his lips twitch, as if he wants to smile back but won't allow himself to. "How's our boy?" he asks, approaching. Rogue spots Reykin, and his tail starts wagging wildly. He barks happily and wiggles to get free of my arms.

"He's a handful," I reply, "and by the look of how happy he is to see you, I'd say he has horrible taste in friends." I set Rogue down, and he bounds toward Reykin.

"She's so mean, isn't she, boy? Heartless." The firstborn Star lifts Rogue and allows the little monster to lick his clean-shaven face.

We eventually sit and lay back on the grass, letting Rogue crawl all over us. I giggle when he steps on my cheek. Turning so his paw doesn't trample my eye, I find Reykin staring at me. He's riveted. He leans forward, his lips near mine. My breath catches. Reykin takes my hand, and his thumb rubs over my crown-shaped birthmark.

I glance at it, and suddenly cold fear trickles through me. I sit up. The puppy bounces off my lap onto Reykin. I scrub the back of my hand with my fingers, trying to rub away my moniker's golden light. *Maybe it's the sunlight*, I tell myself. I hold my hand at different angles, but its color doesn't change. I choke, scrubbing harder, raking my hand along the grass. I lift it again. A gold sword. I search Reykin's face. He stares back at me, his expression unreadable.

"What have you done?" I snarl accusingly at Reykin. The betrayal I feel is horrific. His jaw tightens, but he doesn't deny anything, he just stares back at me. *"What have you done?"* I scream. Reykin doesn't even flinch. "You killed him! You killed my brother!"

He sets Rogue aside and hauls me toward him. I'm sobbing and resist him, but he's incredibly strong. "You killed him!" I sob against his chest. "You killed him!" I repeat it over and over in harsh hacking breaths. Hot tears wet my cheeks. Reykin holds my head firmly against his chest with one hand. His heart thumps wild and loud in my ear.

A shadow falls across us. Through tear-blinded eyes, I realize someone is standing next to me. A girl, breathing hard. Her face is red, and she's crying. "Quincy!" I exhale her name.

"You have to come now! She's asking for you!" Distress puckers Quincy's brow as she reaches for my hand, tugging me in desperation. "Please! She's going to jump! You have to come!" Her long blond braid whips the air wildly. Nightmarish fear is etched into every line of her face.

"Who are you?" Reykin demands from the girl. He won't let go of me.

Quincy sinks to her knees. "He was only supposed to take a little. The Atom told her to give him only a few grams a day, but he found the medicine. He took it all!" She chokes on a sob. "He got so sick, and he turned blue, and we couldn't get him to breathe. He wouldn't breathe!"

Agony and sorrow shine in her red-rimmed eyes. "She needs you! You have to come!"

I put my hand against Reykin's chest and push with all my might. Blindly, I stumble to my feet. Quincy takes my hand, and we run in the direction of the Sea Fortress. Soft yipping barks follow behind me. I turn back to get Rogue, but Reykin has already collected him and is only a few paces behind. I sprint ahead.

The sandbar is still covered by water, but the tide is going out. I wade into the waist-deep surf. I'm soaked by the time I reach the stone walls of the Sea Fortress. The sentry guards posted outside appear not to know what's transpiring within. I allow them to scan my moniker, and then I'm past them, racing across the high-walled courtyard.

The guards won't let Reykin through, and he shouts for me to wait, but I keep going. Once inside, I accost the first person I can find—an elderly Sun-Fated secondborn carrying a multi-tiered tray full of intricate cakes and pastries. I latch on to her arm, nearly spilling the tray. "How do I get to the top of the tower?" I demand.

Her eyes widen, and the lines around them stretch. She starts to answer me, but Quincy's small hand on my arm pulls me forward. She navigates hallways—a labyrinth of stone walls—with me in tow. A winding staircase with carved wooden railings spirals up the middle of the tower, its hundreds of flagstone steps covered by aqua-colored carpet. I move toward the staircase, but Quincy yells, "No, wait!"

Near the staircase are several small hover vehicles, some of them rusted around the edges. Most look as if they are whimsical novelties made for children, resembling miniature ancient sea vessels, but a couple are larger—big enough to carry adults. Quincy goes to a two-seater parked by the wall, near a balustrade carved in the shape of a cresting wave. She climbs onto it and activates the controls. The vehicle's dragon-shaped masthead comes to life, its eyes glowing yellow, and the vehicle lifts off the floor.

I climb onto the glittering golden seat beside her, and she launches the vehicle forward, driving it up the steep stairs. We follow the staircase in a dizzying, ever-climbing corkscrew. Passing stained-glass windows and floors with scores of doors at breakneck speeds, Quincy urges the vehicle on ever faster, slowing only when we arrive at the top floor's landing. I look down over the railing at the ground floor far below. A commotion is forming. People are gathering there. Reykin is one of them. He probably bullied his way in here, using his connection to Grisholm or The Virtue as a threat.

I rush to the open door at the end of the hallway. Sunlight shines in through the stone terrace overlooking the sea. White curtains flap. The breeze is warm. I'm sweating from the run and wet with salt water, but I shiver anyway, as if chilled to my marrow. Gulls squawk and cry outside. Balmora stands barefoot on the wide, lichen-dappled wall facing the cloudless blue sky. Her beautiful hair is long and loose, flowing past her shoulders and over her white nightgown.

In the bed at the other end of the room, my brother's body lays against the white damask pillows. My scalp tingles as my hairs rise in horror. Someone has taken off Gabriel's leaded glove. Apart from his moniker's golden light, it's obvious that he's dead. His ashen skin sags lifelessly over his hollow cheeks.

I ache—a stabbing pain in my chest. Bile rises in my throat and my knees weaken. Hope is a vicious thing. I allowed myself to feel it, and now it's bent on destroying me. My ears ring as blood pounds through them. Beside me, Quincy pants hard, her chest heaving. Wringing her hands, she implores me with her eyes to do something.

I trudge heavily toward the stone terrace, weighed down by fear, my steps echoing on the flagstone floor. "Balmora," I say gently.

Wind lifts her hair. "Nothing ever changes here," Balmora says flatly, without looking at me, from her position on the wall overlooking the sea. "Clouds roll in and roll out. Waves crash in and slide out . . . on and on, day after day, year after year, and I'm always here. Alone. That never changes either. I hate this place."

"Please come down," I beg.

"He said it has to be this way."

"It has to be what way?" I ask apprehensively. "Gabriel was sick—out of his mind—he—" Balmora leans forward a little. I consider rushing her and pulling her off the ledge, but the risk that she'll fall is too great. I inch closer.

Balmora turns and gazes down at me. Wind lifts her hem and stirs her hair. Her waving gown reminds me of the flags that top each tower of the fortress. "He said he couldn't stop your mother, but you can." It's like she's in a trance. Emotionless. Withdrawn.

"Stop her from what?"

"From taking over the world with her monsters."

"What monsters?" I ask. Balmora's foot moves, and her heel now teeters off the edge of the wall. I reach out to her, gesturing for her to take my hand and climb down. "Don't, Balmora," I beg. "We can change the world together—you and me."

"He said, 'Tell Roselle to follow the crow to the trees in the sea.'"

"Kipson Crow? Did he mean Agent Crow?"

The sound of another hovercart crashing into our abandoned one rattles the air behind us. Reykin calls my name, and I hear a few of Balmora's attendants with him. I want to scream at them to leave, but I don't dare take my eyes from Balmora.

"I don't know what he meant," she drones. "He made me promise to tell you, and then, he said, I could join him." Her dazed eyes shift to the young girl next to me. "Good-bye, Quincy," Balmora whispers. And steps off the ledge.

Chapter 17
The Heir

I lurch forward, hoping to grab Balmora, but she's gone. A strangled sob comes from Quincy beside me. Screams tear through the air from the secondborn attendants behind us. I force myself to look over the edge, hoping to find her clinging to a ledge, but the tide is out, and the stones that support the base of the fortress are uncovered. Balmora's body is a mangled mess on the rocks far below.

The wind beats my hair against the sides of my face. I turn away and catch Quincy before she can look over the balcony wall. "Don't," I whisper, holding her to me in a hug. I can't tell which of us is shaking worse. Quincy whimpers softly, the quiet crying of a girl who has been taught not to show her sorrow. I gaze toward the tower. Reykin is standing on the threshold to the balcony. By the grim expression on his face, I think he witnessed what happened.

With long strides, Reykin crosses the balcony alone and peers over the low wall. Rogue isn't with him, and I wonder numbly where my puppy is. Reykin's expression is blank, betraying nothing of what he's thinking.

Alarms peal, distant at first, but growing steadily closer. Death drones converge around us, rising to hover around the balcony. Their bone-jarring tones rattle my teeth. Reykin gets between me and them.

My Halo stingers arm and behave aggressively toward the death drones. The air grows foul with the noise of drones.

Reykin's physical presence buffers me from the chaos. His shoulders arch around me like a shield. Carefully, he herds Quincy and me back inside the tower, away from the death drones. The Halo stingers drift with us. Armed Exo and Iono guards enter the tower bedroom. Balmora's secondborn attendants flutter around, some crying.

The pit of my stomach aches when I cast a glance at Gabriel again. I've been wrong about so many things, but especially him. I can't decide if he was noble or a coward. The one thing he is now is gone.

"This way." Reykin directs me to leave, but we're stopped by the guards. Using his moniker, Reykin contacts Dune, and moments later, the leader of the security team gets orders from my former mentor to bring me to the Halo Palace.

"Quincy comes with me," I growl, trying to hold back my tears. It's strange, this ache. If I could pinpoint its source, I might be able to do something about it, but it's all-encompassing.

We're escorted from the tower. On the way out of the fortress, Reykin collects Rogue from the lap of a middle-aged secondborn woman with a gap between her teeth. The puppy is completely passive, in the grip of a serious nap. I want to bury my face in his fur, but I dare not touch him. I'm not good at loving. I'm only good at killing. Death. Destruction.

"Sad to see him go," the woman says with a grin. In my daze, I mistakenly think she means Gabriel. But then she holds up the puppy and hands the bundle of love to Reykin. He nods, and we cross the shallow water over the sandbar to a waiting aircraft.

Inside the airship, I huddle next to Quincy. Reykin sits beside me. We're so close that our thighs touch. I still hear my heart in my ears. The puppy sleeps soundly on his lap, intermittently wagging his little tail. Reykin watches me. Shame heats my cheeks. I should never have accused him of murdering my brother. Gabriel did that himself. All

I want to do is lay my head against Reykin's shoulder and sob for the brother I once loved. *That* Gabriel was worthy of my tears, but I know my brother wasn't that boy anymore.

"I'm sorry I accused you," I croak. "I thought . . ." I look away so I won't cry.

Reykin's warm fingers close over my hand. "Not a poor assumption, given what I've said to you in the past." He squeezes my hand. "How long?" he whispers. I know what he's asking. How long has my brother been at the fortress, right under his nose?

"Since the night you gave me Rogue," I reply.

"Who knows?" he asks. I indicate Quincy with a dip of my chin. Her cheek rests against my shoulder. "Quincy?" he beckons. The girl doesn't lift her head, but her arm around mine grows tighter. "How did Gabriel come to be in the Sea Fortress?"

Her voice is monotone and distant. "Do you mean the dead man?"

"Yes," Reykin replies.

"I don't know. I only found him like that this morning," she lies. "Secondborn Commander was on the wall of the balcony. She was distraught, so I ran to get Roselle, hoping she'd be able to help."

"Do you know who the man was?" he asks.

She shakes her head. "His moniker says he's a Sword, but I didn't look at him closely."

No one can know what we've done. Now that I'm firstborn and the heir to The Sword, I might get off with some ridiculously light punishment, but Quincy could be killed for helping to bring Gabriel and Balmora together. I can't let that happen. We stick to her story or she dies.

"Quincy," Reykin says softly, "did you know that this puppy is magic?" Quincy side-eyes Rogue, then looks at Reykin. His face shows no hint of humor. "It's true. Nothing bad can happen to you while you're holding Rogue. He's special like that. Do you want to try it and see?"

She looks back at Rogue. Reykin lifts the puppy, holding his little warm body out to Quincy. She doesn't move at first, but then her arm slips from mine, and her small, shaking hands take the furry creature and bring him to her chest. She presses her cheek to the top of his head, and Rogue's floppy ear caresses her skin. A silent tear slips down her face.

Our aircraft touches down on a hoverpad connected to the floating halo. Reykin keeps everyone at bay from Quincy and me. With his arms locked around us, he escorts us inside. The guards here seem different, and the reason isn't immediately apparent until we get to the first security checkpoint. The hostile, suspicious stares that normally greet me have changed to surprise and open curiosity. The golden light of my moniker means I'm now treated with deference.

By the time we reach Dune's apartment, I'm trembling. My skin is chilly. I keep replaying everything in my mind, questioning my decisions. *If I'd gone to Balmora and pulled her off the wall before she had a chance to tell me Gabriel's message, she wouldn't have been able to jump. If I had stayed with her and helped her convince Gabriel not to take his life, they'd both be alive.*

I'm shaken from my daze to find Dune in front of me. His look of concern is genuine, but it's concern for me, not for Gabriel or Balmora. He doesn't share the pain of my brother's loss. Dune may try to comfort me, or he may not, but one thing is true: he wanted this. This is the best outcome the Gates of Dawn could have imagined. But I am unraveling. I feel as though if you pull a frayed piece of me, I'll unwind into ribbon.

"The Virtue has been alerted," Dune says. "He understands that Balmora is dead and that it's confirmed suicide. He's going to want to know what she said before she jumped."

"She gave me a message from Gabriel," I reply. I sound distant, even to myself.

"What was the message?" Dune asks.

"She said Gabriel wants me to follow the crow to the trees in the sea."

Dune's expression grows more intense. "Do you know what she meant by that?"

"No," I reply, "but the only 'crow' I know is Agent Crow."

A woman's shrieks echo in the corridor outside Dune's apartment. He turns to look, and the door is thrown open by a disheveled woman. Her long blond hair is half set, as if she were interrupted in the middle of grooming. Clad only in a long jewel-colored robe, Adora storms into the drawing room.

"Where is she?" The Virtue's wife howls, and then her eyes fall on me. "*You!* What have you done?" Her voice is high-pitched, overwrought. I shudder at the snarl on her beautiful lips. "My daughter would *never* kill herself! She was too strong for that! You killed her!" Adora thrusts her finger at me. Deep lines of sorrow appear around her mouth.

My head shakes involuntarily. "She was my friend," I whisper. Hot tears fill my eyes. "I tried to save her, but she—"

"Liar!" Adora's agony shimmers. Tears drown her eyes. She lunges forward to slap me, but Reykin captures her and thrusts her arms behind her. "Let go of me!" She jerks and twists, but Reykin easily holds her. He nods his head to the Fated Virtue's bodyguards, who have trailed in after her. They come forward to hold her off.

Then The Virtue storms into the room, tight-lipped, flanked by his personal bodyguards. "Adora!" He tries to hug her.

She wrenches away from him. "You *promised* me that if I agreed to keep her locked away in the Sea Fortress, nothing bad would ever happen to my baby. You lied! You're a liar!" Adora spits viciously at her husband. "You're all liars!"

The Virtue motions to his bodyguards. "Take the Fated Virtue back to her apartments," he says. "Call for a physician. Have her sedated."

Gently but firmly, the Exo guards pull Adora away. Her wailing and threats of retribution recede, but the air remains stained with them.

The next few hours are complete chaos. The Virtue paces, grilling me with questions about Balmora's death. Both Quincy and I present the facts of her death without revealing the treasonous part about arranging Gabriel and Balmora's reunion. Most of the questions he asks us are about things I pretend not to know. Ignorance as a defense is weak and unacceptable to The Virtue. I fear for Dune's furniture as the brutal despot crashes around the apartment, laying waste to all the most fragile appointments.

"You were supposedly her *friend*," he rages, almost toppling over a delicate table and sending an iron bowl filled with orbs crashing. The noise feels like slaps to my already taut nerves as his anger escalates from vein-popping to murderous.

"We were friends," I reply with a distinct lack of emotion, not because I'm unemotional, but because I've forced them all down. "But we're also Transitioned secondborns. Relationships cannot be intimate. It's unacceptable to form deep attachments to anything outside one's duties." I use the law as a fallback. If they're going to create ridiculous rules, I'll throw them back in their faces.

"You expect me to believe you're a robot?" he asks. "I've seen you fight. Your passion is why you excel, not your detachment!"

I'm stunned for a moment, not sure how to defend myself from an accusation that's so true. Movement by the door draws my attention. Two firstborns from The Virtue's administrative team creep into the room. Both are young, lithe females wearing terrified expressions. The one with the Virtue-Fated moniker inches forward and interrupts The Virtue's scathing tirade. "Excuse me, Clarity Bowie." Her timid voice quivers.

He whips around at the disruption. "What is it!" he bellows.

"Exos found this in Secondborn Commander's tower room." She holds up a palm-size hologram recorder. "It contains a message from your daughter."

"*Show it!*" he roars.

"But, Your Excellence, it's a very private kind of—"

"Play the bloody thing!" Spittle flies from The Virtue's mouth.

The woman scurries forward, placing the recorder on the floor in the space between them. She activates the message. Holographic light projects up from the cylindrical metal base. Balmora's image appears.

"Hello, father," she says in a brittle, condescending tone. She's wearing the white nightgown she died in. Her hair, beautifully mussed as if she has just woken up, frames her tear-stained cheeks. Puffy eyes attest to her crying. She is perched on the edge of the bed in the Fate of Seas tower. Gabriel's corpse is visible behind her, resting against damask pillows. "It may come as a shock to you that I've been in love with Gabriel St. Sismode since I was very young—and he loved me. We kept it a secret from you and Mother, not by choice, but because you and your perversions forced us to.

"Gabriel has always been kind and gentle, a man who hated being the heir to the cruelest Fate of the Republic. Unlike you, Father, he never thought my being secondborn was a curse, or that it made me inferior. He loved me despite my birth order. We were going to change the world together, he and I, but now it's too late. He's dead, and I'll be joining him soon. So I won't waste much more of your time with my *insignificant prattle*. I know how you hate that.

"Gabriel made me promise I'd give you a message from him. He said his mother is set to bring a wave of war and terror to your shores, the likes of which you've never seen. He said there was no way for him to stop her. He believed that only his sister is cunning and strong enough to do that. So he's stepping aside as the heir to the Fate of Swords. He took his own life so that Roselle could take his place." Bitterness shows on her face. She swallows hard. "Personally," she growls through gritted teeth, "whatever monsters Othala is bringing, I hope they destroy you and your entire dynasty. Good-bye, Father. May your death be long and painful."

The hologram projection blinks out. The Virtue's mouth is unhinged, resembling the severed head from the bronze statue in the Trial Village, locked in its last moment of horror.

"She's mad," he whispers. The Virtue clears his throat. "If Othala wants a war with me, she'll get a war." He points at me. "I'll see that you become The Sword, Roselle. You'll lead the Fate of Swords. Secondborn soldiers will follow you, not your mother! After all, you were one of them!" To the two trembling assistants, he barks, "Assemble all the Clarities of the Fates Republic, except for Swords. I want a meeting today! Roselle shall have a private suite in *Upper Halo*. I need her close to me at all times. *Move!*" The assistants scatter.

I'm herded out of Dune's apartment. Quincy and Rogue get diverted by a pair of The Virtue's assistants. Before they go, the assistants assure me that they'll take Quincy to my new apartment to await me.

Dune and Reykin flank me as we pass through security and into corridors I haven't seen before. The hallways don't make sense at first. The outside of the hovering structure appears to be hollow, but to my complete amazement, it isn't. The architecture is circular, but it's solid throughout, with surfaces that give the illusion of sky.

Arriving at The Virtue's command post in the center of the Halo, I realize that *Upper Halo* is a massive airship. I can't imagine what it's like flying a building, but I'm certain that my Class Seven pilot's license doesn't cover it.

Inside the war room, The Virtue argues with Dune over strategy for the meeting he intends to hold with the other Clarities. Eventually he informs the other Clarities that my brother has taken his own life and that I have elevated to firstborn status. Holographic images of the Clarities extend jovial congratulations. Through all of it, I nod in acknowledgment but say nothing.

All the Clarities, except for my mother, have been apprised of my brother's death. I steel myself for the virtual meeting with Othala, but nothing could have prepared me for her appearance when her holographic image alights in front of us. Seated behind her glass desk in her Sword Palace office, she slouches in her seat with a cocktail in reach. Her red-rimmed eyes stand out in the light of the holographic image. She looks as if she hasn't changed her clothes in days. Her hair is limp and oily. Deep lines of grief carve the sides of her mouth and line her forehead. Her sorrow causes my heart to bleed anew. I have come to despise my mother, but something inside of me is still crushed by her sorrow.

"Return my son to me and I won't torture you, Fabian," she says, her voice deep and raspy, her words slurred. "Do it now and I'll give you a quick death." She lifts the fat tumbler to her lips, drinking a large gulp.

"You're in no position to—"

"I'm not finished, you blubbering man-child!" my mother screeches. She lurches to her feet. "Send me my son's murderer, Roselle, so I can eviscerate her myself. Then, and only then, will I not pluck out your eyes and feed them to my maginots!"

"You've gone insane! How dare you speak to me—"

"I dare, you pompous ass! You won't last a day against me now."

Fabian ignores her threats. "No one had to murder Gabriel, Othala. He did it himself. The first thing he's gotten right in his miserable life! Now we have a competent heir to Swords."

"You're blind and stupid, Fabian!" my mother replies. "Roselle will always be ten steps ahead of you. I'm actually doing you a favor, and you don't even know it. Send her to me along with my son's body."

"I don't think so. I need the right St. Sismode on the throne of Swords to stabilize the Fates and quell the open rebellion. With Roselle in charge, every secondborn Sword soldier will leap to do her bidding. They'd follow her off a cliff. She's one of them. No one will lift a finger if you go against her. Your army will turn on you in an instant."

"And she's your best hope?" Othala laughs derisively. "You're a fool. You'll never be able to control her. She'll run circles around you, and you won't even know it. Won't you, Roselle? Just like you did by aligning with the Rose Gardeners right under our noses. You had one job. All you had to do was die. If you had, Gabriel would be alive. This is all *your* fault."

Her words tear open my invisible wounds, but I don't rise to her drunken logic. Instead, I ask, "Who are your monsters, Mother?"

She smiles sadistically. "Oh, you'll find out," she rages. "You'll all find out! And stop calling me 'Mother.' I never wanted you! I demanded artificial insemination so that I wouldn't have to touch your father again. Did you know that? Did you know that every moment that you grew inside of me was torture? Every time I look at you, all I see is Kennet. I couldn't wait for you to Transition so I could get rid of your pathetic face. You look just like him. An evil little spawn. I had fun planning your death. The Fusion Snuff Pulse was supposed to be the perfect cover, but I was betrayed. Dune protected you. He joined The Virtue and let you live. He's a coward, your mentor. But now, killing you seems too kind, Roselle. No, I should keep you alive long enough for you to understand what it's like to be married to someone you despise. Maybe I'll have you give me an heir to raise before I cut your heart out. How does that sound?" She cackles with glee. "I have just the man in mind. I think he'd be up to the challenge, too."

My stomach roils. I fear she means Agent Crow. "I'm sorry that you were hurt, Othala," I reply, "but I think you know me well enough by now to see that I have no intention of ending up like you."

"How dare you pity me, Roselle! You think you're better than me? I'll make sure you know what a disgusting little insect you are."

I bury any outward sign that I'm affected by her drunken raving. Inside, though, I grieve for her and loathe her at the same time.

Othala looks back to The Virtue. "Send Roselle to me, or pay the price." Her holographic image winks out.

The Virtue wears a stunned expression. He expected my mother to cower on her knees, begging him to spare her life. The fact that she didn't confirms that she's in a much stronger position than anyone imagined.

The Virtue calls for his advisory council, including Dune, Walther, Clifton, and Grisholm, along with Grisholm's closest advisors, which includes Reykin. Most of The Virtue's inner circle now are either Gates of Dawn or Rose Gardeners, or they're simply the inept, privileged offspring of other members of the aristocracy. The Virtue is surrounded by his enemies, and he doesn't even know it. I almost pity him.

As the advisors assemble, Grisholm enters with Reykin. The Virtue-Fated firstborn shows no outward sign of grief over the passing of his sister. I wonder whether he will blame me, too, or has Reykin explained what happened? I'm about to ask him when I hear a deep voice say my name from the doorway.

My heart flutters as my eyes meet Hawthorne's. Dressed in an Exo military uniform, he's a striking figure. I bite the inside of my cheek.

Striding directly to me, Hawthorne offers a military salute. "Firstborn Sword," he greets me, using my new title, "as your acting first lieutenant, may I offer you my condolences for the loss of your brother?"

His formality reminds me not to show weakness. "Thank you," I murmur, feeling my cheeks heat.

He kneels on one leg, bowing his head. "I'm here to pledge my loyalty to you as your acting right hand." When he looks up, I nod in acknowledgment. Hawthorne rises, towering over me. "It's essential that we discuss nominations and appointments to your Heritage Council. Do you have a private space available for this discussion?"

Reykin pushes his way between Hawthorne and me. "No one trusts soldiers from the Fate of Swords," he says. "Especially those in the aristocracy. How can anyone be sure that your loyalties don't lie with Othala St. Sismode?"

Both Hawthorne and I are startled by Reykin's insinuation. "As acting first lieutenant," Hawthorne barks in a clearly military tone, "I'm here to swear my allegiance to Roselle St. Sismode, the Firstborn Sword." His agitation is palpable. "My loyalty is to her, first and foremost. It's my duty to enact the protocols between the Heritage Council and the heir to the Clarity of the Fate of Swords. You will *not* interfere with that duty, Star, or you *will* be subject to our laws."

Reykin isn't intimidated. He goes nose to nose with Hawthorne. "She doesn't go anywhere alone with Sword-Fates."

"She *is* a Sword-Fate," Hawthorne counters, "and she has a duty to uphold."

"I can speak for myself," I interrupt. "Thank you, Firstborn Winterstrom, for your concern. I'll discuss my future council with Acting First Lieutenant Trugrave. Alone."

I pull Reykin aside for a private word. "Reykin, you know I'm capable of handling myself with Hawthorne."

"Never forget that he has had divided loyalties in the past," he insists.

I want to dismiss what he's saying, but it's true. "I'll keep it in mind." To diffuse his anger, I place my hand on his heart. His rough fingers cover mine. It does something to me. My belly flutters. Surprised by my response to his touch, I pull my hand away and drop my eyes. "Thank you for your advice," I manage.

I request a private room to meet with Hawthorne. A firstborn Exo shows us to a lounging room filled with soft, fat chairs. Coverage of the Secondborn Trials training camps plays on every screen in the room. It makes me want to scream and throw things at the walls, but I keep my frustration locked down. Hawthorne already thinks I'm a Fate traitor. I don't want him to think I'm a raving lunatic as well.

"How are you?" Hawthorne asks, taking a seat. I sit in a chair next to his. He doesn't take my hand—doesn't touch me.

"I don't know." I swallow hard against the lump in my throat. "Numb, I guess. Scared. Confused. I shouldn't be surprised, but I am. I'd hoped that Gabriel would somehow come through his addiction. You warned me that he wouldn't. I should've listened to you."

"What can I do to help you with your changeover to firstborn?" he asks. "I have some experience with it. It takes a while to get used to it." His eyes soften. They have a silver tint to them in this light.

"I don't plan on getting used to it, Hawthorne, but you know that."

He looks around. It's possible that we're being monitored, and he knows it. "I'm in, you know," he whispers, "for everything."

My eyebrows rise in surprise. "Everything?"

"Whatever you want, Roselle. I'll fight for it—for you." He reaches out and covers my hand with his. He squeezes, and I grind my teeth so I don't sob.

"I need you to put together a list of candidates for Heritage Council positions and a list of who currently fills them," I tell him. "I don't care about rank and privilege. I want smart people, not entitled ones. I want inter-Fate advisors, not just Swords. To start with, I want you to focus on finding the most innovative Stars and Atoms. I'm looking for forensic investigators not affiliated with Census. And I need a list of all Census holdings, maps of bases, lists of personnel, budget reports. I want to know where Census allocates its assets." He frowns and begins to take notes on his moniker. I stop him with a hand on his sleeve. "We can't use monikers to communicate or to do research. I need you to devise another form of communication. Census is inside most of our systems."

"What other form of communication?" he asks, grinning. "Carrier pigeons?"

I sigh. "Write it down if you have to, but burn it when you're done. We no longer use monikers for anything. Do you understand?"

"Yeah, I got it," Hawthorne replies.

"Before Gabriel died, he warned me about my mother," I continue. "He said something . . . he said, 'Too many zeros.' Do you have any idea what that could mean?"

"Zeros?" Hawthorne holds his hand to his forehead. "I heard him say something like it before, but only in drug-induced ramblings about freedom and freewill. None of what he said before I left made any sense."

"What about Census?" I ask.

Hawthorne drops his hand. "I haven't been back to Swords. Your mother wants me dead. Reports from my friends tell me Census is everywhere in Swords now, like they own the place."

"I think they do, Hawthorne. I think they're Othala's allies." I lean forward and put my elbows on my knees, holding my chin in my hands. I stare at his eyes. They're cloudy. He must be as tired as I am.

"What do you plan to do about that?" Hawthorne asks. He's as close as he can be without touching me.

"I don't know yet." I scrub my face with my hands, trying to think. "Census is entrenched everywhere that secondborn Swords are. They're the roots of every Tree on every Base. They control our monikers—they have access to our communications. They have a stranglehold on every Fate, not just Swords. The advantage is theirs. We have to take out their leaders."

"We don't know who *they* are," Hawthorne says. "Census acts like every one of them is a leader."

"Census has leaders," I insist, "or you never would've gotten me away from Agent Crow when I was his prisoner. He answers to someone higher up, or he would never have let me go." There's a faraway look in Hawthorne's eyes, and I wonder if he's thinking of Agnes and what Agent Crow did to her for helping me. I reach my hand out and tangle Hawthorne's fingers in mine. "Remember when I promised you that I'd help you kill Agent Crow and avenge Agnes when the time was right?"

"Yes," he replies.

"The time is now, Hawthorne."

Chapter 18
Planning My Crash Landing

No funeral or memorial is planned for Balmora. The official cause of her death is ruled an accidental drowning. Her body is incinerated within hours of the pronouncement and her ashes disposed of. The coverup of my brother's drug overdose is a much more elaborate conspiracy. The Virtue pushes it forward with the same swift efficiency and whitewash as his daughter's death. Gabriel's corpse is loaded into an exquisite aircraft and an accident is staged so that it looks as if a tragic malfunction occurred near his estate in Lenity. The fiery crash, with Gabriel's body inside, is executed with the utmost care. By nightfall, it's reported on by every Diamond-Fated media outlet the world over. When the flames die down, there's very little left to send to Othala for burial.

The speed with which this all happens is significant. This way, there's no chance of Othala getting Gabriel's body back and making accusations against me or The Virtue that could be medically corroborated. The Virtue has no intention of letting me return to Swords for a memorial either. Instead, an official announcement states that, in light of the tragic circumstances surrounding my father's memorial in Swords, a small, private ceremony will be held at the Halo Palace, which means there won't be one.

It's almost midnight by the time I'm released from The Virtue's presence. I'm shown to my new quarters by a member of his staff. My new suite befits my stature as firstborn. Decadently appointed in shades of gold, it's excessive to the point of gaudiness. My footsteps echo against the high ceiling in the drawing room. Projections of the cosmos play upon its lofty heights, but I can change the image to whatever I want, from storm clouds to a sun-filled sky.

One arching glass wall affords a view of the sea. Dismissing my new secondborn staff, I walk to the window, staring at the moon shining on the water.

"How are you?" Reykin asks from behind me.

Startled, my pulse speeds up. I want it to be because I wasn't expecting him, but my heart thumps more from a combination of his deep voice and his extremely handsome appearance in tailored dinner attire. "I didn't know you were here."

He comes closer. "Quincy's here, too—sleeping in one of your unoccupied bedrooms with Rogue. I've been keeping an eye on her. She's taking the events of today very hard."

"I think she loved Balmora. As for how I'm doing, the answer is I don't know," I reply truthfully. My emotional self-awareness shut down hours ago. Now I'm simply numb. "Where's Dune?"

"Strategy meeting with his brothers." My eyes flare with alarm. I look around at the opulent furnishings, any number of which could be spying devices. "Don't worry," he reassures me, "I've secured the room. No one will overhear us."

"Where's Phoenix?" I ask.

"You want me to get your mechadome?"

"Of course," I reply. "It's part of my . . ." I was going to say "family," but I don't want to sound crazy. "Why are you here?" I ask instead. His eyebrows rise. I sigh and rub my forehead. "I didn't mean it like that. I'm just surprised they let you in here. Did you sneak in?"

"I didn't have to sneak. You're firstborn now. You can do whatever you want. Entertain whomever you'd like, whenever you'd like. But I am here on official Halo Palace business."

"Oh?"

"The Virtue and the other Clarities are planning to present you to the world as the heir to the Fate of Swords tomorrow night at the Secondborn Trials Opening Ceremonies."

"Why would they do that? It's too soon! My brother just died!"

"In everyone's eyes, Roselle, you're still secondborn, and that's a problem. The Virtue and the aligned heads of the Fates need to change your narrative, and quickly, if you're to overcome your mother's perceived authority as The Sword. They're out of time, so it's going to happen now."

"What are they expecting me to do?"

"They want a new opportunity to showcase your mastery in the realm of warfare. It's something your mother doesn't have, and you excel at it. Grisholm suggested to his father that you and I give a display of your skill at the ceremony tomorrow."

"I'm sorry. What?" I rub my forehead.

"They want us to mock duel." He says it softly, like I might explode if he's too loud.

I shake my head in disbelief. "They want us to fight each other?"

"Mock duel, like we always do. An exhibition with fusionblades, to show your skill."

"And you agreed to this?" I teeter between amazement and derision. "Fighting with a sword is not the same as 'mastery in the realm of warfare.'"

"I agreed to be your sparring partner because I'm not going to allow someone else near you with a sword," Reykin insists. "Especially not a Sword soldier."

"You know how insane this is, right? There should be a period of mourning for Gabriel."

He frowns. "Like I said, there's no time for that. Listen, I know you're grieving. I know you wanted things to be different with your brother."

"And I know you got exactly what you wanted," I reply with a total lack of emotion. I have no energy left.

"I did," he admits, "but I am sorry that it hurts you."

"I can't talk about this right now, Reykin. I just need a moment of peace. Is that too much to ask?"

"No," he replies with an air of contrition. "It's not too much to ask."

"Good night." I turn and walk to my bedroom. Closing the door, I lie on the bed and cover my face with a pillow so no one will hear my sobbing.

No matter what I say or do, I won't be able to avoid attending the Secondborn Trials.

The realization gives me no small amount of anxiety. I walk the open-air corridor of the rooftop cloister, listening to Clifton Salloway give our supreme leader a status report regarding the security measures he's directly overseeing. The picturesque cloister, built atop the floating Halo, shades us from the bright sunlight. The pace Bowie sets is brisk. He walks beneath the barrel-vaulted ceiling at such a clip that the other members of Fabian's Council of Destiny fall behind, holding their sides as we make another lap.

The Virtue's advisory council members are mostly Virtues. I assume that their duties usually don't require much exercise, because only Clifton and I aren't winded. I shouldn't judge them too harshly. A few of the women are over a hundred and fifty years old, not that one could tell by looking. They have excellent Atom technicians who keep them appearing middle-aged or, in some cases, younger.

Walking with my hands clasped behind my back, I gaze through the rosette framework between the columns that line the corridor. The soft scent of roses surrounds us. The formal rooftop gardens are also laid out in rosette patterns, mirroring the framework. In the center are interconnected bathing pools and ponds.

The Virtue stops abruptly when Clifton sums up his assessment of the threat level we face if they go forward with the Secondborn Trials. "So," Fabian Bowie replies impatiently, "what you're telling me is, although you cannot discern any major troopship shift or Sword soldier migration that would lead you to believe that the event is Othala's target or that of the Gates of Dawn, you still want to postpone the festivities to some indefinite date?"

"Yes," Clifton agrees, flashing his most charismatic smile. I fail to see how Fabian can resist it, but resist it he does.

"The threat level is minimal," he argues. "Othala is running scared. She's all talk. In any case, they haven't had enough time to prepare."

Clifton frowns. "You assume they haven't been planning for months."

"Why would they choose the Secondborn Trials?" Fabian asks. "It's a social event. Othala risks turning her people against her if she leads an attack. The same could be said for the Gates of Dawn. Killing innocent people doesn't win hearts and minds."

"May I remind you that our social club was attacked in that manner?" Clifton asks.

Fabian truly doesn't know how hated Virtues is by many of the Fates, by the Gates of Dawn, by secondborns—or maybe he just doesn't understand the magnitude of my mother's hatred. Regardless, he's being shortsighted. "What about the threat of a Census alliance with The Sword?" I ask.

"Bah!" He scowls, turning to me. "It's hearsay! Until you can show me a shred of proof, I consider it a huge fantasy that you've concocted in your mind."

Some of the council members catch up, panting hard and sweating through their silken clothing. The Virtue takes one look at them and says, "Dismissed." Clifton and I turn to leave. "Not you two. You will join me for breakfast." He slips through the archway and out into the sunlight. Crossing the lawn, we near a tranquil pond filled with glistening koi. We enter an opulent gazebo made of stone, where a round table is set with delicious fare. Secondborns stand at attention, awaiting us.

The Virtue takes a seat with his back to the water. Clifton holds a chair out for me. His eyes dance, as if he's thinking of a delicious secret. Once I'm seated, Clifton claims the chair beside mine. From his position across the table from me, The Virtue dives into the minutia. "The Opening Ceremony," he begins, "is the perfect opportunity to present you, Roselle, as the heir to The Sword. As far as it being your first public event as firstborn, it couldn't be more suited to your particular appeal."

Dread filters through me, even though Reykin already told me what was being planned. I set down the piece of buttered toast I was about to eat. "Won't it appear strange," I ask, "when my mother isn't by my side as I accept the honor?"

The Virtue chuckles. "You've already accepted the *honor*," he replies, as a secondborn attendant refills his coffee, "the moment your brother killed himself. It will look stranger if we don't announce your ascension. You can't return to Swords for a proper ceremony at the St. Sismode Palace until you replace your mother as the leader. This is a compromise. Not to worry, though. Soon you'll become The Sword, and everything in that Fate will be yours."

Perhaps the strangest part about all of this is the fact that he's openly discussing the demise of a member of my family, who I would've taken a fusion pulse to protect only a short time ago. I once labored under the notion that only secondborns were expendable, but it seems that all value for life perishes in a power struggle. I'm not delusional, though. There won't be any tearful reconciliation with Othala. One of us will have to die. I'd change that if I could, but I can't. Nothing good will come from my mother's rule if she's aligned with Census. I shudder, thinking about Agent Crow in an even more powerful position than the one he holds now.

"Are you cold?" Clifton asks.

"I'm fine, thank you," I reply with a fake smile.

"I'm glad to see you two getting along so well," The Virtue says with a smile of his own. "It makes me less worried about the future of Swords. Salloway will make a much better Fated Sword than Kennet ever did."

I choke on my water, slamming down the glass goblet, gagging and wheezing. Clifton reaches over and gently pats me on the back until I can take a breath.

Nervously, and with a rueful smile, he says, "I haven't told Roselle yet about the engagement. I was going to explain it to her in a few days—after she'd had time to recover from the grief of losing her brother."

The Virtue waves his fork in a gesture of dismissal. "She's a soldier. She understands alliances and strength—she's a St. Sismode, for Virtue's sake! You don't have to romanticize it. This needs to happen. Her family is on the verge of decimation. She needs someone on her side that she can trust. She already trusts you. I see it between you two. Don't make her go through this alone."

"Excuse me?" I gasp, wiping my teary eyes with my napkin, trying to regain my composure. "Am I to understand that you made an alliance on my behalf?"

Fabian nods. "I've accepted Firstborn Salloway's offer for you. He'll be your husband, the Fated Sword. You'll be wed as soon as we can settle things in Swords." He takes a bite of his meal and chews, gesturing at me with the knife in his hand. "You'll want to start trying for an heir right away. Your brother was an idiot. He refused to choose a Fated Sword and provide an heir. It would've kept the Rose Gardeners from becoming so powerful. Not one for strategy, your brother. Although they tell me that he might not have been able to reproduce near the end of his life. Whatever he was taking made him sterile."

"How do you know that?" I ask defensively.

"His autopsy was very revealing. We'll spare you the details. It wasn't pretty. I'm surprised he lasted as long as he did."

"How did his addiction start?" I ask. "Do you know?"

"That's a question for someone at the Sword Palace, I would think," The Virtue replies.

I plan to pursue the question if given an opportunity.

The topic turns to logistics. Clifton is to accompany me to the Silver Halo, where the Opening Ceremonies will be held. My introduction as the Firstborn Sword will take place as the competitors are brought to the field.

While Fabian drones on, Clifton's eyes are on me, trying to gauge my reaction to the announcement that he's my fiancé. When the meal finally ends, Clifton and I stand. The Virtue bids us a good day, with a promise to see us both this evening, and then he strides away.

I walk from the table with a piece of toast in my hand, feeling Clifton trailing me. The fat koi swim to the surface near when I tear off pieces and toss them into the water. Standing next to me, Clifton waits until I'm bereft of bread to take my hand gently in his. The contact is sensual, and my heart doubles its pace. My belly fills with butterflies. My cheeks color for some reason. *It's still just Clifton. Don't be an idiot.*

"Oh, my swords!" Clifton gasps with a soft chuckle. His green eyes sparkle. "Are you blushing, Roselle?"

"I'm not blushing," I mutter. "You're blushing." I try to take my hand back without hurting him, which I *so* could. I could beat him senseless for not telling me that he petitioned for me.

"I *am* blushing," he says softly. He puts my hand against his chest so I can feel his heart. It's racing, like mine. "You're going to have to tell me what you're thinking, because I'm back-footed right now," he says, putting it in fighting terms we both know. "You're aching right now, and this is the worst timing in the history of the world, but you're not alone. I need you to know that I'll always protect you. No matter what. I don't know how we'll work out together, Roselle, but I'd like you to know that I want us to."

"Is this . . . never mind." I try to lift my hand, but he tangles his fingers through mine.

"Please, ask me anything," he begs.

"Why did you petition for me? Is it power that you want? Because I'll give you power. You can be my right hand anyway. You wouldn't have to—" Clifton leans down and kisses me. I wasn't expecting his perfectly full lips on mine. It scares me—the intense ache that his exquisite kisses cause. I shouldn't feel anything. It's Salloway. Inter-Fate Playboy. In a league of his own. Arms dealer. Massive ego. Unrelenting cunning. Extremely dangerous. String of broken hearts. *That* Salloway. But . . . my pulse flares. My fingers clutch his shirt. My knees weaken. This feels like when I handled explosives for the first time—formidable, deadly, like something is about to be destroyed.

I step back, breaking our kiss. "Clifton—" But he pulls me back to him.

"I've wanted to do that since the day we met."

"You mean the day you asked me for private lessons?"

He groans and bites his bottom lip, adorably, before saying, "You cannot blame me for that. I'd just been introduced to the most confident and poised women I'd ever met. I thought I knew you. I'd been expecting the girl I'd watched for years. Nothing could have prepared me for the reality. You were no girl. You were a goddess. You had me at your mercy."

"I don't remember it like that."

"How do you remember it?"

"My mother had threatened me with severe consequences if I didn't perform well at the press conference. You were an interesting thread in a terrifying web."

The light in his eyes fades a little. "I'm sorry. You shouldn't have been in that situation. It took me too long to tear you away from our enemies. Nothing about your Transition went as planned."

"You didn't *fail* me," I reply, reaching up and smoothing the hair away from his eyes. His expression softens. "I don't want you to be disappointed, Clifton. I care about you deeply."

It's true. I do care about him. I don't want to see him hurt. But I know a union will never happen. If I become The Sword, it will only be for as long as it takes for the alliances that I've made to bring down the empire. After that, there will be no Swords. No Fates. No Fates Republic. He'll more than likely end up despising me for destroying what he has worked so hard to achieve.

"Why would I be disappointed?" he asks.

I can't answer him honestly, so I don't. Instead, I change the subject. "Are you as worried about tonight as I am?"

His expression grows grim. "Worry is a wasted emotion. We need to instead be vigilant. The Virtue is reckless for the sake of popularity, but I plan on making sure that, whatever happens tonight, we never lose the advantage. Do me a favor?"

"What?"

"When we're in power, and someone gives us good advice, let's remind each other to take it."

We walk together, discussing our plans for the night. My arm tightens on his, and I can't help worrying about what will happen the day that Clifton discovers my betrayal. I refuse to feel too bad about it, though. The Virtue and the Rose Gardeners have been planning my crash landing, right into their arms, for far too long. But I intend to keep flying.

Chapter 19
Zero Rise

Floating above the Secondborn Trials training camp, the Silver Halo gives the illusion of being hollow, like the one The Virtue resides in. It isn't. Inside, it's an enormous, bowl-shaped colosseum. Massive airships shuttle excited attendees to the venue. Glass gondolas the size of city blocks also transport crowds to the Silver Halo. I watch the spectacle from the safety and luxury of The Virtue's private balcony.

This mezzanine is reserved for Clarities and their guests. Nine distinct balconies circle the Silver Halo, each named for one of the Fates and comprising an open-air balcony, supported by Gothic pillars, for the exclusive use of a Clarity and his or her entourage. Three extravagantly large thrones stand prominently at the fore of The Virtue's balcony, one each for Fabian, Adora, and Grisholm.

Directly across is the Sword balcony. Blue banners with golden swords hang behind it. Normally it's reserved for Othala, Kennet, Gabriel, and their guests, but two of my family are dead, and one is glaringly absent. But that's not to say that the balcony is empty. Today it's occupied by Census agents dressed in formal evening attire. They're my mother's guests, which isn't going unnoticed by the masses as they find their places in the arena. People point to the Sword balcony and look to each other, wondering about the unique spectacle of Census agents in such a place of honor at the Secondborn Trials. The agents toast each other and sip from tall, fluted glasses as last-minute preparations are made on the field below.

Streams of firstborns fill the arena until nearly every seat is taken. I remain at the back of the balcony, near the rustling silken white banners adorned with enormous golden halos. I'm hoping to avoid Adora. She hasn't noticed me, but then again, she might not notice much of anyone or anything. Her expression is dopey. She's not entirely present, as if she has been given something to subdue her.

Clifton doesn't let me far from his side. I'm not sure if he's guarding me or if he just likes being near me. He wastes no time introducing me to The Virtue's guests as his fiancée. He knows everyone. Everyone wants to be his friend. Every woman who gets near him wants to rub against him. Delicate fingertips touch his sleeve. Smiles grow broader. More teeth. Louder giggles when he smiles. I'm not sure he even notices.

A Diamond-Fated production assistant interrupts a rather pointless story that the saintly bank chairman is telling us about his excursion in the secondborn training camps. "Excuse us, Firstborn Salloway, Firstborn St. Sismode," the assistant says, "it's almost time for Roselle's presentation." He scrutinizes me. "We should get you closer to the front of the balcony. Is Firstborn Winterstrom here as well?" The man scans his moniker, going over a holographic checklist.

"I am," Reykin says from over my shoulder. Attired in an all-black sparring outfit, he's lethal-looking, his dark hair tied back in a knot, his fusionblade—the one with his family crest on it, the one that burned me on the battlefield—in its sheath at his side. My finger grazes the small star scar on my palm.

"Do you have a St. Sismode sword?" the attendant asks me. He eyes my white sparring outfit, settling on the hilt of the fusionblade sheathed on my thigh.

"I prefer a Salloway blade," I reply.

The woman next to me murmurs, "Wouldn't we all."

Reykin's jaw ticks tensely.

The production assistant gestures to the front of the balcony, motioning us forward. "If you two would just come this way. We're going to start soon."

"Go easy on the poor Star," Clifton says, leaning down and giving me a chaste kiss on the cheek. Those around us laugh, except for Reykin. Clifton's lips linger a bit longer than is exactly polite. "Show him what a Sword can do," he whispers. "I'll wait for you down by the field."

I nod. "Please excuse me," I say to those gathered around us. "It was lovely to meet all of you."

As we walk toward the railing, the Diamond-Fated attendant gives me and Reykin last-minute instructions. "The sparring diamond will elevate from the field. It will latch on to the side of the balcony, and you will both enter the diamond. Begin your demonstration as the hovering platform makes a circuit around the arena. It will land in the center of the field at the conclusion of the demonstration. Do you have any questions?"

"No," we both say.

Dune joins us. He hugs me. "I'm proud of you," he says. "I know this is difficult, but you're strong. You'll get through it."

Some of the devastation I feel is assuaged by his words. "I know this is the beginning of a new world," I say, my voice hitching, "but it feels like the end."

Dune's arms tighten around me. "That's grief you're feeling," he says, "but there's joy ahead for you. You've taught me what happiness is, Roselle. Not the distorted version of it that the world would have us believe—but true joy. Having you as a daughter is the greatest gift my life has brought me. You taught me what love is."

I choke back tears. *I love you, too . . . Father.*

"We have a purpose now," he says. "No matter what happens, we endure. And we never stop striving for what we believe in."

Suddenly trumpets blare. It's time.

Dune squeezes me a final time, then lets me go.

Spotlights illuminate the field, and the ceremony begins. Competitors parade through the arena to a heroes' welcome. The applause is deafening. Clad in all-black fighting gear, the secondborn men and women slowly make their way around the field. Some smile and wave, but most appear as though reality is setting in. Tears stream. Trembling hands wring in terror. A few pause along the route to vomit.

The Diamond-Fated firstborn popstar Sarday, attired in a glittering evening gown, sings a heartfelt rendition of "Stay Alive for Me," which her grandmother, also named Sarday, made famous decades ago. Firstborns sing along to the melodramatic song with tearful voices. A colossal holographic projection emerges in the air above the Silver Halo like a domed roof of light, footage of past seasons' Trials, highlights of the more gruesome deaths.

A silver platform shaped like a diamond rises from the field, hovering up to The Virtue's balcony. Reykin and I step onto it. Our images splash across the holographic dome. The crowd roars, but I don't react. I already despise my part in this.

I vow to make this the last Secondborn Trials ever.

We face The Virtue, Grisholm, and Adora, seated on their garish golden thrones. Reykin and I sink to one knee. When we rise, The Virtue gives us a limp wave. We face each other on the hovering diamond, and the platform begins its slow lap around the arena, hemorrhaging rose petals in its wake. I draw my sword and ignite it, choosing the lowest setting. Reykin does the same. From the first thrust, it's clear that my Star-Fated adversary intends to give these firstborns an exciting show.

In long, elegant maneuvers that play to the crowd, Reykin wields his energy blade, and I am coerced to retreat using a series of high-powered back handsprings. As I come out of my tumble, he catches me near the edge of the platform. I ward off his attack and counter with one of my own. "When were you going to tell me," Reykin growls as our swords lock and our foreheads nearly meet, "that you agreed to marry Salloway?"

I let him lean into me, and then I pivot to the side, using his momentum against him. He stumbles past me. "What did you think would happen when my brother died?" I shout back. Our swords whine and blur, coming together in epic clashes of molten energy. We stalk each other in a circle, looking for an opening. "The Virtue wants powerful allies."

We turn in spirals. Our swords fly together in sizzling swipes. Reykin breaks from me, steels himself, and then swings his sword at me in a two-handed arc. I crouch, barely keeping my head. Bits of my hair shrivel, burned by his fusionblade. I tumble back.

"It'll never happen!" Reykin pants with a murderous glare.

We fight on, ever conscious of the platform's edge. I find an opening and take it, making Reykin pay for his crooked left elbow with a thrust that burns his upper arm. The fabric of his uniform singes. The crowd erupts in adulation.

"Why does it matter?" I stalk him as he resets. "You don't care, remember?"

Reykin attacks, driving me back. His sword arm is a golden blur, and I'm forced to take a burn to my thigh so that he won't reach my heart. I wince, feeling the sting and smelling the smoke from my skin. I break away from him and circumvent his position. Lurching forward, I run at him, and Reykin simultaneously lunges toward me, his knee bent. Our swords meet. I step on his bent knee, intending to wrap my other leg around his neck, but he avoids the takedown by swiveling and pushing me up and over his shoulder. I tumble to the mat.

"Ahhh," the crowd moans.

We're now coming abreast of the Sword balcony. As we do, I glance at the Sword thrones, where three Census agents, two men and one woman, are seated. I recognize Agent Crow, slouched, his feet up on the railing. His long black leather coat seems a bit warm for the occasion. An amused grin plays upon his lips. The kill tallies notched near his eyes highlight the blue of his irises.

In his hand, a silver orb shines.

I've seen its like only one other time in my life: on my Transition Day.

And then he presses the button, igniting the Fusion Snuff Pulse.

Instantly, everything powered by fusion energy dies. All the lights go dark. Our swords blink out. Fear grips me. I tense, expecting the entire arena to plummet. It doesn't. The colosseum isn't fusion powered. Our platform doesn't crash either. Both must use the same magnetic technology employed in gravitizers. Our platform continues its slow hovering path around the arena. Since I have a Salloway Dual-Blade X16, I flip the switch and reignite my sword with hydrogen power. It glows silver in the sudden darkness.

Anxious voices ripple through the crowd, and then a different glow begins to emanate. Silver light shines from the eyes of firstborns scattered throughout the arena, at first just a few, then more and more. Soon they're everywhere. Goose bumps rise on my skin. The silver-eyed silhouettes seem to be in a trance, as if watching something the rest of us can't see.

Suddenly they twitch, in unison, as if collectively possessed, and simultaneously hiss like one seething creature, "Zero rise!"

Emergency lighting kicks in across the arena, and in the next instant, horrific screams break out everywhere. It's hard to believe my own eyes. Moments before, the entire crowd was rapt, rooting for me or Reykin, but they've changed. They sound like demons screaming. It's as if they have their own language. The silver-eyed firstborns scream streams of words that sound like negotiations, but for what I have no idea.

My eyes are drawn to one man in the crowd with a silver stare. His moniker's light turns dark and assumes the shape of a shadowy zero. I see another moniker change, and then more. Like dark matter bullying light, black zeros ignite throughout the crowd.

Then the deep, demon-like voices cease, all at once, as one.

Then they attack.

The firstborns with black zero monikers launch themselves at the others like ferocious beasts, tearing into flesh with their teeth, ripping open throats. Clawlike hands eviscerate anyone in their paths. It all happens in the blink of an eye. There are as many of them as there are average citizens. A chaotic stampede begins, but the attackers are horrifyingly efficient, disemboweling people with their bare hands, aided by steel claws that project from their fingertips.

The monsters move in a collective wave. They pile on top of each other, a tide of bodies climbing up each other, cresting toward The Virtue's balcony. Exos fire hydrogen-powered weapons at them, blowing pieces off some, exploding the heads of others. But the convergence continues until it reaches the balcony's edge. Sheer numbers overwhelm the Exos, and Fabian, Adora, and Grisholm are immediately surrounded.

Then the pack turns on Dune.

He fights the first few off with a hydrogen blade, but it's futile. The monsters are not deterred by the deaths of the others. Dune can't fight them all. Their numbers swiftly overwhelm him, and he succumbs, falling beneath a pile of jaws and claws. They devour him like maginots would.

And then everything begins to move in slow motion.

The Exos on The Virtue's balcony are killed with agonizing efficiency. Each murder plays out in gruesome detail. Adora doesn't even flinch when a silver-eyed monster rips into her jugular with razor-sharp claws. Grisholm tries to defend himself with his fusionblade, but the mob takes him down, biting off pieces of his face as he screams in vain. The Virtue is the last one standing. At first, the monsters seem careful not to kill him. They slowly tear his limbs, one at a time, prolonging his suffering. Then they rip his head from his torso, and I snap back into the moment.

Reykin is frantically screaming my name.

On every balcony in the arena, the monsters are slaughtering Clarities, their families, and their guests. All except for the Sword balcony, where Census agents are celebrating, toasting, smoking fat rose-colored cigars, and slapping each other's backs.

"They're Gabriel's monsters!" I scream to Reykin, trying to be heard above the cacophony of demonic voices. "The Zeros!"

Another crest of Zero monsters nears our floating platform, jumping over each other in a grotesque wave of bodies. Reykin rushes the control panel of the hovering platform. We begin to rise, but we're not fast enough. The Zeros climb nearer. We only have my hydroblade between us.

"You have to fight!" Reykin yells.

I grip my sword, though my hand trembles.

At my feet, fingers begin to creep over the edge of the platform. I slice them off, and the steel claws, implants extending from beneath the monster's fingertips, remain embedded in the platform. A woman's face looks over the edge, her silver eyes shining. I shear off the top of her head, exposing her brain, and see circuitry sparking in the rippling pink flesh of brain matter before the woman drops into the undulating sea of bodies beneath us. I kill everything that attempts to gain purchase on our small floating oasis, and Reykin furiously works the platform's control panel, but the Zeros are gaining.

We need to shed weight. Reykin must be thinking the same thing, because he runs to the back of the platform and begins stomping on the machine that's spewing rose petals. The bolts bend with each kick until the metal casing dislodges. It falls from the platform, striking crazed monsters on the way down. Still the creatures rise.

Desperation shows in Reykin's eyes. He looks at me, then over the edge. He takes a step closer to it, his shoulders rounded in defeat. He looks back to me, and the sadness in his eyes is the same sadness I saw when he intended to kill himself on the battlefield when we first met.

"Don't you dare jump, Reykin!" I yell. "I'll kill you myself if you try. Do you hear me? You sticketh closer than a brother!"

"You'll be okay, Roselle," he says. "Take this hovering piece of crap to the training field. Find transportation. Get to Stars—to Daltrey. He'll know what to do."

"No!" I scream. "They'll tear you apart!"

"I love you," Reykin says, inching nearer to the edge.

"Wait!" I fling my unlit sword to him. Reflexively, he catches it. "Agent Crow won't let them kill me, Reykin. He wants me alive." I don't know if that's true, but I'm willing to gamble. I know Agent Crow. If there's one thing I can count on, it's his need to lord his victory over me. It wouldn't be enough to let me die here. He needs to witness my suffering.

A monster lurches up onto the platform. Then several others. I punch and kick the first one that comes at me, but it's as if he doesn't feel pain. Another throws his arms around me, snorting as he presses his nose to my throat, sniffing my neck like a maginot. His claws retract.

"Reykin!" I scream, struggling as I'm hauled to the edge.

"Roselle!" Reykin shouts, swinging the sword as more horrifying creatures stumble onto the platform.

"Find me!" I shout, just as the monster leaps from the platform with me in his arms.

We plummet, but then I'm jolted, caught by upraised hands and cushioned like a fragile egg. I'm moved along atop the bodies, clutched and passed from one to the next, surfing over a sea of Zeros. Above me, the hovering platform accelerates above the fray of bodies until they can no longer reach it.

I'm carried by the wave to the Sword balcony and thrown at the feet of the celebrating Census agents. Agent Crow breaks away from the revelry and approaches me.

"Ah, Roselle." He beams. "Right on time. The party is getting rather dull, and I'm ready to leave now."

"You're a monster, Crow."

He tsks me. "Is that any way to treat your host?" He lifts his hand and places a small black disc to his temple. It adheres to his head, and a glowing blue dot lights up in its center. The horde of monsters surrounding me take a step back in unison. A familiar face emerges from the back of the balcony.

It's Hawthorne, but it isn't. His eyes glow with silver light.

My breath catches. "Hawthorne!" I sob.

Agent Crow chuckles. "It's no use talking to him when he's in Black-O mode. He'll never understand you. They don't speak our language, or so the technicians tell me. Collectively, they stopped using it a long time ago. It's barely above gibberish to them. He's a new conversion, but he has all their technology embedded in his brain now. And, of course, I can use that technology to make him do whatever I want."

Hawthorne stalks toward me. His eyes don't show an inkling of recognition. I thrust out my hands to stop him, but he winds back and punches me in the stomach.

"Hawthorne," I gasp in utter despair.

And now I know I was right. Agent Crow won't kill me, even if I beg him to.

He reaches out and lifts my chin so that I meet his eyes. "Welcome to the future, Roselle."

Sneak Peek: Rebel Born

THE POISON OF OUR AGE

My wrists are bound with steel cuffs.

Hawthorne viciously prods me forward. I stumble behind Agent Crow, through the blue banners and out of the Sword balcony. I glance over my shoulder, but it's not the ache of betrayal that wrenches my heart. It's fear that whatever has happened to Hawthorne is irreversible. His eyes glow with a distinctive silver light. I might have caught a glimpse of it the last time we were together, but I can't be sure. I can hardly process what's happening now.

Shrill screams of terror echo throughout the Silver Halo's corridors. I am surrounded by no less than a dozen Zeros. None of the others approach us. Instead, the monsters busily butcher everything with a pulse. Unafflicted firstborns and the secondborn competitors attempt to escape from the floating colosseum, but hordes of killers intercept them.

My pulse races. *I can't help anyone!*

Another shove compels me forward. We pass by a gondola station. Blood and carnage litter the platforms. Some firstborns jump to their deaths from the floating colosseum rather than be caught by the Zeros. The hairs on my scalp stand on end.

"Why are you killing firstborns?" I growl at Agent Crow.

"Why not?" he replies in a blasé tone, reaching to brush wisps of my hair from my face as we walk. I recoil from his touch. "They won't do well in our new society, Roselle. We're doing them a favor." His mouth curves up at the thought, exposing the steel teeth that stand in stark contrast to his supple lips. The black disc adhered to his temple blinks with eerie blue light. It must be how he manipulates the silver-eyed cyborgs. Their obedience to him seems absolute. He doesn't have to say a word. He somehow just *thinks*, and they respond.

I shudder. *He's depraved.* The inky tattoos around his eyes and on his throat are deceptive. Although there are hundreds of the so-called kill tallies visibly etched into his skin, they only represent a fraction of the deaths he's caused. He would have to be covered from head to toe to represent all the people whose slaughter he has brought about tonight.

Agent Crow guides us to a staging area where a nondescript medical supply airship awaits with its ramp down. No cargo is on board. The Census agent enters the front of the ship, and I'm shoved up the open ramp by the demonic-sounding killers behind me. Inside the tail, I find that the airship doesn't have seats. I'm flung to the metal floor by the monster that was Hawthorne. Sitting up, I push myself to the wall, lean back against it, draw my knees up to my chest, and rest my forearms on them.

I'm not sure how smart these things are when they're in Black-O mode. The silver-eyed woman who latched the cuffs on me made the mistake of securing my arms in front of me. If I can reach a sword, it will be no problem to cut them off. But there aren't any swords. No weapons of any kind here in the cargo hold. It's just me and the Zeros.

The airship door closes, sealing us in. My throat tightens. Dim lights come on, but it's still dark. The Zeros' eyes glow like small moons in the night sky. Gore mottles their mouths, their clothes, and their fingers. The steel claws seem to have retracted into their fingertips, but I know they're there.

The airship rumbles and lurches upward. The Zeros don't move. They don't talk. They gaze straight ahead. They seem barely alive. Hawthorne sits across from me and several bodies away. He isn't smeared in carnage like the others. I don't think he was in the fight at the Silver Halo, which means Agent Crow wants to use Hawthorne some other way. More than likely against me.

My wrists tremble on my knees—or maybe it's my knees trembling—or maybe it's both. I thread my fingers together, but it doesn't stop. Panic seizes me. It's hard to breathe. I feel dizzy. Sweat soaks the back of my white sparring outfit. Wisps of damp hair cling to my cheek.

I have to wait for several minutes in the grip of the attack. When my panic finally subsides and my breath isn't coming out in hacking pants, I try to get up, and all the creatures look at me at once. It makes me want to vomit. I press myself against the wall and rise. Carefully, I walk between the Zeros until I'm across from the ghoulish Hawthorne.

I kneel in front of him. He stares, but it's as if he isn't really seeing me. "Hawthorne." I try a normal tone, but it comes out in a breathless whisper. "Remember when we first met? It was in Swords, when the airships fell from of the sky. Remember?" My voice quivers. Tears spill down my cheeks. "You tried to help me, and I hit you in the nose?"

He doesn't even blink.

I sit down and cross my legs. "You rescued me when I was Crow's prisoner in Census. You were so brave. Nobody else lifted a finger. It was you. Just you." I touch his hand, wanting so badly for him to hold me.

Suddenly his eyes focus. His hand pounces, wraps around my throat, and squeezes. My face flushes. My windpipe feels crushed. I hold up my hands to him, palms out, in surrender. He lets go.

I cough and sputter, gulping breaths. "Okay, so no touching," I gasp when I finally get my voice back. I wipe my tears from my cheeks with my sleeve. I touch my ravaged neck. "I know you're in there some-where, Hawthorne. We're a half-written poem, you and me. Wherever you are—whatever basement in your mind they've got you trapped in—I'll find you. I won't leave you down there alone."

I talk as if we're alone, reminding Hawthorne of everything we've shared together. Every stolen moment when we were secondborns. Every kiss. Every touch. My throat aches, but still I talk.

Hawthorne stares straight ahead. No reaction. No indication that he hears me or understands me. Hours pass with no sign of recognition from him. The pain of it is too much. It's too real. It threatens to bury me. I hold my head in my hands and give in, sobbing quietly.

The cargo ship begins to descend. The touchdown is smooth. I try to pull myself together, wiping my face with the back of my sleeve. The tail opens. Humid air rushes in. The sky is still dark, but tall lights loom above us, like those that line the secondborn military Bases in Swords, throwing stark white light on everything.

Hawthorne stands in unison with the other mind-controlled monsters. He grabs my arm and roughly hauls me out of the hold. Agent Crow waits on the hoverpad. The black beacon on the side of his forehead blinks blue. Around us, palm trees sway in a salty breeze. Balmy air blows loose strands of my hair.

"Pleasant trip?" Agent Crow asks. He smiles, baring his wretched steel teeth.

Normally I try to have something scathingly ironic to say back to him, just so that he remembers he hasn't beaten me. This time I don't. This time he has destroyed me, reached inside me and torn my heart out, and I know this is only the beginning.

"Where are we?" My voice is gravelly.

"A little place we call The Apiary," Agent Crow replies. "It's a small island near the Fate of Seas, one of the first military Bases to have Trees. It's been decommissioned, as far as most people are concerned. Not a lot of people outside of Census know of its existence."

I can just make out the ocean in the distance. All around lie the relicts of a decrepit military Base. Ancient airships that I've only seen in holographic history files rust out in the open. Everything is at least a few hundred years old. The only lights shine from the Base's Trees and infrastructure. Nothing but water lies beyond the Base from what I can tell. Behind us, rough tree-lined, rocky crags dapple the horizon. No other signs of civilization.

Viable airships hang from the Tree's branches, but they're not current models. I wouldn't know if I could fly one unless I got inside the cockpit. Behind me, the cyborgs form two lines. Each of them is spaced the same distance apart. Efficient. Mindless. Controlled and manipulated by a psychopathic Census agent.

Agent Crow strides ahead of me into the Tree's trunk. I'm prodded to follow. A familiar dimness greets me inside the Tree, but the smell isn't the same as the military Trees I inhabited as a soldier. This structure has been resurrected to fit the needs of madmen. We enter a warehouse for hundreds of thousands of adult-size vials—cylindrical tanks filled with fluid. Blue neon light glows from the tops and bottoms of the transparent cylinders. Inside each is a person, curled in a fetal position, floating. Some resemble modern *Homo sapiens*. Others don't. Some are amalgamations of different species. Others are unifications of human and machine. Above us are levels of vials as far as I can see, arranged in concentric rings like the cross section of a real tree.

Energy thrums and snaps in the air. There's an overcharged, singeing scent. If I licked my fingers, I could probably taste it on my skin. As it is, I feel it in my chest. My hair rises, from the smell and from fear.

Agent Crow teeters on the edge of mania. His insolent smile cuts through my haze of disbelief. "Would you like a history lesson of the Fates Republic, Roselle?" he asks. "Not the one you've been taught in Swords about the nine Fates forming for the common good to create perfect symmetry between the classes. That's mostly propaganda. I'm talking about a *real* history lesson."

"Enlighten me," I reply.

He clasps his hands behind his back, and we stroll together through a ring of the glowing tanks. "As you know, our species has made such medical strides in the past centuries that we live significantly longer now than our ancestors did—sometimes a hundred years longer or more. Advances in medicine and technology keep driving those ages higher. Once, our population exploded. We were on the brink of exhausting all our natural resources, bringing catastrophic destruction to the planet. We were wasting away. Something had to be done. At the same time, a powerful ruler by the name of Greyon Wenn the Virtuous came into power. Have you heard of him?"

"Of course," I reply. We continue between the glowing containers like lurking rats. "Greyon was a ruthless warlord and a brilliant strategist. Brutal in his tactics, he slaughtered his rivals when they surrendered, and he set about systematically toppling every other government until he became the first supreme ruler to dominate the world. He formed a single unifying government and presided over it with ruthless aggression."

A sudden spasm of motion explodes in the cylinder next to me. I lurch away. Hands press against the transparent surface. An open mouth with sharp fangs gropes the glass. The eyes of the creature are completely black. Gills cover its neck. Webbed fingers paw at us through the fluid. I'm not sure if it was once a person or not. I shudder. Hawthorne shoves me away from the tank, propelling me in Agent Crow's direction.

Agent Crow chuckles and keeps walking. "You surprise me, Roselle. You know our true origins. Your mentor, Dune, taught you well," Agent Crow says. "You're not as ignorant as most people I encounter."

"Dune always said, 'Know your past so you can avoid it in the future.'"

Agent Crow chuckles. "What else did he teach you about Greyon Wenn the Virtuous?"

"I know Grisholm Wenn-Bowie was said to be a direct descendant of Greyon," I reply numbly.

"Yes, you could trace his family line all the way back to the supreme ruler . . . but the same could be said about you, Roselle. The St. Sismode line directly descends from Greyon. Some say that the Wenns and the Bowies have the name, but it's your family that has the blood."

"They're all dead now," I say tonelessly. "You and your minions decimated them."

"All except for you and your mother. But the Wenn and Bowie lineages lost their nobility and intelligence years ago. We simply rectified the genealogical error. We relegated them to where they belong—a footnote in history. But getting back to Greyon . . . The world was staggeringly overpopulated, and growing more so in peacetime. Greyon Wenn decreed restrictions be enacted on procreation. His government began issuing birth cards, a rudimentary way to give permission to a couple to have a child. Firstborns weren't the only ones allowed to have birth cards. It was based purely on genetics. Once undesirable traits were expunged, it became an issue of privilege. Cards were dispensed at higher and higher prices. Families died off. Inherited wealth became a way to ensure the survival of the family name. Finances were pooled and given to firstborn heirs to keep family lines alive. Only the elite could afford to have children.

The government began issuing cards for secondborn children, but with the explicit provision that the child be given to the government when the secondborn reached adulthood. And voilà! The Fates Republic was formed. Of course, there will always be rule breakers, and enforcement of laws is essential—so Census was born."

I consider trying to choke him to death, like I did when we first met. I could probably do it if I could get my cuffs over his head. Hawthorne lingers so near to me, though. It wouldn't take much for him to break my arms. I contemplate other killing scenarios as we pass more tanks. The beings inside these appear more human, but these people have machine parts grafted to them. The fine-boned lines of one woman's face are covered in a shiny coating of metal. Her left eye has been replaced by a protruding lens. She doesn't move as we pass.

Agent Crow drones on. "Over time, the population scales tipped, and we slid back the other way. Our low birth rate threatened us with extinction. Depressing the birth rate was never meant to be a permanent solution to overpopulation, and even though we were living longer, the population was declining. So again, something had to be done."

He has led us to a Census bunker. He scans his moniker under a blue light near the security doors, and they roll open. We walk a short corridor to the lifts and enter an elevator car. The last time I was in a Census elevator, it filled with lake water, and I almost died. I feel like I'm drowning now, too. The elevator doors close, and we descend.

And still, Agent Crow continues his history lesson. "Scientists were put to the task of finding a solution to our complex problem. Cloistered away from society, they lived like kings and queens on this island oasis, creating generations of offspring we affectionately refer to as zeroborns. A harvesting plant was built right here on this military Base."

I scoff. "Why not just repeal the laws and let everyone repopulate the world naturally?"

Agent Crow scrunches his face like I've said something distasteful. "Bah! I never took you for a simpleton!" He looks down his nose at me and sneers. "You'd let every dirt farmer have as many brats as he wanted, wouldn't you? You'd let the lawbreakers go unpunished?"

"My way would make Census obsolete."

"Your way will never happen."

The elevator doors open. Before me sprawls a state-of-the-art laboratory. It's eerily dim, lit by a low blue haze that seems to come from the floor. Incubation capsules resembling giant wombs hang from tubing in neatly lined rows and columns. I stand frozen, mouth agape. Agent Crow exits the car, turns, and gazes at me, his hands still clasped behind his back.

"Beautiful, isn't it?" he asks. Technicians in gloves and black lab coats tend to the wombs. "The next generation of zeroborns. We use zygotes taken from captured thirdborns before we execute them. We used to genetically engineer our batches through cloning, but we're getting much better results now—from diversity, of all things. Diversity has been the key to hiding our progeny. Clones don't blend in well, but clones *are* useful in running our secret facilities."

Hawthorne shoves me in the back, and I stumble from the elevator. Agent Crow turns and continues walking, passing rows of swollen, veiny, synthetic-flesh bladders filled with fluid and floating fetuses.

"Once the first generation of zeroborns was created," Agent Crow says, "the operation became self-perpetuating. Zeroborns manufacturing zeroborns to work in the embryo centers, as caretakers, as population insertion specialists—chemically mapping the brains of our progeny with false memories so they can be inserted, undetected, into the population in any Fate we choose." The technicians resemble one another, some right down to their freckles. They have zero-shaped monikers.

"How did you keep the zeroborns a secret for so long?" I ask.

"The zeroborns who are inserted into the population receive new monikers representing whatever Fate they're assigned to. Take, for example, zeroborns earmarked to become Sword soldiers. We create them here, in our underground facilities. Other zeroborns care for them. They leave this facility when they're infants. The zeroborn soldiers are raised at other secret military facilities, where they're trained and given false memories of a life and family in Swords that never existed."

I can't believe what I'm hearing. "How do you give someone false memories?"

"Reality and perception are easy to manipulate. Your eyes, as it happens, aren't the best way to perceive the world. They're horrendously inadequate filters. We don't perceive most of what there is to see. Perception is a guessing game for the brain. Once you understand that, then you know that everything you perceive with your senses can be altered and manipulated, especially your visual perception. Take our cornea implants—the silver shine results from an alteration to the visual acuity. The Black-Os aren't seeing what you and I see. They're being fed a virtual reality on top of the world at large. Their cornea implants, coupled with alterations to the chemicals and electrical impulses in the cerebral cortex, override their higher cognitive reasoning, replacing it with artificial intelligence that we control. We can implant any memory we see fit."

I glance at the black disc on his temple. "How do you control them?"

He pauses next to a fleshy womb. In the translucent sack, a fetus floats, blissfully unaware of its very unnatural environment. "The Virtual Perception Manipulation Device, or VPMD, began as a toy," Agent Crow explains. "It was a form of amusement—tricking our brains with enhanced optics. Recreational visual deception. Eventually, Census created our own virtual worlds by implanting devices into the brains of zeroborns. The implants, once embedded, create their own unique neural pathways. Biochemically, we manipulate visual and aural perception, and with implants in the cornea, show them images they perceive as 'real.' We have complex programs and protocols. When we send Black-Os out to perform a mission, there are 'laws' that they have to follow, but the program also incorporates artificial intelligence. How the collective reaches the goal is almost entirely up to them. They just have to adhere to certain rules."

"Rules like 'Don't kill Roselle. Bring her to the Sword balcony while you slaughter everyone else'?"

Agent Crow's eyes dance with amusement. "We gave them your scent. Did you know that? They smelled you, like maginots would."

"So they have olfactory enhancements as well?"

"And so much more."

"You use that device on your temple to communicate with the Black-Os," I say. It's not a question.

"That information isn't part of the tour, Roselle," he admonishes. "We've already created our own population—our own elite forces. The time for a great change in power has begun. No longer will we be subject to the idiocy of the Clarities of the Fates Republic. Census will make the laws now. Your mother, of course, is the exception."

"It always comes down to power, doesn't it?"

"Everything is about power, Roselle. The war between the Fates Republic and the Gates of Dawn has accelerated the transfer of power. Census has been hiding our declining population with zeroborn replacements masquerading as Swords, but we've been having trouble keeping up with your mother's production demands. If things continue at the current rate, secondborn Swords will go extinct in a generation. The Gates of Dawn keeps throwing their martyrs at us, and we can't grow new organic soldiers from infancy fast enough. We had to find a way to convert existing assets."

"Assets?" I spit. "You're talking about *people*!"

"Oh, you don't know the half of it, Roselle."

"If the ban on procreation were lifted," I snap, "Census would lose its power. So instead, you kidnap people like Hawthorne and insert VPMDs to make them obey you?"

"It's called *conversion*, Roselle. We implant devices that allow us to control the host. Let the Gates of Dawn throw as many bodies at us as they want. We'll just keep killing them and producing enhanced reinforcements until there's no one else left."

"My mother knows?" I can barely contain my rage.

"We needed each other, Census and The Sword."

"How long will that last?" I ask him. He smirks but doesn't answer. "How long has Hawthorne been your convert?"

"Not long. A few weeks. We grabbed him at his home after that little stunt you two pulled at the Sword social club. I must admit that I was impressed with how you handled our non-converted zeroborns.

It showed just how weak they are compared with our enhanced AI versions."

"Non-converted?" I ask.

"None of the assassins you fought at the Sword social club had cerebral enhancements. It was too risky. If the implants and other enhancements had been found before we were ready to unveil them, it could have ruined everything."

"Other enhancements?" I think of the steel claws that sprang from the Black-Os fingertips.

"Lethal enhancements, Roselle. We're on the cutting edge of tapping into other perceptions, what some would call a sixth sense. The new neural pathways that the VPMD creates have presented us with some tantalizing opportunities. We've commissioned Star-Fated engineers to help us with our research—only the brightest." I haven't seen these Star-Fated technicians around.

"You've commissioned them or you've kidnapped them?" I ask.

"'Kidnapped' is such an ugly word, Roselle. Most of them are secondborns. We appropriated them."

We leave the room and enter a stark white corridor. The light hurts my eyes. Windows afford a view of a nursery. Swaddled in temperature-controlled cocoons, infants rock gently in nestled bins. Above them, holographic images of faces hover, talking and smiling, giving the impression that a real person is attending to the infant. These are interspersed with other images, flashes of light that I can't make out.

"They haven't gotten their cornea or other implants yet," Agent Crow says. "The holographic images simulate mothers and fathers—a sibling—obedience to Census."

Thousands and thousands of cocoon cradles fill the nursery. It reminds me of a morgue. "Cranston Atom, the mortician at the Halo Palace," I surmise, "somehow figured out that something wasn't right about the assassins at the club."

"He was clever. At the morgue, Cranston noticed that the zeroborn monikers were all cut out of the Death Gods, but he also detected that the zeroborn moniker had left behind unique imprints inside the corpses' flesh. The markings were different than 'normal' Fates Republic monikers. His discovery meant I had to kill him."

"How did you get away with that?"

"We're Census. No one questions us."

We've reached the end of the corridor. Another elevator opens before us. Agent Crow steps in. I have no choice but to follow. Hawthorne enters after me, the doors roll closed, and I'm relieved to feel the car rising.

Hawthorne's sandy hair lies over his eyes. I want to brush it away, but if I touch him, he'll hurt me. He gazes straight ahead, emotionless. My heart aches with sorrow.

"How is it that Hawthorne was converted weeks ago?" I ask. "I just saw him yesterday in the war room of *Upper Halo*."

Agent Crow laughs. "Hawthorne has no idea that he's a Black-O when he's not being actively redirected. Unless VPMD is turned on, you'd never know he is one of us. His eyes have the implants, true, but they won't shine. You'd have to examine him closely. He's the perfect spy because he's unaware that he's spying. We have but to question him."

"You're disgusting," I growl.

"And you'll make a fine Black-O, Roselle."

A cold shiver slips down my spine.

We return to the trunk of the Tree. I'm escorted to a heartwood in the center of the facility. Agent Crow gestures for me to enter the heartwood with him. I clutch the pole and step onto a rising stair. Agent Crow is on the step beside mine. We're lifted upward together through the tube. "There is something I want to show you on level five," he says. We pass storehouses of neon vials containing people—his experiments. On level five, we step off the heartwood and walk together to the area that, in a normal Tree, would be used for the intake of new Transitions.

Inside, secondborn Atom- and Star-Fated technicians are busy at work. They don't appear to be mind-controlled. No silver light shines from their eyes.

Agent Crow commands the attention of the nearest Star-Fated man in a yellow lab coat. The tall, handsome man stops what he is doing on his holographic screen, climbs off his chair, and walks toward us. Dark hair falls over his brow. His eyes are focused on his moniker, but his inattentiveness doesn't seem to bother Agent Crow. "I need you to prepare Roselle St. Sismode for Black-O conversion."

My heart pounds in my ears. I turn to bolt, but I'm caught and restrained by Hawthorne and several other Black-O soldiers. I struggle, but they're ridiculously strong.

The technician doesn't miss a beat, ignoring my outburst. "I just need a requisition, and I can take her back to an exam room now. I'm sending you the appropriate files." His fingers swipe the light of his star-shaped moniker.

Agent Crow uses his moniker to send the requisition. They're still using the Fates Republic communication system. They must have ways of blocking access by nosy Star-Fated firstborns like Reykin, but for my sake, I hope not.

The technician draws a tranquilizer gun from the holster on his thigh. I kick him in the stomach and try again to get loose, but I'm immediately tackled by the nearest Black-O. He growls in my ear until I exhaust myself and stop struggling, and he hauls me back to my feet. I pant in frustration. Agent Crow leans in, touches my cheek, and smooths my hair away from my eyes. "I'm looking forward to your conversion more than I have with anyone else's, Roselle. What will it be like when you fall into my arms instead of trying to rip them off?"

I spit in his face. He scowls and pulls a cloth from the pocket of his black leather coat. Methodically, he wipes away my spit. "Hand me the gun."

The technician places the tranquilizer gun in Agent Crow's palm. He places it directly over my heart. My eyes defy him, even as the dart penetrates my skin. I jerk at the impact when the needle hits my breastbone. My eyes blur. My ears ring. Everything mutes. A dreamy, faraway feeling sets in.

"Let her go," Agent Crow orders. It sounds distant.

I'm released. My knees weaken and I almost collapse, but the technician reaches out and catches me, clutching me to him. He smells like lemongrass.

"Opa," he groans. "It must be too much. You're such a little thing."

His deep voice sound so familiar.

"Don't be deceived," Agent Crow warns. "She's a killer."

"Oh, I know who she is," the technician says. "Everybody knows Roselle St. Sismode."

"Her mother expects her conversion to begin as soon as possible," Agent Crow growls, "so quit the rhetoric. Prep her for conversion and tank her. Alert me the moment she's ready. I'm leaving the Black-Os to guard her. Don't let her out of your sight or you'll regret it."

Agent Crow leaves, and the technician says nothing. My head lolls on his shoulder. He lifts me in his arms and takes me to an examination room, followed closely by Hawthorne and several other Black-Os.

The technician lays me on an examination table beneath a bright-white spotlight. Beside it is a tall tank filled with briny fluid, like the ones I observed earlier. I drift in and out of awareness, trying not to succumb to the tranquilizer. The technician removes my cuffs. I feel him tug off my clothes and wrestle me into a wet suit. He inserts IVs into my arm. Using a powered sprayer, he coats my exposed skin with something.

Then he takes my hand and lifts it.

His thumb rubs over my palm.

He pauses and lifts my hand higher, inspecting it closely.

He rubs his thumb over the small star again.

"That's—" He leans over the table, his head blotting out most of the white light above. A halo remains, ringing his aquamarine eyes, which bore into mine. "How did you get this star?"

I recognize the chiseled lines of his face, the way his dark eyebrows slash together. My pulse jumps as he lays a hand on my shoulder and shakes me. "The star is unique to *my* family crest." He holds my hand in front of my face. "Seven points—a seven-three prism, with three long points that form a W. And my brother's initials in relief—mirrored? What *is* this?"

My lips curl into a dopey smile. "Ransom . . . Winterstrom." I squeeze his hand. "Reykin is . . . looking . . . for you . . ."

Rebel Born *is forthcoming from 47North in 2019.*

Glossary

air-barracks. Kidney-shaped dormitory airships that dock on the military Trees in Bases like the Stone Forest. They transport troops and house them.

air elevator. Also known as an air lift, a glass-framed elevator that transports riders to and from the lower building of the Halo Palace to the crown level. The elevator cars travel in open air as well as elevator shafts.

air lift. *See* air elevator.

The Apiary. An outwardly decrepit-looking military Base on an island near the Fate of Seas. A Census stronghold.

Barleycorn. The high-end restaurant shaped like a spike of barley and located in the Trial Village at the center of the Secondborn Trial training fields.

Black-O. A Census soldier enhanced with advanced military-grade artificial intelligence technology embedded in his or her brain. Each soldier is subject to mind control by programmers and handlers who are often Census agents.

Black-O mode. The state of being a Black-O soldier. It can entail being mind-controlled by a third party or using artificial intelligence to solve problems, follow commands, and complete tasks.

Burton Weapons Manufacturing. A Sword-Fated weapons manufacturing company owned by Sword-Fated Edmund Burton.

Census. A branch of the government comprised of agents whose mission is to hunt down and kill unauthorized thirdborns and their abettors. Their uniform is a white military dress shirt, black trousers, black boots, and a long tailored leather coat. Their Bases are underground beneath the Sword military Trees at Bases like the Stone Forest Base and the Twilight Forest Base.

chet. A nonaddictive substance that is used to relieve tension and induce relaxation. Looks like a white stamp.

Class 5Z Mechanized Sanitation Unit. A robot designed to repair and maintain sewage and septic lines. The unit has no artificial intelligence capacities.

conversion. The process of implanting a VPMD (Virtual Perception Manipulation Device) in the brain of a person other than a zeroborn.

conversions. People who are unwillingly implanted with mind-control technology. Implanted people can be detected by the cornea implants in the eyes that shine with silver light.

Copperscale. A defensive fabric developed by Salloway Munitions Conglomerate that acts like armor. It can conduct an energy pulse, either fusion or hydrogen, away from the wearer.

Council of Destiny. The Virtue's advisory board made up of members from the Virtue-Fated aristocracy. Experts are brought in to advise the panel on a myriad of topics.

CR-40. A topical polymer dispensed in an aerosol device that, when sprayed on the skin, temporarily blocks the signal of an implanted moniker. It can be scrubbed off the skin or it will wear off in a few hours, making it ineffective.

crella. A type of donut.

Culprit-44. A sidearm, also called a fusionmag. A fusion-powered gun-like weapon with a hydrogen-powered option.

death drone. An automated robot with a black metallic outer casing. It's shaped like a bat and used primarily on the battlefield to interrogate and execute captured enemy soldiers. The drone is summoned by a black, blinking "death-drone beacon" that emits a high-pitched sound, prompting a drone to respond to the location. Once the drone interrogates an enemy, it decides whether to kill the soldier or take him or her back to a containment airship for further interrogation.

drone camera. A spherical-shaped automated floating camera that has a multitude of lenses. Some are automated and can be programmed to follow a specific target, while others are operated remotely.

Dual-Blade X16. The Salloway Munitions brand name for the dual-sided sword—fusionblade/hydroblade—designed by Star-Fated secondborn Jakes Trotter and Sword-Fated secondborn Roselle St. Sismode. It was sold to the company by Roselle St. Sismode.

Exo. A rank in the firstborn Sword military. It is higher than all of the secondborn ranks. Only the Admiral and Clarities are higher. Black uniforms. Clifton Salloway is an Exo.

fatedom. The realm of a Fate, like a kingdom.

Fated Sword. A title given to the spouse of The Sword (the Clarity of the Fate of Swords). Kennet Abjorn is considered the Fated Sword because he's the husband of Othala St. Sismode.

Fates of the Republic. Also known as the Fates Republic. A society comprising nine Fates or "fatedoms." The Fates highest to lowest in the caste system are Virtues, Swords, Stars, Atoms, Suns, Diamonds, Moons, Seas, and Stones. The leader of the Republic is the Clarity of Virtues.

Firstborn Commander. A title given to the heir to The Virtue and the heir to The Sword.

First Lieutenant. A position on the Sword Heritage Council that is considered the "right hand" to the Firstborn Sword (the heir to The Sword).

Five Hundred. A drug that acts as a stimulant. It's lethal when taken in large doses.

fourthborn. The fourth child in birth order.

FSP (Fusion Snuff Pulse). A device that acts like an EMP (electromagnetic pulse) delivering a short pulse of energy that disrupts the fusing of atoms that creates fusion energy. The device is a palm-size sphere with a silver metallic outer shell with a trigger button.

fusionblade. A fusion-energy-driven laser-like sword. The sword resembles a broadsword without the expected weight. Fusion cells reside in the hilt of the sword and create a stream of energy when engaged. The hilt is constructed of a metal alloy and usually personalized with a family crest or some other distinctive marking. The St. Sismode family is the originator of the fusionblade.

fusionmag. A gun-like weapon that fires fusion energy in bullet-shaped pulses.

gravitizer. The antigravity mechanism in a combat jumpsuit. It uses magnetic force to repel against the molten core of the planet in order to slow the descent of a soldier after he or she jumps from an airship. It disengages once the soldier is within feet of the ground, allowing him or her to land safely.

Hazy Daze-99. A drug that induces euphoria and sleepiness. It comes in aerosol form.

heartwood. An escalator-like machine that carries occupants up or down levels through a vertical tube within a Base Tree.

Heritage Council. A committee comprising firstborn members of the Sword aristocracy. The leader of the council is the Firstborn Sword. It's a junior council of sorts in which firstborn heirs hold positions of power until they assume their parents' roles as the leaders of the Sword aristocracy.

hologram pad. A handheld device used to correspond with the administrative arm of the Halo Palace. The unit uses prerecorded messages as well as real-time holographic messages in the form of light projections for communication.

hoverdiscs. Small round metallic discs about two inches in diameter that attach to the sole of a boot or a shoe. Once turned on, the discs keep the wearer aloft. They allow him or her to ascend by making motions as if walking up steps, and they allow the person to fall in elevation by using descending stair motions.

hover mode. The ability to levitate and self-propel using antigravity technology.

hovertruck. A large wheelless vehicle that hovers above the ground and is propelled by various means.

hovervan. A large wheelless vehicle that hovers above the ground and is propelled by various means.

kill tallies. Black line tattoos that extend from the outside corners of the eyes to the hairline of a Census agent, denoting the number of thirdborn kills the agent has amassed. The marks can also be found tattooed on the neck or temples of an agent.

Killian Abbey. An abbey and collection of tombs where heads of the Fate of Swords are buried. Roselle's grandfather is buried there.

Lenity. A city in the Fate of Virtues where all of the wealthiest country estates are located. It is considered the "sister city" of Purity.

looking-glass moniker. *See* mirror moniker.

maginot. A canine-like cyborg that resembles a wolfhound. They patrol the grounds of the Sword Palace, acting as sentinels.

mechadome. *See* mechanized domestic.

mechanized domestic. A domestic robot with rudimentary artificial intelligence or advanced artificial intelligence designed to do a multitude of domestic tasks. Models vary in physical form.

mirror moniker. A device that reflects the identity of the moniker closest to it. Used as a tool in espionage. Also known as a looking-glass moniker.

moniker. A symbol implant each person receives at birth to denote class/caste. It is a brand that covers a holographic chip. The chip is loaded with the person's identification and other vital information, such as rank, family members, fatedom, status, and so on. The holographic chips can be activated by checkpoints manned by security personnel. They are used to track people entering and leaving districts, to process secondborns, to denote firstborn status, and more.

Neon Bible. The high-end bookmaking establishment located in the Trial Village at the center of the Secondborn Trials training fields.

night owl bots. Surveillance robots made to look like owls that perch in areas around the Halo Palace. Used by Iono security as covert audio and visual recording devices to gather intelligence.

phantom orb. A small silver ball-shaped device that provides resistance to infrared scanners and pings from Virtue-class stingers. It cools a person's body temperature to camouflage the individual from detection.

Phoenix. Nicknamed "Phee," this automated robot was recently converted into a mechanistic domestic or mechadome. In a former role, this robot was a sewer maintenance unit known as a Class 5Z Mechanized Sanitation Unit, but it was taken from a scrap heap, upgraded with limited artificial intelligence, and recommissioned to be Roselle's valet at the Halo Palace.

Purity. The capital city of Virtues.

Pyramid Conspiracy. A high-stakes card game people bet on, in which one must remember every card laid and the order in which it was placed. Every level, new cards are added.

Rose Garden Society. A secret club dedicated to the preservation and welfare of Roselle St. Sismode. They have a vested interest in seeing her become The Sword (Clarity of the Fate of Swords). One of the most influential members is Clifton Salloway (firstborn Sword aristocracy), an arms dealer who owns Salloway Munitions Conglomerate. Members are called Rose Gardeners.

Rose Gardener. A member of the Rose Garden Society.

Rush. A highly addictive drug that causes paranoia and delusions of grandeur.

secondborn deserter. Any secondborn who fails to report to his or her designated post and is considered a runaway.

Secondborn Deserter Bulletin. An all-points bulletin profiling a secondborn who has failed to report for duty and is considered a runaway.

sky platform. A hoverpad located in the crown level of the Halo Palace.

The Sword Social. An on-moniker news source that covers a variety of news items and topics.

Transitioned. The state of any secondborn who has undergone the mandatory indoctrination of the Fates Republic and who is now the property of a Fate. The secondborn's surname is replaced with the name of the Fate served.

transporter pod. An automated, self-driving pod of a variety of sizes and functions. It's used to transport items by using hover technology to levitate and fly.

Trial Village. The name of the area in the one-mile circle at the center of the secondborn training camps. It's an exclusive area for aristocratic firstborns to socialize and find food and entertainment within the Secondborn Trials atmosphere.

Verringer. A very expensive airship with the ability to dock on land, water, and air.

Vicolt. An antiquated hovercar made of chrome and glass that the aristocracy of the Sword Palace uses in ceremonial precessions.

VPMD (Virtual Perception Manipulation Device). A system of automated and biochemical mechanisms implanted in the brain that can alter reality, including enabling mind control, hallucinations, and false memories. In elite cases, it can stimulate biochemical reactions that enhance one's senses and physical makeup.

whisper orb. A ball, usually metallic, that, when activated by touch, produces an iridescent sphere of light capable of containing sound frequencies. They can come in several different sizes.

zeroborn. A person manufactured in a laboratory and implanted with mind-control technology. The person isn't "born" in the traditional sense. Noncombat zeroborns have red monikers. Black-Os have black monikers.

Acknowledgments

Jason Kirk, that sunny day at Amazon in July 2015 sparked all of this. Thank you for your words of wisdom and inspiration. I'm eternally grateful.

Thank you to the best agent in the world, Tamar Rydzinski. Without your guidance, the Secondborn series would not have been possible.

To the staff of 47North and Amazon, it is a great honor to work with all of you. Thank you for making my dreams come true.

Tom, Max, and Jack, you are my heart. "I love thee best, oh, most best, believe it."

Mom, thank you for always reading my manuscripts before anyone else and giving me your strongly worded opinions. Honesty is love.

To the Four Horsemen of Facebook, no one gets me like you ladies do. Where would I be without you?

Amber McClelland, thank you for always being a shoulder to lean on (or cry on?) when deadlines loom nearer. You have the best take on life. I'm grateful for your friendship.

Arcade Fire, I listened to your songs *Neon Bible* and *Everything Now* on repeat as I wrote this manuscript. Your music inspired me. Thank you for sharing your talent with the world.

Thank you, God, for Your many blessings.